PRAISE FOR

LAST OF HER NAME

"Get ready for a nonstop, action-packed thrill ride. Perfect for fans of Marissa Meyer, *Last of Her Name* will keep you guessing until the last page. I gasped, I swooned, I cried. Stars, I loved this book!"

—JESSICA BRODY, BESTSELLING AUTHOR OF THE UNREMEMBERED TRILOGY

"This is no mere romp through the stars: Romantic, smart, and brimming with intrigue, *Last of Her Name* is a sparkling gem that will truly transport you to another world where no one is quite what they seem."

—SARAH GLENN MARSH, AUTHOR OF *REIGN OF THE FALLEN*

"Ripe with complex yet reachable world building and multifaceted characters, the real hook in *Last of Her Name* is the raw, unflinching way Khoury presents themes of revenge and generational inheritance. Clear your schedule before starting this book. Once you start, you won't be able to stop."

—SARA RAASCH, *NEW YORK TIMES* BESTSELLING AUTHOR OF THE SNOW LIKE ASHES SERIES

"Brilliantly realized, epic in scope, *Last of Her Name* simply soars. A glittering, intricate, and completely thrilling adventure with characters you'll adore and a plot that will pull you along at breakneck speed. I was so busy reading, I missed my station."

—AMIE KAUFMAN, *NEW YORK TIMES* BESTSELLING COAUTHOR OF *ILLUMINAE*

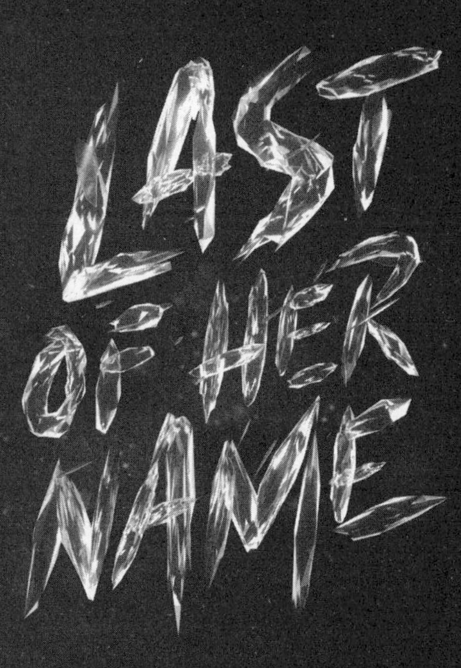
LAST
OF HER
NAME

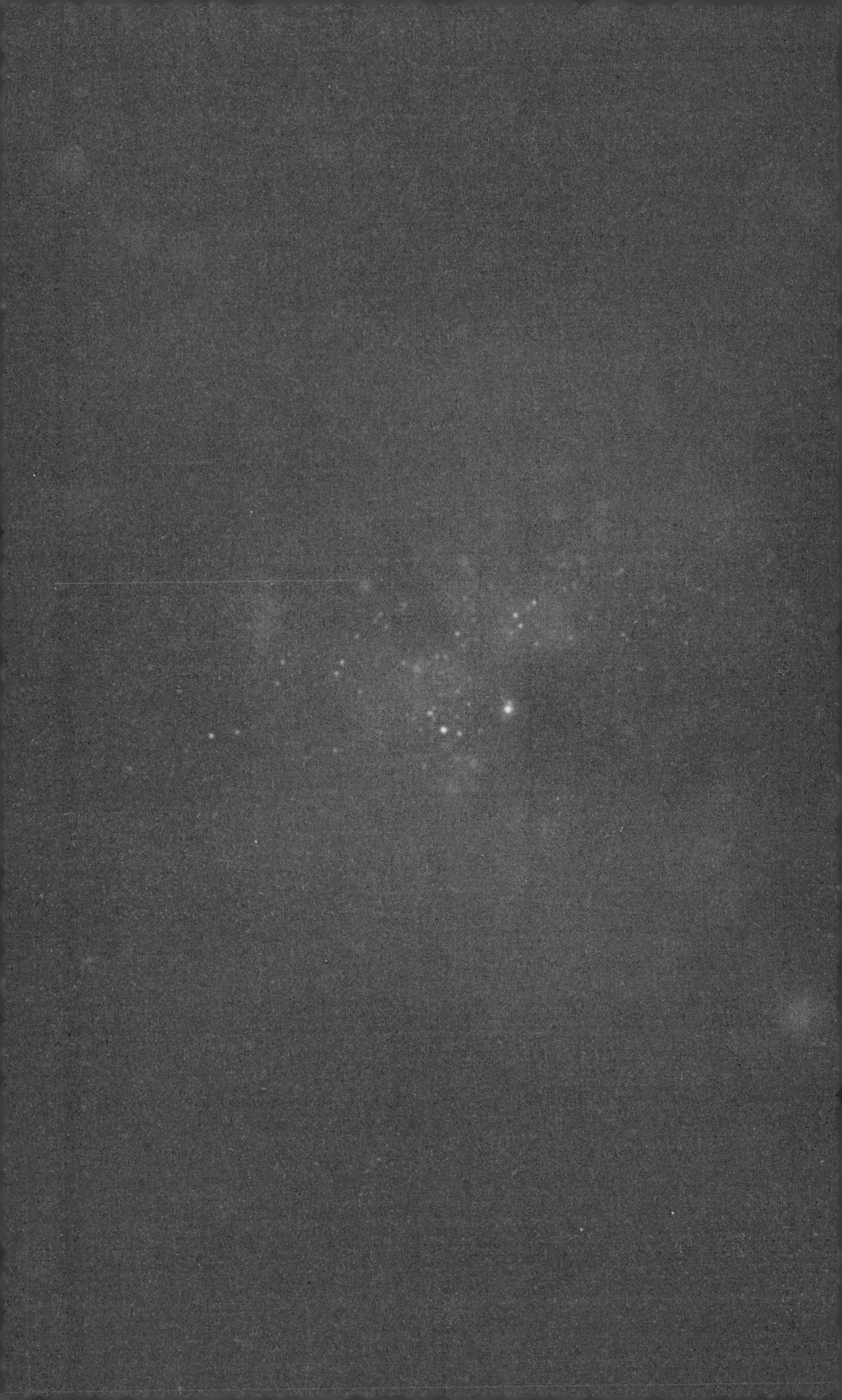

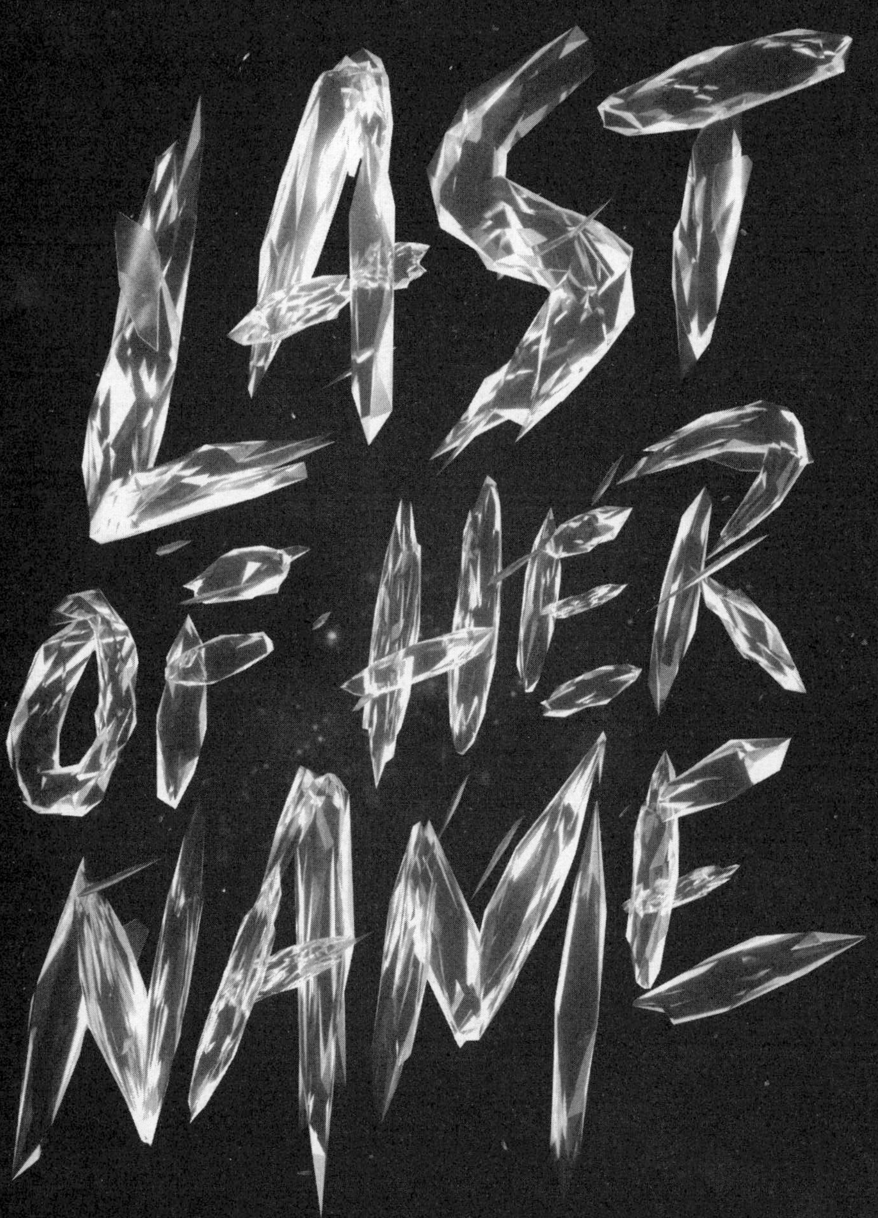

JESSICA KHOURY

Scholastic Inc.

This book was originally published in hardcover by Scholastic Press in 2019.

ISBN 978-1-338-58212-3

10 9 8 7 6 5 4 3 2 1   20 21 22 23 24

Printed in the U.S.A. 23
This edition first printing 2020

Book design by Nina Goffi

For Katharine

CHAPTER ONE

The black ship breaks atmo like a falling star, burning up the sky.

Pressing a scanner to my eyes, I squint and adjust the settings until the ship sharpens into focus. It's a big one, sleek and fast. Fire licks its hull as it descends, and then it passes across the great violet sun, turning to a silhouette.

Balanced precariously in the crooking branches of a slinke tree, its noodle-like leaves tickling the back of my neck, I have a grand view of the landscape below. My father's vineyards stripe the land from east to west, a thick tangle of leaves and sweet grapes. Houses and winery facilities cluster at the north end of the property. Made of honey-colored wood and glass, the buildings sparkle in the late afternoon sun, the windows cast in hues of soft purple.

Glancing away from the scanner, I see the vineyard workers moving to and from the warehouses, rolling barrels onto hovering dories, taking tallies of the stock. Harnessed to the dories, red-furred pack animals called mantibu bray at one another, tossing their antlers at the flies that are the bane of the wet season.

As I'd expected, the black ship angles for the east, where the city of Estonrya waits over the horizon. It's the usual flight pattern of the interstellar vessels that come and go.

But this is no ordinary ship.

Leaning outward for a better view, I put too much weight on the branch, and it cracks.

With a shout, I tumble down, landing hard on my back and feeling the wind rush from my lungs. Bits of twig and leaves rain around me. I blink at the sky, momentarily stunned.

"Stacia! Oh my stars! Are you okay?"

Clio's face appears above mine, big blue eyes wide with concern.

"Fine," I groan, pushing myself up. I've sunk into the spongy lavender moss that carpets the ground. "Astronika."

"What?"

"The ship." With a wince, I pick up the scanner, which shattered when it hit the ground. "It's an astronika. Class nine."

I could add that it's powered by a Takhimir reactor and insulated with a premium magnetic RAM layer. But Clio wouldn't care. She tends to nod off when I drone on about ship specs. Everyone does.

"An astronika?" Clio shakes her head. "What could a ship like that be doing way out here? I mean, I love our planet, but Amethyne's not exactly the hub of the galaxy. Or the hub of *anywhere*, for that matter."

I shrug and click open the bulky metal cuff on my wrist. What looks like a large silver bracelet is actually the universe's greatest invention—or at least a mechanic's best friend—and I'd rather run around stark naked than go without my multicuff for a day. Pushing my fingernail into little grooves along it causes several miniature tools to release—a screwdriver, flashlight, and pincers. Bending over the scanner, I start piecing the parts together. "I'll bet it's military."

"Which makes it even weirder." Clio presses her lips together, eyeing the trail of smoke the ship left behind. Then she asks softly, "Is it the draft, you think?"

I shake my head, but my chest tightens involuntarily as I turn a screw on the scanner's back panel. "It's too early in the year. We have five months at least. They always come in the dry season."

But when our eyes meet, I can see my friend isn't convinced.

Not that Clio need necessarily worry. She's not the soldier type, with her delicate frame and dreamy eyes. Me, on the other hand . . . Well, with my muscular build and mechanic's certification, I'm just the type that the drafting committees love to haul off to boot camp on distant Alexandrine. I've always dreamed of exploring the other systems that glitter in the night sky, but not as some grunt on a military vessel, confined to strict schedules and rules. No, thank you.

"It's probably just some rich Alexandrian tourist with nothing better to do than slum around the outer systems."

"Yeah." Clio gives a wistful sigh. "Maybe a *handsome*, rich Alexandrian tourist, with a troubled past and a broody air and a heart yearning for love."

With a groan, I haul myself to my feet. "You can have his heart. I'll take his ship."

She points at the scanner in my hand. "That was fast."

The scanner is whole again, its circuits operating normally despite the tumble. I snap the multicuff back on my wrist. "Good thing too, or my dad would've skinned me."

My eyes fix on something over her shoulder, and my brow furrows.

"I told you to stop frowning like that," says Clio. "I swear, Stace, you'll be nothing but wrinkles by the time you're thirty."

"The ship," I murmur. "It's not heading to Estonrya."

"Of course it is. All the ships go to Estonrya."

"Clio, *look*. It's coming here. To Afka."

"What?" She turns and squints at the horizon, where the astronika's growing larger in the distance.

The black ship must have passed through Estonryan air space for security clearance, but instead of touching down in the city, it turned around, heading straight to our little town.

Seconds later, the astronika swoops overhead, a low, silent shadow. This close, I can see the call sign stamped on its sides, along with the emblem of the Galactic Union: nine stars in a circle, representing the nine Jewel systems. Each one a different color, with purple Amethyne between green Emerault and red Rubyat. The ship descends into the valley, where Afka is huddled between the hills.

"That's weird." I break into a grin. I'll probably never get another chance to see an astronika up close. "Let's go check it out."

But Clio hesitates.

"Oh, it'll be fine!" I prod. "Don't you want to see your handsome Alexandrian bachelor up close?"

Clio's lips curl into a slow, wicked smile. Then she raises an eyebrow. "You want to change first?"

I look down at my outfit: black tank top beneath a ragged jersey, baggy gray cargo pants tucked into dusty boots—in other words, my usual ensemble. I like that I can carry my tools in my pockets without having to haul around an extra bag. You never know when one of the vineyard lorries is going to break down, and anyway, the smell of engine oil that's permanently worked into the fabric keeps away the gnats.

"What's wrong?" I ask. "This is how I always look."

"Yeah. Like a sentient toolbox." She releases a puff of air and rolls her eyes. "Forget it. Just so long as we stop at Ravi's and get strawberry ice after."

"My treat," I promise her. "Now where did Elki get to?"

Slipping my fingers between my teeth, I give a sharp whistle. Moments later, the foliage behind us rustles, and the large mantibu comes ambling out of the trees, his saddle knocked askew by the low branches. I run my hand down his side, from the reddish fur on his shoulders to the leathery skin on his hindquarters. Then I leap into the saddle, holding out a hand for Clio, pulling her up with practiced ease. She's wearing a knee-length blue sundress over white leggings, and her skirt bunches around her waist as she straddles the mantibu. Below us, Elki grumbles and huffs, shaking his antlers until we're settled in.

We follow the dirt track that runs between the vineyard and the slinke forest. Birds flit overhead, their long, scaly tails flicking in frustration as they try to get the grapes. Their every attempt is foiled by the invisible shield projected over the vines; at a bird's touch, it flashes and sizzles, a grid of white that fades as soon as the bird flees. No harm is done to the birds, but they still squawk angrily, dashing their tiny horns in frustration.

A rumble of hooves catches my ear, and I peer into the rows of grapevines to see a blurry shape racing toward us—a mantibu doe, with a rider clinging to her back.

I glance at Clio over my shoulder. "Trouble incoming. Try not to make a fool of yourself, will you?"

"Ooh," Clio purrs, her eyes going soft. "Forget strawberry ice. I found something yummier."

The boy perched in the mantibu's saddle rides with easy grace, reins tight in one hand. Sunlight glints off the pale horns atop his head. He's dressed in tight-fitted riding pants with a loose gray tunic, and his boots are glued to the stirrups. He's so intent on the timer in his other hand, he doesn't notice us ahead.

"Whoa!" I shout. "Pull up, Pol!"

Mantibu and rider burst through the security shield. It flickers and parts, resealing behind them and fading into invisibility as the boy reins in, pulling his mount into a tight circle.

"Stacia! Sorry. Didn't see you there."

He and the mantibu are both breathing hard as they pull up alongside us, and sweat dampens his shirt, making the fabric cling to his skin. His hair tumbles in dark curls around his horns, shining with the grapeseed oil I know he slathers on every morning.

"Did you see that?" he says, grinning as he waves the timer. "New record. Tinka's ready for the Afkan Cup. We have a real chance of winning this year."

"And to think, three months ago no one could even get a saddle on her." I shake my head. "I don't know how you do it."

"Oh, that's easy," he laughs, scratching the creature's ears. "Sheer bribery. Feed her enough and she turns to putty. Don't you, girl?"

"Not unlike Stacia," Clio points out.

"Oh, you're a funny one, Clio Markova." I elbow her while Pol gives a weak grin, as if he's afraid I'll jump on him if he dares laugh.

Pol slides to the ground and rubs the mantibu's neck, and the beast swats him playfully with her scaled tail. Laughing, he reaches through the security shield to grab a cluster of grapes, which he feeds to Tinka and Elki both.

"We're on our way to Afka," I say to Pol. "Come with us."

"I don't know. I've got to clean the stables, and there's that trellis by the pond that needs repairing . . ."

"Pol, you never stop working. Come have fun with us! Like the old days. Anyway, I don't think Clio's going to take no for an answer."

She grins.

"Oh, all right," he mutters, his cheeks flushing. "If *Clio* insists. Tinka needs to cool down, anyway."

He falls into step with us, scratching Elki's chin and feeding him the rest of the grapes. The mantibu grumbles with pleasure, slowing his pace.

From my position on Elki, I have a view of the top of Pol's head. I'm surprised to see how much his horns have grown lately, poking through his hair where they've usually been half-hidden.

As Amethyne's adapted race, the aeyla tend toward lavender-gray complexions and pale hair and lashes. But Pol is only half aeyla, lacking the species' more distinct features. He inherited his human father's bronze Rubyati skin and dark hair, but he has the ivory aeylic horns—or the beginnings of them, anyway. They won't fully grow in for a few more years, and until they do, he's still considered a child in the eyes of the aeyla, even though he's already taller than half the men in town. Ever since his growth spurt last year, he's been putting on muscle as well as height.

I'm still not quite sure what to make of this *man* replacing the boy I grew up with, running wild in the slinke forest and jumping into the turquoise lakes that pool in the hills. Though by aeyla tradition, he won't be considered an adult until his horns grow all the way in—a painful ordeal they call the Trying. Pol's got a few years to go before that happens—something I probably remind him of a bit too often . . . and a bit too smugly.

"So what's in Afka?" Pol asks, startling me from my wandering thoughts. I realize I've been staring at him.

"An astronika."

"There's an astronika *here*?" Pol stops walking abruptly, and Tinka nudges his shoulder blades in reproach.

"See it for yourself." Reining in Elki, I pluck the scanner from around my neck and toss it to him. "It's landed in the docks."

"Stacia's smitten," Clio adds.

He peers through the lens at the town below, zooming in on the docks. "We should go back to the house."

"Why? I want to see what's up."

"Me too," Clio adds.

He shakes his head, handing the scanner back to me. "It's an Alexandrian ship. Nothing good comes from those."

"Except handsome Alexandrian bachelors," I point out, eliciting a giggle from Clio.

Pol frowns. "This isn't a joke."

"What do *you* think it wants?"

"At best?" His jaw tightens. "Your father's finest vintage. They'll clean out your cellars, pay you nothing, and tell you they need it for the good of the Committee. They'll even strip the vines just for the fun of it." He reaches out, fingers briefly closing on a cluster of grapes. Rich, fat, and as purple as the sun, they'll make for a good harvest this year. An excellent vintage. Unless Pol is right, and the ship is here to rob us blind and get away clean, the power of the law behind them. I've heard of it happening to other vintners on Amethyne, usually by roving bands of soldiers on leave. Not from ships as important as an astronika.

"What about at worst?" I ask quietly.

He only shakes his head.

I stare toward the docks, where the ship shines like obsidian, no larger than the tip of my thumb at this distance. I feel a quiver of nervousness in my stomach.

But Pol has always been a bit paranoid. He routinely rebuilds the vineyard comm network because, as he put it to me, "you never know who might be listening in." Same with the security system. It drives me crazy, always having to relearn the codes for the doors.

The afternoon is waning; the violet sun slips lower in the east, while the Twins rise in the west, one moon full, one gibbous, each tinged pale blue. We won't have much light left. It'll be a dark ride home for me if we don't hurry.

"Well, we're going," I say. "You go hide in the cellars if you like."

Pol gives a growl of frustration. "Why don't you *ever* listen to me?"

"Because you're allergic to fun."

"I'm allergic to always saving your neck when you go poking things bigger and meaner than you. Just last month you jumped on a snaptooth, thinking it was a floating log! If I hadn't been there—"

"I had everything under control. Clio, what do you think?"

Pol groans and looks away as Clio raises her hands. "Whoa! You know I stay neutral when you two are fighting."

I sigh. "Look, Pol. If there's trouble, I'll drop Clio at home and come straight back. Feel better?" Before he can answer, I put Elki into a trot. Clio yelps and wraps her arms around my waist to keep from being thrown off. We leave Pol standing in the middle of the road, holding Tinka's reins.

He'll probably change all the door codes while we're gone, just for spite. I'll have to bang on the window to be let in.

"What if he's right?" Clio murmurs in my ear. "What if it's trouble?"

"Then at least something exciting will finally be happening around here."

"He's only trying to look out for us."

"You're just saying that because you've been in love with him since you were eight."

"So?"

"So, you can do better than Pol, is all I'm saying," I grumble. "Someone who uses less oil in his hair, for starters."

"I like it." She leans forward, resting her chin on my shoulder, the way we used to ride as children. "Why haven't *you* ever had a go at him? You two already bicker like you've been married twenty years."

I sit up as if I got a jolt from the security fence. "Are you insane? He's—he's— Bleeding stars, Clio, when we were toddlers our parents let us *bathe* together!"

"Oh?" Clio tugs my ponytail. "Is that why your face is red? Picturing Pol in the bath?"

I growl at her. "It's because I'm furious that you'd even *suggest* it."

"Well, that's good to hear, because I've got dibs."

"Fine! Marry him and have all his little babies. I don't care."

Clio laughs. "And what about our plans? Our little starship we're going to fix up and roam the galaxy in? You and me against the universe."

"No boys allowed," I add emphatically, but I feel a tug of sadness.

As much as Pol is like an irritating brother, Clio is . . . not a friend. The word isn't big enough for her. Clio is my sister, my balancing force. As bound to me as the twin moons of Amethyne are to each other, caught in eternal orbit. It's been that way since we were four years old. Where I end, she begins. Her parents died in the revolution sixteen years ago, and ever since, she's been practically a member of our family.

"You and me against the universe," I murmur, half to myself.

Clio's hands wrap around my middle and hug me tight. "No matter what."

It's a half hour ride to Afka, following the dirt road that snakes out of the hills down to the valley. Our vineyard overlooks the town; from my bedroom window I can see most of it, tucked into the green hills. Beyond the town, the slinke forest tangles over the lowlands.

As the sun sinks, the sky deepens into heavy shades of violet and red. I never grow tired of that, the way the light stains the world in the late afternoon, as if the whole place has been doused in my father's best wines. With the smell of the grapes ripe in the air, it's almost perfect.

Almost.

There *is* the problem of the rattling hum that now reaches my ears, coming from behind. I turn and look past Clio to see my family's dory come skimming along the road. Hovering a few inches off the ground, it moves at a swift pace, noiseless pads glowing along its underbelly.

"Dad!" I shout, pulling Elki to the side of the road.

My father slows the dory until it hovers beside us with a soft hum. The top is open to the air, and there Dad stands at the controls—with Pol at his side and Pol's father, Spiros. The old vineyard manager, my father's best friend, is a bigger version of Pol, but his black curls are threaded with silver.

"Stacia!" Dad hits a button, releasing a small metal stair that lowers to the road. "Get up here. Hurry!"

"We're just going to Afka to—"

"No, you're coming home with us. *Now.*"

"But—"

"Stacia! For once, I *need* you to listen to me!"

Relenting, I throw Pol a suspicious look. He must have ratted us out.

"What about Clio?"

"Clio too. Hurry!"

I slip off Elki, Clio jumping down beside me, and then I pat the mantibu's flank.

"Home, boy," I murmur. He turns and ambles back up the road, his cloven hooves kicking up dust. Behind me, Clio ascends into the dory. I bound up the steps behind her and hurry to my father's side. "Dad, what's wrong? What does that ship mean?"

"It means the Committee is taking interest in Afka, and we don't want to be anywhere near there until the astronika is gone." His lips pinch together. "I know you love your ships, Stacia, but this time, it's better to walk away."

Seeing the look in his eyes, I feel my lungs squeeze with apprehension. Dad is one of the most laid-back people I know. Even the year we lost an entire season of grapes to beetles, he only shrugged and began planning the next year's crop. But now he seems almost . . . frightened. His frame is tense, poised for trouble. He keeps rubbing the stubble on his cheeks, which I know is a sign that his thoughts are racing.

We've barely settled on the bench behind him before he guns the engine. The pads angle, turning us back toward the vineyard. At the controls, Dad, Pol, and Spiros bend their heads together, whispering.

I frown. What can Dad tell Pol that he can't tell me?

Before I can find out, a blast of air hits us from above, seemingly from nowhere. We all cry out, ducking low as another dory descends from the sky. Twice the size of our craft, it's much faster and louder. As it sinks to a stop, blocking our way, its pads send up a cloud of dust. My father curses.

"Pol, with me," snaps Spiros. They both move to stand in front of me and Clio, as if to shield us. I peer around Spiros's bulky frame, eyes wide.

The dory is marked with green shields, the symbol of the local

Green Knight peacekeepers. There's one at the controls—Viktor, a townie who trained with me at the little flight school outside Afka—but the rest of the men on board aren't familiar.

They must have come in the astronika. I know everyone in Afka and none of them dress like that, in red armor stamped with the Union seal on the chest . . .

Then it hits me.

These strangers are vityazes, the Red Knights. They're elite military who answer directly to the Grand Committee on Alexandrine. I've never even *seen* a Red Knight before, except on the news—usually conducting mass arrests or gunning down protestors in the central systems. Now there are three of them in front of me, and one is jumping aboard our dory.

"By order of the Grand Committee!" the man shouts. "You are to turn this craft around at once!"

I spy Dad's hand reaching under the control panel, where he keeps his gun. Sucking in a breath, I grab his arm. I don't know what this is about, but I know if Dad shoots a vityaze, not one of us will leave this dory alive.

For a moment, he seems like he's going to grab it anyway. But then he relaxes, putting his arm around me instead. He holds me so tight I can barely breathe.

"What's this about?" Dad says, putting on a confused smile, like he's just some fringe system bumpkin. "Gentlemen, I'm a simple vintner on his way home to his wife. You how the ladies get when you're late coming home."

The vityazes don't smile.

"Viktor?" I breathe. "What's going on?"

Aboard the dory, Viktor looks pale beneath his green helmet. Instead of answering, he glances away, as if ashamed.

My pulse quickens.

Something is wrong.

The vityaze, ignoring Dad, regards me instead, staring so hard it's like he's trying to read my thoughts. I glare back.

"All citizens must report to the town hall," the vityaze says at last. "*Immediately.*"

Dad puts on his most ingratiating smile, the one he usually only pulls out when important buyers come to sample his wine. "Sir, if you could just tell us—"

With a swift motion, the vityaze pulls his own gun and places it against Dad's forehead.

I stare at the weapon, unable to breathe, as Clio gasps behind me. It isn't like Dad's, which is only capable of stunning a target. The vityaze's gun is bigger. Uglier.

Deadlier.

Dad doesn't move, but his face drains of color. Pol looks on the verge of attacking the man, but Spiros puts out a hand to hold him back.

"It was not a request," the vityaze says quietly.

"Well, then, to town we go," I say carefully. "Won't we, everyone? No problem. Thank you, officers."

The vityaze's eyes flicker to me, and he lowers the weapon. "You should listen to the girl."

Dad nods, his eyes burning.

The vityaze returns to their dory, and the larger ship follows us all the way down the road, hovering like a large predator. I watch it as dread seeps through me.

Vityazes, on Amethyne.

Vityazes in *Afka*.

It's wild. It's surreal.

I think of all the war films I've seen in school, of the revolution when the Red Knights stormed cities and executed everyone who resisted. And the film we've all seen but never talk about: the murder of the imperial family—of Emperor Pyotr Leonov, his wife, all their little children—recorded and spread throughout the remains of the Alexandrian Empire, now the Galactic Union.

It was the people's victory, they'd said.

It was the end of tyranny.

I've never really questioned it before. I've never thought much—*cared* much—about the world outside Amethyne. That's Pol's obsession. He always follows events in other systems, political uprisings, Committee crackdowns, the sort of stuff that makes me zone out during our history lectures, to his irritation. "People are vanishing!" he often tells me. "They're thrown into prison camps or never seen again. No trial, no explanation. This stuff is *important*, Stacia." It all seemed so far away, the concerns of the central systems, hardly real for us living in fringe territory. I felt bad about the unrest, but there didn't seem to be much I could do to help those involved.

But now I wish I'd paid more attention. Then I might have a clue why the Committee's killers are here, in my *home*, threatening my *family*.

"You okay?" I whisper to Clio.

She lets her head fall on my shoulder, her hand gripping mine tightly. "I'm scared, Stace."

Dad parks our dory outside the town hall just as the sun sets. The dory with the vityazes continues on, once the men on board seem content that we won't suddenly take off again. Running would be a stupid move, given that the street around the town hall is bristling with more Red Knights. There must be a hundred of them in sight. They all carry the same deadly guns as the man who'd threatened Dad, and they all look like they want an excuse to use them. Between the vityazes' armor and the dying sun's rays, the whole scene seems washed in scarlet.

Behind the town, the astronika looms larger than I could have imagined; the whole of Afka could fit inside the ship. But my excitement over seeing it has dissipated. Now I only want it far from my home.

I catch sight of my mom standing among the crowd and let out a cry, running to embrace her. She still wears her physician's coat and cap. She must have come straight from her office down the street. Her dark hair is twisted into a loose bun, but tendrils have pulled free and are stuck to the sweat on her temples.

"Mom, what's happening?"

She squeezes my hand. "I don't know, but we'll find out soon."

She's worried. More than worried—terrified. I've never seen my parents like this before, looking ready to run or fight, as if this were some central system where uprisings are a weekly occurrence.

Way out here on Amethyne, we were supposed to be safe. We were supposed to be beyond all that, but now I wonder if I've been a fool to believe such a thing.

Dad whispers to Spiros, who nods and slips away after squeezing his son's shoulder. He vanishes in moments, but in the chaos, I barely have time to wonder what he might be up to.

People are coming in from every direction, many hurrying from the red-armored vityazes who push them along. They seem to be sorting us, sending many back to their homes, pushing others toward the town hall. A few of the citizens are horned aeyla who've chosen town life over the communes of their own kind, and all these the vityazes turn away. They only seem interested in nonadapted humans.

The mayor of Afka, a tall, befuddled-looking man named Kepht, is in the midst of it all, trying to help. "Please, everyone! Just do as they say!"

A vityaze prods Dad with an odd metal staff. "You three! Inside! Now!"

Dad throws up his hands. "Easy, friend! We're going."

"What about Clio?" I ask.

Dad gives me a harried look. "Bring her along. Keep moving, now."

The vityazes don't seem to care one way or another, so I loop my arm through hers and we walk between my parents, while Pol follows close behind.

Until the vityaze with the staff steps in.

"You," he says through his helmet, his hand closing on Pol's shoulder. "What are you, the family pet? Get away, *d'yav*! Back to your own kind."

I gasp.

I know few people who'd ever stoop to use the slur—demon it means, in the common tongue. The knight now seizes Pol by his hair, spinning him around and kicking him back toward the street.

I step forward. "Stop!"

Pol half turns, his eyes catching mine. "It's all right, Stace."

Then the vityaze brings down his staff. It cracks on Pol's spine, knocking him to the ground. A current of electricity sizzles down its length, and Pol jolts at its touch.

"NO!" I lunge at the knight, but Dad catches me around the middle, holding me back.

Pol clutches the grass, pulling it up by the roots as he convulses. His lips pull back, teeth grind together, and for a moment I think he'll fight back. But the vityaze kicks him so hard I can hear the thud of the boot against Pol's spine. The aeyla gasps, hands curling around his head and knees pulling up to his chest.

"He's just a boy!" Dad snaps at the man. "Let him be!"

The knight only laughs as we are pushed through the doors. Over the crowd, I can see his staff still rising and falling. I can hear Pol crying out in pain. My skin flushes with heat, with fury. I fight against Dad, trying to get free.

Clio lets out a cry. "We can't let them do this!"

My stomach is turning over; each cry from Pol strikes me like a kick from the vityaze's boot, leaving me breathless and gasping. "Dad, Mom, we have to stop them!"

"Not now," Mom whispers.

I stare at her. I've never known her to ignore a person in pain. As a physician, she's sworn to aid the sick and wounded, and Pol is practically family.

Dad drags me away, murmuring, "Stacia, if we try to intervene, they'll kill him. Keep moving."

I push against him, but it's no use.

With the Red Knights taking up positions at all the doors, it's clear there'll be no helping Pol now. There are too many knights, too many guns. I press shaking hands to my face, feeling the hot tears running from my eyes. Heat prickles on my skin; rage pulses at my center. But there's nothing I can do with it except try to hold it in, for Pol's sake, because I know Dad's right.

They search us as we file into the lobby. They take Mom's and Dad's tabletkas, tossing them into a box with dozens of others. Are they worried we'll try to call someone, or that we'll record whatever's about to happen? They even take my tools out of my pockets—my wrenches and pliers, and the scanner hanging around my neck. But they overlook my multicuff, probably thinking it's a piece of jewelry. Finally, they push us through to the main hall.

With its glass dome ceiling and clean white walls, the town hall is the biggest building in Afka. It was here that Pol won the district wrestling championship, and I received my mechanic's certificate after my apprenticeship at the docks. The dome above has witnessed some of the most important events of our lives.

Looking up now, I can see the rest of the Belt of Jewels arcing through the sky, a dusty strip of stars. Somewhere up there is Alexandrine, circling its yellow sun. How strange that a place so distant could reach us here. Sometimes, it's easy to forget there are others out there, that there are other worlds than this one. It's easy to forget that not too long ago, all those worlds were set on fire by the fury of the Red Revolution.

And it's easy to forget that not all those fires have completely burned out. I feel the heat of them now, embers flaring hot beneath my feet. I feel it, but I don't know what it means yet. I only know that the trouble I thought we were safe from has rooted us out, and if Amethyne is no longer safe, then no place is.

Whatever this is, it's not going to end well.

Fourteen Afkan families are now gathered beneath the dome, all bewildered, all frightened. Looking around, I see the common thread that connects us, and why we've been sorted from the rest of the townsfolk: each has a daughter around my age, give or take a few years.

My palms begin to sweat. I start twisting my cuff again, unable to stop even when Clio elbows me.

Most of the parents are shielding their girls, holding them tight. I've known them all my entire life: Honora, Ella, Ilya, Mischina, others whose names I'm not sure of, but whose faces I've seen around town. They look as scared as I am. Mayor Kepht has joined us, and is holding tight to his daughter, Ilya.

Wordlessly, I meet Clio's gaze. She's seen the others too, and her message is clear in her eyes: *They didn't even bother to look at the boys. This is no draft.*

"Teo," Mom hisses, her hand closing on Dad's shoulder. My heart pinches at the naked horror in her voice. I turn to see them both drained of color.

"Mom? What's wrong?" I follow her and Dad's gazes to the front of the room, where a tall vityaze is walking onto the stage.

When I realize who he is, I gasp.

Heads turn; whispered conversations are cut short. It isn't long before every eye in the room is trained on the man. The same mask of shock and fear on my parents' faces is reflected on everyone else in the hall; the silence deepens until you could hear a pin drop. No one dares move. No one dares breathe.

And at the center of it all, as if the gravity of his presence were enough to stop the stars in their tracks, stands Alexei Volkov.

The direktor Eminent himself.

Head of the Grand Committee, effective ruler of all the Belt.

He led the Unionists to triumph over the Empire years ago. But perhaps most famously, he's the man we've all seen in that horrible recording, shooting the emperor, empress, and their little children point-blank. I can still picture his eyes as they look into the camera after the murders are done. He wears an almost sheepish smile as he declares us "free." Alexei Volkov is more legend than man, and not the good kind, either. He's an improbable figure here in Afka, a startling intrusion into our quiet existence.

He wears a deceptively simple uniform, red coat and trousers and polished black boots. No hat, no decorative insignias or medals, like some of the other vityaze officers. And yet looking at him, it's obvious he is in charge. He has a "propaganda" face, as Dad has told me so many times, in a low voice soured with hate. The man possesses the sort of natural charm and pearly teeth that make people unwittingly prone to believe and obey. He looks almost boyish, his cheeks round and soft, his thick yellow hair parted down the center of his skull, but looking closer, I see wrinkles starting at the corners of his eyes.

Volkov swirls a glass of violet Amethyne wine in a white-gloved hand, looking absorbed in thought, as if completely unaware that there are dozens of us waiting and trembling before him. He wears absolutely no expression, betraying nothing of his thoughts or mood; you'd find more emotion in a metal plank.

"Why is he here?" Clio whispers in my ear. "What have *we* done?"

I give a small shake of my head, wishing I had an answer for her.

How many times have I seen Volkov on the government channels? Giving speeches, smiling and waving, pinning medals onto soldiers' chests, signing laws into effect? His picture hangs in this very hall's lobby, above the mayor's and the Amethynian governor's. His is the most recognizable face in the galaxy.

I don't think Alexei Volkov has ever even set foot on Amethyne until today.

At last, he looks up, blinking as if a bit surprised to see us all there. Now he drinks the wine, the muscles of his throat clenching and unclenching, like my dad's fist beside me. We can do nothing but wait in strained silence, and he makes us wait until the glass is empty.

When he finishes, he licks his lips and nods to himself, eyes thoughtful as he regards us.

"An excellent red," he says, lips lifting into a thin smile that doesn't reach his eyes. "My commendation to you, people of Afka. I was told your vineyards were good, but this is truly sublime."

He speaks so quietly I find myself leaning forward to hear better. His words are carefully enunciated, every consonant crisp, as if he takes his voice out of a silver box each morning and irons it smooth before swallowing it.

Volkov flicks a finger at one of the officers, handing him the empty glass. "Place an order for me, General. I'd like to take a case back to Alexandrine. The rest of the Committee will no doubt appreciate it as much as I do. This one taste was well worth the trip."

He gives us another smile, but it does nothing to hide the calculating sharpness of his eyes, which probe us restlessly.

I'm not about to believe the direktor Eminent is here just to sample our wine. And judging by their faces, neither are Mom and Dad or anyone else. As much as I dread the *real* reason behind his surprise visit, I wish he'd just blurt it out and get it over with. The suspense is eating at me like acid.

"Now," Volkov says, his smile fading quickly, as if it pained him to hold it this long, "I apologize for interrupting your day. I'm sure you are anxious and confused, and I understand. I do. But put yourselves at ease. My men and I are, as always, *your* servants."

I think of Pol outside, in terrible pain. I think of the little Leonov prince and princesses dropping to the floor as Alexei Volkov shot them. I glance at the bristling vityazes waiting to shoot or shock anyone who flinches in the wrong direction, and wonder if anyone could possibly seem *less* servile. Behind me, my parents radiate silent alarm; I can feel it in Dad's grip on my arm and hear it in the thin, rapid breaths Mom is taking.

Volkov presses his hand to his chest. "When the citizens of the Belt begged me to take up this office years ago, I swore that I would root out every enemy to our safety and freedom, and that I would crush them. I made that promise to *you*, and I'm here to keep it. Though it breaks my spirit to say it, there are some among you, Afka, who hide treason in their hearts. We've received a report that renegades, dangerous enemies of our glorious Galactic Union, are harbored among you. Perhaps for many years, hiding in plain sight."

Murmurs rustle through the crowd; a few eyes shift, confusion morphing into suspicion. I shake my head, lips pressing together. My family has no love for the Committee or Volkov, but neither do most of the people in Afka, or the rest of the Belt, for that matter. But that doesn't make us *traitors*. If Volkov wants to round up everyone who's ever uttered a word against the Union, he'll need a whole planet just to put us all on.

My parents fled Alexandrine during the war, after their homes were destroyed, like most of the people in Afka. It's a town of refugees and offworlders, now putting down fresh roots. We found a new life here, away from the chaos and aftershocks of the revolution. I was a baby then, so I don't remember what it was like. But my dad rants about it when he's had a bit of wine, cursing the Committee for promising freedom from the Empire but only bringing tyranny to the galaxy. My mom never speaks of it, but when Dad goes off, she gets a faraway, angry look in her eyes, and she'll nod at all his words.

I've heard nearly everyone in this hall—parents and kids alike—complain about the Committee's censoring of broadcasts, the military draft, the strict travel and trade restrictions, the stripping of rights from the aeyla. But that doesn't make us all traitors. That doesn't mean we want *war*.

We're not like the infamous Loyalists I hear about on the news, starting riots and attacking government buildings, still clinging to the glory of the fallen empire like things were any better when we had an emperor on a throne. Those are the sort of people who get arrested and thrown into gulags, or executed outright.

"Daughters of Afka," Volkov says, lifting his hand. "No doubt you've guessed we called you here for a reason. So come forward now. Don't be afraid."

My stomach drops.

The most powerful man in the galaxy crossed thousands of light-years, spent weeks in transit, leaving behind stars know what sorts of pressing galactic crises—to find a teenaged girl in Afka? He thinks one of *us* is this dangerous outlaw? Glancing around, I imagine petite Ilya holding a gun or wide-eyed Honora smuggling Union secrets to Loyalist rebels. I would laugh, if I wasn't focusing so much on simply breathing through the terror that grips my throat.

Dad holds me in place, preventing me from going forward even if I wanted to. I grip Clio's hand, wishing I'd never suggested coming to town. If we'd stayed home, we might be hiding in the cellar now with Mom and Dad and Pol. Safe from this man's cold, probing gaze.

No other girls step forward, either. Parents hold them tight, like mine do me, like I do Clio.

She looks up at me. "Stace . . ."

"Shh," I say, squeezing Clio's arm, trying to keep my voice from shaking. "We're going to be fine. You and me against the universe, remember?"

I'll do whatever it takes to keep her safe.

Because that's my job. It's what I've done for as long as I've known her. *Protect Clio*. When I see Antonin and his gang roaming town, looking for girls to bother, I steer Clio away from them. When we go hiking in the hills, I lead the way so she doesn't get bitten by snakes. Even though we're the same age, sometimes I feel like she's my younger sister. The urge to shield her is instinctual.

Alexei Volkov winces, shaking his head wearily, as if this is what he'd expected us to do all along.

"Very well," he sighs, and he waves to the vityazes.

The Red Knights jump forward and begin prowling through the crowd, grabbing girls from their parents' arms. One seizes me by my collar. It's the same man who threatened us aboard the dory. But my dad clutches my shoulder, the veins in his forearm bulging and his face red. The expression on his face terrifies me, not because of the anger there but because of how *scared* he looks. It makes my chest cave in, to see him like that, to realize how powerless even he feels right now. He's my dad. My rock. He's supposed to have all the answers, even when I don't want to hear them. He isn't supposed to look like this—defeated, trapped, as helpless as I am.

"Sir," says the vityaze in a low, cool voice, locking eyes with my dad. He begins to reach for his gun.

"Dad, let go," I say. *"Please."*

Without breaking gazes with the vityaze, he finally releases me, and my mother takes his hand, as if to restrain him if he changes his mind.

"We'll be right here, love," she says to me. She's still watching Volkov, as if he's a diseased animal that might bite at any moment.

The man pushes me into a line with all the other girls. Clio follows, sticking close, her hand clammy in mine.

My free hand curls into a fist, my heart hammering. I imagine grabbing a gun from one of the vityazes, but my own frightened muscles betray me and hold still. What would I do with it, anyway? Get myself killed, and Clio and my parents too. But still something in me itches to fight back, to not be pushed around at this man's whim. Being powerless makes me angry. Being powerless to protect Clio makes me ashamed.

At last, the room settles again, with us girls lined up in a sniffling, trembling line and our parents silent and pale behind us. Clio is on my right. Mischina, a girl from my mechanics course, is on my left. She's anxiously chewing the end of one of her black braids, and we exchange glances. She looks as angry as I feel, and I reach out and briefly clasp her hand too. Whatever's happening, we're all in this together.

The direktor's eyes creep along the row; he looks frustrated, as if our frightened faces and tears perplex him, as if he cannot understand why we're afraid. He walks to the sobbing Ilya Kepht and pulls out his own handkerchief, handing it to her.

"What's your name, child?" he asks.

Ilya answers in a voice too soft for me to hear. Her father, the mayor, stands behind her, separated by a broad vityaze. He swallows repeatedly, his skinny throat bobbing. The sweat on him is visible even across the room. But he's attempting to smile, as if to assure himself and all of us that everything is fine. I hate him a little for that tepid smile; he's our leader. Why isn't he fighting back? Why is he letting Alexei Volkov lay a single finger on his own daughter?

"Ilya," echoes Volkov. He leans down a little, to look into her eyes. "Do you know what my first duty is, Ilya, as the direktor Eminent of the Belt?"

She just stares at him, eyes round.

He smiles, and this time, it's almost a believable one. "My first duty is to protect my people. It is not a task I take lightly. You, dear Ilya, and all your friends and family here, they are my people, whom I love. As far as I'm concerned, you are all my daughters, for whom I would lay down my life. Ilya, you're a virtuous daughter of the Amethyne, are you not? Do you love our great Union?"

She sniffs. "Y-yes, sir. I sing the Unity Hymn every morning in school, like everyone else."

"Good girl." He pats her shoulder. "And as an upstanding young citizen, what do you think should be done with the traitors among us? Should I let them go about their business, planting the seeds of war, plotting against the safety of the whole Belt?"

Her eyes widen. She glances at the rest of us, but Volkov's fingers lightly turn her chin back to him.

"I—I suppose they should be caught," she says. "And perhaps . . . put in jail."

"You see?" He straightens and looks across the crowd. "Even this child knows what must be done. I can see you are good people. Once I weed the warmongers from your midst, I'll leave you to the peace you deserve."

How gentle his voice is, and how noble. It's at odds with those flat and expressionless eyes. I would almost believe him, if not for the eyes. But some of the girls relax a little. Ilya even manages a smile for the direktor. She clutches his handkerchief tight as he walks on, his eyes softening as he studies each of us in turn. I meet his gaze when he reaches me, trying to remain unswayed by that synthetic smile and soft voice. But still a shiver runs through my bones until his stare moves on. He has the same empty gaze as a snaptooth.

Finally, he returns to the stage, where he begins to remove his crisp gloves, finger by finger. He tucks them in the inner pocket of his coat, then removes a slender white gun. It's almost like a magic trick—transforming leather into metal, stitches into bolts. I flinch; Clio sucks in a breath.

The direktor looks up, his smile gone.

"The warmongers have been very clever indeed, hiding themselves here at the galaxy's edge. But their cleverness forces my hand, much to my sorrow. For we now know that not all the Leonov tyrants died on Alexandrine sixteen years ago. One escaped. One has hidden from us, here among you good, honest folk. So I speak directly to *you*, Anya Petrovna Leonova, princess of the fallen Alexandrian Empire: Save these people. Because unless you step forward in thirty seconds, no one leaves this room alive."

CHAPTER THREE

I wait for someone to laugh, to explain how ridiculous the direktor's accusation is. But the room is utterly silent, the air stretched tight, as if there isn't enough oxygen. We're all slowly suffocating.

"Come now, Princess," Volkov murmurs, eyes probing each of us, "don't make your friends suffer pointlessly. You will not be harmed. This I swear."

Anya Petrovna Leonova.

It's a struggle to recall the day we discussed the fallen imperials in history class. Anya had been the youngest of the Leonovs, just an infant when this very man murdered her and her family. Didn't he? I can't remember if the baby was there in the execution video. I'd all but forgotten the little princess had ever existed.

What sort of terrible joke is this?

Anya, alive? In *Afka*?

It's absurd.

But my stomach rises and twists, like I'm falling out of orbit, faster and faster, hurtling toward the ground. The direktor wouldn't come here himself unless he believed this rumor to be true. He could have sent anyone—a general, a less important Committee member, anyone—but no, he had to come *in person*.

To finish what he started all those years ago. To murder a child.

I try to look around for my parents, to see what they must think, but when I start to turn, I get a rap on my head from the vityaze standing behind me. I stiffen, Clio's arm curling around mine.

Volkov waits for half a minute, but no one raises her hand to say, "It's me you're looking for!" And why would she? What's waiting for her but a hot white bolt of energy to the brain? I glance sidelong down the row of my classmates, friends, neighbors, wondering if one of them is more than she claims to be.

"Perhaps she doesn't know who she is," murmurs the direktor. "But someone here does. Someone here knows the truth, and until one of you speaks up, I'll be forced to assume you are *all* complicit." He turns to the vityazes. "Take the girls to the ship and we'll run genetic tests on the way back to the capital. We can't waste any more time here. When we've cleared the room, kill the rest."

"What?" I whisper.

Shouts of protest break out. I'm still reeling, trying to make sense of what's happening—when Ilya's mother, Mrs. Kepht, bursts through the line of vityazes holding the parents back.

"Stop this!" she cries. "You can't take my dau—"

Volkov fires so smoothly, so swiftly, that it's over before I even have the chance to process what is happening. There's a flash of hot white energy, momentarily blinding us all.

The hole that appears in Mrs. Kepht's forehead is no bigger than a pinprick, but smoke curls from the wound and she slumps to the ground, landing at an awkward angle, one arm twisted beneath her. And I know that behind that tiny puncture mark, her brain has been reduced to liquid. My stomach heaves, and all around me, the other girls scream. Ilya's wail of grief is the loudest of all. She drops to her knees, one hand outstretched toward her mother's body, but a Red Knight holds her back. Mayor Kepht stares at his wife's body, motionless and ashen.

The crowd of parents surges and ripples, but vityazes shock anyone who gets too close to us. Screams of protest turn to screams of pain, and a few more adults hit the floor, seizing from the electric currents. I glance at Mom and Dad, willing them to stay silent and still. But it's as if they didn't even notice Mrs. Kepht's murder. Dad is whispering in Mom's ear, and she's nodding, her expression blank. The world seems to be shrinking around me; all I can hear is my own heartbeat. This can't be happening. It's all too fast. I want to pause the scene and catch my breath, make sense of the chaos.

Tears run down Clio's cheeks. "Poor Ilya," she whispers.

I wonder if she's thinking of her own parents, killed in the war. Where had they died again? Alexandrine? Emerault? My mind struggles for the answer—I should *know* this—but my thoughts go fuzzy. There's too much happening around me to focus on anything else. But for a fleeting moment, I look at my friend closer and feel a shiver of doubt. Could she be . . . ? No. No, that's ridiculous. I know Clio better than I know myself. There's no way she's some sort of long-lost princess, even an unwitting one.

But why can't I remember where her parents died?

"Someone here knows something," Volkov says. "*You* have the power to end this. *You* have the power to save yourselves. But until you do, I regret that we must be firm. Your daughters will be safe, but we cannot allow any Loyalist sympathizers to escape. I must now assume that means *all of you.*"

The reshuffling of the vityazes, the hum of their guns warming up as they turn them on the crowd of adults, underscores his meaning. None of our parents will leave this room alive.

"No!" cries a voice, and I whirl to see Mayor Kepht rising from beside his wife's body. He looks as if the heart has been carved from his chest. But I feel a tinge of hopeful relief. He's in charge of Afka. We voted for him to speak for us. And finally, he is taking a stand. He won't let this happen. I try to ignore the sensible voice in my head that points out the mayor is as powerless as the rest of us; that's his wife, after all, dead at his feet. I wait, we *all* wait, for him to reason with the

direktor. Prove to him that the very idea of a Loyalist faction hiding in Afka is ridiculous.

Instead, what he says is: "I'll tell you who you're looking for. Is that enough? Will you give me back my daughter?"

I've never seen such agony in a person's face. The mayor looks like a ghost, gaunt and racked with pain.

The direktor gives him a single nod.

Mayor Kepht turns and raises a finger. "It's her. She's the one you want. She is the last of the Leonovs."

A murmur runs around the room. I hear a scream of rage, and someone shouts the word "Traitor!" before the hiss of a vityaze's shock staff cuts them short.

But all this I take in in an instant.

Because far, far more electrifying is the finger Mayor Kepht is pointing.

At me.

The chamber falls silent.

I feel every eye like a laser trained on my face. Ivora, Mischina, my friends—they all draw back as if I am contagious. Only Clio remains, fingers locked around mine. But I'm still watching Mayor Kepht, or rather, that accusatory finger, that finger more terrifying and deadly than any gun.

"She's the one you want," he whispers again, and then he drops his hand and looks away.

"No!" my mother calls out. "That isn't true. She's our dau—"

She cuts off with a pained grunt, and I whirl, seeing the vityaze who punched her stomach raising his fist again. My father steps between them, hands up, trying to block any more blows. Mom swears, her eyes wild as she shakes her head at me. I fight the urge to run to them, knowing sudden movement now would only exacerbate the situation tenfold. Dread seeps through me, turning me to stone.

I look from my parents to the direktor and find myself trapped in his gaze as his attention narrows on me. The air seems to harden around me like cement, locking me in place, weighing me down. The rest of it—the crying girls, the shouting parents, Mayor Kepht's accusation, the *impossibility* of what he's saying—I can barely grasp. For now, all that matters is that Alexei Volkov is looking at me and me alone, as if we two were the only people in the hall. So far, I've only been spectating at this twisted circus; now I find myself shoved with no warning into the lion's pit.

But I'm not alone. I'm not the only one in danger.

"Get away, Clio," I whisper.

She shakes her head. "You wouldn't leave *me*."

"Clio, *go*." Whatever's about to happen, I can't let her get mixed up in it.

Her hand locks around my wrist. She looks at me, eyes blazing, and whispers, "No."

I push her, hard. She stumbles away, eyes widening with shock.

"Get away from me!" I shout at her, as tears burn hot in my eyes. "Get as far away from me as you can! I don't want you here!"

She slips away, face pale, as the vityazes close in on me. I have nowhere to run. No escape, no weapon. I lose sight of Clio altogether. I hope she finds my parents, that they can keep her safe.

"You, girl," Volkov says. "Come here. Don't be afraid. I will not harm you."

He's going to kill me.

Whatever the direktor says, I don't believe him. He's going to kill me and I'll never get the chance to explain the truth. That I'm not what they think I am. I can't *possibly* be. I'm so terribly ordinary. Just Stacia

Androva, just a vintner's daughter, an apprentice mechanic, a nobody. I could explain that to them, I could make them understand, if I could just find my voice. But I can barely see straight; the room closes in around me. I feel myself shrinking, vision shrinking to a point. This is all wrong, wrong, *wrong*.

"Alexei!"

My mom's voice rings across the room. I stiffen, then whirl to see her pushing her way forward. Dad is behind her, eyes intent on the direktor.

Alexei. She called him Alexei, his first name.

"Elena?" says the direktor, his eyes widening a little. Then, for the first time, I see a glint of real emotion touch his gaze: fury. *"You . . ."*

He knows my parents.

The room tilts around me, and then my mom shouts: "Stacia! *Run!*"

She grabs the vityaze's gun from his belt and shoots, aiming for Alexei Volkov, but the vityaze throws himself in the way, taking the energy bolt meant for the direktor. He drops, and my mom curses, firing again, but Volkov is already moving behind a wall of his own men; the shot goes wide.

The hall erupts into chaos; I lose sight of my parents as the sound of gunfire erupts, the vityazes shooting into the crowd. Volkov shouts, his words lost in the noise. Everyone is screaming, bodies are colliding. The crowd of parents crashes into the wall of vityazes. Hands reach for daughters, trying to pull them to safety, only to be ripped apart by searing bolts from the vityaze guns. A terrible smell fills my nose, and I realize with a sickening twist that it's the smell of burnt flesh.

For a moment I cannot move, shock immobilizing my every atom. But then someone bumps into me—a vityaze, reeling from a punch thrown by someone's dad—and I burst into motion, my hands closing around his staff. We're nose to nose. I can see through his red helmet to his green eyes, which are wide and surprised. He's younger than I'd have thought. He twists the staff hard, but all the climbing and running I do in the hills behind Afka have made me strong, and I wrench the other way, almost getting the staff free—

Then the wall behind Volkov explodes.

I'm thrown off my feet, landing hard on my back as the glass dome overhead shatters. Instinctively I curl up, hands over my head as glass and plaster crash all around. Smoke and dust fill my lungs, and I gasp for breath, ears ringing, stars dancing in my eyes. Dimly, over the high note singing in my skull, I can hear screams, but I'm too disoriented to tell whose voices they are. And the air is too thick with smoke to see anything at all. Someone stumbles past me, little more than a vague, sobbing shadow.

What happened?

Are we under attack?

Feeling a wave of heat from my left, I turn to see flames spreading along the far wall. Choking on the smoke, I search for something to grab on to amid the rubble.

My hands lands on something soft and warm.

I look down, and bile rushes up my throat. I jerk my hand away and fall back.

It's a face, belonging to a body sheathed in red armor. Green eyes stare up at me through a helmet that's been half blown apart. A shard of it is lodged in the young vityaze's cheek, but he doesn't feel the pain.

He doesn't feel anything, and he never will again.

I stare at him blankly, then push myself to my feet and stumble through the chaos. Pressure expands in my chest, squeezing my heart and making my ribs ache. Is it from the explosion, or just rising panic? My parents are in here, somewhere. Clio is here. Alive? They have to be. They *have* to be—

"Stacia!"

Out of the smoke looms a tall figure in a gas mask. I'm still clutching the dead vityaze's staff, and I punch a button on its rubber grip. White lightning sizzles along the rod.

"Stay back!" I raise it, arms shaking.

"Stacia, it's me!" His hand raises the mask briefly.

Pol.

"Come with me!" he shouts, hooking an arm around me and helping me to my feet. We stumble over the vityaze's body. I blink hard, trying to make sense of his appearance. The world spins around me the way it did that time I crashed one of the dories, driving too fast through the vineyard. It had rolled six times, with me bouncing around inside. I feel the same dizzying disorientation, breath suspended as I wait to see where I land, if I will live or die or find myself horribly injured. No space in my head to think beyond that. Every moment is a jumble, and my brain can't keep up.

"My parents and Clio—"

"It's you he wants, Stacia. They'll be fine. We have to *go*!"

"No!" I try to push him away, but a sudden flare of pain seizes my left leg and instead I end up gripping him just to stay upright. I can't worry about that right now, though, not when I could be searching for my family. We pass more bodies, and not all of them are vityazes. In one horrible moment, I find myself staring into Ivora's open eyes, but she isn't staring back. I try again to pull away from Pol.

"Stacia!" He only tightens his arm around me and I'm forced to turn and face him, his featureless mask smeared with—is that *blood*?

"Pol, let go of me!" The pressure inside me is still growing. I feel like I'm going to explode any moment. I *have* find my parents, have to find Clio.

"A war is about to break out," he says. "And this is where it starts, Stacia. Here, in this room. And I have orders."

"Orders?" I shake my head. "No, Pol! I'm not leaving until I find them!"

My hand tightens around the staff, but I know I won't use it on him. He pulls me away, through the gaping hole where the explosion was centered. I don't see any sign of Alexei Volkov.

We plunge out of the town hall and into the street, which has erupted into chaos. The sky, now dark, is filled with smoke from a dozen fires. I blink at the scene, unable to believe this is Afka. The houses across the street are burning. People run every which way, screaming or shouting or begging for help. Pol passes by them all, dragging me along with him. With the pain in my leg, I have no choice but to follow. I can barely stand on my own, and it's getting worse. He's limping too, obviously still in pain from the beating he took.

"Pol—" With a cry of pain, I stumble to my good knee and drop the staff. Letting go of him, I put a hand to my calf and find it covered in blood. Shrapnel is buried in the muscle. I stare at it, not accepting that the ugly, mangled flesh is my own. It looks like a bad makeup effect. But the pain feels real enough. *Too* real. I sway, nauseated. My head pulses and I freeze up, half expecting to wake up and find myself in bed, sweating and disoriented, but free of this nightmare.

"Stacia! Snap out of it!"

Pol lifts me in his arms with surprising ease, then takes off at a jog. I bounce against his chest, suppressing a whimper as each step sends a jolt of pain through me, excruciating reminders that the nightmare is real and there will be no waking up.

"It wasn't supposed to be like this," he pants. "It was supposed to be a distraction. No one was going to get hurt!"

I squeeze my eyes shut, trying to make a plan. I have to go back. I can't just leave Clio and my parents in that burning building. But my mind is squeezed with pain and confusion. I can't even follow what direction Pol is taking me in. My town, which I thought I knew blindfolded, seems suddenly foreign, everything turned inside out. The smoke and flames and screams have turned Afka into a grotesque mockery of itself.

Volkov's face haunts me, a ghost I cannot shake. *You* . . . I keep seeing the dawning recognition in his eyes when he looked at my parents. It makes me sick.

Pol carries me through a patch of trees, away from the town center. Sharp branches bristling with rust-colored needles claw at us, but he wrenches free of them, stepping into a trimmed backyard. I blink, vaguely recognizing the large house ahead. Pol has shed his gas mask; I hadn't even noticed. There's an angry red scratch across his cheek, probably from the trees we crashed through, and an ugly bruise on his temple is evidence of the vityaze's kicks. There must be a whole patchwork of bruises under his clothes.

"The Kephts' place?" I murmur. A wave of dizziness passes through me. I've lost a lot of blood, and my strength seems to be draining away with it.

Pol goes to a door and enters a passcode, and it opens to a dark staircase going down to the cellar. "The Kephts are part of our cell. Or *were* part of it, before the mayor betrayed us. Doesn't look like he told Volkov about this place yet, but we have to hurry. With any luck, the direktor died in the blast."

Why is he so calm? Why is he acting as if he'd *expected* all this to happen? He should be freaking out right now—like me. Instead, he's collected and sensible, and that frightens me more than if he were running around screaming.

The cellar is crammed with boxes and old furniture and smells weirdly of onions, but the center of the room is open. I stare, confused; the room is huge, much larger than the house above, and built like a war bunker. The cellar must expand beneath the Kephts' yard.

Pol clicks on a dim light and eases me onto a pile of folded canvas. He curses when he sees my leg.

Tearing my pants up to my knee, he exposes the gash in my calf. I hiss, gripping a shelf and trying to focus on the cans of slinke jam stacked there, instead of the pain. I think of how Mrs. Kepht gave me one of those homemade jams last year on my birthday. I think of how she's now lying dead in the town hall, shot by the direktor Eminent.

"No shrapnel left in it, I think," Pol says, dragging my attention back to the pain in my leg. "But you need a skin patch to close that up. And an antibiotic."

"Well, I don't think we're going to find any down here." I grind my teeth together as the pain travels up my leg in fiery spikes.

"You might be surprised," he mutters. Then he rushes to pull a sheet off some sort of control panel across the room. It lights up, buttons and holos flickering in the shadows.

"Pol, what is happening? Why are we down here?"

"You weren't supposed to get hurt," he says softly. "No one was."

I remember something he said earlier, about the blast being a distraction. I was too out of it to understand at the time, but now horror turns my blood cold. "Pol—are you saying—did *you* do this? People *died*! And what about my parents? What about Clio? She could be—" Stars, I can't finish the thought. It's too horrible. I push up onto my good leg, wobbling a bit. "I'm going back."

"No, you're not."

"You don't give me orders! Especially not after you nearly *blew me up*!"

"We had to get you out of there. A minute more and Volkov might have shot you."

I shake my head. Volkov is the last person on my mind. Nothing matters, nothing makes *sense*, except going back to the town hall and looking for my parents and Clio. They could be bleeding out right now.

"What's your plan, anyway?" I shout. "You can't just expect me to hide underground like a scared—"

"We're not staying underground."

He presses his hand against a pad on the control board, and suddenly the floor begins to rumble. The entire center of the room splits into receding panels, revealing a dark space below, while above, the ceiling—and the Kephts' grassy lawn—also begins to peel apart. Clumps of dirt rain down, and with a hiss, vents below me release pale, cold mist. I press myself against the pile of canvas, eyes wide as before me a large object rises from under the floor. Blue spotlights flicker on, illuminating the shape.

I gasp.

It's a G-Class caravel, slightly larger than a dory and the color of rust. Shaped like an almond, with retractable gliding wings and a diamantglass-sealed cockpit, the little ship is clearly several generations old, a now-obsolete model. How long has it been down there?

"Stacia," Pol says, "meet the *Laika*."

Why in the blazing stars did Pol never tell me the mayor had a secret *spaceship* under his house? A spaceship Pol apparently has clearance to access?

It's like I've awoken into some bizarre alternate world. The ship is just the latest in a sequence of impossible revelations, proof that when

I thought things couldn't get any stranger, the universe is still playing me for the fool.

So I stop trying to make sense of anything. My mind shrinks away and slams the door, leaving my skull hollow. I blink at the ship, feeling wholly disconnected. Somewhere inside me, a plug has been pulled, and a wire is frayed and sparking.

As I stare, my vision begins to fade. My head swims and my eyelids drag. At first I think he might have drugged me, but then I realize I'm losing too much blood from my leg. *Hypovolemic shock*, I think vaguely. My mom told me about it, after I gashed my head racing the dory through the vineyard. *You have to* think, *Stacia, before you do these things!* she'd lectured.

Think, Stacia. Think . . .

I try to call out to Pol, but I'm too weak. My vision begins to dim, and I raise a hand feebly, but he's too focused on the controls to notice.

"I have to get to Clio . . ." I whisper. "Please . . ."

I slump over. The last thing I see is the hatch of the caravel slowly lowering open, and then I pass out.

CHAPTER FOUR

When I come to, I find myself strapped into a rickety seat with an array of buttons, levers, and holos in front of me. Numbers tick and needles sway over gauges. For the first few moments of consciousness, all the lights seem to wobble, like they're underwater. The seat harness digs into my shoulders.

Pol must have put me in the caravel.

I fumble for the harness, dimly hearing him say my name. He's to my left, also seated, hands on the controls.

"Hey!" he says, glancing at me. "Easy. You passed out."

I groan and reach for my pants, pulling one side up to reveal the wound. Pol stuck a pain patch on my ankle, so everything up to my knee is completely numb. He also managed to wrap a bandage around my calf, neat and tight enough to make my mom proud.

"I gave you a hemo supplement," he says. "You lost a lot of blood, but you should be feeling better soon."

"Don't launch," I groan. "I have to get out of here. Have to—"

I cut short as my eyes rise to the front window, and the view outside.

Pol pauses on the controls to murmur, "Beautiful, isn't it?"

I'm too late.

Amethyne is a violet pearl hovering above us, visible through the caravel's glass roof. We've dropped away from the planet, a shining tear falling through space. From here, I can see the contours of its continents, the lines achingly familiar to me despite the fact I've only ever seen them on maps. Now, with my own eyes tracing the curves, it doesn't seem real. Raising my hand, I pinch my home world between my thumb and forefinger, as if it were a jewel I could pluck from the sky.

"No," I whisper. "No no no no—"

"We're still not safe," Pol says gruffly. "Union ships are already setting up a blockade, and three minutes ago someone took a scan of our ship. They've got a tag on us now. We'll have to detour, try to lose them in the noise of the central system, or they'll follow us straight to the rendezvous point. How do you feel about seeing Sapphine?"

He's talking fast, trying to distract me from the fact that he's prepping for warp.

"Pol." I feel tears in my eyes, sharp as acid. I'm still fighting through the fog of unconsciousness, still coming to grips with the fact I'm in a starship, floating in space. The curves of the caravel's interior swim around me, surreal and undefined. "We have to go back. My parents and—and Clio. My best friend."

His hand tightens on the lever until his knuckles whiten. He draws a few breaths, and I stare at him intently, both to get his attention and to steady the nauseated tossing of my stomach.

"You know this is wrong," I say. "What about your father?"

Pol shuts his eyes. He's a wreck, with dirt and soot streaked across his face. His skin is mottled with purple bruises. There's blood on his tunic—not his own, as far as I can tell. His dark curls are bound into an aeyla warrior's knot at the back of his head, parting around his ivory horns, but several strands have pulled loose and are glued to the sweat on his brow. I notice then that he's wearing a red scarf—his father's. I've never seen Spiros without it. He must have given it to Pol during the chaos in Afka.

Pol looks unraveled, inside and out. If I could just find the right words, I know I could sway him.

"If the vityazes truly believe that I am some Leonov princess," I say slowly, "they *will* kill them, Pol, for no reason other than their connection to me. Or worse, they'll torture them, trying to find out where I am. But if I go back, if I just *explain* that this is all a mistake—"

"It's not."

"What?"

He opens his eyes, sighing heavily. "It's not a mistake, Stacia."

My stomach twists. "Of course it is."

Holo numbers over the control board tick down—*11, 10, 9* . . . I blink at them, finally realizing, with a sickening jolt, what they are.

It's the *Laika*'s core temperature gauge, indicating when the engine will be cool enough to engage the Takhimir drive, putting us into warp speed. Once the Takhdrive kicks in, there'll be no turning back, not in time to save the people I love.

"No!" I lunge across the controls, through the blinking holos, trying to pry Pol's hand from the lever.

"Stacia!" He peels my fingers away with his other hand. "Stop it!"

"I'm not leaving them!"

3.

"And *I* can't let them kill you!"

2.

"POL!"

1.

He throws back the lever. The *Laika* hums, blue holo lights tracing the interior from nose to tail. The core temp gauge shoots up. I feel an odd, weightless sensation, as if the ship's gravity generator has quit working. But I know from my mechanic training that it's the Takhdrive throwing up its invisible shield, preparing to warp the space-time around us.

We both look up to Amethyne. My home. Where my family and my best friend and all my people are suffering stars know what horrors. Without me. *Because* of me.

The violet planet blurs, then shrinks to the size of a pinpoint.

Then is gone.

◇

Fifty-eight, fifty-nine, *sixty*.

Panting, I collapse onto the floor of the caravel's bridge, sticky with sweat and my arms aching from the one-legged push-ups. Even though I didn't use my bad leg, it still hurts. But the pain is a welcome distraction.

It's been four days since we blipped out of Amethyne's system; four days I've been trapped in the *Laika*'s warp bubble. Pol and I have barely spoken since then, settling into a staggered sleeping schedule so we're not often conscious at the same time. He knows I'm furious with him and doesn't seem eager to press me. Or maybe he's avoiding me because I stink like I've been working out for hours on end. Which is exactly what I have been doing, desperate to fill my time and release the anxiety coiled in my muscles. It's an awkward undertaking with one bad leg, but the pain patches have helped. By now, the rest of me aches enough that the wound has become just another repeating note in my symphony of pains.

Rolling over, I tuck my hands under my head in preparation for crunches, but then I relax, taking a minute to catch my breath.

I stare up through the diamantglass ceiling as infinity stretches on. Pol has disappeared into the back of the ship, behind a thin partition where there are two narrow bunks, a galley, lavatory, and little else. The *Laika* is small, meant for fast, solo trips. It can fit two passengers, but just barely.

Through the window stretched over the front of the cabin and beyond the unseen bubble of negative energy the Takhdrive is producing, a pale glow spreads over space, a fuzzy film of cosmic radiation. The tinted diamantglass dims the brightness of the light, protecting against the massive radioactivity of the cosmos.

No stars, no planets, no galaxies.

We're moving too fast to see them, and the effect is that we're standing still, trapped in a globe of pale, sourceless light. If it wasn't for the navigation system indicating our rough location, I'd think we were not moving at all.

With the sense of motionlessness comes oppressive boredom. When my tired body cries out for a break from exercise, I've been taking apart every nonessential piece in the bridge. I've broken down and reassembled the controls for the ship's exterior robotic arm, the heat exchangers, the spare oxygenator, and even burrowed beneath the control panel to tinker in the nose of the craft with my multicuff in hand. By now, I'm pretty sure I could build a caravel from scratch. There isn't a nut or circuit board on this ship I haven't touched, with the exception of the crucial Takhdrive and a few life-support functions.

And the Prism, of course.

My eyes drift down to a small glass dome on the controls. Inside it spins a crystal shaped like a diamond. The Prism powers the Takhimir drive, generating the massive amount of energy it takes to warp. Without Prisms, faster-than-light travel wouldn't even be possible. A crystal like that costs as much as Dad's vineyard makes in a lifetime. They're an almost infinite power source, the foundation upon which our entire society is built.

There's no opening that case, and if I did, it would interrupt the specialized gravity field inside it that keeps the Prism spinning.

No spin, no power.

No power, we die.

When I was younger, we once took a trip to the energy plant outside Afka, where three Prisms in diamantglass boxes spun, generating enough power to fuel the whole town and all the surrounding homesteads. I remember feeling awed by their gentle, steady light, and the knowledge that they were more precious than any other element in the galaxy. Rare, expensive, immensely powerful and strange, Prisms are the greatest mystery and most valued resource in existence. Every interstellar ship has to have one in order to warp. And all this time, this little specimen has been hidden in Mayor Kepht's basement, the heart of a secret network of Empire Loyalists living in Afka.

Empire Loyalists including my *family*.

I glance back, making sure Pol is still busy sleeping or whatever he's doing back there. Then I lean forward and access the ship's computer. Pulling up a historical index, I run a search and then sit back to watch the results pop up in holo. My nerves twist into knots; this is something I've been avoiding over the past four days. But there are no more panels to pry open or generators to tinker with, and my arms are trembling from the push-ups. I finally give in to my morbid curiosity.

I'm staring at a famous bit of looping footage, the last known recording of the Leonov family before the execution video would emerge months later. They're in some kind of sitting room, a sleekly appointed space with a window that looks out to the stars. There's Emperor Pyotr, reclining in a chair and speaking to the eldest child, Princess Kira. The two younger ones, Prince Yuri and Princess Lena, play a game on the floor, while the Empress Katarina cradles her round, pregnant belly.

I lean closer, studying Katarina's face, trying not to note how similar our upturned noses are or how the shade of her hair is only a little redder than mine. Instead, I focus on the differences—she has freckles, she's paler, she's taller and rounder.

But when I look at Pyotr and I see his dark, wavy hair and thick eyebrows and large eyes, something tingles at the bottom of my stomach.

Drawing a shaky breath, I look at the children, but not too closely, because I can't forget the other famous footage of them taken soon after this. When they were shot, point-blank, by Alexei Volkov and his Unionist forces. I've never managed to watch that film directly; it always turned my stomach.

They feel like strangers, like they're not even real people, just actors in a film. I don't remember much about them from my history lessons, but I do know the revolution started after the emperor blew up a moon and everyone on it because the rebel Unionists had a headquarters there. We were taught that the Imperials were strict, extravagant, and unpredictable. The Committee made sure we all knew just how tyrannical the Empire was, so that we would always remember how they saved us in that brief but bloody revolution.

Their favorite point to bring up, over and over again, is the Leonovs' notorious "curse": insanity ran in their genes. They couldn't be trusted, because sooner or later, they all went crazy. The stories about that vary. Some say they suffered from delusions. Others think it was extreme paranoia and fits of senseless violence against those around them. But everyone agrees that the Leonovs were not at all sane. And an unstable mind wielding great power is guaranteed to inflict only suffering and disaster. All the lives lost on Emerault's moon are a sad testimony to that.

With a shudder, I close the photos and pull up a game of Triangulum instead, trying to distract myself with complex strategy. The board is a hologram, shining neon lines tracing out a geometrical map, all arcing lines and grids. The pieces flicker; the ship is old and the hologram projector glitches. I have to knock the controls a few times before the game is even playable. Then I direct my pieces with hand gestures, rushing a little, forgoing strategy in favor of a crude frontal assault on the enemy position. As usual, the computer wins. Frustrated, I swipe my hand across the hologram, knocking the pieces aside. They dissolve into shimmering bursts of light, then fade.

"You're never going to win, playing like that," Pol comments.

I stiffen, then turn to see him leaning in the doorway to the bunk-room. "How long have you been there?"

"A minute or two. Long enough to see you still keep forgetting the first rule of Triangulum."

I roll my eyes. "You sound like my dad."

I can't count how many rainy evenings Dad trapped Pol and me at the kitchen table, to lecture us about Triangulum strategy, making us play for hours and critiquing our every move. It always frustrated me, when I'd rather have been fooling around in the garage or watching movies with Clio, but now the memory brings a pang of longing to my chest. What I wouldn't give to be back in our kitchen, listening to Dad drone on about the importance of capturing the outer spheres before worrying about the middle ones.

"Your dad is the best player I've ever known." Pol takes the captain's chair next to mine. "Remember what he told us? Triangulum isn't about focusing on your own pieces. It's about controlling your opponent's strategy, forcing them to make decisions that benefit *you*."

I sigh. "I know, I know. When you can't beat them—"

"—make them play by *your* rules," he finishes.

Pol tilts his head, studying me while I shut down the game and bring up the navigation system. The *Laika* appears as a blip on the galactic charts, continually vanishing and reappearing farther along, since we're traveling by warp.

"How are you holding up?" Pol asks.

With a shrug, I click open my multicuff and fiddle with the tools, using the pincers to scrape engine grease from beneath my nails.

"You're afraid it might be true," Pol says. "That you're Anya Leonova."

"You don't know what I'm thinking."

"I know when you've got a problem on your mind, you tinker until you solve it. And you've been taking apart this whole ship screw by screw. Though honestly, Stace, when the only thing keeping you alive is a metal can, you don't go popping open the lid to see how the hinges work."

"*I* do."

"Yes," he sighs. He stares through the window at the foggy expanse, eyes weary, and his fingers rub the fabric of his father's scarf.

"When I was twelve, my dad and your dad and a few other Afkans, including the mayor, showed me the secret bunker beneath the Kephts' house."

I tense, my eyes hardening on the navigation screen as I flick the multicuff's tools open and shut, open and shut, with raspy little hisses of steel. So after days of us both avoiding this conversation, it's Pol who's going to crack first. I turn to stone in my seat, knees against my chest, my injured leg starting to throb.

He sinks into the other chair and rests his hands on the control panel. "They showed me this ship and how to operate it if we ever had to get offworld in a hurry. Then they . . . told me about you."

Now his eyes flicker to me. They seem grayer than they did last week, back when our lives were still normal.

Well, when *my* life was normal, or seemed that way. I realize now that I know very little about Pol or what his life was really like, but *normal* is definitely the wrong word.

"You were barely a year old when they smuggled you out of the palace," he says.

I start shaking my head.

I want to tell him how wrong he is, but my throat is so dry I can barely breathe.

"Your parents and mine, they fought together during the siege of Alexandrine. Your dad—or the man you *know* as your dad—was the emperor's bodyguard, and your mother was a court physician."

Elena? I remember the flash of recognition in Volkov's eyes when he saw my mother. Her name on his lips.

Pol continues. "My parents were pilots, tasked with flying the ship that took you across the galaxy. They and a dozen other Loyalists were charged with your safety and took vows of fealty to the Leonov heiress. *You*."

"Stop."

"My father asked me that day if I could take that vow too. And I did. Because even at twelve years old, I hated the Committee, Stacia. I hated the Union. Under your family's rule, the aeyla were safe. We were equal. But now, we're not allowed into universities or to take high-security jobs. We're not even allowed off Amethyne. We've been stripped of our rights, and that's only the start of the Union's tyranny. I knew I had to help. So I trained to protect you, learned the protocols to follow if you were ever exposed."

"Stop." I lean over, elbows on knees, face in hands, trying to control the chaos inside me. "It's a lie!"

"My father didn't die for a *lie*, Stacia."

I drop my hands to look at him.

"What?"

He stares ahead, his hands in fists on the control board. "He set off that explosion as a distraction, so I could get you out of there, but he didn't get away in time. The bomb was supposed to go off three blocks away, in an empty warehouse. But a vityaze spotted him and shot him just outside the town hall, detonating the blast early."

"Pol . . . Oh, Pol."

I slide my hand across the control board until our fingers meet.

For a moment, I think he'll pull away. But then his hand closes around mine, squeezing so tightly I half worry he'll break my fingers.

The events of my life seem cast in a wholly new light. All those times Pol stopped me from getting too close to the snapteeth or the top of the waterfall above our house. His obsession with the vineyard security. The way he followed the uprisings in the central systems. I'd always thought him a bit paranoid.

But all along, he was acting out of duty to some vow he made as a *child*, before he could possibly have understood what he was committing to. But he made that vow because my own parents urged him to, because all along they had a secret past life I never knew about. And Spiros, my friend, Pol's father, *died* for that vow.

I lurch to my feet, shaking from head to toe.

"Stacia?"

"Don't," I murmur. "Don't say anything else. Please."

I push through the cockpit and into the back cabin, where I can be alone. There, I curl up on the lower bunk and pull a pillow over my head. I can hear him pouring water in the tiny galley outside and try to shut out the noise. Really, I'm trying to shut out my own thoughts, but the more I attempt to ignore them the louder they get.

Princess Anya Petrovna Leonova.

It's a mistake. A colossal mistake. If Pol's father had waited one minute more, maybe I could have told them that. Maybe none of this would be happening, and everyone in Afka would be okay and I'd be at home right now. Pol would still have his dad.

But a part of me—a very strong part—knows that isn't true.

Even if I'd managed to convince direktor Volkov that I'm not the girl he thinks I am, he would have found someone else to call Anya, if only to save face. Maybe Clio.

I stroke my bottom lip with the pad of my thumb. If I were a kid,

I'd pop it in and suck on it for comfort, the way I used to when I was four.

But I'm not a kid anymore.

I can't hide from my problems or scream for someone else to fix them. I have to face them head-on.

And that means, as much as it turns my stomach, that I have to at least *consider* that Pol's story is true.

That thought lights like a fuse, setting off an explosion of panic. I jolt upright, only to smash my head against the upper bunk. Swearing, I roll off the bed and pace the tiny area, punching the wall every time I reach it. My knuckles sing with pain, blocking out everything else. The third punch leaves a streak of blood on the wall.

In moments, Pol is there, standing in the doorway.

"Stacia, stop."

"Shut up."

"You'll hurt yourself."

"Shut *up*."

He slides between me and the wall just before I can punch it again. My fist strikes his chest instead.

Pol's hand wraps around my wrist. He doesn't let go until the tension seeps from my shoulders and I sag against the bunk. I stare at my bloodied knuckles.

"Who else knew?" I whisper. "You, my parents, your dad. What about Clio?"

He hesitates, then shakes his head. "No. I don't think Clio could have known. The Kephts were in on it, though, obviously. The Drugovs, the Vitsins, the Sokolovs, the Ngetes, the Naparas . . ."

Each name lands like a smack. My neighbors, my friends, the mechanic I apprenticed under, even some of the aeyla clans. What excellent liars they were, never letting on that they were all complicit in treason, conspiring together behind my back. A whole cell of Loyalist rebels, fighting for a dead empire.

Living for an unwitting princess.

"And now where are we going? What's your plan?" I gesture at the ship around us. "What was all this *for*? Who cares about Princess Anya? It's not like I—*she*—is any threat to the Committee or the direktor Eminent. It's not like I'm going to lead some revolutionary army into battle."

He waits until I'm finished, his hands deep in the pockets of his baggy pants. He's taken off his ripped tunic and is only wearing a sleeveless black undershirt, ragged at the hems, the same one he's worn since he was twelve or something, only now it's a good bit tighter than it was back then. He looks like a renegade or some equally ridiculous thing. Not my Pol. Not the boy I used to drag all over the hills, in search of hidden treasure and pirate dens.

"To be honest . . ." He raises a hand to scrub at his hair, the skin around his eyes crinkling as he winces. "I don't know *where* we're going, or what the plan is after this. All I know is we're going to a top secret Loyalist base. The coordinates are locked inside here." He holds up a clear data stick with delicate blue circuitry inside. "Trust me, and you'll see we're the good guys here. We're on *your* side."

"I did trust you," I whisper. "Of all the people in the galaxy, I trusted Clio and I trusted *you*. But then all this happens and—don't you get it, Pol? I *can't* trust you anymore!"

He stares at me, speechless, and I know I've stung him. I feel monstrous; his father just died and here I am yelling at him, but I can't contain the terror and guilt welling up in me. Caged up in this tiny ship, I feel like I'm about to explode.

Pol shakes his head. "Then try to trust *yourself*. You must feel, somewhere deep down, that it's true?"

"All I *feel* right now is—"

I'm cut short as the ship lurches around us. I'm thrown into Pol, both of us crashing into the bunks with startled cries. The walls groan and creak and flex. The caravel shudders, then goes still, the engine throbbing beneath our feet.

"What happened?"

"We've dropped out of warp. We must have reached Sapphine's system, but we'll have a bogey on our tail." He pushes through to the cockpit. "Now we've got to reset the coordinates and warp out of here before they catch up or—"

His reply is drowned out by an earsplitting crash. It sounds like some monster has ripped off the engine and is grinding it in its teeth. My stomach lifts as I go weightless, my boots leaving the ground and my head bumping against the ceiling.

The gravity generator has gone out.

The caravel pitches wildly through space. I grab hold of the bunk rail, feeling sick in the sudden zero g. Pol is shouting, but I can't hear him over the noise. He pushes off the wall and makes for the doorway into the cockpit, but the ship spins and he slams into the ceiling instead. His eyes roll back and he falls limp in midair.

"POL!"

I lunge for him, managing to grip his shirt, just as everything goes silent.

Too silent. The engines have cut out entirely.

One by one, the lights in the cabin go out, until I'm floating in total darkness.

CHAPTER FIVE

For a moment, the only sound I hear is my own breath, amplified by the close space. I feel the rough texture of the scarf around Pol's neck, and pull him closer with it, but I can't see him in the darkness. I can't see anything at all.

Then, with a hum, emergency lighting kicks in and a dim red glow fills the cabin.

Pol drifts past me, eyes shut, body limp. Drops of scarlet blood pop from the cut on his brow and float by my face.

"Pol!" I turn him toward me and press fingers to his neck, breathing in relief when I feel his pulse.

I push him onto a bunk—easy enough in zero gravity—and tie him down with his own belt, to keep him from smashing his face into anything else. Then I push through the flimsy door to the cockpit—and gasp.

A blue planet fills the space ahead.

I recognize it at once as Sapphine, though of course I've only ever seen pictures of it. An ocean planet, Sapphine is three times the size of my home world. Off to my left, its yellow sun is just setting over the horizon, and shadows slowly devour the planet.

I pull myself into the captain's chair, snapping the harness on to keep from floating away. Even so, I hover an inch off the seat, my hair drifting around me like tentacles. I tie it back quickly, assessing the controls. The emergency power should be stored in cells somewhere on board, holding just enough energy to keep the minimum systems running—life support, a bit of light, and the control board. But there's not much point in controls for a dead engine.

I do a visual check of as much of the caravel as I can see and don't find any evidence of physical damage. So we're not under attack. What went wrong, then? Something must have caused the gravity generator to go out, taking most of our power with it.

The Prism is still glowing, but only faintly. And instead of spinning in midair inside its dome, it's lying on the bottom. Like a dying bird.

No spin, no power.

Thinking back to my lessons on Prism mechanics, I remember that the crystal has to spin inside a specific gravitational field, much stronger than anything a human can stand. My instructor pointed out that this is the weak point of any interstellar ship. Take out the generator that controls the Prism's gravity field, and you cripple the ship. Most vessels carry a spare generator or two for this reason, but the caravel is so small, there's barely room for the original parts, much less backups.

That's the downside of relying on a single crystal to power your ship. You don't need any fuel, but unless you have backup Prisms, you're screwed.

"Now would be a really good time to wake up, Pol," I mutter.

I glance back to see him still anchored to the bunk. He's not bleeding anymore, thanks to a patch I slapped onto his forehead, and I can only hope there isn't any internal damage. He got knocked around pretty hard. The best thing I can do for Pol is to fix our ship.

I unclip the harness and go back into the cabin, where I find a hatch in the floor that takes me down to the cramped engine room. Clinging to a pipe, squinting in the pale red emergency lights, I study the apparatus jammed into the small chamber, trying to make sense of it all.

The gravity generator is set between the air recycler and a heat converter. Squeezing into the small space, I take off my multicuff and pry open the tiny flashlight, shining it on the generator.

What I see makes my stomach coil.

The generator is *crushed.*

The parts around it are perfectly intact, but the machine that controls the ship's gravity looks like a crumpled piece of paper. The metal is hopelessly mangled. Even if I were the best mechanic in the galaxy, I couldn't fix this mess. The only thing to do is replace the whole unit.

"What in the stars happened to you?" I mutter, cautiously touching the warped metal.

I've never seen or heard of anything like this. Generators don't just spontaneously twist up like that. *Nothing* does. The more I stare at it, the less sense it makes.

"Stacia?"

Hearing Pol's moan, I push off the floor and float back up into the cabin. He's rousing, a hand pressed to his forehead.

"Pull it together," I say ruthlessly. "We're in trouble."

While he struggles to take stock of things, I swoop back into the cockpit and into the pilot's chair. A red light is flashing at the corner of the screen, but I ignore it; everything's in emergency mode right now. I pull up a list of measurements—the distance between us and Sapphine, the planet's gravitational pull, orbital charts. Thank the stars that much of the ship's systems are still up. I start running simulations, hoping I'm not about to get us killed.

Then I laugh darkly, realizing that either way, we die. If we stay up here like this much longer, we'll run out of emergency power. The controls will go out first, then the temperature will drop. But we'll suffocate long before we freeze to death.

"What are you doing?" Pol asks in the doorway.

I raise a finger to quiet him, waiting until I've input all the parameters for the simulation. Then I sit back and say, "Either I'm about to save our skins, or . . ."

He sighs and takes the seat to my right. "Or you're about to fry them."

I give him a weak smile.

"Okay, Captain." He winces and presses his fingers to the patch on his temple. "What's the plan?"

"I'm a mechanic, not a pilot." I draw a deep breath, watching the simulations run at hyperspeed. "But I *think*, if we put on the space suits, then vent our remaining breathable air through the stabilizing thrusters, we might make it."

Pol stares. "Wait. You want to shoot all our oxygen *into space*?"

"At our current speed, it would take *days* to reach the atmosphere, even factoring in the gravitational pull of Sapphine. We'll run out of air long before then, anyway." I tap a schematic of the ship's O_2 system. "We need accelerant, and this is the only accelerant we have."

He lets out a long breath. "Okay. But even if your insane plan works, we have a bigger problem."

He taps the blinking red light that I'd been ignoring, and a message expands on the comm screen. I realize it's a hail from a Sapphino patrol ship.

Pol grimaces. "They're asking for our clearance credentials, which we don't have, of course."

"What do we do?"

He pulls up a comm channel and keys in several numbers. A moment later, a reply message pops up. "Okay, I sent a distress code, and they've given us clearance to land if we can, but that's it. We're on our own, and they'll expect us to check in with security as soon as we touch down."

"Nice work," I murmur. "So they'll wait to shoot us until *after* we've landed."

"It gives us a chance, at least," he returns edgily. "By the way, I saw the gravity generator."

I pause to meet his eyes.

"Stacia, what in the ever-blazing stars happened down there?"

"Why are you asking me? It's *your* secret spaceship."

"I've never seen anything like it."

I look back at the controls. One of the simulations has settled on a course that should get us to Sapphine's surface on what accelerant we have, but there's little margin for error.

"We can worry about the gravity generator when we're safely on the ground. Or, uh, ocean." Right. There is no dry surface on Sapphine. "For now, let's just land this thing."

Once we're in atmo, I can activate the ship's emergency gliding function to navigate Sapphine's skies and find safe harbor. But the wings won't do us any good up here, where there's no wind to sail upon.

I grab the space suits from a narrow storage compartment in the cabin, tossing one to Pol. We put them on in silence.

"Here," he says, when I have trouble latching my helmet to my suit.

I stand still as his fingers work under my chin. He looks pale, blood crusted on his temple, and his breath mists on his visor glass. I've always teased Pol for his seriousness, but now there is an even deeper set to his eyes; shadows cling to him that I've never seen before. I've been so angry with him the past few days I hadn't even noticed how haggard and tired he looks.

"Stace . . ." He pauses, his helmet nearly touching mine, but his eyes still lowered. "If we don't make it—"

"We'll make it."

"Yeah, but still, there's something I . . . need you to know." He raises his eyes to mine, and they burn with such intensity that my stomach twists with sudden apprehension.

"Stop. We're *not* going to die today."

I turn and sit down, strapping into my harness. Oxygen vents from a tube by my ear. It tickles, a minor annoyance that seems magnified by my heightened nerves. I swat at it, but it stays in place, like a tiny snake hissing into my ear canal.

My thumb hovers just a moment over the lever that will divert the ship's air supply. Then, with a heady rush of recklessness, I flip it.

The interior hisses as the air is sucked out of the cockpit and cabin.

"If you're wrong," Pol says, "then you've just killed us."

"Thanks for the vote of confidence," I growl, and I punch in the command to commence venting.

The ship creaks and groans as it tilts. The thrusters are meant for minor directional adjustments, not for propelling us across vast distances, but we're in no position to be picky. We can't hear the air leaving the ship, but I see it spurt from the caravel's nose as it turns us to the left. That was two or three hours of life, gone in an instant.

Stars, I hope I'm right about this.

"These suits hold seventy-five minutes of air," Pol says. "How long till we break atmo?"

I mumble a reply, and he has to put a thick-gloved hand on my shoulder to make me speak it louder.

"Ninety minutes."

Pol's hand drops. He sits back, face white. "Stacia . . ."

"No talking. Skip breaths. Make it last."

The next hour passes with excruciating slowness.

If I'd known just sitting there—trying not to breathe, not to move, not to use up any excess air—would be so mind-numbingly awful, I'd have just vented all the oxygen *without* a suit on and saved us both time by getting it over with.

But I'm too stubborn to die.

And I have people waiting for me.

So I think of them during the eternity it takes to reach Sapphine's atmosphere: of Clio forcing me to try a popular romance show, and laughing when she caught me bingeing it obsessively through the night. I think of Mom, explaining some complicated surgical procedure with fiendishly grisly detail while I helped her clean her office. I think of Dad after too many glasses of his own wine, banging away on our ancient piano. He would urge me to dance, telling me stories about his wild younger days back on Snow, his home-moon in Alexandrine's orbit.

Alexandrine.

He and Mom would have been right there in the thick of things when the Unionists laid siege to the imperial city. They never told me what they did during the war. Only that they'd fled the tumult and emigrated to Amethyne.

They *could* have been at the palace that day, when the Leonovs were murdered by the direktor Eminent and his men.

They *could* have left with a baby, smuggled her out the back door and onto a ship where Pol's parents were waiting.

There's nothing I can do except let the ship follow the pattern I already locked in, but now I wish I'd taken manual control. Then I'd have something to do besides sit here, trapped in this suit, trapped in my own head.

To distract myself from that unsettling thought, I ponder the crushed gravity generator instead.

I lean forward and pull up a digital notepad, keying in a quick message. Then I flick it, and it slides down the board to Pol.

What if this wasn't an accident?

He glances at me, then types a reply and sends it over.

I was thinking the same thing.

Our eyes meet. Then rise to the glass roof, searching the inky space around us. Someone tagged us before we left Amethyne's system. If it was a Union ship, we'd have a fleet on our tail already. Our plan to warp out of Sapphine's system and shake our pursuer was crushed along with the gravity. We're easy prey, limping along in our broken caravel. All anyone would have to do is pluck us from the sky—or shoot us out of it.

We don't see any astronikas lurking in the darkness, but from the stories I've heard, orbital pirate fleets have ways of cloaking themselves from both radar and the naked eye—maybe Union ships do too. I've never heard of pirates who could crush a gravity generator, however. I've never heard of *anyone* who could do that. Not even vityazes with their top-of-the-line tech. But then, it's not like the Committee has been sharing their secrets with me. Who knows what they've got up their sleeves?

Pol slides over another note.

We land, pick up a new generator, and we get out.

He follows it up with, *FAST.*

I nod and power down the holo to save power, then look out the window to my left so he can't see the fear in my eyes. It's a good enough plan, except it's missing the most difficult step: surviving the landing.

◇

Fifteen minutes later, my suit begins to beep, a red light flashing on the lower left corner of my visor.

Ten minutes of oxygen left.

The ship begins to rattle as we near the outer fringes of Sapphine's atmosphere. I can feel sweat running down my face. The oxygen tube by my ear is still hissing, and suddenly it doesn't seem annoying at all. In fact, I hope it goes on happily hissing for ages, for eons, for epochs. Because the moment it stops, I'm dead.

Sapphine fills the window, no longer just blue but every shade of blue, from palest gray to deep cerulean, all partially veiled by a ragged sheet of white cloud. We're fully in her grasp now; the great planet pulls us in, lassoing the *Laika* with her immense gravity.

Two minutes of air left. The beeping seems to get louder. My stomach lurches as I reach for the controls, preparing to take over for reentry. I swallow hard, trying to focus on keeping calm. If I throw up, it'll all float around in my helmet, making it hard to see.

Also, gross.

"Stacia?"

"I got this. Quiet."

"Stacia . . ."

Alarmed by his weak tone, I look over just as his eyes roll back and he goes limp.

He's out of air.

Pol is suffocating right beside me.

Desperately, I unclasp my harness and rip off Pol's oxygen tube, then yank out my own. Flipping back my visor, I suck down one deep breath, then shove the tube into the receptor on his helmet. The ship rattles harder, starting to gather speed.

One minute, Pol.

That's all I can give you.

Pol sits up with a gasp as the caravel lurches forward. I redirect every last bit of power left in the ship to the thrusters, in an effort to control our plummet. The control board goes dark. The lights go off. We're lit only by the ambient light of Sapphine's sun.

"Stacia, what did you *do*?" he shouts, his hand going to the O_2 line connecting my tank to his suit.

I can't reply, because I don't have a breath to spare. My mouth opens and I gasp, but there's nothing to breathe.

It's the most terrifying thing I've ever felt in my life.

Panic is an animal instinct, and it claws me from the inside out, as if my heart is trying to escape my body. I suck dryly for air that isn't there, barely noticing Pol's hands as he shoves me into my seat and buckles my harness around me. He's trying to free the oxygen tube, but it's too late. He's out of air too.

The caravel begins to shake as we break into Sapphine's atmo. Flames lick the hull, and with the coolant system down, the interior heat is already rising.

I'm starting to black out. My head nods, and I whip it up again. I can't tell if Pol is conscious or not. I can't turn my head to look at him for the force of the g's pushing against me. I can barely reach the ship's controls.

Just a few more seconds. I have to hang on that long.

I watch the atmospheric scanner, waiting to see even the faintest O_2 levels outside. Still nothing.

My head's spinning, my vision shrinking to a point. I need air *now*. Involuntarily I gasp, but my lungs find nothing. Frantically, I flip open my visor, and feel the heat of atmospheric entry wash over my face. My brain is shutting down, my consciousness like fingers gripping the edge of a cliff, slipping one by one . . .

There!

The scanner's picked up an O_2 reading. It's weak, but it's there.

I reverse the vents and flood the life-support system with salty Sapphine sky just as my eyes go dark and my head pitches forward. My hands slip from the controls; the ship starts to tilt, leaning into that deadly spin.

Then oxygen fills my lungs.

With a long, straining gasp, I lift my head and grab the controls, my body coming alive again. I haul on the manual stick, pulling the caravel up before it can tumble out of control. And below, the blue surface of Sapphine appears beneath layers of thin white cloud. The sun is behind us, burning across the face of the ocean.

"Stacia!" Pol shouts. "Angle east! There's a settlement—"

"I'll try!"

There's not much I can do with a dead ship except fall, but with the vents sucking in air that I can now reroute to the thrusters, I can at least nudge us a bit. The thrusters are useless against the planet's gravity, so there'll be no flying, no easy, soft touchdown. We're still hurtling toward the planet at a lethal rate, but if I can strike at an angle, we might skim to a halt like a stone skipping across water. It'll take a ridiculously perfect approach, though, and I never was much good at manual landings in the simulators. My mechanic training focused on *fixing* ships, not flying them.

"There, there!" Pol shouts, pointing at something in the distance. There's a smudge on the water, some sort of human settlement. But I'm too focused on controlling the ship to study it.

"Brace!" I shout. "Brace hard!"

I engage all the starboard thrusters, trying to slow our descent as much as possible while turning us horizontal to the surface. The altimeter drops at an alarming rate. A thousand feet, eight hundred, six, four, two—

We strike the ocean and the force snaps my head forward. Everything goes black.

CHAPTER SIX

The first thing I'm aware of is the stench of fish, so rotten it's like a punch to the olfactory nerve.

I crack open my eyes to see nothing but darkness, gagging on the foul odor. For a moment, panic grips me. My body is immobile, locked in place, every frantic jerk of my limbs met with resistance.

Then I realize I'm still in my seat, and the spongy darkness around me is the ship's emergency foam, sprung from the chair to expand around me, keeping me from feeling the brunt of the crash. I'm like a fragile vase packed inside a box.

The ship is rocking gently, and it occurs to me that we're floating, being tossed by waves, instead of sinking to the ocean's depths.

Which means . . . we might actually survive this.

I feel about, pushing against the foam, as panic wells in me. I can't find the release button. I'm going to suffocate in here, in a bubble of black, never knowing—

The foam releases with a hiss, contracting and falling limp, a spongy sheet folding over the sides of the chair. Hands unlock my helmet, and I gasp down salty, fishy, humid air, so gloriously *oxygenated* that I want to cry.

A face—tinted blue and scaled on the cheeks and chin, with large, dark eyes and no hair to speak of—blinks back at me. I recognize the man as an eeda, the race of adapted humans native to Sapphine. But even having seen them on holo before, I'm still slightly taken aback by how . . . aquatic he looks.

The eeda takes one look at me and grimaces.

"Oh, just an easy scrap haul, Ma said," he moans. "Just an easy bit of money. Didn't count on salt-brained survivors, did she? Blasted inconvenient. Oh, c'mon, offworlder. Up, up, before I change my mind and leave you to drown, eh?"

◇

Pol and I stand on a metal dock, watching our crumpled caravel as it's lifted out of the sea. Water pours from the engine, and seeing the shape it's in, I'm still shocked we survived relatively unscathed. The eeda was all too happy to accept the ship as payment for our rescue, but as Pol pointed out to me, we didn't have much choice. If we'd resisted, he'd simply have taken the ship and left us behind. The *Laika*'s useless now, but the scrap will be worth something—and its Prism a small fortune. I suppose it's the eeda's lucky day, for all his moaning about having to rescue us "blasted fool offworlders."

"Well," I say, turning away from the wreck, my stomach still queasy, "now what?"

This is the floating city of Junwa Quay, according to our reluctant rescuer. We're facing a vast network of floating docks, cobbled together from sheets of aluminum, metal grates, and rope, and buoyed by what look like crates full of kelp. Dozens of ships come and go, jockeying for landing pads. I watch them closely, wondering if any are bound for Amethyne. But most of them are small local vessels, hauling cargo crates or fishing equipment. All around them, automated skiffs lift containers to and from the ships' bays, while eeda and humans barter and shout along the quay.

Pol coughs and gently redirects me, turning us both so we're facing the caravel. Green Knight peacekeepers are approaching; the eeda told us they pay them off, so they won't report the scrap haul to the dock master, but he said nothing about us. If we're registered as undocumented arrivals, we'll be in trouble.

We keep our backs turned until the knights go past, then hurry down the quay toward the city.

A ring surrounds the entire settlement, a great floating wall that keeps out the strong waves. The water inside is relatively still and stunningly turquoise. A network of aluminum quays connect massive floating platforms, on which rusty buildings huddle. We stop as a warning light flashes in front of us; the quay ahead lifts, allowing a small, agile vessel manned by an eeda to skim through. Once the quay lowers again, we walk across. I remember seeing aerial shots of Sapphine's famous floating cities and thinking how they looked almost alive: branching, growing organisms spread across the water. Every part is mobile, the platforms like vast barges that can connect and disconnect, so the footprint of the city is always shifting. Most of Sapphine's cities are concentrated on its equatorial current, so while they seem to stand still when you're in them, they're actually constantly on the move, like space ports orbiting the planet.

Eeda children dive effortlessly into the water and pop up with fish in their hands. Glass aquaculture domes protect thriving plant life. The quays form a maze through markets and residential districts, and I'm struck by the almost complete lack of wood, which is our primary building material on forested Amethyne. But here, everything is made of glass and metal, and it's clear nothing is wasted. Many buildings look like they were cobbled out of old boat hulls, some of them still stamped with the fading names of the ships they once were.

When we reach a market barge, we pass rows of beggars holding up credit pods, pleading silently for deposits. Each of them has a vertical line tattooed between their eyebrows. I reach into my pocket, where I usually keep my own pod, then remember it's long gone, seized by the vityazes along with my scanner and tools. All I have left is my multicuff.

"We're in the center of the Belt now," Pol whispers in my ear.

"Things will be different here. The Committee's presence is stronger in this sector."

"These people . . . Why does no one help them?"

"They're the lucky ones. Most are relatives of dissenters and protesters, stripped of their property, money, and rights. Those tattoos mark them as ineligible for jobs, so they'll always serve as warnings to the rest of the people. Stay in line, or get forced outside of society altogether."

"If this is what happens to the *families*," I whisper, "where are the actual criminals?"

"They're not criminals," he returns sharply. "They're just trying to find freedom. And they'll be in one of the gulags, if not dead."

The market swallows us up; the air is thick with the smells of smoke and salt and above all else, *fish*. I've never seen so many types of seafood, from raw, tentacled things to pallets of kelp. To our left, a bar is serving bowls of steaming noodles. The smell makes my stomach grumble, and I remember I haven't eaten in ages. All this food, right next to all those starving outcasts.

Back on Amethyne, are my parents being tattooed with that line of shame? Is Clio being forced to beg? I doubt they'd get off that easy.

"We should go back to my original plan," I say. Putting a hand on his arm, I meet his eyes. "We try *talking* to them. Maybe it's not too late to clear things up. If we . . . if . . ."

Pol frowns. "Stacia?"

I can't speak.

Can't *think*.

Because my eyes are fixed on a holoscreen booth behind him, where a dozen different displays are broadcasting the same scene: a group of prisoners marching onto a transport ship, their hands shackled and heads bent.

"Clio," I whisper.

Pol turns to look. "What?"

I shake my head and point. The prisoners are all Afkans, my neighbors and friends. And there she is among them, her eyes downcast, her shoulders hunched. She looks traumatized. Her hair is slung down her back in a messy braid. Her clothes—a brown, shapeless prisoner's uniform—are too big for her, swallowing her up.

"They've got *Clio*, Pol."

He takes my hand and says nothing, eyes fixed on the screen.

The camera pans slightly to Alexei Volkov. He's dressed in combat gear, but he doesn't look like he's been doing much fighting. There's too much polish on him, his yellow hair too perfect. The uniform is just for show. I can't hear the broadcast over the noise of the market, but I can read the words on the holo plainly enough.

UNION FORCES QUELL UPRISING ON AMETHYNE

Below that reads, *Committee refutes claims that Anya Leonova is alive.*

"Where are they taking them?" I whisper. Pulling away from Pol, I approach the booth, until I'm close enough to hear the announcement. Behind me, people are pausing to look up curiously at the screen. A man carrying a load of fishing nets spits on the floor, muttering about rebels making everything worse.

A woman's smooth voice is narrating the broadcast.

"A recent terrorist incident on the fringe planet of Amethyne has led to an increase of insurrectionist activity. Claims have been made that Anya Leonova, youngest of the imperial family, may in fact be alive and involved in the event."

The screen now shows scenes of the destruction of Afka. Not just the town hall but most of the other buildings are on fire, belching clouds of black smoke.

The world seems to tilt around me. I lean against Pol, nauseated.

Then the direktor himself speaks. "These claims are false, of course. Princess Anya Leonova perished sixteen years ago, alongside the tyrannical Emperor Pyotr. This imposter, this Stacia Androva of Afka-on-Amethyne, will be found, I assure you, and brought to justice for this senseless attack. We hope Ms. Androva chooses the peaceful option and turns herself in, but rest assured, we will do whatever it takes to bring her into custody. In the meantime, we will be questioning her known associates at our secure facilities back at the Autumn Palace."

And there we are: holos of me and Pol, rotating under the words *wanted* and *dangerous.*

"A reward is being offered for information leading to the capture of two individuals believed to be behind the attack," says the announcer.

"We have to get out of here," Pol murmurs in my ear. *"Now."*

"They took her. They took *Clio.*"

His face is pale, his grip hard on my arm. "It's a trap, Stacia. He wanted you to see the prisoners, so you'd come running into his hands."

"So? They're going to torture her!"

"No," he breathes. "She'll be fine. I swear to you, no one will hurt Clio."

"How can you know that? You can't possibly know that!"

He pulls at me. My shouts are drawing attention.

All thoughts of returning to Amethyne evaporate from my head. Clio, my Clio, has been ripped from home and taken across the stars to some Alexandrine prison. She must be terrified. She must believe that I abandoned her.

But I haven't. And I won't.

"If I turn myself in, maybe they'll let her go," I say. "You heard him: They're going to interrogate her. That means *torture*, Pol." Tears burn in my eyes; I can't even say the words without my voice sticking to my throat. The Sapphine air is hot and humid, but I'm chilled to my core.

"Let's just focus on surviving *this* planet, okay? Then we'll worry about what comes next."

Pol starts pulling me away. I catch one more glimpse of her on the screen, as the Afkan prisoners settle in for transport to Alexandrine.

I'm coming, I promise. *I'll do whatever it takes to reach you. I'll tear every star from the sky if I must.*

"Stacia, let's *go*!"

◇

We walk through the city's less populated streets until we find an alley that dead-ends into the sea. The buildings on either side—apartments, ratty and rusted—lean overhead, reducing the sky to a sliver and casting the alley in shadow. A sign squeaks as it sways in the wind, advertising a psychic's services, but the shop looks long closed. My leg is starting to hurt again, and we have no more pain patches. Pol leaves me to rest on the steps and goes off in search of a transmitter, hoping to contact the Loyalists.

While he's gone, I unclip my multicuff and remove the hinges from the psychic's door. After making sure no one is watching, I slip inside.

The shop is dusty and piled with junk, boxes of charms and gems and carved totems. I shuffle through the mess to the far wall, which is covered in heavy drapes. Pulling them down, I find a wide window looking out to the sea, with no buildings or quays to interrupt the scene. A rusted panel on the wall opens to reveal electrical wiring. I study it a moment, then pull out my tools again and set to work.

Within a few minutes, I've got a few lamps lit. They're shaped like crystal balls and glow softly blue. Dragging cushions from a box, I pile them by the window, and that's where Pol finds me an hour later, lying back and watching the waves lap at the city's barrier ring.

He's sporting a new hat—a wide-brimmed, conical thing I've seen the eeda wearing. It looks ridiculous on him, but it hides his telltale horns that are basically antennae transmitting *I'm not from here.* He's also got on a fisherman's coat that hangs to his knees and makes him look vaguely piratical.

"Nice," he says, looking around. "No transmitter, but I swiped these."

His pockets are full of ration bars. I open one, sniff, and grimace. The bars are made of seaweed and taste awful, but I'm hungry enough to not care too much.

"Wait," I say, pausing over a mouthful of seaweed. "Where did you get *that*?"

He brushes his coat, trying to conceal the gun tucked in his belt. "Doesn't matter."

"Pol—"

"We can't be defenseless here, Stace. Don't worry. The guy never knew I took it. He'll wake up in an hour and think he got mugged by some gang. There are enough of them running around this place." He sits beside me and opens another pocket in his coat. "I thought we'd better wear disguises, since our faces are popping up all over the news."

I take the bottle of hair dye he hands me and lift a brow. *"Purple?"*

He blinks. "It's your favorite color."

"Yeah . . . but I never thought to use it on my *hair*."

He flushes and mutters, "Fine, I'll go get another—"

"Oh, sit down. You'll have to help me with it, though. My leg's killing me."

"Right, I got something for that too."

He hands me a wad of pain patches, then finds a bucket amid the clutter behind us. The taps still work, probably pulling water straight from the sea below.

Pol sits behind me and carefully rinses my hair. His hands are surprisingly gentle, his fingers teasing out the knots. He squints at the instructions on the dye before carefully applying it. I'd half worried he'd scrub it into my scalp as if I were one of his mantibu, but he seems almost afraid to touch me, as if my hair were made of glass and he fears it will shatter if handled too roughly.

I can only imagine what Clio would have to say about this. My cheeks grow hot.

"We have to go to her, Pol. We have to get her back."

"We can save all our people once we have the Loyalists' help. You'll see. We'll take back the galaxy and free everyone."

"I promised her we'd get strawberry ice," I whisper. "I have to keep that promise."

"You'll keep it. Look, I swear to you, Clio is going to be fine."

I lean back, letting him rinse out the excess dye. I never knew Pol could be so gentle. Tingles race over my scalp and down my spine, and I start to shiver.

"You all right?" he asks.

"Uh . . . the water's cold."

He takes off his coat and wraps it around my shoulders, then finds a ream of gauzy cloth that he uses to wrap up my wet hair.

"You look ready to tell my fortune," he says, grinning.

I sigh and huddle in his coat. I wish someone could tell me *mine*, could promise that soon my family will be together again, happy like we once were. But I know it's impossible; even if I get home somehow, even if I get Clio back, Pol's dad would still be dead. Spiros was a part of our family, like my big, hairy, laughing uncle. I can picture him in his scarf, sharing a joke with Dad—probably at my or Pol's expense.

Thinking of him brings tears to my eyes, but I don't want Pol to see them, so I blink hard until they're gone.

We sit side by side, watching the water. The sun is setting to the west, out of sight, but its riot of color splashes the horizon and shimmers on the water. A few boats move in the distance, and a space-bound ship angles upward, trailing blue lines across the sky.

After my hair dries, I let it down and shake it out, studying my reflection in the window. Now that I see it, the purple *is* actually sort of cool.

"Stacia . . ." Pol turns slightly, not quite meeting my eyes. "Did you mean what you said back on the caravel? About . . . never trusting me again?"

I draw my knees to my chest and hug them. "Pol, I . . . don't know. Look, this is all *nuts*. Right now, all I can think about is getting Clio out of the Committee's hands."

"You've always looked out for her, ever since we were little," he murmurs. "Stacia and Clio, the Twins, your dad called you. As bonded as the moons of Amethyne."

I nod. "I'm the only person she has."

"No," he says, and he reaches out to grip my hand. "She has me too."

I look down at his fingers, stained purple from the dye. My hand briefly tightens around his, but then I pull away, inhaling deeply.

"Look at us," I say, trying to lighten my voice. "Not much of a rescue squad, are we?"

"Nonsense. All we have to do is steal a spaceship, join up with a hidden resistance army, battle our way to the center of the galaxy, retake the throne, and somehow not die in the process." He shrugs. "We're Afka's wrestling champion and top mechanic. This will be a piece of seaweed cake."

I make a face and brush crumbs from my lap. "I'll settle for just saving Clio and getting as far away from the rest of it as possible."

His lips part like he's about to say something more, but then he sighs and falls silent.

We lie back as darkness falls, nestled in the musty cushions. One of the lamps is pricked with tiny holes, so it casts soft beads of light across the ceiling, like a net of stars. I turn off all the others but leave that one on. Pol nods off first, and I listen to him breathing beside me. When he sleeps, some of the worry drains from his face, but there's still a crease between his eyes. I stare at it, reminded of the tattooed outcasts in the market. Impulsively, I reach out and softly touch the line, and Pol's face scrunches reflexively. When he relaxes again, the crease is still there.

As I drowse off, I try hard to think about Clio, and how we're going to get off this planet, and not how warm Pol's fingers were in my hair.

e next day, we scour the market barges, searching for a transmitter Pol can try to contact the Loyalists. While he digs through a scrap-r's junk pile, I slip to the stall next door, where a female eeda is sell-g passage credits.

"Anything to Alexandrine?" I ask her softly so Pol doesn't hear rough the thin stall partition.

She's smoking a long pipe; when she pulls it from her lips, the oke releases through gills in her neck. "Sure, if you got a thousand edits."

"A thousand—" I swallow hard. "What about Amethyne?"

"See for yourself," she says, sliding a tablet toward me. I press the tion for Amethyne. Every departing vessel comes up as *canceled*.

"The Purple Planet's gone full revolt," she says. "Crazy Loyalists d those savage vityazes, blowing each other up. Bleedin' shame too. here's gonna be a wine shortage now."

"Surely *someone* is going there?"

She shrugs. "Committee's put up a blockade. No one in or out. n't even transmit a message to the planet. Fools have got themselves o stormy water now. Dunno what they were thinking, kidnapping e princess."

"She wasn't kidnapped. And the direktor himself said she *isn't* the ncess."

The eeda shrugs. "Makes no difference to me. Leonovs, Committee, ey're all the same. Alexandrine thugs looking down on us adapted k, always busting down doors and making up charges."

Groaning in frustration, I turn away—only to bump into the next stomer.

I stumble as the man reaches out to steady me.

"Get off!" I snap, pulling away.

"Pardon me, I didn't mean to offend."

The stranger's voice is deep and polite. I blink, looking closer, but there's not much to see. He's got a gray hood pulled over his face so most of his features are cast in shadow. All I can make out is that he's younger than his voice implies. He holds a wooden staff in one hand, which makes me think he might be an offworlder too, given how little wood I've seen on this planet.

"If you want passage," I say, "better look elsewhere. This place is a rip-off."

"Hey!" The eeda glares at me, jabbing her pipe in the air.

The stranger gives a half smile. "Actually, I have a ship of my own. I was thinking of registering it here, in case anyone might be looking for passage."

My eyebrows rise a fraction. "Oh? Where you headed?"

"Alexandrine."

"Really? I was just—" I cut short when I spot a pair of local Green Knight peacekeepers strolling our way. The sight of those uniforms is so achingly familiar, reminding me of all my friends on the force back home. But these knights are no friends of mine.

"Something wrong?" asks the stranger.

"No, nothing . . ." I turn around, hiding my face in case the knights look this way.

The eeda notices my evasive behavior and narrows her eyes. Panicking, I slip away before she can put two and two together, hoping my violet hair is enough to fool her. The stranger calls out, but his voice is lost in the noise of the street.

I spot a man walking with a pole across his shoulders. Wriggling eels hanging along its length create a useful curtain. I duck in front of him, letting him shield me from the knights until I can dart into the junk shop where Pol is still digging through piles of parts.

"Nothing," Pol growls when I tug at him. "Not a single blazing—"

"We've got trouble," I say.

"Maybe if we got aboard a ship, even just a fishing trawler with an old radio. We could—"

"Pol!"

I drag him out of the stall just as the knights at the fare booth look our way. The eeda is leaning across her counter, pointing right at me.

Pol curses.

We break into a run, pelting along the barge and leaping to the first quay we see, which crooks across the water to an aquaculture farm. We bust through glass doors into a massive floating greenhouse, past startled botanists bent above rows of plants.

"Sorry!" I shout over my shoulder as we trample over their soil beds. They curse at us, then make way for the knights. We break through the back door and onto another quay, this one taking us into a residential area. Rusty metal apartments are stacked five and six blocks high, their walls seeming to dance where wind turbines spin, drawing power from the air. The creaking, whirring sound fills our ears as we run. Children shriek and laugh as we fly past, jeering at the knights.

My lungs burn from the salt air, but Pol pulls me relentlessly onward. His hat has flown off; his horns glint in the sunlight. This quay seems endless, leaving us exposed for too long. We have no choice but to keep running. I can only hope that their guns aren't set to kill.

We finally reach the next platform—a junkyard, by the look of it, with scrap metal in heaping mounds all around us. Pol turns the first corner, but we only find ourselves in a dead end.

"Back, back!" he shouts, and we spin, only to see it's too late. The knights have us pinned.

Pol draws his gun. "Don't come any closer!" he warns.

"Stacia Androva! Appollo Androsthenes! You are wanted on charges of terrorism, murder, and illegally entering Sapphine. Come quietly, and you'll have a chance at trial. Resist, and we'll bring in your bodies."

Pol and I stand shoulder to shoulder, completely out of options. His free hand finds mine and squeezes it.

Never in a million light-years would I have thought I'd die in some stinking Sapphine junkyard with Pol Androsthenes. It's so ludicrous that I find myself, absurdly, wanting to laugh. But fear twists in me like a cold eel.

He glances at me. "Stay here."

"What—"

He raises his gun and fires while running headlong at the pack of knights and yelling at the top of his lungs. They shoot back, a barrage of Prismic energy rays slicing the air. I duck behind a rusty generator for cover, and when I look up again, the gunfire has stopped—thanks to Pol.

He's in their midst, ducking and grabbing, twisting and kicking. I've trained with Pol and his dad most of my life, learning self-defense techniques, but I've never seen him like this. He's unstoppable. He knocks a knight's gun away, then pulls the man's arm, using him as a shield to take the pulse from another weapon. Then he drops the unconscious peacekeeper and lunges at the shooter, while managing to kick the legs out from another. The knights shout to cease fire so they don't hit more of their own, and I spot one activating the comm on his helmet to call for backup.

I sprint for him.

"—suspects in Gamma Sector, Karn's Junk Barge—" He cuts short when the blade of my hand chops his throat. Choking, he drops to his knees, and with my good leg, I plant a roundhouse kick to his temple, laying him out cold.

When I look up, fists still on guard, Pol is standing surrounded by the rest of the knights, all unconscious or groaning.

"Nice hit," he says. "You all right?"

I nod, hiding the pain shooting through my wounded leg. He's breathing hard, but he's unhurt. Something warm and strange spreads through me as I look at Pol, standing there with his hair wild around his horns and his foot still pressing an unconscious knight to the ground. I realize—with a shock—that it's a feeling of *awe.*

That little revelation, for some reason, leaves me deeply uncomfortable.

We hear shouts from farther in the junkyard.

More knights. *Loads* more.

Pol steps in front of me as I stoop to pick up one of the fallen guns. But then more peacekeepers appear from behind us, and in seconds, we're surrounded. There must be two dozen of them, all screaming at us to drop to our knees.

I press against Pol, squeezing the weapon, bracing myself for the pulses that will knock us out.

But instead of the hiss of Prismic rays, I hear startled shouts.

Opening my eyes, I see the peacekeepers drop one by one. Their guns hit the metal floor plates with dull thuds, and the men follow, crashing to the ground and pressing into it as if an invisible heel were crushing them. They cry out in strangled voices, eyes wide and pained. But strangest of all is the distortion in the air around them, a pattern of transparent triangles that shimmer and shift with a sound like sizzling electricity. It's as if I'm looking at the world through a kaleidoscope; air and quay and peacekeepers appear to warp and fragment, broken down into sharp planes and angles. I blink hard, but the illusion doesn't clear.

Pol and I look up, bewildered, to see a hooded man stepping over the writhing knights, his staff raised before him, his gray robes brushing the ground. Through the distortion in the air, it takes me a moment to make out his face.

"You!" I shout.

The stranger from the fare stall approaches us slowly, and I can just see his two silver eyes glinting beneath his hood.

"Stay back!" Pol warns, raising his weapon again.

The man freezes, then slowly lowers his hood. The distorted illusions in the air vanish as he relaxes his grip on the staff.

He's even younger than I first thought, no older than we are. His head is clean-shaven, his dark brown scalp traced with silver tattoos. Around his eyes, dark lines smear from his temples to the bridge of his nose, like he's rubbed engine grease across his face. But as I watch, the lines begin to fade, until I almost think they were just a trick of shadow.

"What are you?" I whisper.

His eyes flicker over me. "You must come with me."

"Not a chance, pal," says Pol, raising his gun.

"There are more knights coming," says the stranger. "I can't fend them all off, but I can get you off this planet."

He turns and walks away, cloak swirling, not even looking back.

"He's a tensor," Pol growls. "A gravity witch. You saw what he did to these guys."

I glance at the peacekeepers, most of whom seem unconscious, but a few are still groaning and clutching their ribs.

"You mean these guys who were about to kill us? Pol, he saved our skins. I'll take him over the knights, thank you."

I dart after the stranger and hear Pol follow with a curse.

As I trail the cloaked boy through the market—he dodges the groups of guards as if he knows where they are before he sees them—I struggle to remember what I've heard of tensors. Not much. They always seemed more legend than reality, monks from the fringes of the galaxy who can manipulate gravity enough to crush a man into the size of an Amethyne grape. They make for good stories, but they aren't supposed to show up in real life.

Then again, I'm not supposed to be on Sapphine, branded a terrorist and a princess, while my best friend is in the clutches of the most powerful man in the galaxy.

I guess my idea of normal is a bit obsolete these days.

The tensor leads us through the flotilla city, taking furtive routes to avoid the crowded markets and neighborhoods. He leads us to the docks where the eeda dropped us off yesterday.

"There," he says, pointing to a ship. "Hurry, now. They'll be onto us soon."

"Stars above," I sigh, melting with awe.

It's a J-Class high-end clipper. I've never seen one before, except on holovision. Larger than our caravel, shaped like one of Sapphine's graceful manta rays, it shines in shades of black and silver. Its name is engraved along the hull: *Valentina*.

It's easily the most beautiful machine I've ever seen in my life, and I wish there were time to stop and admire it properly. But there are more knights nearby, starting to give us suspicious looks.

A hatch opens in the belly of the clipper, extending a stairway for us. Pol races up first, disappearing inside. The tensor waits, holding out a hand to assist me up. As if I need assistance climbing a blazing little stairway, but I take it, anyway.

"Why are you helping us?" I ask.

He pauses, my hand still in his. His dark eyes bore into me, more black than silver now.

"Please forgive my lack of manners," he says, his tone almost *too* polite. "I assure you, once we're safely in warp, I'll properly introduce myself."

"That's not an answer."

He glances at the knights, who are talking into their comm patches and approaching the ship.

Looking back at me, the tensor says, "You and I have a common enemy. Alexei Volkov. I think we can help each other."

I raise my eyebrows. "Are you a Loyalist?"

A dark look flashes in his eyes. "Stars, no. I'm more of an . . . independent."

That works for me.

We hurry into the clipper and up a ladder inside, into a wide, sleek bridge. This room alone is twice the size of Pol's caravel. The door shuts behinds us, and over the comm system, Sapphino security is ordering us to identify ourselves. The tensor ignores them.

Furnished with sofas, tables, holoscreens, and even a bar, the *Valentina* is the height of luxury after the clanking tin can that got us off Amethyne. Stairs lead up to a balcony where the ship's controls glow and blink, beneath a curving dome of diamantglass.

"Welcome aboard," says the tensor. "You can sit there—"

"Drop the act," Pol says, raising his gun. "I want some answers."

I groan. "Pol . . ."

"Who are you?" he demands, moving between me and the tensor. "What do you want with Stacia?"

I look at the boy over Pol's shoulder. "My friend is a little overprotective. Please—"

The tensor raises a hand, and the air around Pol's gun folds like paper. Behind the strange, broken geometic panes, Pol's hand appears stretched in two dimensions. The sound is terrible—like scraping, jagged glass on stone—making my ears ring.

Pol's gun bends and crumples, the metal folding inward on itself. He drops it with a startled cry, and when the weapon hits the ground, it's nothing more than a ball of steel no bigger than my fist.

We both look up at the stranger. The black lines have appeared around his eyes again, and his irises gleam silver.

"I'm sorry I had to do that," he says softly, in his same cold, controlled tone. "And I'm sorry I must do this. Truly, I am. But you see, I'm in a somewhat desperate circumstance."

Before Pol or I can move, he flexes his fingers, and we both hit the deck. I gasp as my body is pressed into the floor, gravity dragging at my every atom. I feel like I'm back in the caravel, suffocating. The weight on my lungs makes it impossible to draw more than the thinnest of breaths. My head swims and my vision blurs. The tensor's power is terrifying. Unnatural.

And like a fool, I walked right into his trap.

CHAPTER EIGHT

"Let . . . her . . . go!" Pol demands, his voice strained.

The tensor keeps his hand out, pinning us down as he lifts himself into the air. His robes swirl as he settles onto the balcony overhead, where the control board curves along the window. In moments, he has the clipper powered up, and we pull away from the docks and angle for the upper atmo. I can feel the ground dropping away, but I'm still pressed hard into the floor, Pol sprawled beside me.

Then the tensor finally releases us. I flip over, gasping down a breath. Beside me, Pol coughs and raises himself on trembling arms.

The tensor collapses into the captain's chair, panting. His hands press to his face, but he can't fully hide the black lines that have spread around his eyes.

Pol pushes himself onto his hands and knees. *"Witch,"* he breathes.

The tensor turns his back to us, calling weakly, "You'll want to strap in before we accelerate."

Pol takes a step toward the stairs to the balcony, but the tensor only raises a finger to bring him to his knees. But I can see the effort is draining the boy. The use of his ability seems to exhaust him.

"I don't want to hurt you," he says, almost pleadingly. "You have to understand, I don't have a choice."

"Just sit," I say to Pol. I settle onto a seat and pull a harness around my chest. Pol, looking furious but surely realizing that attacking the tensor is futile, sits beside me. The ship accelerates, and the crumpled gun rolls past us with a clatter.

I stare at it, my mind seizing on the way the metal is bent.

"*You* crushed our gravity generator," I say to the tensor.

He sucks in a breath, as if about to deny it, but then nods.

"We almost died!"

"I'd planned to rescue you, but the effort of taking out your generator knocked me out. By the time I woke, you'd already entered Sapphine's atmo. I've been looking for you ever since."

"It was you who scanned us back at Amethyne," Pol says. "You *followed* us here. Do you work for the Committee?"

A look of anger flashes across the tensor's face. "Of course not."

"Then why are you after us?" I ask. "What's all this for?"

He turns back to the controls. The metallic silver tattoos on his scalp glint when he moves. "Volkov. I was trying to get to him on Amethyne, but there were too many Reds around. When I intercepted a military bulletin, saying a small caravel had escaped the planet and that it had to be brought in at any cost, I decided to go after you myself." Glancing back at us, he adds, "Volkov has something I want. I intend to trade you for it. Considering the expense he went to to go after you, I figure you might be the only thing valuable enough for him to make the deal."

My stomach drops, partly from his confession, and partly from the ship's Takhimir drive engaging. The stars outside blur and then seem to turn to mist as the hazy glow of warp surrounds us. Stillness overtakes the *Valentina*.

Pol unclicks his harness, but the straps remain in place. I try mine, but it's also stuck.

"Forgive me," says the tensor, cool as ice. "I've overridden your locks. I'm afraid you'll have to stay put until we reach our destination. But I thought you'd be more comfortable out here than in the brig. I have snacks, if you're hungry."

Snacks! What does he think this is, a blazing pleasure cruise?

"You don't understand!" I shout. "I have to save my friend! She's a prisoner on Alexandrine."

"In these skies, everyone's trying to save someone." He opens a cabinet and pulls out waters. Crossing to us, he offers us each a bottle. Pol refuses, but I take mine, drink it, then spit it on the floor.

Even in the worst of circumstances I still have a petty streak as wide as the Belt.

The tensor sighs and holds out a hand. The water rises, weightless, and he holds out the bottle. This time, only a few spidery black lines creep from his eyes. When he releases the liquid, it falls gracefully inside. "You could have just said 'no, thank you.' "

He opens a few ration bars, and my hunger wins out. I break off cube by cube, savoring each bite. They taste wonderfully of grainy mush, not a fleck of seaweed to be found.

"My name is Riyan, by the way. It's only fair you know it, since I know yours."

"What do you know about us?" I ask.

"I installed a vityaze scanner a while back, so I can eavesdrop on some of their comms. For the past fifteen hours, all they've talked about is the pair of you. You're quite the notorious duo. 'Dangers to the freedom of every Jewel in the Belt,' they're saying. Impressive." The tensor sits on the couch across from us, watching me curiously. "You don't look like a princess, or a terrorist."

"That's because I'm neither."

"Doesn't surprise me. The Committee often defaces their enemies, branding dissenters as violent psychopaths or insurrectionist spies, just so they can shoot them without public outcry."

He unclasps his cloak and folds it neatly, setting it on the cushion beside him. Underneath it, he wears all black, some sort of armored cloth that accentuates his lean form. He's of a height with Pol, but perhaps half his weight, sinewy and long. When he sits, he caves into himself, arms crossed and one ankle propped on the opposite knee. His shaven scalp makes him look older than he is, and I can't help but study his silver tattoos with curiosity. They're perfectly symmetrical and stand out in sharp contrast to his dark brown skin, circles and lines and arcs stamped in a complex geometric pattern. They march down the back of his neck, and I wonder if they continue down his spine.

I realize he's staring at me, fully aware of my wandering eyes. Heat rising to my cheeks, I look down, locking my jaw.

"We could work together, you know," I say.

At that, Pol snorts and Riyan just sighs.

"What?" I look between them. "We all hate the Committee, right? I want Clio back, Pol wants a revolution or something, and you . . ." I wave a hand at Rian. "What do they have, exactly, that you're after?"

His eyes lower. "Something important. Something I should have kept a better eye on, or it would have never been stolen in the first place." Then he shakes his head. "But I'm not interested in a revolution."

"Either you're on our side," says Pol, "or you're on *theirs*."

Riyan rises to his feet, arms rigid at his sides. "Your side? Ha! Where was *your side* when pirates attacked one of our cities and razed it to the ground, killing nearly a thousand tensors? We called for aid, but did the Empire come? No, but they had the audacity to call on *us* when the Unionist army knocked at their gates. Did they send food when we went through famine twenty years ago? Oh, they sent it, but they charged us thrice the cost because they knew we had no choice. When has *your* side ever been on *our* side?" Now he looks at me, his dark eyes shining with cold anger. "What makes the Leonovs any better than the Committee?"

I flinch under his gaze, my eyes lowering.

"That's why we have to fight back," Pol says. "We have to change things, make the galaxy equal for all."

"You don't get it, aeyla," Riyan replies. "You can knock down one tyrant, but another will always rise to take the crown. When has the galaxy ever been equal? When have my people ever been free of persecution and fear? I left Diamin for one reason only: to recover what Volkov stole from me. I'm not here to make bargains or treaties with anyone."

He stalks past us, his dark form reflecting on the polished white floor. With a wave, he sinks a panel from the back wall, stepping through into a hallway beyond. The panel rises again behind him, sealing itself seamlessly.

I groan and rub my temples. "I thought I'd break through to him."

"We don't need his help."

Twisting to elbow him, I growl, "If you'd been nicer to him, maybe—"

"Nicer! He nearly crushed us alive! And you want me to be *nicer*?"

"All I'm saying is that we could use an ally right about now, not more enemies!" Removing my multicuff, I pick at the harness lock with the nail file, jamming the narrow point into various grooves and screws, trying to find a way to cut the power to the override mechanism Riyan activated. "Wherever he's taking us, Volkov's going to be waiting with a hundred Red Knights."

Pol lays his head back and shuts his eyes. "We're not going to Volkov. We're going to the Loyalist stronghold, as planned."

"Um, Pol. I'm all for optimism, but let's be realistic. This guy could squash us into the size of a pea with his *mind*."

He shrugs. "Maybe. But he's not handing us over to Volkov. I already took care of that." He opens his coat and pulls out a familiar clear stick. "I switched his data core and overrode the navigation system with the Loyalist coordinates, all encased in a shell program. The computer will display his destination but set course for ours."

I look up from my tinkering. "When did you do all that?"

He closes his jacket again. "While you two were wasting time holding hands on the docks."

"He was helping me up the stairs!"

"Since when do you need help *walking*?"

"Ugh!" My face goes hot again. I clip the multicuff back onto my wrist; my prying revealed no weak points in the lock. "You're just mad he got the better of you."

"It was *your* idea to follow him. This is just like that time you bought that tabletka from the seedy guy in Afka. Only it turned out to be stolen, and *I* was the one who nearly got arrested for it. You never think before you do things."

"Well, you think too much." Scowling, I twist away from him, as much as the harness will allow. "Anyway, as I recall, our descriptions of the thief led to his arrest. So as I see it, I was sort of a hero."

Pol groans.

◇

Seven hours later, I awake to my stomach floating out of my body and dragging the rest of my insides with it.

Or at least, that's what dropping out of warp feels like. The cabin lights, which must have dimmed after I fell asleep, swell brighter.

I don't remember nodding off, but stars, did I need the rest. My muscles feel tight and creaky, my head thick, like I've been passed out for hours. And I have a serious need to pee.

The deck is quiet. There's no sign of Riyan.

Beside me, Pol jolts awake. "Stacia?"

"Shh. We're here." I wonder where "here" is exactly. What if Pol was wrong about overriding Riyan's coordinates? What if I'm hours away from being taken by Volkov and shot?

"Can you tell what system this is?" I ask.

Pol and I stare through the diamantglass roof to an unfamiliar pattern of stars, but there are no planets that we can make out. I tug in vain at my locked harness. My mouth feels like sandpaper, and I wish Riyan would show up and give us some more to drink. Thinking about that only exacerbates the pressure in my bladder. He better show up quick, or he's going to have to gravity-magic more than just water off the floor.

As if hearing my thoughts, the tensor comes stumbling from his rear cabin, eyes red-rimmed and groggy.

"Hey!" I call. "I could really use a trip to your lavatory!"

He blinks at me, then looks up at the stars. "We stopped." He leaps up the steps to the control deck and lets out a startled shout as he bends over the navigation system.

Pol grins. "What's wrong?"

Riyan whirls, hands gripping the rail above us. "What did you *do*, aeyla?"

"Tweaked our course. Now release us, and we might ask our friends to go easy on you for laying a finger on Anya Leonova."

"*Allegedly* Anya," I amend. "I still haven't seen any proof."

Riyan works the controls, frantically entering commands that Pol's data core must be overriding. He hasn't yet realized that Pol switched them, and the only way to stop the ship would be to yank out the stick.

"I have to make this work!" Riyan says. There's a catch in his voice, an edge of desperation. "What did you do? Tell me!"

His hand rises, and the air around Pol begins to crack. That horrible sound fills the cabin—crunching, grinding, shrieking, reality warping in ways it was never meant to bend, all at the tensor's command. He's gone off his head. Before, he looked in control when he used his power. But now he looks deranged, that black mask spreading until it reaches his temples.

Pol bends over, hands clasping his head. He cries out, and blood trickles from his ear. The air twists around him, space-time warping into a mosaic of glimmering shards.

"Riyan!" I buck against the harness. "Riyan, stop it! Stop it, you're killing him! *Please!*"

But he doesn't seem to hear me. His eyes flash silver, his jaw rigid.

I unsnap my multicuff and hurl it. It flies true and strikes Riyan squarely in the forehead.

With a shout, Riyan releases Pol. His eyes clear and he stumbles backward, panting.

Pol sags, whimpering and cradling his head. His entire frame shakes like paper. When I touch him, he recoils.

I look up at the tensor. "Let. Me. *Go.*"

Riyan stares at me, eyes wide, then he turns and punches a button. The harnesses retract.

Freed at last, I burst up and kneel in front of Pol, my hands on his knees.

"Look at me, Pol. Are you all right? Say something."

"I'll be fine," he croaks, barely raising his head. "Once I've killed the witch."

"No." I push him back. "No more fighting. I've had enough! From both of you!"

Turning, I glare up at Riyan. "Get down here, *now*!"

To my surprise, he obeys. He looks almost as shaken as Pol. When he reaches the lower deck, he sinks into a chair, hands pressed to his temples. He murmurs something to himself over and over in another language. It sounds like *"Imper su, imper fata, imper su, imper fata."* Then he says in a choked whisper, "I've lost her."

"Lost who?" I demand.

He shakes his head, staring wide-eyed at the floor. "Natalya. My sister."

Staring at the top of his smooth head, I feel a shift inside me as understanding settles in. "That's what Volkov took. Your sister."

He shuts his eyes, a shudder passing through him. The metallic tattoos on his scalp glint, their precise geometry reminding me of the pattern on a Triangulum board—or the way the air factures into hard shapes when he manipulates gravity.

Pol rises and goes to a cabinet, taking out a canteen of water and draining it. His back is turned to us, muscles taut and angry, and I can't blame him—the tensor nearly crushed his skull. But I find I can't quite blame Riyan, either.

I sit by the tensor, which seems to surprise him. He raises his head a little but doesn't look at me. I can feel his desperation like a fever's heat. This cool, polite exterior he projects is a thin shell; I wonder how close he is to splitting open. What happens when a tensor loses control? Again, the darker stories I've heard bubble in the back of my mind, but I shake them away.

In these skies, everyone's trying to save someone.

"When did he take her?" I ask softly.

His reply is flat. "It's been one hundred and eighty-three days."

I swallow. "And you've been looking for her all that time?"

"Every minute of it. Even in my sleep, I . . ." He releases a shaky breath, his eyes boring into the open palms of his hands. "It's no use. The Union is too strong, too well defended. Even if I knew where she was being held, I couldn't get to her. And now I know I'm too weak to play *their* games."

Meaning he won't trade us for Natalya, I suppose. But it's hard to feel relief when I know what he's experienced, the pain of seeing your loved ones ripped away and knowing you're powerless to help them.

The grief and anger I'm feeling now, he's been living with for more than six months.

He's a tensor. I've seen his incredible power. If *he* can't rescue a prisoner from the Union, what hope do *I* have?

I push back against the despair snaking around my lungs. "Maybe the Loyalists can help us both." I have to grind out the words, the taste of them bitter on my tongue. "I don't trust them. But they have to be better than the Union, right?"

Pol is watching us now, from across the deck, but thank the stars he's keeping quiet.

"I met a Loyalist spy once," says Riyan. "We were both trying to infiltrate a gulag on Emerault. She was looking for someone too, and I told her if I saw her man, I'd find a way to help him. All I wanted was for her to agree to the same, to help Natalya if she could."

He sits up, and though he doesn't look at Pol, I can feel the air simmering between them. His words are directed at the aeyla more than me. While I don't think he'll try attacking Pol again, I still can't help but tense.

"She told me to crawl back to whatever black hole had spawned me," Riyan says through his teeth. "She said if the Union had my sister, then they were welcome to her. She said she hoped they'd already shot her and rid the galaxy of one more freak. *That* is what the Loyalists think of my people."

A painful silence seizes the deck. I glance at Pol, and see him gazing at Riyan with a queasy expression.

"Look, mate," he says, his voice rough. "I'm sorry for the whole *witch* thing. I should know better. I . . . *do* know better."

I know he's thinking of the vityazes in Afka, and the vile slurs they hurled.

"But we're not all like that spy you met," he adds.

"No?" Riyan's gaze turns dangerously cool. He rises to his feet, and I rise with him, electrified with alarm. But he doesn't attack Pol. Instead, he presses a series of buttons on the arm of the sofa, and a hologram activates, a wide cone of light beaming down from a projector in the ceiling. It fills the empty floor between him and the aeyla. The threads of light twist and coalesce into a shape that makes my heart twinge.

Emerault's moon.

The moon the Leonov emperor destroyed, sparking the war that split the galaxy apart.

I let out a long, thin breath, knowing this won't end well. And judging by Pol's expression, he knows it too. He's already shaking his head, preparing a defense, but Riyan doesn't give him time to speak.

"Forty-eight of my people died the day Emperor Pyotr Leonov destroyed this moon. I knew the name and face of each one. They were there to attend a mathematics conference. Half of them were schoolchildren." His tone is clad in ice. "One of them was my mother. Then, when the war began, the Empire had the audacity to ask us for aid. When we did not come, they branded us traitors and oathbreakers. Is this the cause to which you've sworn yourself? Is this your good to the Union's evil?"

Pol looks at me, perhaps expecting me to step in and defend the empire he thinks I should inherit. But I can't.

I can only watch him and wait to hear his answer, because Riyan has found the words for the question I've been too afraid to voice: Is Pol's faith in the Loyalists as blind as I fear it is? Has he given himself wholly to their cause?

Who is Appollo Androsthenes? A Loyalist soldier, or my friend?

But he doesn't give an answer. He just stares at the shining hologram moon, his face pale but impassive.

Riyan shuts down the hologram. "I can't trust your people, but I won't keep you from them. As soon as we reach your base, let's agree to part ways and forget we ever met."

Pol nods once, ashen. He looks like he's had the wind knocked from his lungs.

Riyan leaves the deck, disappearing into one of the cabins in the rear of the ship. Left alone with Pol, I sink onto the sofa and feel his eyes on me. A long moment of silence passes between us. If Clio were here, she'd try to lighten the mood by noting how the blue lighting inside the *Valentina* makes Pol's horns look sexy, or something stupid like that. Stars, I miss her so much I can hardly breathe. Everything in me is out of balance without her by my side. I'm careening out of control, faster and faster, all thruster and no brakes.

"You think he's right," Pol says at last.

"Maybe."

"Maybe," he echoes in a hollow voice. "Well, then maybe you two should turn around and run to Volkov, like the tensor wants. Hand yourself over if you think the Union is so much better."

"That's not fair. You know that's not what he's saying." I shoot him a cold look. "Pol, who are these people we're meeting? What do they want?"

"Peace. Justice. The rightful heir on her rightful throne."

"And what do *you* want?"

He throws up his hands, as if that should be obvious. "I want to see you where you belong. An empress restored to her place, the galaxy set right again."

An empress. Not a friend. Not *me*, Stacia.

He wants Anya.

Maybe that's all he ever wanted. Maybe all this time, whenever he looked at me, he saw *her*—this girl I'm supposed to be, this role he thinks I can pull on like a mask.

"I trust them," he says. "I hope you will too."

Trust.

Trust is a luxury I've always taken for granted—trusting my parents and Pol, trusting I'd wake up each morning and find my loved ones near and safe, trusting that the universe could be a fundamentally fair place. Trusting that my life wouldn't implode in the course of a single hour.

Trust yourself, Pol urged me, just before we crashed onto Sapphine. Just before my intincts led us into Riyan's trap. So much for that advice.

But there's still Clio. I can trust her, even when I can't trust myself. Especially then.

Whatever it takes to reach her, I'll do it. With or without Pol, with or without his Loyalists, I'll do it. Whoever I have to use or betray or leave behind, whatever the universe demands of me, I'll do it. I'll go with Pol until his road deviates from mine, and then I'll go alone.

Worlds may burn and stars may fall, but I will never give up on her. No matter how far away she is, or how impossible to reach, as long as she is waiting at the end of it, my path is clear.

CHAPTER NINE

An hour later, we sail into a cloud of asteroids, guided by the data stick Pol inserted into the *Valentina*'s control board. As far as I can tell, Riyan still doesn't know it's there.

I'm standing at the control board with Pol, having freshened up and washed my face. A search of the clipper's rear cabins uncovered several closets stocked with clothes, and I'm now dressed like a tensor in a complicated wrap of gray tunic and black leggings. The cloth itches. I think it might be actual wool, like, from an *animal*, instead of the synthetic stuff I've always worn. Pol is dressed similarly, his tunic black and his pants looser than mine, but with his red scarf hanging around his neck.

Riyan appears beside me with no warning, and I nearly jump out of my skin. He moves like a ghost, gliding around in his own little zero gravity bubble.

"You have got to give a warning," I say, my skin still crawling.

"Sorry." He doesn't appear sorry. He still seems angry and is very pointedly not looking at Pol.

The deck sizzles with tension. Pol stares straight ahead, as if the tensor isn't there at all. I make sure I'm squarely between them. I can't risk another fight, one that might push Riyan over the edge and cause him to break his own ship in half. The memory of the *Laika*'s crumpled gravity generator is still fresh in my mind.

Riyan's staff is across the deck, leaning on the wall. He opens his hand toward it, finger curling, and the air over his palm splinters. The staff scrapes across the floor and then lifts, falling into his grasp.

"It's called a *stress field*," Riyan says, catching me staring.

"How does it work?"

He thinks a moment, then says, "Space-time is like a fabric, right?

When I tessellate, I'm putting pressure on the threads in that fabric, so things around them are naturally pulled in—or repelled away. Gravity is just a distortion of space-time, after all. A tensor can provide that distortion in the form of a stress field. Whatever *some* might think"—he slides a narrow look at Pol—"it's not magic or witchcraft."

"It's incredible," I breathe.

Pol looks up, his jaw hard. "We're almost there. So how about we stop with the science lessons and focus on finding the base?"

Riyan's hand tightens around his staff. "I hope you're not wrong about these people, aeyla."

Pol savagely bites a ration bar and says nothing.

I stare at the navigation unit, frowning. "Granitas System. What's that? It's not a part of the Belt."

"It's a dead system," says Riyan hollowly. "No habitable planets. A dwarf star that can't support life. Nothing but rocks out here."

"And plenty of them," says Pol.

The asteroids seem to come out of nowhere: irregular, unwieldy lumps that look small until they're right on us, and then seem ten times the size of the clipper. One hit and we'd be obliterated.

The eerie emptiness of this system seeps through the ship's walls; it feels unreal, like we've passed into some nightmare. I've never been in a place that felt so utterly devoid of life. The asteroids seem to go on forever, and I wonder how long they've been here, drifting in the vacuum of space on their strange, ancient journey. My skin prickles, as if the asteroids have hidden eyes and are watching us, waking from their billion-year sleep.

"Look at that," murmurs Pol. He points at an approaching rock, which at first looks no different from the others. But then I realize how slowly it's approaching, and how large it already is.

"It's *massive*," says Riyan.

So that's our destination. I know at once it must be. The ship isn't changing course, and we've passed the window to avoid collision. Either that rock has a secret, or we're going to smash full into it.

I notice Pol gripping the edges of his seat. So maybe he's not as confident in this plan as he makes out.

"Could you shift that?" I ask Riyan.

He shakes his head. "Far too big. With ten other tensors, maybe. Not alone."

The rock grows bigger and bigger. Soon it fills the whole width of the diamantglass window. Its shadow closes over us, the monster's breath before it bites. I lean back in my seat, licking sweat from my upper lip.

"There's a door," Riyan says.

Pol and I lean forward, peering ahead.

"There!" I shout. "Lower left, you see?"

Pol nods. "Here we go."

My stomach rises as the clipper angles for the rectangular hole carved into the underside of the asteroid. In moments, we're sliding through rough-cut walls into total darkness. Only the clipper's lights are visible, reflecting off the stone walls. But ahead—inky blackness.

I feel a slight bump and realize the ship has set itself down. For a moment, we sit in silence, listening to the hum of the engines.

We're here.

I can't see anything except a few patches of rock, lit by the clipper. No sign of people, no sign this hole in this asteroid is anything other than just that—a hole in an asteroid. I picture someone collapsing the tunnel behind us, shutting us inside the belly of this rock forever, in darkness and stone with no way out—

"That's it, I'm going to investigate," announces Pol. "Wait here till I know it's safe."

I jump up to follow him down the stairs. "As if!"

Riyan is on my heels, clipping on his cloak and picking up his staff.

Pol hurries down the steps to the main hatch and the exit ramp, which slowly lowers to the ground. It hits the rock floor with a thunk, and Pol slides down into the darkness.

"Gravity!" he says. "Either this rock's big enough to generate its own, or—"

He cuts short as lights blast on from every direction.

Blinded, I throw up a hand and stumble backward into Riyan. For a few seconds, I can't see anything. My eyes fill with spots of white. But I can hear well enough—hums as machines power up, the pounding of boots on stone, and voices.

"Freeze! Hands out! Drop the staff!"

I blink furiously, trying to see what's going on. Slowly my surroundings blur into focus. The large gray blobs in the distance become ships of various classes and sizes. The nearer, moving blobs become people. They wear white uniforms, emblazoned with a red bird on the breast. I recognize it, vaguely, as the symbol of the old Empire. More and more of them appear, surrounding the ship with guns ready.

They close in on us, and before I know it, they grab me and press my face into the ground while my hands are pinned against my back. The barrel of a gun is inches from my face.

"Get off her!" Pol shouts. "She's—"

He goes quiet with a grunt. I can hear a boot kicking him in the stomach. Meanwhile, Riyan, standing with his feet spread, plants his staff and tessellates the air around him. The soldiers trying to grab him are lifted up, where they hover like they're in zero g. One by one, their guns hit the ground, crumpled balls of useless metal.

"It's a blazing gravity witch!" someone screams. "Shoot him!"

"No!" I yell. "Riyan, stand down! Please!"

He glances at me, then relaxes. The men around him drop hard to the floor.

"Enough!" A commanding voice rips through the room, and at once the soldiers go to attention. I push up onto my knees, freed as the soldier holding me snaps a fist-to-chest salute. Beside me, Pol is also kneeling, one hand clutching his rib cage.

"You all right?" I whisper.

He nods, but I can hear him struggling for breath.

The woman comes to a halt several paces away, regarding us.

She holds a very small gun, almost like a toy. Her uniform is dazzlingly white, with a half cape and severe shoulders. Her short, spiked hair is as pale as her clothes, though her face is only middle-aged. She's beautiful, in a menacing sort of way, like a glinting shard of ice. Her black eyes study each of us in turn.

"Identify yourselves," she says softly.

Pol rises stiffly to his feet. "I'm Appollo Androsthenes, son of Spiros Androsthenes, who was formerly of the Imperial Interstellar Navy. And this is Anya Petrovna Leonova, heir to the Crescent Throne, the Firebird Princess, the last of her name and Guardian of the Jewels."

"Allegedly," I add, with a sideways glance at Pol. Blazing stars, what a mouthful of absurdity.

"We've come from Afka on Amethyne," Pol adds. "Nearly two weeks ago a traitor—"

"I know about the situation at Afka," the woman interrupts. "We received word of it six days ago, and we expected you in half that time. And on a different ship. And . . . with different hair."

I glance at the purple locks hanging over my shoulders.

The woman asks, "Why should I believe you are who you say you are?"

"I know the codes." Pol reels off a string of numbers, which the woman listens to closely. Even before he finishes, the woman's gaze shifts, tightening on me like a vise.

"So it's true. You are Princess Anya." She considers me for a long, torturous moment. I've never felt so exposed in my life as I am underneath those eyes of hers. They suck at me like the vacuum of space.

But then, finally, she releases me. I let out a breath, feeling like I've just passed a test where the consequence of failure was death. Her demeanor shifts; she snaps a salute, then bows at the waist. All around me, the other soldiers do the same.

"Highness," says the woman, "I am Lilyan Zhar, commander of the Loyalist Remnant Force. We are very glad to see you safe, and it is my honor to meet you at last. But I must ask, what in the stars are you doing with one of *them*?" Zhar nods at Riyan, who stands with his staff still on guard.

"We ran into a bit of . . . engine trouble," I say. "Our ship malfunctioned and we dropped out of warp near Sapphine. This tensor helped us. He should be allowed to leave in peace, if he wants."

Zhar studies Riyan, who looks back steadily, not intimidated in the least.

Then she shakes her head. "The boy is one of the Unsworn, who broke faith with the Empire when we needed them most." Her jaw twitches, then she adds, "He's a traitorous freak, like the rest of his kind."

She raises her gun at the same moment that Riyan lifts his staff, and I burst into motion before I have a chance to even consider what I'm doing. I slide between them, ignoring Pol as he shouts my name.

"No!" I shout. "Don't shoot him!"

Zhar's lips pinch together. "Out of the way, Princess!"

"I won't let you hurt him."

"Grab her, soldier!"

I realize with a start that it's Pol she's talking to, ordering him to pull me away. He's the closest to me, within arm's reach.

"Soldier, that was an order!" Zhar snaps.

Pol blinks, then looks at her. "Stacia—*Anya*—is free to do as she likes. As the Leonova heir, she is the one in charge here, not you."

A look as cold as stone crosses Zhar's face. "You are on my base now, and my rules will be followed. The princess's safety is our first priority, and if she won't let us protect her, she will be *made* to comply. Anya, you will stand down."

"No." I look at Pol. "If Riyan isn't safe here, then we're leaving. Now. All three of us."

Pol's eyes flicker to me. All the color has left his face.

"We tried it your way," I whisper to him. "Now it's my turn. Pol, *please*."

The next moment that passes seems like an eternity.

Where does Pol's true heart lie? With these Loyalists and their cause—or with me? As a heartbeat passes between us, I see that question weighing in his eyes.

Then he lets out a breath, his chest collapsing, and I know he's reached a decision.

"Stacia," he murmurs. "Get back on the ship."

I stare at him, my heart unfolding with relief.

He's mine. He's still mine.

"Don't do this, soldier," Zhar warns.

"Stacia, go!" Pol shouts. He turns—then collapses, knees hitting the ground, tilting sideways with a look of confusion.

By the time I realize that Zhar has shot him, Pol is sprawled on the rock floor, blood spreading in a dark pool around him.

CHAPTER TEN

"It's so beautiful."

"That means it's poisonous, Stace. Don't touch it."

"You're not my boss!"

"You're seven and I'm eight and I say it's poison."

"And I say you're a bossy grouch."

"Stacia, no! Stop!"

The memory is so bright it's like I'm standing inside a holo, watching it play out all over again. I remember how the air smelled of wine that day, even though we were miles from the vineyard. The wind swept the heady scent over the forested hills. It chased us through the slinke trees, me leading, Pol following, as usual. It was just me and him, exploring the pastel hills, arguing every step of the way. Rivals in all things: For dibs on the swing. For the last cookie. For my mother's attention.

I picked the flower, just to spite Pol.

He'd been right, of course. He usually was. The poison caused a reaction, and in moments my throat closed up and I could barely breathe. Pol picked me up and ran the whole way home, me bouncing in his arms. A mile from the house he twisted his ankle, but I didn't find out about that until later, because he didn't let it slow him down.

Pol saved my life that day.

And he was only eight years old. That was four years before he would make a vow to protect the girl he thought was a princess. He saved me for no other reason than that he was my friend.

When I see him fall in front of Lilyan Zhar, it's like my heart is

I know I'm screaming, but I don't hear it. I can't hear anything over the roar in my ears. My knee bursts with pain; dimly I realize I fell forward, driving it into the ground. My nails dig into the stone floor. Someone grabs me. I shove them away, crawling toward Pol, turning him over, his head in my lap. I rock as I hold him, shaking my head, murmuring his name. My fingers threaded through his hair, I lean over to press my forehead to his.

His eyes are shut, a trickle of blood at the corner of his mouth. I can't find a pulse, can't see his chest rise for breath. I shake him but he doesn't stir. His dark curls spread across my lap, and one of his horns digs into my leg.

"Help him!" I scream. "Someone help him!"

A hand slaps a sleep patch against my neck. It's almost a relief, to feel darkness overtake me and silence the inferno inside my head. I cling to Pol as I slump onto the floor beside him.

◇

I wake facedown on a spongy surface and, with a groan, try to roll onto my back. Instead, I drop onto a hard floor. For a moment I lie there, blinking away the sudden pain, taking in the room.

White walls, stone floor, harsh lights in the ceiling. A white metal box in the upper corner that I'm sure is a camera. A panel to my left is a fold-out lavatory. The bed I awoke on is really no more than a soft pad on a metal frame.

It's a cell.

The door is diamantglass, unbreakable but transparent. I scramble toward it, finding nothing but a dim white corridor outside, lined with closed doors like this one. I bang on it for a while, but no one comes.

"I want to see my friend!" I shout. "Where is Pol? Where is he?"

With a cry of rage, I beat on the door harder and longer. I yell and scream and curse, until my already raw throat feels like I've been swallowing knives.

Exhausted, I sink to my knees, hands still pressed against the glass. I breathe in and out, trying to stop the trembling that overtakes me.

My throat is thick and scratchy from the sleep patch. I find the papery thin square still on my neck and rip it off savagely, then begin shredding it into fragments, breathing hard.

I'm still dressed in my tensor tunic and leggings, but my feet are bare and my pockets are empty. They even took my multicuff. Without it, I feel naked.

When the patch is shredded to nothing, I fold my feet, one atop the other, and wrap my arms around my knees. The air in here smells stale, like it's been filtered too many times; this is air that's never blown through a forest of leaves or rustled fresh grass. It's manufactured and sterile, and it burns my throat.

"He can't be dead," I whisper. "He can't be."

I think back, hoping it was all a nightmare, or at least that the sleep patch somehow altered the memory, making it seem worse than it truly was. But it comes back clearly: Pol falling at Zhar's feet, the weight of his head in my hands, the absolute stillness of his eyes.

All because he stood up for me. All because, in the end, he chose Stacia over Anya.

Guilt squeezes my lungs. I did this. I pushed him to choose a side. I begged him to choose *me*. And he paid for it with his life. I as good as shot him myself.

Rocking in place, I hold down sobs but can't stop the tears. A part of my brain works, nonsensically, to figure out how to reverse time, how to go back and stop it all from happening. It's like watching a rat in a maze with no exits. I know how it will end, but I can't convince the creature to stop trying.

Hours seem to pass, but it's probably only twenty minutes or so before a muted tap catches my ear. I track the sound to the fold-out lavatory, which I practically rip out of the wall in my frustration, thinking it's just a water drip.

But there's no water in the little white bowl, and I can still hear the tapping.

"Hello?" I say, then I shake my head and lean back.

Stars, Stacia, you've really lost it. You're talking to a toilet.

But then I hear a soft "There you are," and I clutch the little lav harder.

"Riyan?"

"I'm next door. I think our lav pipes are connected."

"Are you hurt?"

A pause, then he says, "I'm alive for now, so that's what counts."

I rub my forehead, sighing as guilt overwhelms me. "I'm sorry, Riyan. I'm sorry we got you into this."

A dry chuckle comes echoing through the pipes. "It's no worse than what I'd have gotten *you* into, if Pol hadn't hijacked my ship."

"Is he—did you see what happened to him?"

"They knocked me out right after they got you. But . . . he took a hit to the chest, with a nano gun. Nobody survives that, Stacia. I'm so sorry."

I can't reply. My throat's too choked. If I say it, there's no going back. There's no fixing things.

If I say it, I have to believe it.

I bend over the lav again. "Can you, you know, gravity-magic us out of here?"

"No. They . . ."

I catch a strain in his voice. "Riyan?"

He takes a moment before replying. "They dosed me with a lethal metal compound. I'm using all my strength to tessellate it in the lower half of my body, but if it reaches my heart, I will die."

He says it so matter-of-factly, as if informing me he has a headache.

Fury rolls through me, scalding my mind. "How long can you hold on, Riyan?"

"I don't know. Can't keep talking. Have to focus."

"Riyan?"

I push my face into the lav, ears straining to hear him.

"Riyan! Riyan, are you—"

Sensing movement to my left, I turn just as my cell door opens and white-clad soldiers pour in. I scramble to my feet, back to the far wall. Six of them crowd my little space, all shoulders and stony eyes.

But one is dressed differently, in plainer clothes, no armor. His skin is warm brown and his hair is white, neatly combed into a thick wave that falls to his shoulders. He peers at me over his large, hooked nose with something almost like sympathy. He extends a hand, which I don't take.

"Princess, I am Dr. Faran Luka. Things got out of control in the hangar, but I promise, we will take the best care of you from here on out."

Before I can reply, he jams something into my arm. I shriek, leaping back, but he's already finished, and now peers at the little device that punctured me.

"Don't worry. Just making sure your system has stabilized." A note of anger creeps into his voice. "That was quite a strong dose of sedative they gave you."

He steps closer, and I flinch, but he only briefly clasps my wrist and whispers, "You have friends here, Anya Leonova. Let me help you."

I spit in his face.

He blinks, then backs off, wiping his face with his sleeve and regarding me with a sigh. He nods at the guards, leaving them to close in on me.

"Come with us, Princess," one says.

"Why? Are you going to shoot me too?"

Instead of responding, they just grab me and march me out. I dig my heels in front of Riyan's cell. "Wait! Stars curse you, *wait* a moment!"

Dr. Luka nods to the guards. "Let her go."

I wrench free and press my hands to the glass of Riyan's door. He's sitting cross-legged, eyes shut and fingers steepled in front of his chest, like he's meditating. If he hears me, he doesn't show it. Sweat beads his brow and neck. His feet are bare, the tendons of his ankles standing out in evidence of his concentration.

If he lets up for even a moment, will the poison destroy him?

"You have to stop this!" I grab Dr. Luka by his coat. "He'll die!"

The doctor coughs and lowers his gaze, his brow furrowed. "The commander has her reasons, Princess."

With a snarl, I shove him away and turn back to the door.

I barely know the tensor. Just yesterday he was trying to abduct me and hand me over to my enemies, but right now I feel like he's the only ally I have left in the universe. Clearly these Loyalists are not trustworthy. Maybe Riyan isn't, either, but I am not going to let him die here.

I'm not going to lose anyone else.

"I'll get you out of here," I whisper through the glass, hoping he can hear. "I promise. Just . . . just stay strong."

Right before I turn away, his lips part and he whispers in a strained voice, *"Hurry."*

CHAPTER ELEVEN

They lead me through a maze of stone corridors, each one looking exactly the same as the last. We pass more soldiers in white, with tha red bird incorporated into their uniforms. How long have they been here? Why are they so loyal to a dead regime? And if they think I'm their princess, why are they handling me like I'm some sort of danger-ous criminal?

My parents trusted these people. If Pol hadn't brought me here my mom or dad would have. I wonder what they would have done in Pol's place, in that horrible moment. Would they have let Lilyan Zha shoot Riyan? I don't know. I don't know if I ever truly knew them not the *real* Elena and Teo. As difficult as it is to imagine them here, in white uniforms with imperial crests emblazoned over their hearts these *are* their people. Maybe there are faces here they would recognize from their old life, before they were my parents. Or maybe they neve truly were my parents—just imperial babysitters, doing their duty fulfilling some oath. The thought lodges in my gut like a splinter, cut-ting deeper with every breath.

Finally, we come to a wide, brightly lit chamber, stone walls and high ceiling over a floor of polished asteroid. A long conference tabl dominates the space, but the rest of the room is clear. The far wal sports a massive imperial crest. This bird seems to glare at me with one red eye, its wings raised and its tail morphing into a flame.

There is Zhar, surrounded by twenty or so children. She's sitting cross-legged on the floor, a tiny boy in her lap as she reads a holobook to them. The image of a planet hangs above her, turning slowly, green and blue.

"Ah, look who's come to join us," she says, looking up with a smile

The kids all turn to stare at me.

"This, my loves, is Anya Leonova. Our princess and the heir to the Autumn Throne."

"A *real* princess?" squeals a girl in braids.

"A real one," says Zhar coolly, her predatory eyes fixed on me. "And the last one. Bring her over, Taysie."

The girl jumps up and runs to me, grabbing my hand. I want to pull away, but Zhar has me smoothly trapped. It's not like I can knock over a child.

I follow Taysie into the circle, shaking with fury. This is all a pretense: The children. The playful tone. Zhar is using them as a shield.

"That's better," she says, once I'm sitting in the circle. Taysie plops into my lap uninvited, knitting her fingers through mine.

"You see, Highness," Zhar says, "we have been waiting for you. *All* of us."

Not just soldiers, she means. She wants me to see that they have families and children who need me to cooperate. To be the obedient, loyal symbol Zhar wants. Because on *her* rock, she's the one in charge. Challenge her, and you get shot.

She kisses the head of the boy on her lap. "This is Adi, my nephew. Adi, tell the princess about the story we're reading."

He smiles. "It's the one about the Motherworld."

"Ah, Zemlya," she sighs. "Our lost paradise."

I glare at her. "Whatever game this is—"

"Adi," she cuts in, "why don't you tell the princess the story? I think she has forgotten it."

Adi nods, taking the book from her and opening it on his lap. The blue planet spins above us, and the children look up with wide eyes. Zemlya reminds me a little of Amethyne; it's a bit larger, and its sun was yellow, not violet, but the green continents and blue seas are similar. And like my home planet, the Motherworld is said to have been lush and forested once.

"Zemlya was dying," Adi says, reciting more than reading. "Humans had used up all her water and plants. So they built ten ships."

"Ten arks to sail to ten distant stars," murmurs Zhar.

Adi nods, turning a page, and the ships appear above us, each going a different direction. They were bulky, ugly things, built to house generation after generation. Millions of humans living and dying without ever standing on any planet at all, in the hopes their descendents would one day find solid ground again.

Adi says, "But they were so slow because they didn't have . . . um, what's the word, Aunt?"

"Prisms, dear. They lacked the energy to exceed the speed of light, and so they limped through the universe."

Adi flips patiently through the book, the holo overhead changing with each turn of the page, recounting the ancient story. Of the ten ships that left Zemlya, nine reached their destinations. But by the time the arks reached their planets, for some, hundreds of years had gone by. And once they arrived, they were alone, isolated from the other arks, unable to communicate. They didn't know if their sister tribes lived or died. And so they developed their own cultures, languages, even genetic code, adapting to their new worlds in strange and wonderful ways.

My genes are Alexandrian; I don't look much different from those first humans who left the Motherworld, just built a little smaller, because of Alexandrine's slightly higher gravity. I think miserably of the aeyla, of Pol and his ivory horns and his quick reflexes.

"In the end," Adi continues, turning a page, "there were nine races in nine systems, seeds fallen far from their mother tree. And so it would have gone on forever, humanity split into nine new species, growing ever more separate."

"Then a pair of scientists on Alexandrine, the sisters Danica and Zorica Leonova, discovered Prisms," I rush in, trying to bring the story to a close. Taysie shifts on my lap to look up at me, her braids tickling my chin. "The Leonova sisters used them to develop warp ships, found the other eight tribes, and formed the Belt of Jewels. That was a thousand years ago, so why does it matter now?"

Zhar smiles at the children, taking the hands of the ones on either side of her. "From the beginning, it was House Leonov of Alexandrine who brought peace and unity to the galaxy. They paved the way for the exchange of goods, languages, genes, cultures, between all the people of the Belt. We need *you*, Anya Leonova, last of your name, so that we can restore the unity and vision of Alexandrine and bring down the self-serving Committee for good."

My blood rises. "You speak of peace and unity, but you're a monster. You *shot* my friend!"

My shout frightens Taysie, who scrambles away. I lock eyes with the commander. Zhar's motherly facade begins to fracture, revealing the adamantine woman beneath. "Adi, children, go on to lunch now."

"But, Aunt—"

"Now."

He sighs and storms out, throwing me a dirty look. The others follow, holding hands. Once the doors hiss shut behind them, Zhar stalks toward me. She is all steely commandant now, cold and relentless as a comet churning through space.

"Is Pol alive?" I whisper.

"Princess—"

"Is he?" My voice cracks with desperation.

Zhar purses her lips, her gaze falling away. "I sent his body to the crematorium hours ago. They'll have deposited the ashes in space by now. It is an honorable end."

My heart shatters, a star gone supernova.

I can't speak. Can't look at her. Can't *breathe.*

I imagine Pol, dust among stars. He'd have hated that. *Hated* it. The aeyla bury their dead. It's their most important tradition, that reunion with their beloved Amethyne. I owed Pol my life. I couldn't even give him a proper death.

With a roar, I lunge at her, tackling her to the floor and reaching for her throat. It's like an animal has awoken inside me, hungry and clawed.

My hold doesn't last but a moment. She manages to throw me off, and then I'm the one pinned to the ground, facedown, arms wrenched behind me. Zhar is breathing a bit harder, but it's clear I'm no match for her. I snarl, my face pressing into the cold stone floor, but can't do anything to free myself. I peer up at her with one eye, anger like a hot rash on my skin.

"You love your people, Anya," she hisses. "Just as I love mine. I grew up in the Leonov court, and I was honored to serve your family. But I saw them fall. And later, I saw Adi's father hanged for smuggling refugees off Alexandrine. My sister was assassinated for speaking out against the Committee. A ruthless enemy requires ruthless resistance. They may call you a monster, as you call me one. But I become the monster so that years from now, the ones I love—those *children*—don't have to."

She releases me then. Several locks of her hair have come loose, and they hang over her forehead like icicles. Slightly undone, she seems younger than I first thought.

I turn onto my back, feeling the last of my fury fade away until I'm as limp as a slinke leaf, without the will to even lift my head.

"Shooting Pol was *wrong*," I say hoarsely.

She looks at me, eyes weary. "I know it hurts, but it was necessary.

He disobeyed a direct order, and I have to know that I can trust my people. One weak link on this rock could lead to our destruction. Our families are here. Our children, Anya."

How dare she speak of her loved ones when mine are torn from me, one by one?

"So why let Riyan live? Why poison him? It's torture."

Zhar sighs. "The tensors betrayed the Leonovs when they needed their aid most. They could have turned the tide during the rebellion, but they refused our call and hid on their cold moon. That boy is not one of us, and he never will be. Even the Committee has the sense to outlaw his kind, for the tensors' power is volatile and unnatural." Her eyes narrow. "You've seen it, haven't you? You know what they're capable of."

I shake my head, jaw tight, but think of Riyan nearly crushing Pol's skull.

But he *hadn't*. He'd stopped himself. And now he could die for that mercy.

"He doesn't deserve this," I whisper.

Zhar pulls something from her pocket and tosses it to me. It's a vial, fragile and no bigger than my pinkie. Inside is a clear liquid.

"That is the antidote for the tensor," says Zhar. "You're lucky it didn't crack when you attacked me. It's the only supply we have. Cooperate with me, and you may give it to him soon. I know you think us harsh, but we have to be."

I cradle the vial, feeling how delicate it is. This is Riyan's life, literally in the palm of my hand. And he's not the only one waiting for me.

"Volkov took my friend," I say quietly. "She's being held prisoner on Alexandrine. If I do what you want, can you save her?"

"Become who you were born to be," Zhar replies, "and you can save her yourself."

I shut my eyes and say a silent apology to Pol for letting his killer outplay me. But I have to reach Clio. I can't sacrifice her safety for the sake of revenge.

"What do you want me to do?" I ask tonelessly.

Zhar's satisfied smile makes my blood burn. "Come with me."

She stands and starts for the door again. I follow, hating her and hating that I have no choice. She takes me down the hallway and into a medical ward. Metal grates plate the walls and ceiling, revealing the asteroid rock behind them. I recognize some of the beeping machines from my mom's practice, but these ones look older and show evidence of many repairs.

Dr. Luka is there, busy at an arrangement of equipment. He turns when we enter, brushing his hands together.

"Ah, here you are, Princess, excellent."

Zhar gestures to a chair. I eye it warily, but it looks fairly normal—a metal folding seat, no shackles or electric wires hooked to it. "What is this?"

"Nothing to worry about." She nods to the doctor, who rolls a squeaky table in front of me. "We need to be sure you are indeed our Anya."

"I just need a bit of blood," Dr. Luka says, far too cheerfully. "Skin and hair are too easy to replicate these days, you know."

"Ouch!" Before I realize it, he's already stabbed my arm and drawn the sample.

While I grind my teeth, he and Zhar sit at a table on my left, in front of a little white machine. Dr. Luka deposits the sample inside it, then nods.

"Scan checks out. She's a Leonov, all right."

I stare at the tiny hole he left in my arm and press a finger to the bead of blood welling from it. Something shifts inside me, another wall of defense crumbling. They have DNA proof. No more pretending this was all some colossal misunderstanding, that they had the wrong girl from the beginning. The evidence is written in my blood.

Dr. Luka looks down at me and smiles. "I served your family, you know, as the imperial physician. Your foster mother, Elena, was my top apprentice."

I look up, surprised. "You know my mom?"

He gestures at my leg. "Let's have a look at that wound, shall we?" As he inspects the bandage around my calf, he continues. "I knew her, and I knew your true mother, Empress Katarina. I knew all the imperial family quite well—or as well as anyone could. They kept so many secrets, even from their doctor." He tilts his head. "You've heard, no doubt, of their supposed curse."

"You mean how they were all insane?" I say flatly. That's not something I've let myself think about too directly in the past few days, like trying to ignore a bad toothache. You know it only means trouble, but you don't want to deal with it any sooner than you have to.

"They had their demons," he concedes. He unwraps the bandage and studies the wound where the shrapnel cut me; it's starting to heal over. "And what about you, Anya Leonova? What is your demon?"

"Oh, I've got plenty." I glare at Lilyan Zhar. "And my name isn't Anya."

Dr. Luka chuckles. "If you are not frank with me, I cannot help you. I know Elena would have kept a close eye on you, but I must ask: Do you have any history of psychological irregularities?"

"Meaning?"

"Oh, you know. Hallucinations, paranoia." He smiles, trying to put me at ease. My leg flinches as he injects something into the muscle and then deftly begins binding it again.

Something flickers in my mind—a memory, or a fragment of a

memory—my mom holding my hands while I convulse with sobs. She's saying something over and over . . . *Not real, not real, Stacia* . . . Then the memory is gone. I'm not even sure it truly happened, but it leaves me shaken.

I swallow. "Maybe I'm hallucinating *you*."

He sighs. "You have Elena's attitude."

"Look, what do you *need* me for? Why not stage your rebellion on your own? It's not as if people will rise up to follow some girl from the outer fringe, no matter what her name is."

"Believe me, we aren't ready for this fight," Zhar says. "The plan was to ignite a widespread revolution when you turned twenty-one, giving us time to assemble the strength and giving *you* time to grow up. But then Volkov captured one of our best spies. He has ways of getting answers even from the most loyal tongues, and by the time we realized our man had told Volkov all about you, it was too late. He got to you before we could alert your foster parents. And so here we all are: starting a war four years early."

"If you want to rebel, then rebel. But leave me out of it."

Zhar taps the table, studying me. Then she turns to the doctor. "Give us the room, Luka."

He nods and heads out, pausing only to give me an inscrutable look before closing the door and leaving me alone with the commander.

Zhar turns back to me. "I'm afraid you don't have a choice in this matter. There is a reason we risked everything to smuggle you out of Alexandrine sixteen years ago. Anya, you're the key to this whole war."

"Why?"

"Because 'when she is ready to rule, the Firebird will guide her.'"

My patience is wire thin, and I feel on the verge of snapping again. "Is that supposed to mean something to me?"

A shadow passes over Zhar's face. "Those were the words your father, Emperor Pyotr Leonov, said to me the day he placed you in my arms. The palace was under siege. He knew it would fall. So he gave you to me, to keep you safe. You're our hope for the future. You are the custodian of the Leonov legacy, and it's time you learned what that means."

She rises and walks to a cabinet and takes out a small metal box. This she places on the table and opens to reveal a glass case with a Prism spinning inside. The crystal shimmers with iridescent tones, pearl and gold and silver. Light flashes along its edges, beautiful and strange.

"Anya, what do you know about Prisms?"

I shrug, staring into the crystal's mesmerizing dance of color and light. "They power everything. Ships, cities, pretty much the whole galaxy."

"Do you know where they come from?"

A dozen heated replies crowd my brain. What does this have to do with anything? If this is some kind of object lesson, like her trick with the kids and the Zemlya story, and she's just wasting my time while Riyan is dying downstairs and Pol's ashes are spreading through space . . .

But my hand goes to the little vial of antidote. If she wants to play games, then I have no choice but to go along, for Riyan's sake.

"I always heard they were harvested from deep space," I say. "That they just drift out there."

She nods. "Prisms are the foundation of our civilization. They are the reason the planets are united, and for our advancements in technology like the Takhimir warp drive and cross-system communication. And the Leonovs were the original discoverers of the Prisms, the only people in the galaxy who knew where they could be found. This was the base of their power. The secret upon which they established an empire."

She leans across the table, her long fingers extending to tap the case. The Prism's light glows on her skin, casting pools of shadow above her eyes.

"Somewhere out there, Anya, is the mother crystal, the source of all the others. The Leonovs called it the Prismata. And it is the key to everything—defeating the Committee, ruling the Empire, and guarding against future threats." She lifts the box with the Prism inside and holds it between us, staring at me intently over its spinning light. "Through the Prismata, we can connect with and control every Prism in existence."

I stare at her, wondering if this is all some elaborate story to make me fall in line. But the zeal in her eyes seems real enough. "What do you mean, *control*?"

"You've heard of Emerault's third moon?"

I picture Riyan's hologram, the blue threads of light reflecting on Pol's eyes. "The emperor blew it up, trying to stamp out the Unionist's secret base. That's what started the rebellion. Everyone said Pyotr had used some superweapon . . ." I look down at the Prism. "You're saying it was this Prismata?"

She nods. "Pyotr used it to send an enormous surge of energy into the moon's Prisms, causing them to overheat and explode."

An icy tentacle slithers down my spine. I gape at her. "But . . . that's a terrible power to have! Prisms are *everywhere*. On every ship, in every city, keeping the lights on. That means anyone could be targeted by whoever controls this Prismata."

"Exactly. Which is why we cannot let it fall into the Committee's hands. Its location is the greatest kept secret in the galaxy, one the

Leonovs guarded with their lives. All I know is that the location of the Prismata is hidden inside a device called the Firebird, but when the Empire fell, the Firebird was lost. And I believe you might be the only person who can find it."

She leans forward, handing me the case. I take it stiffly, staring down at the little crystal.

"That's why you want me," I whisper. "And that's why *they* want me."

I was right in thinking no one would follow a girl from the fringe into battle. The Loyalists were never interested in me leading a revolution—only in using me to reach the Prismata. Whoever finds it, this source of all the galaxy's energy, will control everything, just like the Leonovs once did.

To Zhar and Volkov, I'm not just a lost princess.

I'm the key to the greatest weapon in existence.

"Alexei Volkov has been seeking the Prismata for years," Zhar says. "The only reason we've lasted this long against the Committee is because they too have been unable to find it. Once *we* control it, they'll be forced to comply with our demands." She leans forward, eyes aflame. "Work with me. Tell me where the Firebird is hidden."

I shake my head, setting down the Prism as if it were poisoned. "How would I know that? I don't even know what it is."

"The emperor wouldn't have smuggled you off Alexandrine without some way for you to find it. Perhaps it is an object you've had since childhood? A necklace, or a trinket of some kind, that might contain it?"

"I have no idea how to give you what you want." The only piece of jewelry I keep with me is my multicuff, and I've taken that apart enough times to know there are no secrets hidden inside it—and certainly no maps to some Prismic superweapon.

"*Think*, Anya! With the Firebird, we can prove who you are. We can show the galaxy that you are the rightful ruler—"

"If you want answers so badly, why don't you ask my parents? My *real* parents, Teo and Elena?"

She sighs. "Believe me, I'd love to talk to your parents. We cut off all communication with them long ago, so our messages wouldn't give away their—and your—location. But now that we *want* to reach them, we can't."

She pulls a tabletka from a drawer and powers it on, cycling through clips of raw footage.

Afka, on fire.

Warships gathering in the sky above Estonrya.

Aeyla being herded onto prison barges.

The slinke forests burning, blackening the sky with smoke.

While I stare, horror-struck, Zhar circles the table and stands behind the holos, the images reflecting in her eyes.

"Thanks to the Committee's blockade, we've had no communication with Afka, your parents, or the any of the Loyalist cells on Amethyne. War has engulfed the planet. But take hope in the fact that they are fighting back. And they're fighting back because they believe in you, Anya. They believe you can give us the only thing that will win this war."

Zhar clicks off the tabletka and holds it up. "Stored in here is a reconstruction of the Autumn Palace. Explore it. See if it jogs something in that head of yours. We need to know where the Firebird is hidden. And we need to know *fast.* If we're going to save your people on Amethyne and put an end to the Committee's tyranny, then we have to act quickly. Find it, and I will let you give your tensor friend the antidote."

I stare at the empty air where the images of my broken, burning home had been.

"When she is ready to rule, the Firebird will guide her." Zhar places the tabletka in my open palm and closes my fingers around it. "Find the Firebird, Anya. It's our last and only hope."

CHAPTER TWELVE

Instead of sending me back to the cell, Zhar gives me a room on the barracks level. One wall is rough rock, the others smooth and white. In lieu of a pad, I have a bed, with a nightstand and a cabinet filled with clean clothes. Soft blue lights glow from round globes on the ceiling. It feels military, all clean lines and stark surfaces, but at least the lav isn't five inches from my pillow.

I change into fresh clothes, a sleeveless black shirt and leggings. But I keep my boots. There's still a bit of Amethynian dirt on the soles. My multicuff, I'm relieved to see, is sitting on the bed—but that's not the only thing.

There's a square of folded red cloth, and even before I touch it, I know it is Pol's.

My hands shake as I press the fabric to my nose, still smelling him in the threads—grapeseed oil, my family's last batch of wine, the faint, salty tang of the Sapphine sea.

There's a note under the scarf.

My deepest sympathies on your loss, Princess. Though it is no comfort, I am sure, I ask you to remember that the amethyst gambit is the noblest play.

—Dr. Faran Luka

The amethyst gambit. It's a Triangulum phrase, referring to a famous move in which the purple warrior piece is sacrificed in the opening play, in order to free the scarlet queen's path of attack.

Fury boils in my chest. I rip up the note and fling the pieces to the floor.

"He is not a sacrifice!" I yell at the walls. "This is not a stupid game, and I am *not* your queen!"

Then I bury my face in the scarf and begin to sob.

◇

It takes me an hour to pull myself together, but my anger doesn't fade. I reluctantly take out the tabletka Zhar gave me, determining to move forward, to do whatever I must in order to save Riyan.

The only program on it is this holo she wants me to explore. I activate it, and a fan of blue light spreads upward and outward, raking the ceiling and walls before assembling into an image that hovers in front of me. I set the tabletka on the floor and stand up, circling the projection. Pol's scarf is draped around my neck, his scent in my nose.

Alexandrine spins before me, green continents set into a swirling crimson sea. The heart of the galaxy, home of emperors and conquerors.

But the Autumn Palace isn't on Alexandrine at all. The planet is carpeted in cities, all grand and vast and sparkling. They are the centers of trade and military and craftsmanship, but the palace is a whole city of its own—the City in the Sky, a satellite compound orbiting the planet like a moon.

Dismissing Alexandrine itself, I spread my hands and widen the floating city until it's all around me. The Autumn Palace is composed of hundreds of buildings, all locked together in a vast network of struts, like a complex molecule. Two white rings, one vertical, one horizontal, encompass the array, enclosing it in an artificial atmosphere.

Once, the palace was home to the Emperor's Court, thousands of people who ran the Empire, overseeing every aspect of life in the Belt. Now the orbital city serves much the same purpose, except it's the Committee and their people who occupy it. This holomap must have been constructed before the war, because I can see tiny imperial emblems emblazoned on the buildings.

After studying the array a moment, I turn my focus to the large structure at the hub of the compound. The Rezidencia is an elegant construct, long and sleek and white, a wide, round center tapering to two long arms from the top and bottom, one extended toward the planet, the other pointing outward to the vault of space. I dismiss all the other buildings that float around it, until only it remains. The heart of the palace. The imperial family's headquarters. I've seen it many times in history classes, but now I look at it closer. Will it spark some memory? Will it feel familiar?

But no matter what angle I study it from, the slender structure holds no epiphanies, at least from the exterior.

Time to go inside.

With a swipe of my hand, I go into the palace's heart: a conservatory featuring plants from all across the Belt. There I pause to stare at a small Amethyne slinke tree in a pot, its tubular leaves swaying slightly, always in motion, just the way I remember them. I run my hand through the leaves but feel nothing. They reflect over my skin, just particles of empty light.

The holo is breathtakingly detailed; though every surface is partly transparent, I can make out the tiny patterns engraved around the doorways, the seams in the wall panels, even the details on the clothing of the people who walk past me and through me, beings of light from a lost era. Dressed in elegant robes, hair sleek and shining, they seem lifelike enough that at first I flinch. I float through like a ghost, navigating with small hand gestures, so the walls and corridors flow around me.

I can't deny that the Leonovs had taste. The Rezidencia is stunning: a sprawling, fluid hive of halls, balconies, and incredible vistas of Alexandrine below or the galaxy beyond.

I follow a curving hallway that winds around and around. Windows look out to the stars and the other palace buildings, moving in slow parallax.

I'm so caught up in exploring I nearly forget my purpose here: to find the device Lilyan Zhar is after, this Firebird that will supposedly turn the war in her favor. Maybe if I can find it, she'll release me and Riyan. I can save Clio. We can go . . . well, not home. If what Zhar said is true, then Amethyne is cut off, a war zone. Is there anywhere in the galaxy we can disappear to? Stars, how will I tell Clio about Pol?

I shake my head. That's a problem for another time. And I can't think about Pol right now or I'll crumble.

The winding corridor brings me at last to a network of rooms. These must be the imperial family's chambers. Elegant bedrooms and sitting rooms and libraries all connect together, a sprawling, luxuriant residence. Game rooms show signs of children at play—toy ships and soldiers scattered on the floor, a Triangulum board set up as if the players were interrupted mid-game, a large screen covered with messy drawings of people and planets and animals with too many limbs. Of the children themselves, I see nothing.

Then I find a nursery, and here I freeze.

There they stand: emperor and empress. Pyotr and Katarina. Just steps away from me, so stunningly realistic that I instinctively pull back, as if they might see me spying on them.

The empress is holding a baby. The emperor is leaning over, smiling, a tiny hand wrapped around his pinkie. Swallowing, I step closer, studying them with fascination.

When I looked at their photo after Pol and I fled Afka, the image was small and grainy. Now I see them in exquisite detail. The holo makes them life-sized, nearly as real as if they were truly standing in front of me.

The emperor had a broad, easy smile and brown eyes, with thick eyebrows over dark lashes. When he smiled, his chin dimpled. The empress had a petite, almost feline beauty, large eyes and a pert nose, but with a smattering of freckles that make her seem a little more human, a little less sculpture. Him with dark hair, hers light red, worn in an elegant twist of curls. The baby has no hair at all but her eyes are wide and fixed adoringly on her father.

I stare at the child, heart hammering.

Is this me?

Is this my real family? Was this a real moment in my life? Were these toys mine, this crib mine, these people *mine*?

I step close and peer into the woman's face, searching for myself in it. And at the moment, her head turns slightly and her eyes seem to connect with mine.

I recoil from the room, and the holo repeats its loop. The imperial couple coos over their baby, and I leave them to it, feeling dirty, like I've violated their privacy.

I don't belong here. I'm not one of them. Maybe I started life here, I don't know, but this place is not my home and these people are not my family. Shame heats my face, as if by even looking at them, I've betrayed my *real* parents, who are suffering on Amethyne right now, likely prisoners or worse. I should be with them, not buried on an asteroid in a dead system, searching for something that might not even exist, working for the woman who killed one of my dearest friends.

I shut down the holo. The palace vanishes, and with it, my hope of getting off this rock. There was nothing there that I recognized, nothing that might be a clue to the Firebird's nature or location. I feel like I've been exploring a crypt, treading on forbidden ground.

Hurling the tabletka into the corner, I retreat onto the bed and let out a long breath. My hands are shaking. I grab the pillow and squeeze it against my chest, careful not to crush the vial of antidote. I think of Pol, and my chest caves in and the tears come in a rush.

◇

Dinner is brought to my room, but after I push it around my plate a while, I decide to go exploring. If I get the chance to make a run for it, I'll need knowledge of the base's layout. Besides, sitting trapped in here with my thoughts and my memories is a torture I'm desperate to escape.

I move quietly through the corridors, fearing I'll be locked in my room if anyone catches me wandering. The base isn't as big as it seemed at first. There are three levels, one for mechanical engineering, the cells, the mess hall, and the hangar. The second floor is all barracks for the five hundred or so Loyalist soldiers. The third floor is operations, where they run their comm systems, strategy meetings, and other business.

I stop by Riyan's cell first. A bored guard stands watch, eyeing me as I approach. I raise my hands and try not to stare. The man is a paryan, the adapted race native to Emerault. I've never seen one in person before. He is very thin and tall, with a birdlike skeleton. Emerault's atmosphere is so dense and moist, and its gravity so low, that 90 percent of its life is found in the sky, in floating kelp forests. The paryans, with their light frames, navigate their airborne world like birds, riding on the backs of great sky whales. I've heard they even have wings of delicate skin and bone that they keep folded on their backs, when not using them to glide around their dense, algae-filled skies.

"I just want to see him," I say. "Please?"

The guard shrugs his thin shoulders but doesn't take his eyes off me. They're the color of green Emerault itself.

Riyan has gone into a trance, unmoving hour after hour. He's still sitting with his legs folded, hands on his knees.

"You know he's going to die without this," I say to the guard, holding up the vial on its chain.

The guard grunts. "You can't trust an abomination like him, Princess. The tensors' magic will be our undoing one day. Pulling at the fabric of space like that . . . it's not right."

After a few minutes of no change in the tensor, I continue on to the hangar. There, the Loyalist fleet is arranged in neat rows, but there's no hiding that their ships are outdated and in need of repairs. A team of mechanics is working feverishly to retrofit a battle schooner, but I'd guess their efforts aren't doing much good. The ship looks like it should be scrapped for parts, if not scuttled altogether.

Riyan's ship has been added to the fleet, I note sourly. Someone has opened up the hull, and a couple pilots are admiring the exposed engine.

At the far end of the hangar rests a scuttled scout ship that's been refitted into a bar. Drinks are served on a counter made from the old control board. A tabletka on the wall projects a hologram of a geeball match, with some pilots clustered around, placing bets. The miniature players look like bees dodging and spinning through their zero-gravity arena, chasing a glowing ball from one end to the other.

About half the pilots are human—Alexandrians, Rubyati, one white-haired Opallan—and the rest are adapted: paryans, eeda, a woman with radiation-resistant orange skin, who must be a zheran from Tanzanet. She wears a pair of dark glasses to shield her large, sensitive eyes and curses when one of the geeball teams scores a goal. There are no aeyla, I note with disappointment; I haven't seen a single pale horn since I arrived. If there were, maybe I could have talked them into helping me, for Pol's sake.

I start toward the bar, hoping to find something to drink, but at that moment a red light begins flashing overhead and an alarm blares through the hangar. I freeze, thinking I've been spotted, but no one's even looking at me.

Instead, pilots are running to line up by an empty pair of landing pads, shouting excitedly. They watch the long tunnel leading out of the rock, like they're waiting for something.

Curious, I wander over and try to blend in. There isn't much need; everyone is so focused on whatever's about to come down that tunnel that they don't notice me lurking.

A distant roar reaches my ears, and then I see lights deep in the darkness, growing brighter and brighter.

A sleek little battler is speeding toward us, a one-man ship equipped with guns and hyperboosters for high-speed attacks. The sound of its engine floods the hangar, deafening, making the floor vibrate. I can feel it in my teeth. Its thrusters are at full brake, generating a strong wind that has the light-boned paryans bracing themselves, lest they be swept off their feet.

The battler lowers smoothly onto one of the pads, popping landing struts. Everyone converges on the ship as the top hatch pops open and the eeda pilot emerges, grinning and pumping his fist. He powers down the engine, and the others all cheer. Someone hands him a canteen of water, which he pours over his head to hydrate his scaled skin.

Seconds later, another battler comes speeding down the tunnel, engine whining and rattling. I wince at the sound; this one's clearly experiencing some sort of engine trouble. It sets down next to the first in a cloud of smoke.

The hatch opens and a brown-skinned girl climbs out, scowling and cursing. She pulls off her helmet, shaking loose a pair of braids that start at her hairline and curl over her scalp. After she shuts down the battler, she slides off the nose and to the floor, and is met by the jeers of the other pilots. Throwing them a rude gesture, she storms to the wing of her ship, where the engine underneath it is wheezing.

"That's the third race you've lost this week, Luka!" shouts a pilot.

"Not my fault!" she snaps back. "The engine blew! I nearly smashed into a rock."

"She's lying," the victorious pilot returns. "She lost control of her ship, as usual. How many you gotta destroy, girl, before you realize you should have stayed on the laundry rotation?"

The girl bristles but faces him squarely. "How many times did I have to wash your stinking uniform after you wet yourself in the battle sims?"

The other pilots burst into laughter, and the eeda pilot hurls a curse. The girl, scowling, stalks over to the bar and grabs a bottle of water.

The pilot tending bar grabs it back. "You already used up your ration this week. Thirsty? Open your mouth in the shower, Luka."

With a few steps, I lunge across the counter and grab the water from the guy's hand. "Did I use up *my* ration?"

The bartender rolls his eyes and goes back to watching the geeball match. Twisting off the cap, I grab a tin cup and pour half in, sliding it to the girl.

"Thanks, uh, Your Highness," she mumbles.

"Stacia's fine." I wave a hand. "I guess water's pretty scarce out here."

"No kidding, and the eeda use up half of it just bathing three times a day. We chip it off a frozen comet core that passes through every eighteen months. Trust me, you haven't experienced misery until you get put on water duty and spend a few days tethered to a giant chunk of space ice." She pauses, then smirks into her cup. "We call it Lilyan Junior. But you didn't hear that from me."

I draw a finger over my lips in the universal sign for a secret kept. "So, your name's Luka? Related to the doctor?"

She winces. "You've met my dad, then. Don't judge a girl by her relations."

I hook a thumb at the pair of battlers. "What was all that?"

"What, the race? It was a setup, that's what it was." She scowls at the crowd of pilots, still congregated around the winner. "They knew that was a bum engine, but they gave it to me anyway. Zhar's going to kill me when she sees the mess it's in." With a groan, she turns around and lets her head fall onto the bar. "I can't afford to pay for another one."

"I could take a look at it, if you want."

She tilts her head, one eye peering at me. "Huh?"

"I'm a mechanic. Well, apprentice mechanic." I tap my multicuff. "Broken engines are sort of my thing."

She shrugs. "I guess you couldn't make it any worse. I'm Mara, by the way."

We walk over to her ship, the others ignoring us as they escort the victor to the bar. Mara watches them with narrow eyes, twisting one of her braids.

I grab a wheeled dolly and lie on it, pushing myself under the wing. The engine is housed beneath it, tucked against the hull. Popping a screwdriver from my cuff, I open the panel concealing it. As I work, I glance at Mara, who's sitting a few feet away, nursing her water like she wishes it was something stronger.

"So, Mara Luka. Is rebellion a family business?"

She swirls her cup. "It's not rebellion. It's restoring the rightful order. My mom died sixteen years ago in the Battle of Alexandrine, defending the palace from the direktor's invasion force."

"I'm sorry."

Her eyes darken. She drains her cup, then slams it on the floor. "I'll avenge her when we take out those pigs."

I slide out from under the wing so I can set aside the panel I removed. "So that's why all these people are out here, hiding in a dead system and fighting for a dead dynasty? They want vengeance?"

"Well, not just that. Most of us are here because we had nowhere else to go after the war. A lot of these pilots flew for the Leonovs. What's waiting for them, except death sentences?"

"But do you really want to see the Empire restored?"

She shrugs. "I just want to go home to Alexandrine. And until the Committee falls, that can't happen." With a grim smile, she adds, "It's not always about the big picture, is it? Empires and armies and ideals. I don't know who's right or wrong in the end, but I know what I want and I know what stands in my way."

I slide back under the wing and shine my cuff's flashlight at the engine, spotting the problem right away. One of the energy lines to the left fusion reactor is torn. I go to work on it, splicing and snipping.

"You said Alexandrine's home," I say. "What's it like?"

"Oh, it's a paradise," she says wryly. "The whole planet's covered in cement, and the protected greenspaces are reserved for the wealthy. You have to wait in line for hours just to get your daily meal ration. If you complain about it, you risk getting thrown into a cell for a week. The Committee controls everything—the peacekeepers, the courts, the food distribution, the banks."

"Things are really that bad there?" I'm neck-deep inside the engine now, my voice muffled by the metal walls around me.

"Think about it like this: We left there in order to live *here*."

"Good point." I back out and study the line I've extracted. "You must have really hated it on Alexandrine."

"I didn't hate it. It was just like . . . seeing someone you love get sick, to the point they're not *them* anymore, you know? You want to run away, because it hurts to see someone you love become someone else, always in pain and misery."

"You left Alexandrine because you want to find the magic pill that will heal it."

"Yeah." She nods thoughtfully. "That's it exactly."

I use my pliers to disconnect a secondary line, redirecting the power flow through the engine. "You think Zhar's that pill?"

"I don't know. Maybe. My dad thinks *you* are, once you come into your own, whatever that means."

"Guess you all must be pretty disappointed in me, then."

"I'm withholding judgment for now. Let's see how you handle that engine first."

"Fair enough." Burrowing back into the exposed hull, I reconnect the wires, then replace the panel.

"Okay, you're set."

Her eyebrows shoot up. "You fixed it? In . . . five minutes?"

I stand and wipe my greasy hands on my leggings. "Only one way to find out."

She shrugs and climbs into the cockpit, flipping a switch inside. I step back and hold my breath as I snap my multicuff back on my wrist—and release it when the battler's engine begins to hum. Mara gives it a few bursts of power and the booster flashes blue, burning up the Prismic energy stored inside the power cells.

She shuts down the engine and leans out of the cockpit, her eyes wide. "What did you do?"

I shrug. "Nothing fancy. Just redirected a few lines, bypassing some stuff and getting energy directly to the reactor. I think you'll find she's a little bit faster now too."

Mara shakes her head, her lips curling into a grin as she jumps back to the ground. "Okay, so you've got some tricks up your sleeve. Literally. That's a neat gadget."

I twist my cuff. "It was a gift from my dad, after I graduated from my mechanical training."

"Well, I'm impressed. And I don't impress easy. Maybe you'll fix this galaxy after all, Princess."

I manage a sickly laugh.

Mara circles the battler, inspecting every inch of it the way Pol would study one of his mantibu after a race. The thought leaves me cold, like a hole's been blown through my chest, and it takes me a moment to find my breath.

Pushing away the clawing grief that surges from my gut, I follow Mara. She's wholly absorbed in her ship and is now peering into the engine to see how I rearranged the wires.

I study the girl thoughtfully.

She's my age, she's tough, and she's a pilot. And unlike a lot of the other soldiers here, she's willing to talk to me.

If things go sideways with Zhar, I will need an ally on this rock, and Mara might be the perfect place to start. But I'll have to be careful how I go about it.

"You know," I begin, "my best friend is in a Committee gulag. All I want is to save her." I weigh my words cautiously before continuing. "Do you think Zhar cares about that stuff? About our families and homes? She seems focused on just taking out the Committee, not caring who she has to destroy to do it."

Mara shrugs and closes the engine. "Zhar is doing what has to be done. The path to victory is paved with sacrifice."

"Then maybe that's the wrong path. Did you ever think of striking out on your own? Returning to Alexandrine and maybe seeing if that magic pill's someplace else?"

She stiffens and faces me, her dark eyes suddenly hard. "Look, I'd love to chat more, but I've got work to do." She starts toward the hangar doors, then pauses to add over her shoulder, "Be careful, Princess. If Zhar knew you were trying to turn us against her, she'd lock you up."

I sigh as she walks away, her braids swinging. "She already has."

◇

Three days pass, and when I'm not scouring the holopalace, I check on Riyan to find him still deep in his meditation. How much longer can he possibly last? He looks weaker and weaker, shriveling before my eyes. I notice someone—Dr. Luka, probably—has set up an IV in his arm, so at least he's getting fluid. But he can't possibly hold out much longer.

Sometimes I just sit and stare at him, willing him to wake up and declare that he's somehow cured himself. I clutch the vial of antidote around my neck until I fear I'll break it. The guards watch me but say nothing, and are deaf to my pleas that they open the door.

The third night, I ignore my room with its soft bed and instead curl up in front of Riyan's cell. When Zhar orders I be forcibly removed, I fight them, but they just drug me and dump me back in my room, anyway.

Instead of going back to sleep, I stand in the shower and watch the purple dye run from my hair and vanish into the drain.

I can hear Pol as if he were whispering in my ear.

You can't save me by saving him.

"I can try," I whisper, pressing my hand to the glass. Is that what this is, my desperation to save Riyan? I could save a hundred of him and never be free of the guilt I feel for Pol's death. But I won't give up on the tensor. I'll save him, and together we'll rescue Clio and his sister and everyone else we love. I won't let Pol's death have been for nothing.

These are the lies I tell myself to keep from shattering.

CHAPTER THIRTEEN

After five straight hours of combing the holopalace and coming nc loser to finding what Zhar wants, I growl in frustration and sling the abletka across the floor. I huddle for a moment, arms around my knees ny chest like a cage full of angry, thrashing snapteeth.

Finally, I shoot to my feet and storm out of the room. I roam the orridors, itching for a fight, feeling like I'm about to explode. It mus how in my face, because everyone I pass scurries out of the way.

On the bottom floor, I find a shooting range. There's no one there nd Zhar never said I couldn't use it. So I go in and pick a gun off the vall, noting sourly that it's tagged; if I tried to steal it, alarms woulc o off and it might self-destruct or something. I pull off my multicuf nd study the tag, then decide it's not worth it. These things are usu- lly tamperproof, even against my skills.

An open stone room is spread before me, wired with projectors. ower up the control panel on the wall and pick a simulation. The pro- ectors whir and then spit out beams of light that coalesce into faceless uman forms.

I fire a rapid succession of shots. Concentrated beams of Prismic nergy flash and sizzle in the air, scorching the back wall.

I've fired a gun before; my dad was adamant I learn how to, anc ow I know why. He knew, all along, that one day I'd get caught up ir his war. So much makes sense now—Pol's obsession with the security ystem, Dad's insistence on my learning self-defense, even Mom's ten- lency to drill medical info into my head. All along they were training ne for a role I had no idea I'd one day be forced to play. How did they eep all this from me? How could they look at me every day and lie?

Before I know it, I've finished the simulation. I pick another ncreasing the difficulty, so the ghostly figures appear and vanish in seconds, giving me barely any time to aim before I shoot. The concentrated Prismic energy interrupts their forms when I land a hit, and they burst into a shower of sparkles before dissipating. It's disturbingly satisfying, and I worry a little at how cathartic the exercise is. Even knowing they're just phantoms of light, I don't want to feel good about killing. I don't want to be like Volkov and Zhar and all the others. But with every shot, I feel like I'm slipping further from myself.

Clio would hate this. She never would practice shooting with me, and always said the galaxy would be better off if there were no guns at all.

Maybe she was right.

When the gun's charge is depleted, I put it down and pick up another, setting the sim to the hardest mode. Phantoms pop up and vanish like bursts of light, and my hands move quicker than my mind. My thoughts suspend as instinct takes over, and the gun becomes an extension of myself. Every bolt of Prismic energy finds its mark. Every holo drops with a single hit. Minutes later, it feels as if no time has passed, but the simulation has ended.

I have a perfect score.

I stare at the results as I lower the gun. The weapon is warm from so much firing. My fingers are locked around it, my heart hammering.

All right, I could understand if I had a natural flair for shooting or something.

But this feels . . . different.

Unnatural.

"You shoot like a Leonov."

With a start, I drop the gun. It clatters at my feet, and Lilyan Zhar stoops to pick it up. She slides the depleted battery out and pops in a fresh one, smoothly, expertly. All the while, she keeps her eyes on me.

"I . . . I got lucky," I stammer.

“Not lucky,” she replies, keying in a code to the simulator, then widening her stance in preparation to shoot. “I saw the emperor shoot. He had that same precise eye.”

The simulation begins. Instead of the faceless holos I was firing at, the one that appears before us has its facial features. It’s a man, dressed in a white Loyalist uniform.

“Stars,” I breathe. “Is that—”

“Alexei Volkov,” says Zhar, keeping her gun trained on the figure. He stands at ease, looking off to the side, nodding as if listening to someone speak. The holo must have been ripped from a recording, but an old one. The direktor Eminent looks young here, without his trademark silvered temples.

“He worked for the emperor,” I whisper, noting his uniform.

She nods once. “He was the head of imperial security, before he defected to start his rebellion.”

“I never heard that.”

“Because he didn’t want anyone to know. He wanted to be seen as the people’s savior, one of the common folk. He changed his name, even. Alexei *craves* to be a hero. In truth, he was one of Alexandrine’s most elite, with an inherited command post and a healthy fortune in his pocket. He had the trust of the emperor, but he was a traitor.”

Zhar speaks with venom, her knuckles blanching as she grips the gun.

“You know him,” I realize.

Her lips press together. “Of course I know him. He is my husband.”

She fires. The gun’s ray strikes the holo-Volkov in the temple, and he bursts apart. A thousand shimmering motes of light dance before us, then fade.

Zhar sets down the gun and turns to me. “I am not your enemy,

Stacia. *He* is. He must pay for his crimes against your family. He must answer for his treachery."

I stare at her, as all becomes clear.

Lilyan Zhar, the loyal soldier, her name tarnished by a treasonous husband.

Her legacy stained, her liege-lord slain.

Now I know why this war is happening.

Zhar's husband is responsible for the fall of the Empire and the deaths of the imperial family. He destroyed everything important to her, including her honor. All of this—the hidden base, the complex network of rebel Loyalists—all of it serves *her*. This isn't about bringing justice to the galaxy or restoring order.

This is about vengeance.

Even Pol's death wasn't just about him disobeying orders. The moment she saw he was more loyal to me than her, she had to eliminate him. She can't risk anyone getting in the way of her vengeance, not even the so-called princess she swears to serve.

"Suppose I find the Firebird," I say softly, "and it leads us to the Prismata. What happens next?"

The corner of her mouth curls upward a fraction. "We give Alexei a chance to step down. If he doesn't, we take them *all* out."

My skin turns cold. "What?"

"With the Prismata, your rule will be absolute." She looks me straight in the eye. "You'll use it to destroy the Autumn Palace and every last one of the usurping murderers inside."

"My best friend is a prisoner in the palace!"

"We've all sacrificed people, Anya. If you're going to rule, you have to be willing to make the hard choices. That is how the game is played."

She sets down the gun and walks away, and I stand frozen in place, watching her until she turns a corner. My hands tremble at my sides.

Whatever small hope I had that Zhar would help me save Clio, it's gone now. She doesn't care about Clio. She doesn't care about anyone.

It's beyond time to get off this rock.

◇

There isn't a single guard posted in the medical ward during the night cycle. Even so, I creep along the wall, making no sound, my skin clammy. The first room I come to is the one in which Dr. Luka ran my DNA sample and Zhar told me about the Prismata. The lights are off, but the machines blink and their screens glow enough that I can see as I rummage through cabinets. I can feel time running out; the pillows I piled beneath my bedcovers might not fool the guards for long. And the moment they realize I'm trying to escape, it's over. Stealth is the only real weapon I have.

But the glinting scalpel I find in the top cabinet could also be useful.

I have to climb onto a table to reach it, and now I scurry down, trying to move quickly. But my leg hits a chair and it crashes to the ground.

I freeze, heart pounding.

A moment passes and nothing happens, no one comes running. I slowly slide off the table and tiptoe to the door, the scalpel gripped in my hand. It's no match for a gun, but if I'm quick and quiet enough, that won't matter. I don't think about whether I could actually use the blade on someone. If I think about it, I'll lose my nerve.

We become the monsters so the ones we love don't have to.

Breathing faster, I step into the hallway

And smack into Dr. Luka.

With a startled shout, I jump back—a mistake. Now he's out of my blade's reach, and he's holding a charged gun. He must have heard the crash and come ready for trouble.

"Princess? What are you doing here?" His eyes flicker to the scalpel in my fist.

For a moment we stare at each other; I think he's as surprised as I am. But he's also the one with the superior weapon, and he quickly recovers to wave me back into the exam room.

"Out of sight, quickly, girl! Have you lost your mind?"

My heart slams against my ribs. I suppress the urge to scream. There goes my escape plan. There goes every chance of saving Riyan.

Still, I eye the doctor as he follows me into the room, gauging whether I could lunge at him before he could shoot me.

"I'm done cooperating with you people," I say. "Get out of my way or shoot me, because that's the only way this ends."

The machine by Dr. Luka's head is covered with small blue lights, and they cast a ghostly tone over his face. He studies me, the gun still raised. "So you thought you'd just, what? Sneak out?"

"Zhar is willing to destroy whoever she must in order to get her revenge," I go on. "I won't be part of that. She's just as bad as Volkov. I'm getting out of here, whatever it takes, and I'm going to save my friend."

He glances at my scalpel. "With that?"

I shrug. "If it was Mara out there, if it was her life at risk, what would you do to save her?"

Dr. Luka smiles grimly. "For starters, I wouldn't try to break out of a secure military base with a toothpick like that." He sighs and shakes his head, the skin around his eyes crinkling. "Instead, I'd confide in the people who were on *my* side and always have been. The people who are sworn to serve me and not some suicidal vendetta."

My eyes widen; I stay very still, wondering if I'm hearing him right.

Dr. Luka raises the gun and I flinch, but then he flips it over, extending the grip to me.

"And I'd arm myself properly," he adds.

I slowly take the gun from him, my eyes locked on his.

"You're right about Zhar," he says. "She's lost her way. Many of us here see it, but just as many share her anger, her need for vengeance. Volkov destroyed our lives and killed our loved ones, after all. But, Princess, I was there the day you were born. I delivered you myself, and when your tiny lungs failed to inhale, I breathed air into you and brought you back. You are like another daughter to me, a child I was supposed to watch grow up and become strong like her brother and sisters. I loved your family, Anya. And I won't see you become a pawn in Zhar's game."

I shake my head. "Doc . . . I . . . what do I do?"

"You go and get your tensor and give him that antidote," Dr. Luka says. He heaves a weary groan. "I'd rather do this slowly, laying careful plans and covering all contingencies, but I can see you're not going to wait. And to be honest, I'm not sure the tensor can hold out much longer. I can only do so much for him before the poison wins out."

"So you're helping me?"

"Like I said, I'm sworn to serve the Leonov line, and if this is what you must do, then I have no choice but to help you. Besides, you're just going to get yourself hurt or killed, running around with a blazing scalpel." He ducks through the door and glances down the hall. "It's clear. Go quickly, and meet me in the hangar. I can get us off the base, but I have to take care of a few things first, and find Mara. That's my only condition—if we're doing this, she's coming with us."

"Of course. Thank you," I breathe. Relief and excitement ignite a rush of adrenaline in my veins. Before, I'd been filled with dread, knowing my poorly conceived plan would almost certainly end in disaster. But now I have hope.

More than that, I have an *ally.*

CHAPTER FOURTEEN

There's one soldier on guard in the cells, the pale Opallan I saw in the hangar a few days ago. He's holding Riyan's staff, using it as a prop to lean on while he drowses in the dim night-cycle lighting. His pearly complexion and white hair make him seem almost luminescent. I vaguely recall that the Opallans live underground, which is why they have so little pigment in their skin. It makes him a bright target, even in the dark.

I set my gun to nonlethal, but even so, when I raise it my palms go clammy.

A hiss, a flash of Prismic energy, and the guard drops with a thump. The staff clatters and rolls away.

I smile a little, thinking Pol would have been proud of the shot.

Then emergency lights flood the corridor with red light. An alarm begins screaming overhead, a long, whooping screech that strikes with almost physical force.

I spot the tiny camera mounted above the guard's station. Stupid! I should have checked for eyes before dropping him, but it's too late now.

So much for doing this quietly. Dr. Luka will not be very pleased.

I sprint down the corridor and smash the lockpad with the heel of the gun. It throws sparks, crackling as the bolts disengage and the door swings open.

"Riyan!"

He is so deep in his trance that he doesn't even flinch. I can barely think over the blaring alarms. With a growl, I turn and shoot the speaker in the ceiling. Sparks rain around us, but at least the noise lessens.

I take the vial of antidote from my neck and pop the lid, trying to wake Riyan by slapping his arm. When that fails, I pry apart his lips and shove the vial between his teeth, but he won't loosen his jaw. I can hear boots pounding down the corridor, closing in on the cell.

"Stars curse you, I'm trying to save your life! Wake up!"

I stand behind him, one hand cupped under his chin to tilt back his head. His jaw is like a vise, but I finally manage to tip the vial between his teeth.

"Princess! Stop!"

White-coated soldiers fill the corridor, crouched behind their guns. My hand jerks, and half the antidote spills onto the floor.

"Back away from the witch!" shouts one of the soldiers. It's the eeda pilot from yesterday, the one Mara said wet his pants in the sims. He doesn't look so frightened now. He looks on the verge of blowing my head off.

I dump the rest of the antidote into Riyan's mouth, unsure how much actually makes it down his throat. Just as the first soldier raises his weapon to shoot, I step in front of Riyan, shielding him. My own gun is trained on the soldiers.

"Get out of my way," I warn.

"Just stun them both," the pilot says. "We'll sort them out later."

I fire.

Just like in the range, something takes control of me. I give in to it completely, watching my arm move on its own. The gun fires six rapid shots, nonlethal pulses that fly faster than my eye can even follow. Six soldiers hit the ground, unconscious.

"Oh," I breathe, staring at the gun, my hand beginning to tremble. Then I shake myself, forcing my limbs back into action. I try to get Riyan to his feet, but his muscles are rigid. I manage to drag him to the door before I fall to my knees, panting.

"The guy who can bend gravity, too heavy to carry," I groan. "Nice time to be ironic, Riyan."

Hearing shouts, I look up and see more soldiers coming down the steps. I drop the tensor and start firing, but there are too many. For every one I hit, two more appear. They start shooting back, nonlethal pulses only. I pull back into the cell, dragging Riyan with me.

"Blast!" My gun's run out of charge. The soldiers scattered in the corridor are too far away for me to grab theirs. I have Riyan's staff, but it's just plain wood, not an electric one like the vityazes use.

Letting out a frustrated growl, I drop my useless weapon and stand up. Maybe I can at least bargain for Riyan's life.

"I'm coming out!" I call. "Don't fire!"

Slowly I step into the corridor, one leg at a time to be sure they're not going to blast me into unconsciousness. When nothing happens, the rest of me follows.

Zhar stands flanked by her soldiers, her eyes like black holes.

"This was foolish, Anya."

"Yeah, I'm starting to get that. I'll come nicely, just swear you won't hurt Riyan."

"You're not in a position to bargain, Princess." She turns to the soldiers. "Grab her. Execute the tensor. He's too dangerous to keep any longer."

"No!" I shout, taking a step forward—only to see my foot fly away from me as I go weightless.

With a startled yelp, I pitch forward, my momentum taking me into a full, midair somersault. I bump against one wall and rebound to the other, while ahead of me, the soldiers and Zhar are all lifting up and tangling together. Someone fires, probably by accident, and the pulse hisses past my ear.

"He's awake!" Zhar shouts. "Drop him!"

Then Riyan is there, grabbing my hand and yanking me behind him. He has no trouble navigating his zero-g stress field. His robes float around him, but he walks along the floor as naturally as if he were planet-bound, his staff striking the floor with every step. I set down behind him, able to stand once more, while the soldiers collide and twist in the air over the stairs.

"Finally!" I've never been more relieved in my life.

He tosses me a look over his shoulder, his eyes masked with black spidery lines, his irises tinted silver. "Keep hold of me, Princess."

He needn't tell me; his grip on my hand is so strong I couldn't break it if I wanted to. Riyan starts toward the soldiers, pulling me along, his other hand thrown forward.

The air cracks, the corridor tessellating into a kaleidoscope around us, crunching and splintering. The soldiers and Zhar drop, pinned down the way Riyan took out the guards on Sapphine. But we are unaffected.

Until my hair starts to fall sideways.

Riyan plants a foot on the left wall, and with a shout, I follow, as he tilts gravity around us. I find myself walking along the wall as if it were the floor, while my head spins and my stomach threatens to mutiny. He uses his staff to push off the walls, guiding us through the low gravity. Then he tessellates again, and this time, we drop to the ceiling. I shut my eyes briefly, try to reorient my mind, and then open them again. It helps, but not much. It still feels completely wrong to be walking along the ceiling while the soldiers writhe beneath us. Zhar is on her back, and as we walk over her, I look up to lock gazes with her. Riyan's stress field makes it seem like I'm staring at her through a pane of cracked glass.

"I . . . will . . . find you," she grates, fighting for breath.

Riyan puts us down when we reach the second level, and I have to take a moment to reorient myself. Riyan leans on his staff, trembling. He manages to warp the metal of the door to the cells, a temporary block against Zhar and her soldiers, but then he collapses to his knees, panting. Sweat rolls down his face.

"Can you keep going?" I ask.

He nods. "But I won't be able to do much more. Too weak."

Right. He hasn't had food in days.

"Come on," I say. "Hangar's this way."

"What's going on? How long was I out?"

"Four days. I made a friend, Dr. Luka, and he's waiting for us. I hope."

Hearing footsteps, I yank Riyan into a maintenance closet, just as a group of soldiers rounds the corner ahead. The space is crammed with machines and pipes, the air hot and stifling. We huddle against the door, listening to them run past. I can just make out Zhar's voice crackling through their comm patches.

"Can you run?" I whisper to Riyan.

"I don't think so."

Stars, he's barely even standing. There's no way we'll make it to the hangar.

Unless . . .

I turn around and face the machines humming behind us. "All right, what've we got here?"

An air filtration system, a water pump, an electrical panel . . .

"Ooh, what's this?" I tap a red button on the wall, enclosed in a clear case. There's a label over it, but it's so faded I can't make out the words, just a warning below it.

Riyan frowns. "It says don't press except in case of emergencies."

"I'd say this is an emergency."

"You don't even know what it does!"

"Riyan, Riyan," I mutter, unclasping my multicuff to pry open the case. "If there's one thing you need to know about me, it's that I *always* press the red button."

"Wait—"

I punch it.

A holoscreen pops up, with a thread of data. I scan it, then feel goose bumps ripple up my arms.

"Oh. Oh no."

"Stacia? What did you do?"

I back away toward the door. "We have to go. *Now.*"

"Why?"

"Because I just set off an emergency distress signal. This asteroid is beaming its location across the galaxy." Blast! I was hoping it would be some sort of anti-fire system or a power shutdown. This is worse, *way* worse.

His eyes grow wide. "The vityazes—"

"Will swarm on this place like snapteeth on a wounded mantibu calf."

"I don't know what either of those things are, but I get the gist."

I throw open the door to see the same soldiers running past us again, only this time they're heading the other way. Toward the hangar. One locks eyes with me as he runs past, and he looks surprised, but he doesn't stop.

Because we're not the main threat anymore.

They're preparing for battle.

I drag Riyan out and we limp after the soldiers. The weakened tensor hobbles with an arm over my shoulder, and I strain under his weight.

"We have to get out of this system before the vityazes arrive," I say.

"Really? I thought we might hang around, see if we couldn't settle all this over a nice cup of coffee."

Was that *humor*? I didn't know he was capable of it. Figures that it would only appear under life-threatening circumstances.

Grinning, even as my pulse pounds with adrenaline-spiked fear, I haul him around another corner and see the hangar door at the far end, what seems a light-year away.

"Anya!" a voice screams. "Anya, what have you *done*?"

I look back to see Zhar at the far end of the corridor. She looks unraveled, hair spiking up, clothes disheveled.

"Sorry!" I yell, desperately throwing all my strength into getting us to that door before Zhar can catch up. "You should really label things better around here!"

Riyan pulls his arm from my shoulder and limps ahead. "I think I can hold them off once we're in."

"You'd better!"

We burst into the hangar and the tensor pulls away from me. Riyan's staff is a blur, his robes swirling as he spins to bring down the rock above the doors. The sound is like thunder, echoing through the hangar. Massive slabs of asteroid break away and crash to the ground, sealing off the corridor and sending a cloud of dust into the air.

"Enough!" I shout. "We don't want to scuttle the place! There are kids in there!"

"There were kids on Emerault's moon when the Empire destroyed it," he snarls, but he relents. We run across the smooth stone floor toward the *Valentina*.

The rocks Riyan brought down buy us time, but not much. Already the soldiers are firing through the gaps.

I spot Dr. Luka standing in the hatch of the clipper, waving at us. We run toward him, Riyan using his staff like a crutch. Pilots are running between the ships, shouting and prepping for launch, but when they see Riyan they shout and take a few shots at us.

We reach the clipper in a hail of Prismic energy pulses, and rush up the ramp to tumble inside, landing at the doctor's feet. He grabs my hand and helps me up.

"I'm not even going to ask what went wrong," he sighs. "We have to get out of here before Zhar breaks through your tensor's barricade. If she reaches the net activator, a laser shield will seal off the exit and we'll be fried. I disabled it, but she can override my command."

The clipper hums to life, lights tracing the exterior, the engine snarling. The *Valentina* seems as eager to get off this rock as I am. I scurry up the ladder to the main deck, and see Mara on the balcony above, operating the controls.

I call to her, and she glances down.

"To be honest, Princess, this is *not* how I expected to spend my morning." Despite her light tone, she looks stressed, sweat glistening on her brow. I wonder what her father must have said to get her on board. When I talked to her, she made her loyalty to Zhar pretty clear.

"Glad you could join us."

"I wasn't about to let my dad fly out of here alone. He can barely operate a forklift. Besides, this *is* a J-Class clipper. It's not every day you get a chance to handle a beauty of this caliber."

I could kiss her for that. Finally, someone who *gets* it.

"Princess, if you could handle the air lock doors, I'll get the engine—"

But I don't hear what she says next, because my eyes settle on a stretcher hovering over the floor, its occupant strapped down.

My knees go weak.

"H-how?" I whisper.

The doctor climbs up from the air lock, helping Riyan up with him. "When they brought him to me, I thought he was dead. Had the crematorium all fired up when I noticed his fingers twitch. Lucky thing, or he'd be space dust right now." With a grunt, the doctor pulls Riyan inside, the tensor stumbling. "His aeyla bones are denser than ours and stopped the pulse from killing him. But several ribs are broken and there's been internal damage."

I approach the stretcher slowly, every hair on end. Pol's face is pale, his breathing shallow. He doesn't look good, but he's *alive.*

"Why didn't you tell me?" I ask.

"I tried," says the doctor. "Didn't you get my note?"

I think back. "You compared him to the amethyst gambit. You as good as confirmed he was dead!"

"Anya, think. How does the gambit play out?"

Oh.

I let out a breath, shutting my eyes. In Triangulum, you have the chance to return your first sacrificed piece to the board just before the endgame begins. By letting your amethyst warrior go, you can later bring it back into play.

"You could have been a *little* more specific," I grumble.

"I couldn't risk Zhar finding out, and she was careful not to let me be alone with you. I think she always knew I'd choose you over her. She didn't trust me."

"You risked your life to save him."

"He's important to you, Princess, and he's loyal." He walks to Pol and stares down grimly. "You need to get out of this system and find someplace to lie low for a while. Find a physician for your friend, and quickly. He won't last long in this condition."

"Dad?" Mara runs down the steps from the control deck, her eyes wide. "You're coming with us!"

"If Zhar reaches that shield, you won't escape here. I'm going to hold her off."

"But, Dad! She'll space you! No!"

"Mara, my love." He presses his forehead to hers. "Did I ever tell you that you're my favorite daughter?"

"I'm you're *only* daughter!" She pulls back, eyes wide and afraid.

He chuckles. "Find your place among the stars, Mara. Knowing you are out there, free, that is enough for me."

"Dad, no. I won't—"

He presses something to her arm.

Ah, the old sleep patch trick.

Mara slumps in her father's arms, but he passes her to me. I grunt, struggling to hold the girl up. "If you go back," I say, "she'll never forgive you. *Or* me. Please stay. We can find another way."

Dr. Luka looks at me with watering eyes. "I'm trusting her into your care, Princess. I once swore to protect your family. Will you do the same for mine?"

"I swear it," I whisper. "But, Doctor, you don't have to do this—"

"Hush, now." He swallows hard, his eyes locked on Mara. "You don't have much time. They're almost through. I wish I could explain to you, Anya, but you have to listen to me now: the Firebird. Zhar's got it all wrong."

"What do you mean?"

Now his eyes flick to me. "You've had it all this time, Princess. You—"

He's cut short as a loud crash shakes the clipper. I curse, thinking the ship's been hit, but then Dr. Luka climbs down to the air lock and looks out.

"Zhar's blasted through the rocks! Go, go, *go*! I can't hold her off for long!" He vanishes through the hatch, and Riyan rushes to shut it behind him.

"Get us off this rock, tensor," I whisper.

"You got it." He rises into the air and lands on the control deck, his robes settling around him.

I grab Pol's stretcher and activate the magnetic locks on the bottom, clamping it securely to the floor. Then I drag Mara to a seat and strap her in. On a screen connected to the ship's rear cameras, I see Dr. Luka standing in front of the shield controls. Soldiers are running toward him. He shoots, and they duck for cover. But then Zhar breaks through, furious and ruthless. She fires on the doctor, and he retreats behind a ship.

"Go, Riyan!" I shout as I climb to the control deck. "She's almost at the shield!"

Zhar crosses the floor in three quick steps. She reaches for the controls.

And is blown off her feet as Riyan blasts the thrusters. The soldiers go skidding away, crashing against the far wall. That's all I have time to see before we shoot down the tunnel. I fall into a seat and strap in. The *Valentina* rattles as we accelerate through the rock chute, and I grind my teeth together and watch Pol shake on his stretcher.

Then we burst out of the asteroid and into open space.

"Holy stars," I breathe.

I count the Union ships as they drop from warp: nine, ten, eleven. All destroyers, all muscled and bristling. I'd expected a few scout ships, but not this.

Not a war fleet.

There must have been something in the signature beamed out by the asteroid base that gave away its identity. The Committee knows this is a Loyalist stronghold, and they're coming in hot. To warp into this system with that much speed means burning up entire Prisms, billions and billions of units' worth of the crystals.

"They'll wipe out the asteroid," I say. "All those kids . . ."

Riyan shakes his head. "The Committee will want to take everyone alive for questioning. They'll be all right, for now."

But still the blood drains from my face and I feel nauseated, watching the ships close in on the asteroid. A few Loyalist fighters swoop past us to engage the enemy, but they're shot down by Prismic pulses from the destroyers. All those pilots from the bar, who were laughing and placing bets over geeball just days ago—gone. The ships burst in front of us, fiery, silent explosions that shimmer and then fade like fireworks.

What have I done?

The *Valentina*'s controls blare an alarm as one of the Union ships gets a missile lock on us.

"Warp, Riyan!" I shout. "NOW!"

Cursing, Riyan quickly throws a lever, engaging the Takhdrive.

We dive into the ocean of stars.

CHAPTER FIFTEEN

Once the ship settles into warp, the adrenaline that had fueled me through our wild escape evaporates. I'm left drained, limbs trembling, desperately wanting to collapse and sleep.

But first I have to check on Pol. I unbuckle and stand, and as I make my way toward the stretcher, Riyan lands silently on the floor in front of me, making me jump.

"Riyan!" I raise a hand. "Seriously, you have to give a warning or something before you do that."

"Sorry," he murmurs, looking abashed. "I just wanted say thank you. For getting me out of there."

I grimace. "I got you *in* there in the first place."

"You could have left me, and then you might have gotten away with the doctor."

"That wasn't even an option."

He stares at me as I edge past him. Pol is prone on his stretcher, his skin cold and clammy. His lashes flick like he's caught in the throes of some terrible dream.

"He's in bad shape," Riyan says.

"He needs a physician."

"And we need a safe place to lie low."

I glance up at him. "You have something in mind?"

He hesitates. "The tensors maintain a gravitational ripple in the space around Diamin, making it impossible for any outsiders to approach. It's the safest place in the galaxy, if you can get in. And I can get us in."

"Then take us there."

A groan from the other sofa draws our attention. Mara is stirring, the sleep patch wearing off. She sits up, pressing a hand to her face. I grab a canteen of water; I know from experience that her mouth will be dry as sand.

But Mara ignores the water, instead shoving off the sofa to teeter on her feet. She looks around a moment, and then her face freezes. Her eyes go flat.

"No," she whispers. "Tell me he didn't go back. *Tell me he's alive.*"

Riyan and I exchange looks.

"Mara . . . I'm sorry," I whisper.

"This is your fault," she says.

I stiffen, my mouth opening but unable to form a reply. She's right. I'm the reason her father is dead. And now she's stuck with me, at least until we reach Diamin. She didn't ask for any of this. Shame clogs my throat; I look away, unable to meet her eyes.

She limps past me, her jaw set. The door to the back cabins is open, and she disappears through it, clearly wanting to be alone. I rub my face, wishing I'd never dragged her or her father into this. But then they'd just be prisoners of the Committee now, also thanks to me. It seems I can't leave a place without first destroying it.

"She'll need time," Riyan says. "Let her be."

I nod, and he heads off to the galley, saying he'll make coffee for us both.

With a sigh, I lie on the floor beside Pol. His hand dangles over the side of the stretcher. I reach up and hold it tight. I can't even feel his pulse in his wrist.

"Oh, Pol," I whisper. "Come back to me."

◇

When I open my eyes sixteen hours later, groggy with sleep, the bridge is quiet, lights dimmed. Pol is still unconscious, but his breathing is steady. I gently extricate my fingers from his. Rising to stretch, I study his face, searching for any sign of improvement. If anything, he seems even paler.

Mara and Riyan are in their cabins, presumably asleep. The ship is quiet, frozen while the universe flows around it, a stone in an infinite river. The hum of the Takhdrive pulses steadily, and up on the control deck, the spinning Prism throws beads of light that dance across the ceiling.

I climb to the upper deck and sit in front of the control board, my feet drawn up so my knees tuck under my chin. Staring at the spinning crystal until my eyes burn, I feel a stab of anger.

"All this," I whisper, "because of *you*."

The Prism spins on, uncaring and indifferent, churning out the energy that threads through every circuit and wire on the *Valentina*. And if Zhar is right, the crystal is still connected to its source, the great, mysterious Prismata lost somewhere in the cosmos. Zhar wants it, Volkov wants it, and both of them are willing to kill everyone I love to get it.

I lean forward, the brightness of the spinning shard burning itself onto my eyes, so that even when I blink, I see it shining on the backs of my eyelids. There are more colors in it than I'd first thought; instead of just gold, it's orange and violet and red, a stormy sunset bound in exquisite, hard-edged symmetry.

Stacia.

My spine tingles and I jerk back, blinking hard.

For a strange moment, I could have sworn I felt . . . *something.* A whisper, a tendril in my mind, a ghostly caress on my shoulder.

My own name uttered.

"I'm losing it," I mutter, looking away from the Prism so my eyes can clear.

My brain is scrambled, and no surprise. I've been running on panic and dread for the past two weeks. Maybe Diamin is just what I need—a safe, peaceful harbor to catch my breath. If everyone there moves as silently as Riyan does, it has to be the quietest planet in the galaxy.

I flip through the nav system, studying the warp path. It'll be sixteen days till we reach the moon of Diamin. Will Pol last that long?

Pulling up a holo of the moon, I study the spinning orb. It hovers beside its larger, uninhabitable planetary companion. The pair is so distant from its sun that Diamin only exists in twilight, and that only a quarter of the time. Mostly, it's dark. All I know about it from my studies is that it's cold, forested, and unwelcoming. Our lessons always rushed through the Diamin chapters, with an almost superstitious fear of the little moon. The Cold Moon, it's been called, both for its extreme temperatures and for its secrets.

I'd always thought Amethyne was as far from anywhere as you could get. Turns out, Diamin is twice that. Maybe that's part of the reason tensors always had so much trouble fitting in with the rest of the Belt—besides their ability to manipulate the fabric of space-time, of course.

Riyan startles me when he sets a cup down on the board.

"Riyan!" I groan. *"Warning."*

"Sorry. I brought coffee."

I take the cup, holding it with both hands and letting the heat sink into my palms. Riyan sits in the next chair and runs a brief system check.

"I haven't been home in six months," he murmurs, sitting back to sip his own coffee, watching the streams of data flow.

"Your family will be glad to see you."

"Hm." He raises a hand to massage his neck. "Maybe not. I didn't leave in the best . . . circumstances."

I look up. "Don't tell me we're flying into more trouble."

"You'll be fine." He stares into his cup, grimacing a little. "It's just that I sort of . . . stole this ship, when I left."

My eyebrows inch upward. "So there's some rebel in you after all."

He sighs. "Defying tensor law and leaving Diamin was the hardest thing I've ever done. You wouldn't have found a more devoted, obedient citizen than me. Meanwhile, Natalya would have cut off her own finger just to irritate our father."

"What happened to your sister?"

He sighs. "She said she was going to find Zemlya."

"Zemlya? The Motherworld? Why?"

"She'd heard stories about it, of treasure hunters who went there and returned with priceless artifacts—she obsessed over the rumors. But she never made it. Vityazes picked her up on Emerault. The last transmission I got from her, I could hear their guns going off in the background."

"So you took off after her."

He nods. "Against my father's wishes. Under Union law, of course, we are not allowed to leave Diamin, but we have our own rules against it as well." The air over his cup begins to snap and warp, and the liquid rises into a mosaic of dark triangles. His eyes harden, silver glinting in his irises. "It is feared that the Committee is trying to steal our abilities."

"Steal them? How?"

He opens his hands, releasing the liquid, and it splashes back into the cup, not a single drop spilled. "Our ability is genetic. If the Committee figures out how to isolate the tensor gene, they could replicate it in their own soldiers."

Stars, tensor vityazes. That's not something I want to think about.

"Surely your people can't be too angry with you," I say. "You were only trying to save your sister."

He lifts a brow, his mouth pressed into a sardonic line. "My people are . . . complicated. We have strict codes by which we must abide, and with good reason. I know the stories you must have heard about us, how we threaten the fabric of existence with our tessellating, how we're unnatural and dangerous."

"I know better now. It all seemed more like a myth, anyway."

"There is truth to it." He looks at me, his eyes dark. "When I attacked Pol, you saw how close I was to losing control. Tensors value self-control above all else. *Imper su, imper fata.*"

"I heard you say that phrase before. What does it mean?"

"It means if you control your self, you control your fate. It's sort of our motto." He gives a grim smile. "When you manipulate gravity as we do, you pull on threads that connect to every part of existence. Lose control of that, and the consequences are devastating."

"What," I joke, because his tone is making me deeply uneasy, "are you worried you'll create a black hole or something?"

He just looks at me.

My teasing smile slides away. "Oh. *Oh.*"

"It's only happened a few times in our history." His eyes turn up, toward the fuzzy glow of the cosmos, the light tingeing his cheekbones silver. "But you can see why it's doubly important we never let the Committee steal our secrets."

"No kidding," I mutter. So maybe not *all* the stories I've heard were lies—at least, not the ones about tensors ripping apart the fabric of reality. Stars, imagine being capable of producing something as terrible and powerful as a black hole? No wonder Riyan's so uptight all the time. If he lost control, he could not only bend space-time—he could tear it open altogether.

I hear a groan from below and whirl to see Pol shifting on the stretcher, pushing against the straps. Setting down my coffee, I hurry to the lower deck and kneel by him. He looks terrible, worse than he did yesterday. His skin is sickly gray and his lips are cracked; when I touch his face, it's hot with fever.

"Stace?" he groans.

"Whoa." I gently hold him down. "You're not going anywhere fast. In case you don't remember, Zhar *shot* you. You've been out for days. I thought you were dead."

"Stars, it feels like I was kicked by a mantibu." He groans, shoulders curling as he tries to double over, but the straps have him pinned.

"Stay still. Let me see the wound." I look up at Riyan. "You got a med kit?"

He nods and opens a compartment to rummage inside.

"Your hair isn't purple anymore," Pol notes. His voice is a thick whisper. I have to lean in to hear him.

"What, do you miss it?"

"Yes."

I snort and shake my head. "Well, just try to stay alive, and maybe we'll dye yours next."

"You don't have to look at me like that," Pol grunts.

"Like what?"

"Like you were right about the Loyalists."

"Well, Pol, I sort of *was* right. Look, I don't need you or anyone else to die for me, got it? Enough with the heroics. Save them for Clio, because we are going to get her, after you're better."

"Where are we going now?"

"Diamin."

"Tensor Town?" He tries again to push himself up. "Stars, no! Those people—"

"Riyan says it's safe."

He grimaces. "Oh. Well, if *Riyan* says so."

"I do," says Riyan, approaching with the med kit.

Pol attempts a weak smile. "Hey, buddy."

Riyan kneels and places a hand on Pol's shoulder. "They would have killed me if you'd sided with them. I thank you for my life, and from now on, we are as brothers."

"We . . . are?"

Rolling my eyes, I take the med kit from Riyan. The tensor then leaves to search for cloths to cool Pol's face.

"Brothers?" Pol whispers to me. "What's that mean?"

"I guess it means you're an honorary tensor." I grin and carefully open his shirt.

There are pain patches inside the kit. I press one to his chest, and take the opportunity to inspect his wound, peeling back the bandage Dr. Luka applied. The hole isn't large, no bigger than the tip of my finger. The gun Zhar used was an efficient little machine, compressing Prismic energy into a narrow but powerful bolt. The skin around the entry wound is red and ugly, purpling over his ribs in large bruises. But the real danger is internal, and I have no idea what to do about that beyond basic first aid. I hope it's not infected. Just in case, I find an antibiotic patch and stick that on him as well. Pol watches silently, but I can tell he's hiding the extent of his pain. Sweat beads his face, and his breathing is jagged. My own chest hurts just listening to him inhale.

"So," Pol says, in a softer tone. "Did you have a funeral for me?"

"What?"

"When you thought I was dead."

"I barely thought of you at all." Stars, he better never find out how much I sobbed, or he'll never let me live it down. "I had my hands full with Zhar. She's worse than you know."

I tell him about the days he missed, about the hologram palace and the missing Firebird and that Zhar is married to the direktor Eminent. His eyes widen at that.

"Do you think our parents knew?"

"They must have. They all served together under the old empire. They were like friends or something—her and Volkov, your parents and mine."

"And this Prismata is the key to winning the war?"

"She sure seemed to think so. She was willing to torture Riyan to get me to find it. I think she'd have tortured me too if she thought it would help."

He shakes his head. "I just can't believe our parents would rally behind someone like that."

"Maybe that's not how it started. Maybe Zhar sort of took over, and they had no way of knowing. She did say they hadn't communicated with our families for years."

He nods. "So. Forget her. We can find this Firebird thing on our own and end this war."

"What?"

"If the Prismata is what Zhar says it is, and if we find the Firebird to lead us to it, we could use it to overthrow the Committee. You're sure you have no idea what it might be? Your parents never mentioned it before?" He blinks hard, as if suppressing a wave of pain.

"Pol . . ." I stand up and walk a few paces away, looking up at the Prism spinning on the control deck.

"The Firebird is the imperial crest, the sign of House Leonov. I don't remember anything at home with the crest on it, but maybe you do? What if it's still on Amethyne? We could go back."

I turn to him. "Back? You mean, *away* from Clio? You think we should abandon her to the Committee?"

He grimaces, teeth bared, and I don't know how much of his expression is due to pain and how much is frustration with me. "Once you control the Prismata, you can save Clio. You can save *anyone*."

I clench my fists. "You're starting to sound like Lilyan Zhar."

"Stacia, you have to accept who you are. You can't push it away forever."

"And when do I get a choice?"

"When do any of us? We are who we are, Stace. You can't hide from that, no matter what disguises you put on. I could cut the horns off my head but I'd still be aeyla. You can run to the ends of the galaxy, but you'll still be a Leonov. You'll still be the rightful heir. You have the power to change things—doesn't that mean you have a responsibility to see it through?"

Turning back to him, I spread my hands. "Let's not talk about it, please. Let's just get to Diamin."

Riyan returns, and helps me move Pol into the medical bay, where we transfer him to a proper bed. The med patches are making him sleepy, and soon he passes out with one arm hanging to the floor. I pack cool damp cloths around his head, trying to bring down his fever, hoping we make it to Diamin soon.

◇

Pol gets worse.

He complains of pain in his head, and we run out of med patches. By day four, he's writhing, curled up, hands gripping his horns.

"I don't know what to do!" I shout, kneeling over him. Riyan and Mara are no help. Whatever's wrong with Pol seems to go beyond his gun wound. He was shot in the chest, not his head. I have no idea what's wrong with him.

"If you'd stopped my father from going back out there," Mara intones, "he'd be here now. He'd know what to do."

“Riyan, can we go any faster? The Committee ships jumped to Granitas System in minutes! Why can’t we?”

He scowls. We’re all tense from listening to Pol howl for hours on end. “Even if we burned through all the Prism’s energy, we’d only shorten the trip by a few days, and we’d have no power left to actually land once we got there.”

“Could we change course? Go somewhere closer, where there are doctors?”

“We’ve already passed the last planet before Diamin. Going back now would just take longer. If the wound is infected, there’s nothing we can—”

“It’s not the wound,” Pol groans.

We both turn to stare at him. He looks exhausted, eyes clouded with pain. Slowly, his gaze shifts to me.

“It’s my Trying.”

My eyes open wide. “You’re only eighteen, Pol. It’s too early.”

“I’ve heard of it happening, when an aeyla is almost old enough. Stress, injury, they jump-start the process.”

“What’s he talking about?” asks Riyan.

I turn to the tensor. “It’s a sort of coming-of-age thing with the aeyla. We all go through puberty, but aeyla have a second maturation event called a Trying. Basically, it’s when their horns grow in all the way.”

“It’s more than that,” growls Pol, curling up again.

I let out a puff of breath. “Yes, there’s a ritual about honor and pride and becoming a voting member of the tribe and a bunch of other stuff, but, Pol . . .”

My voice trails off. I stare at him, knowing he’s seized with pain I can’t even imagine, as the bones of his horns grow at an accelerated rate.

"His body attempting to heal has triggered the growth," I explain. "The aeyla usually take a strong drug to numb the pain, but we don't have anything left."

"What do we do?" asks Riyan, looking alarmed. "Will he . . . die?"

"Not from the Trying. But if the ordeal affects his wound, he might. I don't know. I'm not a blazing doctor!"

"I can . . . handle it . . ." Pol lets out a roar, a sound like I've never heard from him before. It's a primal sound, bone-rattling. His entire body clenches.

"All right, this is happening," I say. I pull up a chair and lean over him, gripping his hands in mine. "And I'm not going anywhere."

CHAPTER SIXTEEN

I sit by him for the next ten hours. He grips my hand so tightly I can feel my bones crunching together. He doesn't know he's hurting me. He's conscious but totally absorbed by pain. His horns are growing before my eyes, a half-inch per hour from my best estimate. He curses, he howls, he asks me to put a gun to his head and pull the trigger. I only squeeze his hand and make him drink more water. In his delirium, he rambles insensibly.

"I can't tell you," he whispers. "I can't. I swore. I took a vow."

"Pol, Pol, I know about your vow. It's all right."

He shakes his head, eyes shut. "Clio . . ."

I wipe sweat from his brow. "I know all about you and Clio. She's loved you since she was a kid, after all."

"No, no . . ." He falls to groaning again.

There are moments of relief, when he lies still, eyes shut, limbs trembling. Still clutching my hand, anticipating the next wave of pain. I hate these periods almost more than the painful ones, because of the apprehension that builds up waiting for the next fit to seize him.

"Remember Soro's Trying?" I ask him, to distract us both.

He nods, not opening his eyes, but a smile curls his lips. "He paraded around Afka like he owned the whole town, tossing his stupid new horns for anyone who'd watch."

"He got them tangled in a slinke tree."

"Stars, I forgot that part! Didn't you set him loose?"

"Yes. You and everyone else were laughing so hard, you couldn't move."

He gives a short chuckle.

"I miss home," I sigh.

Pol's eyes open and find mine. They've turned red, some of the veins burst from the pressure in his head. I swallow hard but don't let him know how bad he looks.

"Remember the Vanishing Tent?" he whispers.

I study him a moment, then stand. "Scoot."

He shifts, and I settle onto the bed beside him, still clutching his hand. We lie on our sides, facing each other, and I draw the sheet over our heads. It billows and then settles around us, sealing out the world.

"See?" I say. "I remember."

"You were so terrified of lightning," he reminds me.

"And you said it couldn't find us in the Vanishing Tent. That it was old aeyla magic."

"You believed in it till you were ten or something."

"Older than that," I whisper. "I just didn't tell you."

"Well, you never got hit by lightning, did you? Who's to say it didn't work?"

I laugh, but my breath hitches with longing for the past, for when our problems were so simple that just pulling a sheet over our heads could make them disappear. I recall the nights when storms rocked the vineyard, thunder stampeding over the hills and lightning splitting the sky, glowing in the bellies of the great violet clouds. And Pol and I, and sometimes Clio too, huddled in the house under bedsheets, where the lightning couldn't find us. We would play Triangulum and tell stories and dare each other to spill our darkest secrets. Always, we ended up falling asleep in a tangle, where our parents would leave us until morning.

"I loved Afka after a storm," I whisper. "It was like a new world. Everything washed clean, the colors brighter."

Pol nods, eyes shutting again. He shudders, and I hold my breath, thinking the pain is starting again. But after a moment he relaxes and says, “I remember we picked up the fallen slinke leaves and wove them into hats.”

“You and me and Clio.”

“You and me and Clio.”

I stare into his eyes, seeing my own memories play out in them. But then he shuts them again, his face weary.

“You could be back there now, both of you,” I whisper. “If you hadn’t gotten tangled up with me.”

“Stop.”

“What?”

“Don’t play that game, blaming yourself for everything.”

“*You* do.”

“Yes, well, it’s my job to protect you, not the other way around.”

“Then what do you call this?” I raise his hand, squeezing it.

Now his eyes open, just barely. “It’s starting again.”

“I’m right here,” I whisper, bracing myself as he seizes with pain.

◇

When we emerge from the cabin hours later, I’m more exhausted than I’ve ever been in my life. Pol looks a wreck, and I’m no better. At least he’s cleaned up, after showering and changing into spare tensor robes Riyan found for him. Mara and Riyan are sitting in the main deck, playing Triangulum, but they shut down the game when we stumble in.

“Whoa,” Riyan says. “Nice horns, brother.”

Pol’s horns are now ten inches long, starting just behind his hairline and arcing gracefully behind him, ivory white and ridged. In addition to his horns’ growth, his cheekbones and jaw have sharpened a little, making him look more aeyla than human.

Stars, I’m staring too long. I pull my eyes away, looking instead at Riyan and Mara.

"Did you guys find paint?"

Mara nods and stands up. She brings me a metal tray with several puddles of colored pigment on it. Her eyes are hollow and red from lack of sleep, but she's at least willing to talk to us now. I'm not sure how she's coping—I've been so preoccupied with Pol—but it seems we've struck a fragile truce. Still, she doesn't quite meet my eyes.

"It's not like we had a commissary to shop at," she says, "but we found some flare powder and mixed it with water. Close enough, I hope."

Pol stares at the tray as I turn to him. "What are you doing, Stace?"

"You only get one Trying. Did you think I'd let you skip the actual *good* part of it?"

He clears his throat, his voice rough when he replies. "An elder usually conducts the rite."

"Yes, well." I shrug. "We're a little short on *elders*, so I'll have to do. If . . . if you want me to. I know it's sort of sacred and there are a lot of rules that I don't know about, but I do know the basics and—"

He places his hands over mine, silencing me. I meet his gaze.

"I want you to do it."

Feeling a nervous twinge in my gut, I set up the rest of the ceremony—holocandles burning in a circle around us, cast by tabletkas I set around. Not exactly the traditional burning tallow from the fat of a snaptooth, but they're better than nothing. Then I dim the cabin lights, to simulate night. The Trying rite is supposed to be done precisely between sunset and dawn. I have no idea what time it is on Amethyne right now, but in space, it's always night, so I figure the sacred aeyla laws aren't being *too* violated.

Riyan and Mara slip away into the rear cabins. The rite is supposed to be done in private between the elder and the new aeyla warrior.

Pol kneels in front of me, which feels weird enough, but then he fixes his gaze on mine with such intensity that I almost forget what I'm supposed to be doing. Stars, he's even handsomer than he was before, the new-and-improved Pol. Pol 2.0.

"Okay," I mutter, breaking my eyes away and looking down at the tray of makeshift paints. I've read about Tryings enough to know the gist of the ceremony, but I hope I don't screw it up. He only gets one of these during his life. I don't want to be the one to ruin it.

I dip two fingers in the red paint and raise them to Pol's face. His body is rigid, his brow still damp with sweat. Stars, he's really taking this seriously.

"Son of Amethyne," I murmur, "where is your past?"

"I carry it in my veins: the blood of my ancestors."

I paint two red stripes down his forehead. Then I dip into the blue paint. Pol's eyes don't waver from my face.

"Son of Amethyne, where is your present?"

"I carry it in my lungs: the breath of this moment."

Two blue crescents on his cheekbones. He doesn't flinch as my fingers brush his skin, leaving azure trails.

Next is the green paint.

"Son of Amethyne, where is your future?"

He bows his head, his jaw hardening. "I carry it in my hands: the soil of Mithraya, to be tended, guarded, honored."

He uses the old word for Amethyne, which was the planet's true name before the Alexandrians annexed it to their empire. The aeyla still use it in their sacred ceremonies. His palms turn up, and I slowly print five green dots on each.

"We'll never go back to how things were, will we?" he whispers, pressing his fingers to the dots. "Amethyne is behind us for good. Even if we go back there, it won't be the same."

"For years I dreamed of leaving Afka. Now all I want is to go home." Raising my eyes back to his, I add, "This will sound selfish, but . . . I'm glad you're here, Pol. I'm glad I'm not alone."

His eyes don't flinch as he replies, "I'm sorry I took you to Zhar. I should never have been so blind and stubborn. Can I even dare to ask for forgiveness?"

"You saved my life." I dip my fingers into water, the green paint washing away. "On Amethyne and every day since, you've been there for me. You've lost so much on my account, and I don't know how to thank you."

"I don't need thanks."

"You don't need forgiveness."

The last part of the rite means dipping my fingers in the violet paint and tracing it over his heart. I wait as he pulls off his robe, until he's kneeling in nothing but a loose pair of trousers that hang low on his hips. The bandage over his chest is fresh; I changed it several times throughout his Trying, when his thrashing caused it to bleed even more. But already the wound is beginning to close. The skin around it is healthier, thanks to the Trying boosting his growth hormones. He isn't fully recovered, but looking at him now, I know he will pull through.

"Son of Amethyne," I whisper, kneeling so we are level, "where is your purpose?"

"I carry it in my heart: to serve and protect Anya Leonova, the last true empress."

My hand freezes between us, violet paint running down my wrist.

"That's not how the ceremony goes," I whisper.

"It's how *mine* goes." He takes my hand, bringing my paint-dipped fingers closer to him. "Please, Stacia."

With a short exhalation, I lean forward and stamp a handprint over his heart. Stars, his chest is solid. I can feel his breath warm on my cheek.

His hands close softly on my arm, holding my hand in place, and our eyes lock.

Then his eyes slip, fixing on my lips. Not daring to look at his mouth, I instead stare at his eyelids. I can make out each individual eyelash, and the threads of emerald in his gray irises when his gaze flashes up to mine.

Pol leans toward me.

The tip of his nose grazes my cheek. I freeze, barely breathing, feeling his pulse race under my palm, making my own accelerate. My heart tightens like a knot. I feel like I'm standing atop the highest hill above Afka, with a storm wind rushing around me, stealing my breath, tasting of lightning.

An image of Clio rises bright in my mind: her glowing eyes when she saw Pol riding toward us that last day on Amethyne, her flushed cheeks and wistful sigh.

Swallowing, I turn my face away. "Pol . . . Pol, no."

"Stacia." His tone is heavy, full of unspoken meaning. "I—"

"*Please*. Please don't."

He pulls back, letting out a breath, eyes darting everywhere but at me. I drop my hand, violet paint dripping from my fingertips to the floor. I can barely breathe, and my body is stretched taut, skin tingling from my scalp to my toes.

"Appollo Androsthenes," I say, my voice strained, "you knelt as a child. Now rise as a man, a warrior of the aeyla."

He stands rigidly and bows to me, then turns and strides away without another word. His cabin door hisses shut behind him. I'm left standing with paint all over my hands and my cheek still burning where he touched me.

What in the blazing stars just happened?

I draw a deep breath and let it out slowly, trying to calm my racing heart, trying to cool the heat in my face.

I won't think about it.

I will forget it happened.

Clearly, Pol's head is off from all the med patches we've been slapping onto him. The Trying has sent his hormones into overdrive, and his system is all out of sync. And I'm sleep deprived or something. There must be a limit to how many times a person can go into warp without their thoughts getting loopy.

"Stars," I mutter, setting down the tray of paint.

Then I flee to my own cabin and lock the door.

◇

The rest of the sixteen days pass in a blur.

I drink obscene amounts of coffee, wishing I had a couple bottles of Dad's wine instead. The four of us are a wreck, moving around the ship like ghosts. Pol and I do an admirable job of avoiding each other, given the close confines of the ship. We don't say more than five words to each other the rest of the trip.

He's still fragile from the gun wound, but healing well. I check his wound wordlessly, rewrapping it every twelve hours until the procedure becomes routine. I can't go near him without remembering his touch, his soft breath on my neck. I can only hope he doesn't notice the heat in my cheeks as I bind him, and when it's done, I rush away to splash my face with cold water. I can barely think of Clio without shame curdling my blood.

Mara doesn't speak, either. She spends most of her time in her cabin, sleeping or crying, stars know. I try not to bother her. She never asked to come on this trip, or to sacrifice her dad, or for any of it. I wish I could do more for her, but don't know where to begin. I barely know the girl.

That leaves Riyan for company. But his mood gets darker the closer we get to Diamin.

I spend a good deal of time sourly pondering how I ended up warping to the farthest reaches of the galaxy with three people as wrecked as I am.

And then, finally, we drop out of warp, and there it is.

The Cold Moon of Diamin.

CHAPTER SEVENTEEN

Riyan cuts the engine and engages the forward thrusters, slowing the *Valentina*. All four of us are on the control deck, seated and strapped in. A large reddish planet hangs to our left, the gas giant around which Diamin orbits. But there's no sign of the moon itself—instead, something else is waiting for us.

"What," Pol breathes, "is *that*?"

Riyan gives a tight smile. "The Diamin Wall."

My mouth hangs open, my eyes fixed on the shining black sphere in front of us. Perfectly round and impossibly smooth, the massive stress field is the color of obsidian. It blots out the stars, like a void suspended in the sky. I've seen something like it before—every time Riyan tessellates and the air warps at his command, folding like paper. But this is a thousand times bigger, an orb of condensed space-time, where gravity is shaped and stretched and turned against itself. The sight is enough to liquefy every ounce of courage I had.

I think of Riyan's warning about what can happen when a tensor loses control and try to ignore the anxious knot of unease in my stomach.

"The moon is . . . behind that?" Mara asks.

Riyan nods. "Think of the wall as a sort of gravity shell. And Diamin is hidden inside."

I look at the tensor. "We're going *into* that thing?"

"Don't worry, Princess," he murmurs, "I'll get you through in one piece."

He closes his eyes and rests his hands on his knees, palms up. At first it looks like he's not doing much at all. But I notice sweat start to form on his skin. The muscles in his neck and arms tighten. His relaxed fingers start to curl, as if he's pulling against some unseen force. Like poisoned veins, dark lines spread from his eyes. When his forearms begin to shake, I feel a cold lump of fear.

What if it doesn't work?

The massive stress field in front of us grows larger, and the closer we get, the harder I grip the arms of my chair. I can barely draw a breath for the terror clogging my throat.

"Look," Mara whispers, glancing at the cup of coffee on the board in front of her.

The liquid inside is starting to toss.

She and I lock gazes, and then I feel it—the trembling of the ship as it begins to accelerate. But the engine is idling and the thrusters are off. We're not propelling ourselves.

The wall is sucking us in.

Swallowing, I press myself against my seat. Pol catches my eye and shakes his head, probably still thinking this was a bad idea. Maybe he's right.

Harder and harder the ship rattles. Riyan is sweating and straining in silence, his hands now in fists, the tendons in his wrists like taut cables. His entire frame is rigid, and I can see his pulse hammering in his temple. From ear to ear, his face is masked in black, as if he smeared soot over his skin.

A spine-tingling crunch sounds around us, and I watch in horror as the walls begin to buckle. It looks like some invisible space giant has grabbed the clipper and is slowly squeezing it. The sound gets louder: crunching, grinding, groaning. Mara lets out a soft, frightened cry, and Pol's hand leaps to mine, his fingers tightening.

"He's going to get us killed," he says.

For once, I agree with him. But there's no going back now. The pull of the wall is so strong I'm not sure we could escape it even if we tried. The closer we get, the more I realize it's not as smooth as it appears. The wall bristles with static electricity—forking, bursting webs of light. I'd expected a solid wall, but it's more like a storm trapped in glass. The shadows draw us in and swallow us whole, space-time boiling around us.

The force of it begins to pull at *me*, a pressure inside my chest, pushing forward, trying to burst through my ribs. Struggling for breath, I squeeze Pol's hand back, while my bones cry out and my head reels. Black dots float in my eyes, expanding, and no amount of blinking washes them away. It's like I'm suffocating all over again.

"Riyan," I gasp through my teeth.

The tensor's eyes slam open and he sucks in a breath as the pressure gripping the ship relaxes and we shoot through. The wall's dark tentacles release us, and we sail toward the white moon that waits ahead. A few splinters of lightning crackle over the ship, then fade away.

I let out a gasp and crumple into my seat. Then I realize I'm still clutching Pol's hand. He seems to realize this at the same time, and we pull apart.

"That was a little too close, *brother*," Pol grumbles.

Riyan leans forward to ignite the engine, muttering. It sounds suspiciously like, "I can't believe that worked."

We stare at him.

"You . . . you *have* done that before, right?" Mara asks.

Riyan shakes his head. "The barrier only works one way. When I left, I sailed right through it."

"Oh," says Pol. "Well. That's reassuring. And we're listening to this guy *why*?"

"Be quiet," I mutter, but my heart's still knocking around like a bird trying to escape.

"Don't we need to get entry clearance?" Pol asks.

Riyan gives him a look. "That *was* clearance. Only a tensor can get in and out of the wall. Welcome to the safest bit of space in the galaxy."

◇

Riyan navigates the clipper across the frigid Diamin landscape. Spindly trees flick below us, endless frozen forest cast in muted twilight. They are much taller than any tree on Amethyne due to the lower gravity of Diamin, bristling with short, stiff needles, their trunks pale. Snow clouds gather to the east, thick as foam. From this side, the gravity wall isn't even visible. Instead, the dead planet fills the sky, massive and looming, its rim burning gold from the star beyond. The sight is awe-inspiring but strange, reminding me how far I am from home.

"Looks cheerful," Pol murmurs.

"Nothing out there but frost bison and minki," Riyan says. "Bison are good for eating, minki good for dropping out of trees and ripping your eyes out. Don't go on any long walks alone if you can help it, my brother."

"What are those?" I ask, pointing to dome-like structures that huddle in the distance.

"Those are the glazieries."

Right. All diamantglass comes from here, made by some secret process only the tensors know. Supposedly their people are wildly wealthy, given their monopoly on the glass trade. You can't have Prisms without diamantglass. It's the only material capable of containing the gravitational fields required for the crystal to spin. If it weren't for the glass, I wonder if the tensors would have anything to do with the rest of the Belt at all, or if they would become wholly secluded.

Riyan makes a wide turn, angling for a mountain range in the distance. The ship is so low I half expect to clip the tops of the trees. We skim over the domes, and I can just glimpse tiny figures moving between them, workers coming and going.

Mara emerges from the back cabins with clear masks and oxygen tanks.

"Good, you found them," Riyan says. "Put them on and make sure your tanks are full. Otherwise, you'll pass out within a few minutes of setting foot in our atmo. It's not so bad inside Tyrrha, because we regulate the air, but you'll still need a boost from time to time."

"Tyrrha?"

"Our city. It's more of a stronghold, really. You'll see."

My stomach flutters nervously; Riyan assured me we'd be safe here, but I can't forget the target hovering over me like a holo. After what happened in the Granitas System, the Loyalists will be looking for me as ruthlessly as the vityazes. There's no way of knowing whether Zhar was captured or killed by the Union, or if she somehow escaped. I feel like a minnow swimming between two hungry snapteeth, hoping desperately that neither notices me hiding in its shadow.

"There it is," Riyan says wryly, cutting the ship's power to half. "Tyrrha, ancient home of the tensors."

"Holy stars," breathes Mara. "How is it *possible*?"

Set in a flat vale between two mountains, Tyrrha is an enormous pyramid of stone—turned upside down. It balances on a fine point, sloping upward and outward until it forms a vast flat surface directed at the sky. Its sides are smooth and gleaming, reflecting the jagged landscape around it, so it assumes all the colors of the mountains, forests, and sky. Like an optical illusion, like Riyan's power itself, it bends my perception nearly to a breaking point. The more I stare, the less possible it seems. My eyes search for the trick to the thing—hidden supports or mirrors or anything to explain that impossible structure. It looks like it would tip at the slightest touch of wind, and across those peaks around it, the gales must be powerful.

"It was built by the first generations of tensors who landed here," says Riyan. "There are always fifty of us in meditation across the city, keeping the whole thing balanced."

"That seems . . . risky," I point out. "What if someone messes up? What if you're attacked? The whole place would tip over."

"Exactly."

"It's a defense mechanism," Pol says, his eyes widening. "If the enemy ever breached the city, you could just roll it over, completely changing the battlefield in your favor. Genius!"

Riyan nods. "Just so, brother."

The clipper tilts upward, pressing me back against my seat. We rise, dwarfed in Tyrrha's shadow. The outer wall is so smooth I can see the reflection of our ship flitting across it, chasing us up to the sky.

At last, we overshoot the wide, flat peak, nose pointed at the stars, and Riyan pulls back on the yoke. The ship turns a lazy half loop, diving and swooping toward a large slot in the top level of the pyramid.

Within, a lit hangar awaits. There must be fifty ships anchored there, from cruisers to catamarans. None as gorgeous as the clipper, though.

Once the *Valentina* is inside, Riyan quickly engages the landing system, bringing the ship to rest. The space is stark, open, and polished, a fair bit more sophisticated than the makeshift hangar the Loyalists had carved into the asteroid. And it's quiet—I don't see any pilots or mechanics hanging around. The other ships rest in silence.

"Where is everyone?" I ask. "Do you think they know we're here?"

"They know. They'll have known since we broke through the barrier." He shuts his eyes briefly, then nods. "Here they come."

The wall in front of us rumbles as a stone door sinks into the ground, lowered by a group of tensors behind it. They approach the *Valentina* slowly, cloaked and solemn, shaven heads decorated with the same tattoos as Riyan's, carrying similar staffs. There are a dozen altogether, and they spread out into a line, waiting.

"Let's get it over with," Riyan says, grabbing his staff and heading for the hatch.

We're a few paces behind him as he rounds the ship and approaches the twelve tensors. Pol grips his ribs, wincing a little, still in pain. If it comes to a fight, he won't be much help. I wish I had a gun or something to defend myself with.

I wonder when I became the sort of person who expects a fight at every turn. Riyan said we would be safe here, but his nervousness is making *me* nervous. Little about our welcoming party actually says *welcome*, and I remember all the worst stories I've heard about the tensors. My head spins a little.

Remembering what he told us about the moon's lower O_2 levels, I raise the mask to my face and take a few deep breaths. My head settles and the panic in my chest eases somewhat, but I still watch the waiting tensors with apprehension.

"Riyan Ayedi," says a tall, thin tensor with milky skin stretched over an elongated bone structure.

"Jorian," replies Riyan. His eyes flicker over the others.

"You presume much, boy, by returning here."

"This is still my home."

Jorian scowls and turns to whisper with the others. We all exchange looks, and I can see Mara and Pol are as worried as I am. I glance back at the *Valentina*; we could be inside the ship and out of here altogether in a matter of seconds, if this goes badly.

But then Jorian turns back to us, his face smug. "Riyan Ayedi, you are charged with larceny, desertion, and dereliction of duty. Do you accept these charges?"

Alarm splinters through me, and I turn to stare at Riyan.

He swallows but doesn't look surprised. "I accept them."

"This was a bad idea," Pol whispers in my ear.

"You will be tried in five days' time," Jorian says to Riyan. "Until then, you're not to leave the city."

Riyan bows his head. "So be it. I only ask for asylum for my companions. This one needs to be taken to Damai for healing." He gestures at Pol.

"A lawbreaker cannot claim asylum for anyone," Jorian replies.

"I have not been proven a lawbreaker yet, have I?" returns Riyan coolly, and in the look he gives the man, I sense a long and turbulent history between them. "I've only been charged."

Jorian looks ready to argue again, but the woman on his left puts a hand on his arm. His lips tighten, but he waves a hand. "Bring them, then, but they'll have to be cleared through quarantine first."

The tensors turn, making space for us to pass through. As we do, I grab Riyan's sleeve and whisper, "You knew this would happen, didn't you? Why would you come back here if you knew they would put you on trial?"

"Because you will be safe here." He pauses, then adds softly, "In my people's tradition, when someone saves your life, they become blood to you. Pol is my brother, and you are my sister. What I would do for any of my family, I would do for you."

He walks on, leaving me to follow with Mara. I stare at his back, until the tensors surround us and he blends in with the rest.

CHAPTER EIGHTEEN

An hour later, Mara and I find ourselves in a small room, clutching our oxygen tanks and staring at a single wide bed. Beside it is a wood nightstand, a shaggy hide rug that I can only assume is from one of the frost bison Riyan told us about, and a tiny, narrow window that looks east. Like all the walls I've seen so far in Tyrrha, these are all slightly angled, following the slope of the pyramid's outer walls.

The tensor who brought us here is a stone-faced woman with a shaven and tattooed head. She separated us from Pol and Riyan in order to unceremoniously strip us, push us into showers, then poke and scan us until she was sure we weren't carrying contagious diseases or Committee spying equipment. Now she stands in the doorway, her suspicious gaze making the back of my neck prickle.

"Um," I say. "Is this the only bed?"

"On Diamin," says the woman coolly, "sleeping is a communal arrangement. But we thought you might want privacy, being off-worlders. Perhaps you would be more comfortable in a proper sleeping chamber, with fifty other girls?"

I quail at the challenge in her gaze.

"No, uh, this is great. Right, Mara?"

"Cozy," Mara says, rolling her eyes and breathing from her oxygen mask.

The tensor woman sniffs and steps into the corridor outside. She icily informs us dinner will be served in one hour. Then she shuts the door, which is made of white wood and opens on hinges, thank the stars. Half the doors in this city, it seems, can only be opened by tessellating.

"I'll take the floor," I say.

"Don't be ridiculous. Sleep on the bed—it's huge. Unless you snore."

"No. Do *you*?"

She looks for a moment as if she's going to pick a fight, but then she gives a dry laugh and flops onto the bed. Then she groans, pressing a hand to her side. "Let's both take the floor. This thing is hard as a rock."

"I'm not surprised." Everything I've seen of Tyrrha has been hard, smooth, and sterile. My cell in the Loyalist base was almost more welcoming.

Mara makes room for me to sit beside her. We both end up lying back, staring at the stone ceiling, separated by a wall of silence. How many times have I shared a bed with Clio, just like this? Lying side by side, whispering and laughing, making plans. The dull ache I've lived with for the past few weeks suddenly sharpens. The pain of missing her is as acute as a cold blade between my ribs. I let out a shuddering breath, wondering if she's been crammed into a room with a bunch of other prisoners or if she's in isolation. Is someone looking out for her? Is she with the other Afkan prisoners, who might be able to help her? Does she think I've abandoned her? Does she blame me?

I should never have left her behind, not for a moment.

Mara sits up, raising one eyebrow at me. "You're crying."

I raise a hand to my face and find my cheeks damp. I hadn't even realized the tears were there. Wiping them away, I close my eyes and press my oxygen mask to my mouth. The rush of air helps steady me.

"Look," she says, "if you want the floor that badly, it's yours."

I snort, opening my eyes just enough to glance at her. She looks a bit bewildered by my tears, as if they're a language she doesn't speak. If there were ever a polar opposite to my sensitive, nurturing Clio, it's Mara Luka. But I'm glad she doesn't try to comfort me. Tenderness right now would only send me over the edge, into the dark, sucking abyss of grief that I've been trying my best to stay out of. I envy Mara her toughness. But I know that deep down, she's hurting too.

The silence grows heavy while I search for the words I haven't been able to say in the last sixteen days.

"I'm sorry," I start, my voice thick. "Your dad—"

"Don't," she says. "Don't be sorry, as if you forced him to do anything. He made a choice and I have to respect that." After a pause, she adds, "I just hope you're worth it."

I sit up. The walls seem to press in on me, squeezing the air from my lungs. I want to tell her I'm not worth it. I'm not worth any of the sacrifices that have been made on my account. But the words stick to my throat.

Mara watches me. "I don't hate you, Anya. Or Stacia, or whatever you want to call yourself. This is a war, and in war, soldiers die. Just . . . don't forget what side you're supposed to be on. Promise me that, and I'll be your ally."

I nod, feeling sick.

This may be war, but I don't feel like a soldier. In many ways, we're still just kids. The only thing we should have to fight for is a later curfew. Mara shouldn't have had to leave her father to die. Clio shouldn't be sitting in a gulag, waiting to be interrogated. Pol shouldn't be recovering from a gunshot that came within an inch of killing him. Riyan shouldn't have had to hunt across the stars for his stolen sister.

And I . . . I just want everything to go back to the way it was before. But it never will, even if I save Clio and take down the Committee and find this Firebird thing, whatever it is. Even if everything from here on out goes exactly the way I want it to, I'll never get back what I lost. Something fundamental has changed deep inside me, and I think it's changed in Mara too, and in Pol and

Riyan. I shudder to think of how Clio will have changed, when I finally reach her.

None of us will ever be kids again.

Mara lies back again, eyes closing, her hands folded on her stomach. I kick off my boots and press my feet into the rough hide on the floor, the fur white and coarse. Through the narrow window, the great gas planet is rolling into view, yellow orange and ominous, like a dying sun.

◇

Not long after, the peal of some massive horn sounds through the whole pyramid city in a bone-rattling groan. Mara, who'd nodded off, wakes with a sharp intake of breath.

I panic at first, thinking we're under attack, but in the corridor we find a stream of tensors calmly making their way along. They give us odd looks when we burst out of our room with wild eyes and racing pulses. Then I realize what we'd heard was the tensor version of a dinner bell.

We follow the people at a slight distance, me hopping as I put my boots back on, my oxygen tank swinging from my belt. No one takes much notice of us, at least not openly; I see plenty of sidelong looks and curious glances, especially from the younger tensors, as we stand in a long line to pick up our dinner. Mara yawns and stretches, her eyes still red with sleep.

The mess hall—or Hall of Sustenance, as they insist on calling it—is nothing more than a long, narrow room with a long, narrow table. The ceiling is probably a hundred feet high, and because of the angled walls, it's almost twice as wide as the floor below. Hard to tell, because the shadows obscure it from view. Along one wall, the tensors' motto is carved forbiddingly into the stone: *Imper su, imper fata.* Candles—not holos but actual *tallow* candles—burn along the center of the table in varying degrees of height. At the far end, where the youngest sit, a couple of kids are playing some sort of tessellating game, making candles float around and trying not to spill the hot wax. Mara watches them with a mixture of fascination and bewilderment.

They're a strange, solemn society. No one raises their voice, and there is no shoving in line or racing to get a seat at the tables. I think of Riyan telling me the tensors prize self-control above all else and begin to sympathize with his sister Natalya. I can easily see how a girl longing for adventure would come to feel chafed by the tensors' quiet, restrained world.

Mara and I pick up bowls from an elderly tensor stirring a large pot and carry them to one of the tables. She watches the gruel slide from her spoon to land with an unappetizing plop in her bowl.

"I've learned something today," she says.

"Yeah?" I shovel the stuff in, swallowing the chunks of frost bison meat whole, since they're as chewable as an old rubber gasket. It's best, I realize, to get it all down quickly.

"I am not cut out for tensor life." With a look of distaste, she pushes the bowl away.

Only to have it slide back toward her as if pulled by an unseen string. Mara jumps.

"In Rubyati culture," says Jorian, tucking his hand back into his sleeve, "refusing the food offered by your host is an invitation to a death duel."

"Name the time and place, then, mate." Mara glares at the tensor until he walks on, his eyes sliding mistrustfully from her to me.

"You shouldn't push him," I tell Mara. "He could crush you into a pebble. And he looks like he's waiting for an excuse to do it."

She snorts and looks down the table at the rest of the tensors bent over their bowls. Several of them look just as miserably at their meals as we do ours.

"I'm going to check on Pol," I say, rising to my feet.

"And I'm going back to bed." Mara yawns and raises her oxygen mask to her face for a deep breath. The low O_2 levels make me sleepy too, but I haven't had a chance to see Pol since we landed, and I'm anxious to see how he's doing.

Mara and I split up in the passageway outside the mess hall. She goes up, I go down. Tyrrha is all stairs, it seems, and that combined with the low oxygen levels means I stay perpetually winded. The tensors, of course, just float up and down the stairs like blazing leaves on the wind, and not a few of them with smug little glances at me.

The infirmary is a pleasant room, by tensor standards, anyway. Instead of hard wooden chairs devised to torture one's vertebrae, the seats here actually have soft pillows on them. The sloping outer wall is set with windows that overlook the mountains, and Diamin's distant white sun is just peeking over the shoulder of the nearest summit. Thin, silvery rays slant across the snowy plain far below, where a herd of frost bison moves ponderously through the drifts.

Pol is standing at the window, silhouetted against the rising sun, his back to me. For a moment I almost don't recognize him for his newly grown horns.

Hearing my footstep, he turns. He's wearing only loose tensor trousers, his scarf knotted around his waist like a belt. His chest is bandaged tightly.

"Hey," he says.

"Hey." I scratch my elbow, my eyes slightly averted. "You want to put on some clothes, maybe?"

He looks down at his bare chest, then up at me. "You've seen me like this hundreds of times."

"Yeah . . ." But those times, the sight of him didn't leave me weak. It's like something changed between us on the way here, in that blazing ceremony of his. I'm not sure how to get back to the way we were. I have even less idea where we actually *are*, and what the jitters in my stomach mean. Or how in the stars I would explain them to Clio.

I try, desperately, to lighten the mood. "So! How about that bison meat? Chews like a sock, am I right?" I punch his shoulder in a poor attempt at playfulness, just as a tensor girl emerges from another doorway.

"Easy!" she snaps. "He isn't healed yet. You'll undo all my work!"

"Sorry," I mutter.

"This is Damai," Pol says. "She's incredible, Stacia. All that pain in my chest? Gone."

"Your bones are strong," Damai says, setting down a pile of clean bandages and going to Pol. She is tall and lean, her hair woven into many braids that she piles atop her head. She presses her hand against Pol's chest, fingers lightly probing his sternum, and nods to herself. "He had several broken ribs. But I was able to ease the pressure on his lungs."

"Turns out gravity-magic is great for healing," Pol adds. He grins at the girl.

She smiles back at him. "I'm fascinating by this Trying of yours. You aeyla have such exquisite bone structure. I hope you'll let me study it for my notes. We know so little about your people, and it would be a great service to our medical library."

"Oh," he says, lifting his eyebrows. "Well, I guess if it's *helpful* . . ."

She laughs.

"Right. Damai, thank you." I cough, noting her hand on his chest, her fingers lingering on his bare collarbone. "Pol, you weren't at dinner. I'd thought you died or something. Again."

"That's Stacia," he says to Damai. "Always exaggerating."

I suck in a sharp breath. "Well, at least I don't go around getting myself shot."

"Oh, I got *myself* shot? You're the one who had to jump in front of Riyan—"

"They were going to kill him!"

"Well, better they kill me than him, then. You know, I saw you two cuddling up on the bridge on the way here."

"Cuddling?"

Damai's gaze darts between us. "All right. Enough. You need to rest, Pol. You might feel better, but your bones still need to heal."

She moves to walk me to the door, whispering, "You probably should stay away for a few days, until he's stronger. You upset him."

"I what?"

"When he talks about you, his pulse goes nuclear. Your being here is even worse. You're bad for his blood pressure."

"I'm *what*?"

Damai ruthlessly pushes me out of the infirmary door.

"My patients come first," she says. "I must see to his well-being."

With that, she shuts the door in my face, tessellating it slightly so it sinks into the floor. My efforts to push on it get me nowhere. That's the tensor version of a lock, I guess.

"I am *not* bad for his blood pressure!" I yell through the stone. "What does that even mean?"

No answer. She's probably in there studying Pol's exquisite bone structure with her long, clever fingers. Well, see if I care. I kick the door, then yelp at the splinter of pain that shoots through my foot.

"Whoa," says a voice behind me, and I jump, startled. "While I appreciate the irony of breaking one's foot on the infirmary door, surely there are less destructive forms of self-expression?"

I turn to see Riyan standing there, eyes amused. "For the last time, *please* stop sneaking up on me like that!"

His lips quirk, a grin he's trying to suppress. "Sorry. Is there trouble here?"

"She locked me out!"

He nods knowingly. "You've met Damai."

"Who does she think she is, not letting me see Pol? Who knows what's going on in there! She could be hurting him or poisoning him or . . . or worse."

Riyan's eyebrows arch up. "Worse?"

"Nothing. Forget it." I shake my head, looking at him closer. "I thought you'd be locked up or something. Aren't you a criminal here?"

"They know I won't run. I'll face my trial with honor, or what honor I have left."

"You only went to search for your sister. Anyone would've done the same for their sibling."

"Not anyone. Damai didn't."

"Damai . . ." I blink. "She's your sister too?"

He sighs again, looking suddenly weary. "I have eight of them."

"Eight!"

"Come," he says. "I'll talk to Damai later about letting you in. Meanwhile, we're wanted below. The Lord Tensor wishes to meet you."

"The Lord Tensor? As in, your people's leader?"

Riyan nods.

My stomach sinks to the floor. "Sounds fun."

We walk through passages that remind me a bit of the Loyalist asteroid base, but back there the walls had been rough-cut and raw, while the tensors' structure is so smooth I can see my reflection in the dark stone. When we walk through an open atrium that looks out to the snowy forest, I come to a stop and look out. The trees look dusted with flour, while the mountains to the side are harsh angles of stone and ice. For all its forbidding climate, Diamin is undeniably beautiful.

"Such a strange and lonely place," I say softly. "Why here? Why settle so far away from the rest of the Belt? Aren't the tensors originally from Alexandrine?"

"We didn't have a choice. Our abilities made us pariahs on Alexandrine, so we fled here and the people of Diamin gave us asylum." He stares out at the white landscape, his eyes distant. "Some of the native Diaminicans assimilated into our culture, but the full-blooded ones died out long ago. Radiation hampered their fertility rates. Our tradition of granting unconditional asylum to outcasts is done in their memory."

"Really? I never knew much about the tensors," I admit. "And I think most of what I did know was . . . um, a bit untrue."

He laughs. "At least the stories keep away the tourists." Sobering, he adds, "Most people also have no idea that our order was founded by Zorica Leonova."

I raise my eyebrows. "As in . . . *the* Leonovs?" I still can't say the words *my family*.

He nods. "The Leonovs were originally scientists, you know, before they were rulers. They created the tensor gene, a cybernetic code grafted onto our DNA. But the Alexandrine government of their day had outlawed such biological tinkering, and my ancestors became outcasts, imprisoned or even killed for our abilities. Later, after the Leonovs discovered the Prisms and pioneered warp travel, we would leave that world behind and settle here, where we could be left in peace." He gives me a sidelong look. "I have no love for your family, but there's no doubt they left their mark on history, in more ways than one. And here you are, the very last of them."

"I'm not so sure about that. I may have their blood, but the rest of it?" I shake my head. "I don't feel like one of them. And I don't think I want to. You said it yourself, before we ever even found Zhar and the Loyalists—the Leonovs were just as awful as Volkov and the Union are now. The galaxy needs to move forward, not backward."

He tilts his head, studying me. "And I suppose you'll be the one to lead us forward, from your mighty Alexandrine throne?"

"Stars, no!" A short, acidic laugh bursts from my lips. "What would I know about leading anyone? Back home, my dad barely let me fly a dory unsupervised." I look at him. "Who says we need a throne? Who says we need a Committee? There has to be another option. One that lets the planets rule themselves and gives everyone an equal chance, no matter where they're from or what they want to be. Peace *and* freedom."

"Careful," Riyan says. "You're almost starting to sound wise."

I throw a soft elbow into his side. "What do you care, anyway? I thought you wanted nothing to do with the outside worlds."

He turns to gaze out the window, leaning on his staff. "Sixteen years ago, during the war, the Leonovs called on my people for aid, and we did nothing. They had wronged us. They killed my mother and countless others. Like the rest of the Belt, my people were appalled to see how far the Leonovs would go to rout an enemy." Riyan pauses, taking in the view. "But now we're prisoners on our own planet, and the galaxy hates us even more than they used to. They think we're arrogant because we're reclusive, and evil because we're powerful. Maybe if we were allowed back into society, we could show them that we're more alike than we are different." Riyan sighs and taps his staff on the floor. "We should keep going. The Lord Tensor despises tardiness."

We walk deeper into the pyramid, leaving behind the bright windows for dark, narrow corridors, until at last we come to the heart of Tyrrha. Or what feels like the heart of Tyrrha, anyway. The walls around us seem a mile thick, the air so thin I have to take every other breath through the mask. A triangular door is before us, smooth stone carved with geometric patterns like the ones tattooed onto Riyan's skin. Two wide basins of fire burn on either side, the heat choking the air.

"You *sure* he wanted to see me?" I ask uneasily.

Riyan only nods before raising a hand, and the air begins to crack in response.

The great door depresses and sinks with a sound like thunder and screeching slate, rock crushing against rock, sending a chill down my back. I wince and shift from foot to foot, wishing I'd gone with Mara for that nap.

The door finally vanishes into the floor, and we step through the opening. Riyan is a pace ahead, his hands working around his staff.

The floor of the chamber within is round, enclosed by sloping walls that come to a very high point, so the space creates a sort of hollow cone. Around the perimeter of the floor, candles burn in waxy puddles. The Lord Tensor is at the center, three feet in the air, hovering in perfect silence and stillness on a shimmering stress field. He wears gray robes that hang nearly to the floor, while his legs are drawn up and crossed beneath him and his hands rest on his knees.

Riyan and I come a stop halfway to the levitating tensor.

"Father," he says softly.

Oh.

Looking up at the man, I see it at once.

His eyes are closed, but there's no mistaking the resemblance. The Lord Tensor has the same dark brown skin as Riyan, the same lean build and brooding brow. But his face is more lined and he has a short, graying beard that creeps up to his temples. He does not look like a man who smiles much.

I glance between father and son, wishing I were anywhere else. The air in the chamber is stretched tight. I raise my oxygen mask, sucking down a long breath. The sound of the gas releasing from the tank on my hip breaks the silence, and Riyan's father finally opens his eyes.

"You've come back," he says, in a deep, rumbling voice. His eyes settle on Riyan.

Riyan says, "I told you that I would."

The Lord Tensor slowly descends, as if lowered on an invisible rope. His slippered feet touch the ground, and his robes slowly settle around him, in a motion so seamless it's like he's underwater. He makes me feel clumsy just standing here.

"So," he says, his voice filling the smoky chamber, "what hedonistic pleasures did the universe hold for you, boy?"

Riyan stares hard at the ground. "You know I was searching for Natalya. Your *daughter*."

"I have no such daughter."

Riyan's hands clench into fists. I try to make myself as small as possible, silently cursing the incessant hissing and wheezing of my oxygen tank.

"I expected rebellion from Natalya. Maybe even from some of the others—Damai or Elsid. But you?" The Lord Tensor's lips twist. "You were born to lead our people, and instead, you forsook them."

"Father—"

"You have lost the right to call me that."

Riyan's eyes widen. "I'm your son."

"I have no son."

"Hey!" The word bursts from me before I can stop it. My face heats, but I can't keep quiet. "He only went looking for his sister because you didn't have the guts to do it yourself! I'd say *you're* the one abandoning people, not him."

Riyan lets out a thin breath, his eyes closing. The Lord Tensor turns to me slowly.

"So. You're the one who claims to be the lost Leonova princess."

"I haven't claimed to be anything."

"The Leonovs were nothing but trouble for us."

Riyan lifts his chin. "Stacia saved my life, and I call her sister."

"Pah!" The Lord Tensor storms out of the room, and Riyan hurries after him. With a sigh, I trail behind, sucking down another draft of oxygen.

"Asylum was granted to you, Princess," Riyan's father says, his voice echoing through the smooth stone corridor, "and it will be honored. But I want you off this moon the moment your horned companion is cleared from medical."

Well, I think sourly, *if Damai has any say in that, looks like we'll be here awhile.*

CHAPTER NINETEEN

A lacy snowflake, fine and glittering, lands on my open palm. It survives my body heat just long enough for me to study its intricate pattern, the minuscule rods and swirls of ice frozen in perfect symmetry. I've never seen anything so beautiful, but in a moment, it is gone, turned into a drop of water in the cradle of my hand.

My head starts to feel light.

I raise my oxygen mask, taking a long inhale. The rush of air steadies me, and I hold it in place for a few more breaths.

The frozen forest glitters all around, trees encased in ice over deep banks of snow. Diamin's pale sun plays in the glassy branches, splitting into fractals of blue and silver that shine on the snow's clean surface. The air smells fresh and sharp, tinged with smoke from the diamantglass glazieries a short distance away. The dark domes huddle on patches of bare earth, where the heat from the kilns has melted away the snow. But here, the cold is absolute, and I stand knee-deep in the drifts.

Riyan picks up a handful of snow and rolls it into a ball. "When I was a boy, we used to hurl these at one another from dawn to dusk."

"So, for two hours," I point out. Diamin's daylight is brief and weak; the sun seems to barely rise before it's already setting again.

He gives me rueful grin and lets the snowball fall to the ground, where it breaks apart at his feet. "Speaking of which, we can't stay out here much longer."

The sun is already setting, burnishing the rounded hip of the great planet in the sky. The tensors call the planet Rumiha, which means elder brother. But to me, it seems more like a jailor, allowing only a small window of sunlight before rolling across the sky and blanketing the snowy moon in darkness.

I sigh, watching the shadows creep closer. I could spend a whole day out here—an Amethyne day, with sixteen hours of light—exploring the wintry landscape of Diamin. It took some political maneuvering on Riyan's part to buy these two short hours for me. Mara elected to stay inside, unenthused by the prospect of tramping around in the cold. Pol wanted to come, but he's still under Damai's ruthless control, and she was convinced if he so much as set foot in the snow, he'd drop dead. We've been on Diamin four days now, but Pol carries on like it's been a month.

"She's driving me *insane*," he moaned this morning. It had been our first chance to talk since Riyan made his sister admit me into the infirmary. "She keeps taking pictures of my skeleton. It's creepy!"

But even Riyan couldn't convince the resolute medic to release Pol to us. He's probably pacing the infirmary now, steaming.

I watch Riyan as he wanders on, his shoulders bent beneath the heavy fringe of a frost bison's mantle. Our cloaks are lined with a synthetic material that makes the cold seem almost nonexistent, but the fur is so warm I'm starting to sweat a little.

"Hey!" I shout.

Riyan starts to turn—just in time to get hit smack in the face by the snowball I hurl.

I burst out laughing at his shocked expression. Then he bends to scoop up snow, and I yelp and sprint away. It's slow going through the knee-deep drifts, and his shot hits me squarely on the back of my head. Melted snow trickles down my neck and makes me shiver, but it's an exhilarating sensation. I duck behind a tree and form another ball, but before I can throw it, Riyan sneaks up behind me and steals it right out of my palm.

I put up my hands to shield my face, bracing for the impact—but it doesn't come. Riyan just laughs softly and tosses the snowball aside.

"I couldn't hit an unarmed warrior," he says.

"Do you ever stop being so blazing noble?"

He cocks his head. "Well, there was this time I kidnapped the last of the Leonovs and tried to hand her over to her enemies."

"Right." I wince. "There was that."

We start heading back to Tyrrha. Though the inverted pyramid looms over us, it's going to take a half hour to reach the lift into the city, but I don't mind the walking. The snow is deep, and I love the way it crunches underfoot.

We pass a glaziery, and there I pause to watch a team of tensors move a load of diamantglass sheets into a cargo ship. They seem almost to be dancing, the way they move their hands through the air, sliding the glass along a crackling stress field.

Thoughtfully, I turn to Riyan. "So you are the only people in the galaxy who can make diamantglass, right?"

He nods. "It's our only source of trade, and we guard the process carefully. Of course, few could copy it, since it involves stress fields."

I look around at the landscape: snow, rock, ice. "Where does the sand come from?"

"Hm?"

"For the diamantglass. Where do you get the sand to make it?"

He blinks; his eyes slide away, to the gas giant swelling on the horizon. "From Rumiha."

For some reason, my question seems to have unsettled him. The planes of his face harden, like a shell closing.

I frown, confused, before carefully adding, "You must know a lot about Prisms, then, since you make the cases that hold them."

"I know as much as anyone else, I suppose." He tilts his head. "You said Zhar is seeking control of the Prisms."

I nod. "She's looking for something called the Prismata—the

mother crystal, I guess, that creates all the others. Do you think that's even possible?"

His eyes follow the cargo ship as it lifts off the ground and turns toward a row of warehouses farther to the east. "It's long been thought that the Prisms are connected. They seem to sense one another, and even react when a nearby crystal is stimulated. My father believes it's similar to quantum entanglement, only we can't really know, because we have no idea what element the Prisms are made of. Theirs is a unique energy, unlike the electricity generated from solar, wind, or water sources." He pauses, his eyes returning to me. "We pluck these crystals from deep space, we sell them for a fortune, and we still have no idea what they *are*, or how they generate so much energy." He gives a shy laugh, his breath a white cloud. "Forgive me. I tend to drone about Prismic science when given half the chance. It was my favorite area of study growing up."

I smile. "Trust me, you haven't heard *droning* till I start in about engine mods."

We move on, trudging through the snow. Walking with my head down, I expose the back of my neck, and snowflakes tingle and melt on my bare skin.

"So your trial thing is tomorrow," I say. "What's going to happen?"

He winces. "Everyone will be there, but you might not want to come. Our customs might seem strange to you."

"They already do, but I still want to watch. What will they do to you?"

"It depends, I suppose, on how the judges are feeling. I could be imprisoned for a few months, if they're in a generous mood. If they aren't, well, they may turn to more . . . *corporal* methods."

"Don't tell me they'd whip you or something!"

He says nothing.

I slow to a stop, reaching out to touch his arm. He turns to meet my gaze.

"We could leave," I say softly. "You, me, Pol, Mara, tonight on the clipper."

"Stacia . . ."

"It's ridiculous, making you go through this when you were just trying to save your sister."

"I disgraced myself. I must face justice."

"But you did nothing wrong."

He shuts his eyes. "Without my people, I *am* nothing. We are all threads in a tapestry, Princess, and to deny our people is to tear a hole in that fabric. I have chosen to trust them, and whatever their decision, I will abide by it."

I nod, feeling the wisdom of his words, even if I'm not entirely sure that I agree with them.

◇

We step out of the lift still speckled with snow, into a common area where tensors are gathered to talk and drink their bitter iceroot tea. Even here on the far edge of the galaxy, Triangulum seems to be the most popular game, and several clusters of people are bent over hologram boards, speaking in hushed, intent whispers. In one corner, a girl is playing a stringed instrument, filling the chamber with soft, dreamy notes.

I'm shivering from the snow, which has melted and slipped under my clothes. Riyan shakes his robes, then helps me out of my cloak.

"Thank you," I say. "Today was fun."

He smiles, and I realize how rare it is that he does that. It softens him, makes me remember he's no older than I am. He only carries himself as if the galaxy weighed on his shoulders. "It was my pleasure, Princess. You made me remember how magical the snow seemed, when I was a child. It brought me joy when I needed it most. I think I should be thanking you."

His smile fades slowly, and worry creeps into his eyes. I reach out impulsively and grab his hand.

"It's going to work out," I say. "Your trial, I mean. They have to see you were doing the right thing."

He stares at my hand in his. "It would be easier to face if I'd found her."

"Natalya's out there. There's still hope."

He meets my gaze. "Like your friend Clio."

I nod. "Like my friend Clio. We'll get them back, Riyan."

I hear a cough and realize Pol is standing a few feet away. I drop Riyan's hand and turn to him, my cheeks warming.

Pol looks like an entirely different aeyla from the one I nursed on the trip here, thanks to his Trying and, I have to admit, Damai's expert care. The gold has returned to his complexion and the brightness to his eyes. He wears tensor clothing, loose gray garments that wrap and tie and hang in a way that only highlights his new physique. It's impossible to look at him and not lose my breath, as I'm still adjusting to the changes the Trying worked in him. With his broader shoulders, longer horns, and sharpened bone structure, Pol is almost a stranger, and I feel a disconcerting surge of shyness when he looks at me with those clear gray eyes. I have to remind myself this is the boy who once tripped over me in a footrace and landed in a heap of mantibu dung, just so I can breathe again.

"Have a good time?" he asks stiffly. "I finally managed to escape your jailor of a sister, mate. Guess I was too late to join the fun."

"Oh, come on, you grouch." I grab his sleeve, pulling him toward the lift. "Can I borrow those, Riyan?"

Riyan nods and tosses me the cloaks. I pull mine on, and Pol puts on the other. The fur hood frames his face, making his cheekbones even more pronounced. Swallowing hard, I stare at my shoes and tell myself the tumbling sensation in my stomach is just due to the rapidly rising lift.

At the top of the pyramid, the lift slows and the door opens. We step out onto the immense flat top of Tyrrha, where the cold leaves me breathless. I pull on my cloak and hug it tight, watching my breath frost the night air. Dusty snow blows around us; it pricks my face and glitters on the ends of my hair.

Standing here, I can feel the true immensity of the pyramid. It's three miles across, three miles wide. You could drop a city on top of it.

The moon has turned its face away from the planet, so the whole of the galaxy is before us. We're staring into the unexplored wilderness of the universe. The stars are endless, dust upon silver dust, cold and brilliant in the night. I stare at them and wonder if the Prismata is somewhere in that darkness, a cold and lonely crystal light-years away. The key to controlling a galaxy, just waiting to be found, and somehow, the only map is linked to me.

Maybe it's best I never find the Firebird, and the Prismata remains hidden away. No one should have that much power.

"There." Pol pokes my shoulder, and I turn and follow his pointing finger.

"Home," he whispers.

My eyes fix on the little dot of light that is Amethyne's sun. From this distance, it appears silver blue. It occurs to me that the light I'm seeing would have taken thousands of years to reach Diamin. Under *that* star, there's no war destroying my home. There are no vityazes, no humans, no aeyla. Just a warm little planet turning in the sky. I'm staring into the past, and the past stares back.

"I brought you something," I say. I take a small box from my pocket and open it. A snowball sits inside, kept cool by a tiny generator in the hinge. I take it out and set it onto Pol's palm.

He gives a little laugh, turning it over. Then he pinches off some and sticks it on his tongue.

"I've always wanted to do that," he says.

"How is it?"

"Good." He pinches off another bit and holds it out. I open my mouth, and he pops it onto my tongue. I let it sit there and melt, the coldness making my mouth tingle.

"Not as good as Ravi's though," I point out. "Not even a hint of strawberry."

Pol watches me, his eyes as gray as the snow clouds. "I never thanked you for what you did. For me. On the ship."

I swallow the melted snow, shivering as it races down my throat. "Oh. It was nothing."

"But it wasn't *nothing*, was it?"

"Pol . . ." I look down, frowning at my boots.

"How long are we going to avoid talking about it?"

Heat rushes to my cheeks. "There's nothing to say! We . . . we were caught up in the Trying ceremony, and I'd thought you were dead just days before. Anyway, you're the one who started it, not me."

"So there *was* an 'it'?"

"Ugh! That's not what I meant." I turn away, pressing my hands to my flushed face. I stare across the dark mountains, trying to calm my quickening pulse. I can feel Pol's eyes following me.

"You're right, you know," he says. "I did start it."

I look back at him. "What's that? Did Pol Androsthenes honestly admit *I* was *right*?"

He frowns. "I'm not joking, Stace. Not now."

I don't like the way he's looking at me. I don't like the way my heart is jumping at the memory of my hand pressed to his chest, our skin separated only by a thin layer of paint.

"We should go back inside," I say, turning and walking past him, toward the lift, but stop when he begins to speak.

"Do you remember back when I was thirteen," he says quietly, "and you were twelve, and we found out the mantibu ranch across town was selling all its elderly animals to a slaughterhouse?"

I turn back to him, eyebrows rising. "We ran all the way there, as fast as we could. I was crying the whole way, I was so angry."

"You made me pretend my leg was broken so the ranchers would be distracted while you opened the barn. You chased those mantibu so deep into the hills the ranchers gave up looking."

I snort. "Dad was furious with me. He made me scrub every vat in the winery twice, as punishment."

"And you conned me into doing the work *for* you."

I give him a sheepish grin. "I'd forgotten all about that day."

"I hadn't." He stares straight into my eyes. "Because that was the day I fell in love with you."

I stop breathing.

Pol steps closer, his eyes burning into mine, his cheeks flushed from the cold. I'm pinned beneath that gaze, my body turned to stone.

This cannot be happening.

These words can't be coming from his lips.

I stare at him, snow swirling around him, the stars shining above him, everything about this moment impossible.

"My dad figured it out by the time I was twelve," he continues. "And that's why he told me the truth about you and our family's history. Because he wanted me to understand why you could never be mine. And so I tried to forget what I felt. I really did. Especially since you never seemed to see me the same way."

I turn away from him, my chest pressing tight. I hold a hand to it as my mind spins. "Why are you telling me all this?"

Pol lowers his hood, as if shedding a lifelong disguise. "Because you told me you couldn't trust me anymore. So I'm done lying. Maybe you'll never trust me again, and maybe I deserve that, but I'll still keep trying. Till the day I die, Stace, I'll be trying to earn your trust back."

"I can't . . . I can't think about this right now. Pol, I . . ."

I turn around, and he's there, his hands sliding up my arms. Somehow my fingers find his waist, and I grip the cloth of his cloak.

My eyes meet his—my head tilted back, his bent toward mine. Snowflakes dance around him, melting on his hair, turning to water that slides down his temple and cheeks. The wind ruffles the fur lining of his cloak; it brushes against his jaw. His horns shine silver in the starlight.

He looks at me like I am air and he cannot breathe.

"I know you might not feel the same way," he whispers. "I know you think I'm dull and stubborn. But I can't go on like this, pretending that the sight of you doesn't hit me like lightning. Back on the asteroid, when Zhar asked me to choose between you and my mission, I realized it was never the mission I cared about. It was *you*, Stace. It was always *you*. And, stars damn me, I'm in love with you."

I stare into his stormy eyes, at a loss for words, at a loss for breath.

He is relentless, his hands gripping my arms like I'm the only thing tethering him to the ground. "I love your tenacity, how you'll run miles across town on the hottest day of the year to save something everyone else has given up on. I love how you look at the stars, like you want to peel them from the sky and swallow them whole. I love that you can't see the horizon without needing to discover what's beyond it."

I don't know what to say.

I don't understand the feelings that flutter in me like leaves stirred in the wind. There is something deep down, fighting to be made known, words waiting to be whispered, but I cannot catch them. They come and are gone, like falling stars.

I pull away, brushing back my hair, exhaling long and slow in an attempt to calm my pulse. Stars, this is *Pol*. I know him better than almost anyone. So why do I suddenly feel as if he were a stranger? As if he is calling to some part of me I didn't know existed, as if there's another voice in my head crying out to be heard by him?

My words finally rush out, all at once. "I can't—I can't do this right now. Clio—"

"Clio." His eyes are pained. He can't look at me, and I feel my cheeks heat with warmth.

"Clio's loved you since she was a kid," I say. "I can't do this to her. Neither can you."

"I don't . . . I don't love Clio, Stacia. I can't. She's not . . ." He lets out a growl of frustration, stepping back and rubbing his face.

"Well, maybe you don't love her," I return, "but *I* do."

I run past him, nearly slipping on the smooth, wet surface of the pyramid. I practically leap into the lift and then punch the controls inside, letting out a relieved breath when it sinks back into the pyramid.

I'm enclosed with my own turbulent thoughts, my watery reflection looming on each of the lift's smooth walls. I feel like I've betrayed my best friend. I didn't kiss him, but oh stars, I was close to it. I *wanted* to, and isn't that just as bad? How will I tell her about this night?

My stomach rocks like I'm an out of control shuttle, burning through the atmosphere. I sink down to sit on the lift's hard floor, arms wrapped around my knees, still breathing hard. I can feel him, his hands, his breath, his chest against mine.

The lift comes to a silent, gentle stop, and I rise and stumble out into the corridor leading to the room I share with Mara. I follow it slowly, hand trailing the polished stone wall. Candles burn along the floor, their flickering light making my shadow dance beside me.

I pause in front of our door, collecting my breath, silencing my thoughts. The past few weeks have been a mad race across the stars, from one danger to the next. Who knows what tomorrow will bring? Who can say how long any of us has?

I almost lost Pol twice, when he was shot, and during his Trying. I remember how it felt to hold him as he inched toward death, watching for his every ragged breath, fearing he'd slipped away from me. Shaken by how frightened I was. Even more frightened by how badly I needed him.

I can't love him, but I can't lose him again.

No matter where I go or how far I run, I will have a target on my head. And everyone around me will pay the price. My parents, Spiros, Clio . . . I can't keep letting others get hurt for me. Pol might be the only one left I can save. He's bound his fate to mine, but it's time I set him free—him and Riyan and everyone else who's helped me.

The longer I run, the more people get hurt.

So maybe it's time to stop running and accept the inevitable: I can't save both my friends and myself. The choice has been in front of me since all of this started.

It's time I finally found the courage to make it.

CHAPTER TWENTY

Riyan's trial is to be held in a massive room at the heart of Tyrrha, ominously named the Chamber of Judgment. Mara and I blend in with the streams of tensors heading that way. The corridors echo with shuffling footsteps and hushed voices. The solemnity in the air fills me with dread.

Stone benches, stacked at sharp angles along the sloping walls, overlook a central platform of shining diamantglass. High above, a cylindrical shaft rises all the way to the top of Tyrrha, where a circular hatch has been opened to allow a single beam of twilight to shine down on the accused.

When I arrive with Mara, the place is almost full.

"I feel sick," I murmur, looking across the gathered people.

We find Damai already there, with six more girls lined up beside her. It's not hard to tell by their wiry dark hair and tall, lean physiques who they are. All of Riyan's sisters watch the central platform and whisper to one another.

Mara and I sit by them, leaving a seat open between Damai and me. I push my hand into the pocket of my coat and grip the small tabletka hidden inside. Without turning my head, I glance down at the screen.

I have no way of knowing whether the message I sent this morning reached its intended target, but I have to be ready in case it did. My stomach is in knots. What if the Tensors have jamming equipment to block messages from being transmitted offworld? Even worse—what if they don't, and the message *did* get through, and I've made a terrible mistake?

I try to focus on Riyan for now.

Pol appears and slides into our row, taking the seat between Damai and me. I stiffen, conscious of every inch of space between us.

"Stacia. Did you sleep well?"

I scowl. "You've never asked me that question before. Don't start now."

"Just trying to be nice."

"Don't start that, either. Things are weird enough."

"I'm sorry," he replies softly, and my heart squeezes at the flash of pain in his eyes.

He turns to greet Damai. The two start laughing over something she says. I set my jaw and look the other way.

I've never felt like this around him before—shy, awkward, my heart fluttering like a startled butterfly. Deep down, I know that now we can never go back to the way things were. So where does that leave us?

Stars blast you, Appollo Androsthenes. Why couldn't he have just kept his mouth shut? Why can't he feel for Clio the way she feels for him? And why can't I stop imagining the weight of his hands on me and the warmth of his breath on my neck?

The Lord Tensor enters, and the crowd falls quiet. He wears black robes today, his expression solemn as he slowly proceeds toward the center of the chamber. Twelve tensors follow behind him. Their faces are lined, and the hair of the unshaven ones is silver. Solemnly they spread into a semicircle, each cupping in their hands a small device that looks like a metal rosebud. Once they're in position, they wait in silence.

"What's happening, Damai?" I ask.

She slides me a cool look. "They are the judges, bearers of the Legacy Stones, our most precious heirlooms."

"Look . . . I'm sorry this happening. I wish—"

"This is bad enough without having to discuss it with *you*."

Getting the hint, I sink back into my seat and press my lips together.

A deafening sound swells around us. A man is blowing into a massive horn that winds around the walls and under the benches, incorporated into the very architecture. It sounds like the dinner horn, but deeper and more ominous. The noise is so loud my bones seem to rattle. It fills the cavity of my chest and reverberates in my teeth.

My hand inches reflexively toward Pol's, but then I catch myself and pull it back.

A door across the room opens, and in walks Riyan, flanked by six tensors. Though his hands aren't bound, it still seems like they're treating him like a prisoner. Anger unfurls in my chest, but I know I can't interfere. His people's customs aren't mine to challenge, and he chose to be here. Whatever happens, I'm only a witness. So though it chafes every instinct in my body, I stay still and harden my jaw.

Riyan and the other tensors arrange themselves before the judges. He keeps his head high, expression calm. He bows to his father and the judges, taking his time. I wonder how he can look so serene in the face of such injustice. If I were him, I'd be scorching the walls with my cursing and rage.

"Riyan Ayedi, Son of Tyrrha," says one of the judges, a hunched woman with long white hair. "Charges have been made against you. We will hear them now. Will you accept our judgment?"

Riyan bows his head. "I accept."

One of the tensors—Jorian, of course—begins listing Riyan's litany of supposed offenses. He does so with flourish, making the whole thing a performance.

". . . exposing tensor secrets to uninitiated outsiders, consorting with radical insurgents, stealing the Lord Tensor's own ship, demonstrating an egregious lack of self-control . . ."

To hear him speak, you would think Riyan was an enemy to all humanity and a threat to galactic order.

I roll my eyes and sink deeper into my seat, steaming. Riyan remains calm—but I notice a vein in his temple start to pulse a bit.

Perhaps he's human after all.

"Riyan Ayedi," says the gray-haired woman, "how do you answer the charges laid against you?"

"I refute none of them," Riyan replies. "I stole a ship that belonged to the Lord Tensor. I crossed the Diamin Wall. I risked exposing our secrets to our enemies. I broke our laws, and I will face judgment for it."

Damai gives a little groan and sinks deeper into her seat, her fingers pressed to her forehead.

"Can you offer any explanation for your actions?" asks the judge.

Riyan pauses for a moment. His eyes flicker across the audience, resting on me for a brief moment before settling on his father. "I acknowledge that I transgressed our sacred laws, and fully accept punishment for that. I ask you to consider, however, the circumstances of my crimes."

Damai and her sisters sit up straighter, exchanging surprised looks. I hear her murmur, "That's it, brother. Fight back."

Though he addresses the elderly judge, Riyan's gaze fixes on his father, as if they were the only two in the room.

"My sister Natalya and I have always been close. I knew she was thinking of running away, and I should have done more to stop her. Her disappearance is my fault, and I had to make it right. She is my sister. My actions were taken out of love, and given the chance, I would do them again."

Damai groans, her face falling into her hands.

But Riyan keeps his head high. He stares at his father, unafraid.

As I watch him, I can't help but think of Clio, and the things I've done in the name of saving her. Risking Pol's life, exposing the Loyalists to their enemies, getting Mara's father killed, even landing Riyan in this trial. The list seems to be getting longer with each move I make, the collateral damage piling up.

And yet I know, given the chance to start over, I too would do it all again. Saving her doesn't justify any of the terrible things I've done, but if the price for her life is my soul, it's one I'll pay a thousand times over.

It's seems Lilyan Zhar was right.

Maybe this is me becoming the monster.

"Your words have been heard," says the judge to Riyan. "Now we will cast our Stones."

She looks to the judge on the end of the line, and he raises the object in his hand. Legacy Stones, Damai called them. As the judge focuses on the metal pod, its petals begin to unfurl, revealing a light in the center that glows white.

"A vote for clemency," Damai whispers excitedly.

But the next judge's Stone shines red, and Riyan's sister sucks in a sharp breath.

One by one the judges share their verdicts, and not all of them are in Riyan's favor. I look around the room, gauging the reaction of the other tensors; they seem divided, some nodding when a vote is cast for clemency for Riyan, others when one is cast for condemnation. The lights of all the Legacy Stones seem to swell brighter as each one is opened, soft beams of red and white blending and tinting the faces of the onlookers.

I narrow my eyes.

Then sit up straighter.

The light emitted from the flower isn't just light—it's some sort of hologram that plays over the crowd. I raise a hand to run it through one of the beams and see symbols dance over my skin.

"It's a code," I whisper.

Pol shake his head. "What are you talking about?"

"The Stones are projecting data all over the room—don't you see it?"

"I don't see anything." He gives me a worried frown. "Are you sure—"

"You can read it?" asks Damai, pushing Pol back so she can stare at me.

I nod, eyes scanning the streams of data playing over her face.

Damai's eyes widen. "But you're not a tensor. You shouldn't be able to read the sacred words. They're *ours*, the record of our genetic code, not to be shared with any outsiders!"

This must be the cybernetic code Riyan told me of, the one Zorica Leonova created. I'm looking at the pattern of symbols that comprise the tensor gene, only it reads as garbled text that makes no sense to me—all except for one word, which I see repeated over and over, rippling over the faces and bodies of the gathered tensors, flashing over Damai's cheeks. I blink rapidly, to be sure I'm reading it right, as my skin seems to tighten on my bones.

"Pol," I whisper, my heart beginning to pound faster, "Pol, there's a word I know."

"What is it?"

I lower my hands and meet his eyes. *"Firebird."*

His eyes widen. I sit back in my seat, feeling like I'm sinking into the floor.

"Stace, what does that mean?"

What does it mean? It could mean nothing. It could be a coincidence. The Firebird was the seal of the Leonovs, the great red bird on the imperial crest. Maybe it's just a stamp they left behind when they created the code. Or maybe . . .

Maybe it means *everything.*

"I—"

"No!" shouts Damai, half rising from her seat, her eyes wide with horror as she stares at Riyan.

I look from her to the trial below, where the Legacy Stones have all been opened.

Six red, six white. The judges are at an impasse. Damai pulls one of her sisters close, and they—and everyone else in the chamber—now stare at the Lord Tensor.

"Given the divided verdict," he says, "I will cast the final Stone."

He holds his metal flower up but doesn't immediately open it. His eyes slip to Riyan. His expression is inscrutable, a face carved from rock.

Riyan seems to sway on his feet.

"Father, *please.*" The words burst from him in a rush. At once he lowers his eyes, his hands clenching. Around his shaking fists, the air begins to crackle.

I hold my breath, sitting on the edge of my seat and squeezing Pol's hand. I don't even remember grabbing it.

The Lord Tensor merely gazes at his son, expressionless. "Control yourself, boy."

Riyan nods once, his eyes boring into the glass floor. Gradually, the trembling air around him falls still. He lets out a breath, forcing his hands to relax. Everyone in the chamber is silent and transfixed.

The Lord Tensor waits a moment more before finally opening his Legacy Stone.

A gasp ripples across the room.

Damai lets out a wail.

I grip Pol's hand so hard he sucks in a breath.

Somehow Riyan remains standing, though he visibly sways when he sees that his father has voted against him. His chest begins to heave.

"Of the charges brought against you, Riyan Ayedi," the Lord Tensor says, "you have been found guilty. According to our laws, your tensor gene will be locked and you will serve the remainder of your life in the Rumihan sand mines."

The only sign the man gives that he has any emotion in his body is the small shake of his head as he turns away. The Legacy Stone closes in his palm, and the other judges follow him out of the room.

Beside me, Damai and the other sisters break down, the littlest ones sobbing as the older ones pull them into their laps. I watch, stunned, as Jorian and the other escorts close in on Riyan. They rip away his cloak and staff; they force him to his knees. Before our eyes, they begin to tattoo a new symbol onto his forehead: a red stripe that runs from his brow, over his scalp, to the nape of his neck. It must be painful, but Riyan only shuts his eyes and clenches his fists.

"What does that mean?" I ask. "What are they doing to him?"

"He'll undergo a painful genetic rewiring," says Damai, looking at me as if this were my fault. My skin heats with guilt. "They'll lock the tensor gene, and he'll never be able to tessellate again. Then they'll ship him to Rumiha to shovel sand for the glazieries until he drops dead of exhaustion."

I think of Riyan's face yesterday, when I asked him about the sand, and how his whole demeanor had changed. He'd either suspected or known what his fate would be. My heart sinks.

"This is insane!" Pol shouts, rising to his feet. "How could his own father do that?"

Damai shakes her head at him, her eyes shadowed. "Because he has always been Lord Tensor first and our father second."

"You can't agree with this!" I say.

"Of course I don't! But there's nothing we can do. Riyan will be sent to the mines tomorrow." Her face pinches, eyes fierce but flooded with tears. She turns to her sisters.

Below, the tensors finish branding Riyan, then leave him hunched on the floor, trembling and holding his hands to his scalp. His sisters push through the crowd to get to him, and I start to follow. I don't know what I can do to help him, but I know I didn't save his life at the Loyalist base just to see him get sentenced to death by hard labor. This may be tensor law, and maybe I swore not to interfere, but Riyan is my friend. I have to do something.

But that's when the tabletka in my pocket beeps.

I pull it out, hiding it in the cup of my hand, as my heart begins to pound. I'd almost forgotten it was there, in the drama of Riyan's trial and the startling revelation hidden in the judges' Stones. But now all of that fades away, a hundred light-years distant, as my full attention narrows to the little screen in my hand.

My message *did* get out, I realize, because now a single line of text flashes across the screen: *You have a deal, Princess.*

CHAPTER TWENTY-ONE

The tensors are slow to leave the chamber; everyone wants to whisper about what just happened. The Lord Tensor voting to condemn his own son, sending him to a prison camp—they all seem shaken. Riyan is still kneeling below. Jorian and a few other tensors aren't letting anyone close to him, even his sisters.

I slip away before Pol or Mara can notice. Weaving through the crowd, I duck out a side door and then hesitate a moment. Looking back at Pol, I can just make out his face. He's looking around, probably for me. I press his profile into my memory—the angle of his cheekbones, the line of his jaw, the sweep of his hair around his curving horns—and then turn away, a knot forming in my throat.

I have to hurry.

The pyramid is silent as a tomb. I climb stair after stair; the tensors who operate the lifts must still be below with everyone else. My oxygenator hisses and wheezes at my side, the mask digging into my face.

Up and up, my heart beating faster with every step. But my body drags, as if trying to pull me back, resisting my decision. I press onward until finally, halfway up the pyramid, I stop and sag against a window, partly to catch my breath, partly to harden my nerve. This is the same spot where Riyan and I stood the day he told me about his people's connection to the Leonovs. Where he told me their tessellating was due to a cybernetic code fused to their DNA.

What are you running away from? whispers a voice in my head, a voice terribly like Clio's.

"I'm not," I whisper.

You're afraid of him. You're afraid of yourself around *him.*

"This has nothing to do with Pol."

It's a lie. This is for Clio *and* Pol. They are the most important people to me in the galaxy. If this one act can save them both, how in the stars could I walk away from it?

Snow falls outside in dusty white clouds. Flakes land on the glass and melt, running in thin rivulets that mingle and branch like crystalline veins. While I catch my breath, I watch the clouds forming over the mountains, nebulous, brooding, and full of secrets. Bringing yet more snow and ice to this frozen world.

The more I stand here, the more I lose my nerve.

I push myself into motion, turning from the window and toward the stairway. But I don't make it three steps before I hear the horn from the Chamber of Judgment again, only this time, the sound comes from every direction, flooding the whole of the pyramid. It washes over me with almost tactile force, vibrating in my rib cage. The sound is too loud and urgent to be the dinner horn, or even the peal that signaled the start of Riyan's trial.

It's an alarm. And I think I know what tripped it.

I hurry back to the window and press my hands against the glass, eyes widening at the dark ships that lower from the sky. They're miles distant and indistinct through the haze of snow, but I don't need a close-up to know what they are. Dread turns my limbs to stone. I stand locked in place as the ships approach, all my courage melting like the snowflakes on the glass beneath my fingers.

Can I really go through with this?

Because once I do it, there will be no turning back.

I hesitate too long and hear hasty footsteps behind me. Before I can move, he calls out.

"Stacia! There you are!"

I shut my eyes, let out a breath.

Pol's breathing hard, one hand on the wall. He must have stopped at his room on the way up, because he's got his coat on and his gun tucked into his belt. "Stace, they're here. It's the astronika, and a dozen other Union ships." He curses. "I'll bet the Loyalists told them about Riyan. They'd have guessed we'd go to Diamin."

"They got through the gravity wall," I murmur, watching the ships as they hover over the ice forest. That wasn't part of the plan. How did they get through into Diamin's atmosphere?

"No one knows how they did it, but the tensors are preparing to fight."

The Committee isn't here for the tensors.

"We have to talk," Pol says. "We . . ." His voice falters; his eyes narrow on me. "What are you doing all the way up here? Is something wrong?"

"I'm fine."

"Fine? The Committee is right there!" He points through the window. "We have to decide what to do."

"I've already decided," I whisper.

Pol stares, and I see realization dawn in him as the color drains from his cheeks. His eyes drive into me, unblinking. Unbelieving.

"Stacia."

I back toward the stairs and shake my head. "Go back. Please."

"What are you doing up here?" His voice is soft, the way he would talk to a spooked mantibu. "Where are you going?"

But he knows. I can see that he knows, and just doesn't want to admit it.

I run my hand over my face, feeling weary to the bone. When he takes a step toward me, I raise my hand to stop him.

"I can't spend the rest of my life running, Pol. And I can't ask you to do that, either."

"You don't have to ask me anything. My mind was made up years ago. Where you go, I go, for as long as you'll have me."

"Well, that's just it, isn't it?" I feel tears sting the corners of my eyes; I blink them away. "I won't have you, not anymore. I release you from your vows and whatever lingering sense of duty you have toward me. Go back, Pol. Please."

He closes the distance between us in three steps, his hands locking around my elbows.

"*You* called them," he whispers. "You called the Committee."

"I'm not negotiating this with you."

"You would surrender to them, after everything we've been through to *escape* them?"

"If I'd done it in the first place, Clio would be safe. Everyone would be safe. I was scared then. I thought they'd kill me. But now I know I'm more useful to them alive. I'll be okay, Pol." At least for now. At least until I give them what they want, and then I go from being a valuable asset to a viable threat. But I've already thought all of this through, and I still came to the same conclusion: This is the only right move I have left.

He lowers his face a moment, a struggle playing out across his features. His pale horns glint as he shakes his head.

"No." His fingers tighten on my arms and he looks up, his gray eyes steely. "This isn't how this ends. You're staying here, and we're going to figure out a plan."

"Maybe we do." I raise my fingers to his shoulders, gripping his coat to keep my hands from shaking. "Maybe we slip away to some other system and try to start over, until the Committee catches up and we have to figure out *another* plan, and run away again. Maybe we do this over and over for the rest of our lives."

"At least it would *be* a life. If you go to them now, you'll be a prisoner. I'll never see you again."

"And you'll be free. And if I play this right, so will Clio. You can find each other. You can be together." His protests have banished the last of my hesitation. I'd almost hoped for the opposite—that he could talk me out of this. That he could offer some magical third solution to save us all and make everything go back to the way it was before.

But there is no going back.

There is only this moment, and this choice.

He raises a fist to his forehead in frustration. "I can't watch you run into their hands."

"Then don't watch."

"Agh!" He turns away, raking his hands through his hair, the muscles of his neck taut.

My window of time is closing. If Alexei Volkov thinks I've backed out, he *will* attack Tyrrha. That's probably why they crossed the wall, instead of waiting beyond it like they said they would—it's a warning. I have to follow through, or they'll destroy this city and everyone in it, just like they did Afka.

I have to get out of here, and Pol's the only thing in my way.

"This doesn't end well for anyone!" he says. "Even if it worked out the way you want, they'd still use you to get the Prismata. And if Zhar was telling the truth, that means they'd control *everything*. We'd all be prisoners, theirs to manipulate and destroy and exploit."

I shrug. "Aren't we already?"

"I'm not letting you go."

"What, so *you're* going to imprison me? How are you any different than they are?"

He flinches; I know the words aren't fair, but what about any of this is?

"We'll be okay," he says softly. "I swear. We will disappear. We will change our names and faces. There are places they won't find us, if we're smart. Stacia, I love you."

I swallow hard, gripping my oxygen mask at my side.

"We'll figure this out." Pol attempts a half smile. "Please?"

"Okay," I whisper, my heart crumbling.

"Yeah?"

"Yeah."

The relief on his face is so pure that it nearly breaks me.

I take his hand and step into him, letting him fold his arms around me, tuck his chin atop my head. I lay my ear on his chest and listen to his heart pound; his pulse is racing. His arms tighten around me, warm and safe. Stars, will I ever look at him the same way again, as my overprotective big brother, my best friend's crush?

Clio is the one who deserves his arms around her and his whispers in her ear.

And knowing that the two of them might find happiness together—that would be enough for me. That could sustain me through whatever comes next.

"It could have been possible," I whisper into his shoulder. "But it could never be *right*."

"What?" His arms slacken a bit.

I step backward, drawing his gun with me. It slides out of his belt and tucks into my palm, my finger curling around the trigger.

Pol goes still. His eyes lock on mine.

"She's my best friend," I whisper.

His eyes dart to the gun, then back to me. I walk backward, out of reach, so he can't grab the weapon. My foot finds the stairs and

I slowly ascend, keeping the gun trained on Pol. I don't want to shoot him, not even with the nonlethal setting. But if he makes a move, I will. I will, because every bone in my body knows this is the only way to save him.

"Goodbye, Pol," I whisper. I start to lower the gun and turn, enough distance between us now that I can turn my back to him. But still, it's the hardest step I've ever taken in my life.

"Stacia." His voice is wretched with pain.

I keep walking, my back rigid.

"Stacia!"

My heart tumbles, pleading, tugging me back. I fight against it.

"She's not on Alexandrine, Stacia!"

His shout rings across the room, and I pause.

"Clio isn't there! You'll be surrendering for no reason!"

I turn. He's standing at the bottom of the stairs, looking up at me with such misery that my stomach drops.

"Of course she's on Alexandrine," I say. "We saw the footage of the prisoners."

He shakes his head, his jaw tightening. "She's not there. You have to believe me on this one, Stace."

"What are you saying?" Despite myself, I take a step downward. "Are you saying she's *dead*? Because we have no way of knowing—"

"She's not dead. She— Stars, Stacia. How do I say this? How do I say what I've spent my whole life keeping secret? How do I tell you the truth, knowing it will destroy you?"

My heart climbs into my throat. His words fill me with inexplicable dread. They make no sense. I know he's just trying to stop me from turning myself over to the Committee. But still, fear seeps through me, wet and cold as the snow.

"Stop," I whisper. "Whatever you're trying to do, just *stop*."

I've never seen him with such pain in his eyes. His hands curl into fists until the veins in his arms stand rigid. Distantly, behind him, I hear voices. The tensors are on their way up, probably to the hangar.

I'm out of time.

"I'm sorry, Pol," I whisper.

His eyes grow wide. "Stacia, don't—"

He flinches when the gun's pulse hits him. I hurry forward, catching him as he topples into the stairs, nearly collapsing under his weight.

I ease him to the ground and lay the gun on the floor beside him. My hands find his face, brushing back his hair. Raising his hand, I check for his pulse, breathing in relief when I find it steady as ever. Then I lean over and kiss his forehead.

"I'm so sorry," I whisper into his hair. "Stars, I wish there were another way."

Then I back away, pressing shaking hands to my face. I shot my own friend, laid him out cold, and now I'm turning my back on him. Possibly for good.

We become the monsters so the ones we love don't have to.

The voices are getting louder. I turn and run up the steps, reaching for my oxygen. I press it to my face as I tumble out into the hangar, running across the smooth floor toward the smallest ships, little interplanetary couriers lined up like sleek silver birds.

The one I choose doesn't operate much differently from a dory. There's no Prism to activate, because this is no warp ship; its power is stored in cells, and I turn them on one by one. The buttons flash, and a screen prompts me when it's ready for launch.

Tensors spill into the hangar at the same moment that I lift off, their robes swirling as they run. I'm spotted at once, hands and voices raised in my direction. I punch the thrusters, shooting out into the sky before they have a chance to pull me back down.

The little courier swoops through the dusty snow, aiming for the Union ships hanging in the upper atmosphere. I lean back, letting the autopilot lock on my destination, and release a long breath.

Then I double over and let the tears fall into my shaking hands.

CHAPTER TWENTY-TWO

An impassive general leads me through the sleek corridors of the astronika, with ten vityazes trailing behind. I walk rigidly, my heart in my throat, wondering if I've made a fatal mistake. My hands are shackled behind me, the plastic cuffs chafing my wrists, even though I docked with the great ship of my own volition. I haven't said a single word since setting foot on the astronika, and neither have my captors, except to tell me to follow.

This is the same ship that landed in Afka ages ago. I remember how excited I was to see it, and how eager I was to get a closer look.

How naive I was.

Still, it's an impressive vessel, probably the most luxuriously outfitted ship in the Belt. All glass and light and high-end tech, it's like a flying city, part battleship, part palace. Military decks are tucked between floors devoted to art galleries and ballrooms, but for the most part, the soldiers keep separate from the dignitaries who occupy the astronika's more gilded spaces.

When we reach what appears to be the command deck—every soldier we pass here seems to rank colonel or above—I ask, "How did you get through the gravity wall?"

The only reply I get is a severe look from the general escorting me. I wasn't expecting much of an answer, anyway. But it's been bothering me. Diamin was supposed to be the safest bit of space in the galaxy. If I'd known the Committee could breach the wall, I'd never have invited them to the tensors' doorstep.

Finally, we come to the bow of the ship, and here the general stops and nods to the two vityazes guarding a plain white door. They step aside, allowing him to open the door and wave me in. Apparently

I'm meant to go in alone. I do so feeling like I'm plunging into a snaptooth-infested pool.

Inside, the direktor Eminent is waiting.

The room is some sort of lounge area, its clear walls made of translucent material, so they shift with subtle color, like they're made of ice. Two crescent sofas face each other over a table engraved with a Triangulum board; it has metal playing pieces on it, instead of the usual holo setup.

Alexei Volkov is dressed in a Union red vest that sweeps the floor over a plain black shirt and trousers, a stiff collar hugging his neck. He looks much the same as he did the first time I saw him, but now the sight of him fills me with a rush of violent memories: his cold order to the vityazes to pull us girls from our parents' arms, his passionless murder of Ilya Kepht's mother, the way his eyes settled on me when I was exposed as the princess.

The first time I saw him, I feared what he might do. Now I fear him because I know what he's done.

"Princess Anya Leonova," Volkov says, his voice soft, warm. "It's a pleasure to see you again. Let's get you out of those."

He snaps his fingers, and the old general jumps to release my hands, but he isn't gentle about it.

"Do you require anything?" Volkov asks me. "Food? Sleep? Please, allow me to make you as comfortable as possible. You are, after all, our very important and cherished guest."

I shake my head as the general backs away, slipping out the door. It hisses shut, and I'm alone with the most powerful man in the galaxy.

I feel like I'm going to throw up.

Volkov's smile eases. "Well. You can imagine how pleased I was when I saw your message. That was clever of you, delivering it to your own address."

"I figured you guys had hacked into all my stuff. But we were supposed to meet *outside* the gravity wall. How did you get through?"

He gives a soft laugh. "You know, your father, the oh-so-great Emperor Pyotr, underestimated me too. He thought no one could penetrate the palace's defense shield, and yet." He spreads his hands, the conclusion obvious. "Now. You said you have the Firebird, and that you'd give it to us, if your demands were met."

I nod, my palms starting to sweat. "The prisoners from Amethyne—I want them released. And I want to see them first, to be sure they're . . . unhurt." I don't want him to know it's Clio, specifically, who I'm looking for. I can't risk that he might use her as leverage against me.

He nods. "They're being held at a facility near the palace. I'll take you there as soon as we arrive. Anything else?"

"I want to know that the tensors will be left alone. You've got what you wanted, so leave them out of it. My parents too. I want the fighting to stop."

The direktor smiles. "Absolutely. We don't want unnecessary casualties any more than you do."

I think a moment, then add, "My friend Appollo Androsthenes. There's a warrant out for him and I want it canceled."

He nods again. "Consider it done."

I stare at Volkov, lost for words. This is not what I expected from him—gentility, assurances, giving in to everything I demand. Where is the fight I'd braced myself for?

No doubt this is some ploy to win my trust, but if he thinks I'll give in that easily, he's in for disappointment. I won't forget who he is or what he's done, or what I've lost because of him.

"Would you care to sit?" he asks. "It's been a long day. The journey to Alexandrine will last two weeks, and I hope to get to know each other well in that time. Despite that unfortunate business on Amethyne—your people did, after all, attempt to *kill* me—I think you'll find me not quite the monster you fear."

I perch on the edge of the crescent couch. My fingers leave smudges on the white leather.

Volkov picks up the Triangulum die and rolls it on his palm, then offers it to me.

"Do you know the rules?"

"Doesn't everyone?"

I take the die and roll it; it's made of glass, and its fourteen sides glint as it tumbles across the board. Glancing at the result, I arrange my pieces accordingly. They're shaped like little people, each one carved from a different gem, representing the nine Jewels. My hand lingers on the amethyst aeylic warrior before I set it down with the others. Meanwhile, Volkov sets up his own pieces, humming softly as he does.

With his sleeves rolled back and his approachable demeanor, I wonder how this man came to overthrow a dynasty that had ruled for centuries. An entire galaxy, overtaken by that sheepish smile and that boyish face and those soft, manicured hands. He looks like he's never seen an hour of fighting.

Volkov slides his ruby pirate across the spherical designs of the board, cutting off my attack route. "So, Anya. What do you know of the Firebird?"

"I know that it holds the location of the Prismata, the source of all Prisms and the most powerful weapon in the galaxy. At least, according to your *wife*."

He chuckles, shaking his head. "So you met dear Lilyan. I thought we had her when we captured the asteroid base, but as usual, I underestimated her."

Great. So Zhar's still running around the galaxy, probably even more unhinged than she was before. I guess it was too much to hope that the Committee would have caught her.

I move my sapphire fisherman, defending one of my vulnerable spheres from Volkov's ruby pirate. "It's a shame you two couldn't work out your issues without dragging the rest of the galaxy into it."

He laughs and leans forward, one hand dangling from his knee, the other rubbing his chin as he studies the Triangulum board. His eyes track my hand as I move another piece, stealing one of his spheres. Up close, he looks older and harder.

"Anya, Anya. You know, I grew up in the Alexandrine court, playing this game—this very set, in fact—with Pyotr Leonov. He was the only person who ever beat me at it. I loved your father as if he were my own brother. "

I pause in the middle of moving my emerald priest. "You *killed* the emperor."

Volkov sighs. "No, I didn't."

"I've seen the footage. You executed them, point-blank."

His eyes find mine, green as the emerald piece in my hand. "That is how we told the story, and we created the footage to back it up. But the truth is, Anya, when my people and I breached the Autumn Palace sixteen years ago, the emperor and his family were already dead."

I sit back, blinking. "If it wasn't you, then who—"

"It was Pyotr himself." He pauses. The skin at the corners of his eyes pinches. "He used a poison, gentle but fast-working. By the time we got to them, it was too late. Empress Katarina, the three children, Pyotr himself . . . all had been lost. But of infant Anya, of course, there was no sign. She was small enough to have been smuggled out in a pack, right under our noses."

I shake my head. "Why would he murder his own family?"

"He knew I wanted them alive."

I'm clutching the emerald game piece so hard it leaves the imprint of a miniature priest in my palm. "So they could give you the Firebird."

"Yes. But also because he had been my friend, and because I loved his children—you and your siblings." His sorrowful eyes are almost convincing. "I never wanted them to die. I only wanted them to cooperate with the people's wishes, to ensure our safety. And the Firebird was, and still is, the key to that safety. But Pyotr couldn't set aside his pride and give it up."

He infuriates me, the way he twists history, making himself out as the hero.

I realize he's *exactly* the person to lead a revolution—not with guns and bravado and glorious battle victories, but with words. And now he's using those words on me, distracting me from who he is and what he's done.

"So you faked the executions because . . . what? You couldn't stand for people to know the truth, that the Leonovs outsmarted you in the end?" I shake my head in disgust. "Why not forget the Firebird? It's not like you need it or the Prismata. You already control everything."

He sighs like he's a mathematics teacher and I'm not following the lesson. "This has never been about control. This is about the survival of humanity. Our civilization is in terrible danger, Anya Leonova. You have no *idea* of the threat hanging over us, or what the Prisms really are."

"I know what the Prisms are, like I know *you're* the threat hanging over us."

Anger flashes in his eyes. Just a bit, enough to see there's another layer beneath his pleasant facade. "I assume you've figured out what the Firebird is."

I swallow and look away but can't hide the heat gathering in my cheeks.

"Ah." He leans back, eyes glinting. "I see you have."

I think of the tensor gene, the Legacy Stones, the streams of data dancing across the Chamber of Judgment. Dr. Luka's last words to me: *You've always had it.*

I haven't been able to admit it to myself yet, but during that last climb through Tyrrha, I had nothing but time to ponder it.

To connect the dots and find the truth that's been staring me straight in the eyes.

Ironically, when I first sent Volkov my surrender message, I hadn't known what the Firebird was. It had all been a bluff. I had no idea that only hours later, I'd have the real answer.

"I'm not telling you anything," I say. "Not until my friends are safe. That was our deal."

Volkov looks me in the eyes for a long moment, his lips slowly peeling back into a thin smile. He looks like a viper that's already struck, who knows its poison is working its way through my body and now it's only a matter of time.

And then it hits me—he knows, he's *always* known—and I can't stop the little gasp of dismay that breaks from my lips. My body turns heavy, my skin tight, as I realize he's already a dozen moves ahead of me. I've played right into his hands.

The truth about the Firebird had been my one bargaining chip—the only leverage I had to wield. But he knows it already. And because he knows, all the promises he made to me are worthless. My list of conditions are so many ashes falling through my fingers.

"Yes, Anya," Volkov murmurs, "I know the Firebird is *you*, or rather, it's an artificial segment of your DNA, a cybernetic code passed down through generations of your family."

I set down the emerald priest, but my hand is so sweaty it slips and clatters on the floor.

"Don't worry," he adds. "I'll still meet your demands, provided you offer me your cooperation."

I can only nod.

He considers me thoughtfully, the pad of his thumb rubbing his lower lip. Then he says, "What do you know about the Firebird code?"

"Only that the tensors have it too."

"They have something *like* it," he corrects me. "Before they were rulers, the Leonovs were artists of genetic enhancement, and the tensor code was one of their earlier innovations. They created four Firebird codes in all. The tensors' gyrokinesis one, two others lost long ago—one that fostered superintelligence, the other rumored to grant virtual immortality—and the final code—yours."

I draw a deep breath and look down at my hands.

I am the Firebird.

"But what does that mean? What does the code *do*?"

Before replying, Volkov rises and walks to a cabinet against the wall. As he opens it and looks through the contents, he continues, "I was twenty when your father broke his family's most sacred rule and told me about the Firebird. Pyotr always was the braggart. He showed me the things he could do—the gifts he had, like no other. He called it prismakinesis. Pyotr—all the Leonovs—could *control* the energy the Prisms produce, the same way tensors control gravity."

"They controlled Prismic energy . . ." My hands knit together on my lap, starting to shake. "Zhar said he used the Prismata to blow up Emerault's moon."

"Yes." He finds the bottle he wants and pulls it out, then turns to look at me. "The Leonovs could reach any Prism in the galaxy, and cause it to explode or fade or even manipulate the tech and systems they powered. Any station, any settlement—it was all at their fingertips. They could pluck your secrets from your tabletkas, spy on you through your own security cameras, override any system they liked. If it was powered by Prism energy, it was theirs for the taking." He shakes his head, eyes darkening. "I lost a lot of good people the day Pyotr blew up Emerault's moon, and that was when I knew he would never come to terms with us. The genetic code that granted the Leonovs such great power also cursed them with insanity. Strange visions haunted them; voices woke them in the night. I remember old Feodor, Pyotr's father, holding conversations with people who were not there. And Pyotr finally succumbed to that curse. He had to be removed from the throne."

While he pours the wine, I look down at the Triangulum pieces, thinking of the millions of Prisms in use across the Belt. If this is true, then the Leonovs had power beyond anything I've imagined. They controlled every aspect of the Jewels.

Zhar thought the Prismata was the superweapon—but it's been *me* all along.

But with the Leonovs' power came their curse. I think of Dr. Luka, peering into my eyes. *What is your demon?* I press my fingers to my temples, my skin clammy.

"I don't understand," I say. "If they had so much influence over Prism energy, how did you even have a *hope* of revolting against them?"

He nods, picking up a second glass to pour into. "We built ships that ran purely on solar power. They were slow and mostly useless—but they were beyond the Leonovs' control. We used ancient gunpowder weapons; we didn't rely on a single piece of Prism tech. And we knew we only had one shot at it, because the element of surprise was our only advantage. We couldn't have sustained a full-scale war against their superior weapons and ships, so we had to take the Autumn Palace in the course of an hour, or all hope would be lost. But we did it."

With a sigh, he replaces the bottle of wine. "Humanity was never meant to be ruled by gods, and that is what the Leonovs had made of themselves. Pyotr would do anything to keep the code from falling into enemy hands, and so he killed himself and his family, and the poison he used corrupted their DNA. They even flooded the ventilation system with a toxic agent that scoured any traces of their DNA from the palace. The Firebird had slipped from our grasp, and with it, our last chance at true freedom." He smiles. "Until, of course, we realized Anya Leonova still lived."

"You think *I* can control Prismic energy?" I shake my head. "I swear, I've never felt anything close to what you're describing."

He returns to the sofa, carrying the two glasses of wine. "I believe Pyotr deactivated the code before he had you smuggled away. The Firebird is dormant inside you, waiting to be awoken. All we have to do is figure out how to turn it on."

"And then you can wipe out your enemies, just like the Leonovs did. You'll be no different than they were. You're *worse.*"

His eyes settle on me, and something slinks across them—something dark, something dangerous. Almost as if there are another pair of eyes hidden inside his, and now they've awoken and fixed on me. I freeze under them, swallowing my voice. *He craves to be the hero*, Zhar had said. Calling him a villain is like digging a knife under his armor, I realize, probing the sensitive skin underneath.

"I have no such ambition," he says quietly. "I seek to protect humanity, and if that requires sacrifice, then so be it."

He hands me a glass, and I take it automatically, still tasting the metallic fear those hidden eyes inflicted.

Then I taste the wine, and choke.

I'd recognize my father's vintage anywhere. The liquid in the glass tastes like Amethyne, like violet sunlight and dark soil and the warm wood of the slinke trees.

It tastes like home.

I look up at Volkov, hatred pulsing through me.

"It truly is an excellent wine," he says, studying his own glass. "A pity this was the last bottle."

My hand shakes as I set the glass down.

"Now," he says, "I'll have you shown to your room. You will be treated with utmost respect during your time with us, Anya, rest assured. Despite everything behind us, I hope you will come to see me as a friend."

I stare at him, wondering if he actually believes his own lies.

The door opens and a girl walks in, coming to attention before Volkov. "Sir?"

"Ah, Anya. Meet your new bodyguard."

I stare in shock.

The girl is dressed in vityaze red, but instead of armor, she wears a caped gown that splits at either hip, over tight leggings. Her black hair is gathered into many small braids that are twisted into a bun atop her head. But most arresting is her face—a face I've seen before, on seven other girls and one boy. All with the same full lips, dark eyes, and high cheekbones.

"Natalya Ayedi," I breathe, before I can stop myself. It's not a question, because there isn't a doubt in my mind that this girl is Riyan's long-lost sister. She was here, all along, just like he'd feared—a prisoner of the Committee. Now I know how they broke through the Diamin Wall. "What are you doing here?"

But her eyes don't even flicker. It's as if she didn't hear me.

Volkov smiles, giving me a surprised look. "Don't tell me you know each other?"

"I . . . I know her family. What's wrong with her?"

Natalya is staring straight ahead, her eyes empty, her expression bland. Only when Volkov speaks does she blink, her chin turning slightly as if she is awaiting orders.

"Natalya feels fine," Volkov says. "Don't you, my dear?"

She nods once, robotically.

"Natalya is the jewel of my military," he tells me. "I assure you, you will find no better protection in the galaxy."

"I don't want her as my bodyguard!" I protest. "She should be sent back to her family! I—I want that to be one of my conditions!"

"Very well," Volkov says. "Natalya, do you wish to return to your family?"

She tilts her head, her eyes meeting his and narrowing with confusion. "Family?"

The direktor shrugs, giving me a helpless look. But there's a glint in his eye—he knows he's mocking me, mocking *us*.

Then it hits me.

Natalya is brainjacked.

I heard of it from Pol. The Committee uses chips to override a person's brain, reducing them to automatons who respond only to certain individuals. The technology is supposed to be illegal, and the Committee has always denied their use of it. But I'm staring at the proof, and she's staring right back.

Riyan had feared they were experimenting on his sister, stealing her genetic code.

The truth is so much worse.

Speechless with horror, I draw back, but Volkov catches my wrist. Our gazes lock over the Triangulum board, the game long abandoned.

"Understand this, Anya Leonova: I *will* find a way to awaken the Firebird. Whatever it takes."

When he pulls back, he leaves a single game piece lying on my palm—an alexandrite empress, her hollow eyes staring beneath a scarlet crown.

CHAPTER TWENTY-THREE

Alexandrine shimmers like a drop of blood against the cosmos. As we approach, I begin to make out the coastlines and continents, emerald green set in scarlet seas. The chemical that makes Alexandrine's water look like blood is harmless, but I still find it hard to swallow.

I've been given free roam of the astronika, and I stand in the bridge to get the best view of the planet. The heart of the galaxy, Alexandrine is massive, the largest of the Jewel planets. Not only is it the capital of the Belt, it's also the center of technology, trade, and learning. As the saying goes back home, if you're going to be somebody, Alexandrine is where you start.

It was here the Leonovs rose from obscure scientists to powerful rulers. It was *from* here that, nearly eight hundred years ago, their first Prism-powered ships blasted off in search of the scattered tribes of humanity.

Natalya stands below, staring with that unnervingly hollow look of hers. When I've tried to talk to her, in the rare moments we find ourselves alone together, she doesn't speak. She seems robotic, like a ship running on auto—all minimum function and no personality. I can't see her without feeling a wrench of horror. What would Riyan think, to know the truth about his sister? Will he ever get the chance to hear it? By now, he'll be trapped in the Rumihan sand mines, sentenced by his own father to a fate almost as cruel as his sister's. And I'm powerless to help either of them.

"The palace is night-side currently," says Volkov. "We're an hour away."

I hadn't heard him approach, and I tense automatically. For the past weeks of travel, he has paid close attention to me. He gave me a tour of the astronika, showing off its glamorous cabins, its theater, pools, gymnasiums. The only place I could escape him was in my luxurious stateroom, or in the geeball court, where I'd float in zero gravity and kick the ball with all my strength, trying to release tension. I'd only finally emerge when I was dripping with sweat and my muscles ached. But even then, Natalya was there, watching with her hollow eyes.

For the past two weeks, I've realized the prudence of playing along, pretending to be swayed by Volkov's gestures. When he offers me a drink, I take it and say thanks. When he invites me to the theater to watch a movie, I go and I compliment him on his choice. When he suggests a game of Triangulum, I play and struggle to keep up. He wins every time.

Whatever I have to do to keep Clio safe, I will do it.

And I'm almost there. After nearly three months of endless running and bouncing from one system to the next, I'm so close to Clio I can almost feel her presence, like she's standing just around the corner.

We skim along the curvature of Alexandrine's atmo, through a nearspace cluttered with ships and stations. The planet's population has overspilled its boundaries, and these suburbs sprawl all the way to Alexandrine's white moon. Clusters of stations link together, creating zero-gravity versions of neighborhood blocks, microworlds caught in an orbital dance. Their lights flash as we drift past, neon exclamations advertising ship dealers, casinos, shopping malls, spas. The busyness of Alexandrine's orbit is dizzying; there are probably ten times as many people up here than there are on the whole of Amethyne. I watch it all slip by with a feeling of disconnection; I am a fish in a bowl, unable to touch the world just outside my glass walls.

A path is cleared for us. Lighter ships scurry away, tiny orbital transports that buzz about the astronika's exterior like flies around a mantibu. Several security escort ships flit ahead, bullying aside any vessels slow to make way.

Finally, a golden moon appears around the brow of the planet. Only it's not a moon, I realize, but the Autumn Palace. At this distance, with Alexandrine curving between us still, the hive of buildings looks like a solid object. The nearer we get, the more they separate, and twenty minutes out, the place looks like a molecule hovering in the air. The Rezidencia is unmistakable, a rotating white orb at the center of the compound, larger than all the other buildings. The shield rings spin around them all like a gyroscope, generating an impenetrable, unseen wall. Though it isn't totally impregnable, I remember. Sixteen years ago, Volkov got through with his rebels, in their solar-powered attack ships.

It all feels familiar after my explorations of Zhar's holomap. I recognize each building and its function—trade, travel, tech, military. Lots of military. After the chaos and noise of the orbital suburbs, the palace is stunningly pristine, all its buildings uniformly white. Narrow tubes connect the buildings, incorporating them all into an elegant frame.

I remember as a kid, I was once given a school assignment to re-create the palace by connecting foam blocks with narrow sticks. Clio helped me label each building. It took days to complete, and I remember my mother bursting into tears when I unveiled it. I thought she was crying because I'd mixed up some of the labels and ruined it.

Now I think it might have been for a different reason.

Did my parents live here once? I try to imagine my easygoing dad and my quiet mother in this bustling, floating metropolis. They'd seem as at home here as a mantibu on Sapphine, but maybe I don't know them as well as I thought I did.

The idea leaves me hollow.

Once we're in the palace, everything will change. Volkov expects me to give him the Firebird, but I have no idea how to do that. He hasn't brought it up since our first conversation, and I haven't dared bring his attention back to it. I know he must think of it every time he looks at me, but whatever his plans are for extracting it from my DNA, he hasn't said what they are.

I watch closely as the astronika approaches the palace shield. The space around us flickers blue and parts, just like the vineyard security fence back home, though no doubt a thousand times stronger.

I twist my multicuff, my stomach filling with nervous flutters.

The shield reseals behind us, and we glide through the compound, navigating the framework with gentle nudges from the thrusters.

A memory drifts back to me—a conversation with Pol after we'd finished a history lesson. Instead of sending us to the local school in town, our parents had enrolled us in the same cyberschool. When our courses synced up, we liked to do them together, usually sprawled in the shade of the vineyard with our tabletkas hovering over us. Clio would braid my hair while we studied, weaving in leaves from the grapevines, and Pol would quiz us on the lesson.

"Isn't a floating city a dumb idea?" I'd wondered after one of our civics lectures.

"Weren't you listening at *all*?" Pol explained that the Autumn Palace had originally been the lab where the Leonovs conducted their work, back when they were scientists. The zero gravity of space was the optimum environment for their experiments. After they discovered the Prisms, their orbital station became the center of their growing empire. Scientists turned conquerors.

Only now I know that their research into the Prisms went much further than anyone realized, that they could somehow control the crystals' energy and wield it against their enemies. How twistedly brilliant they were, to seed Prisms all over the galaxy. Making their subjects dependent on the very thing the Leonovs could use to destroy them.

The astronika makes a hard dock in the palace hangar. I'm escorted out of the ship by a cloud of vityazes, Volkov walking beside me. The hangar is massive, and there are four more astronikas docked there, each as shining and vast as the first.

A white, egg-shaped lift waits to whisk us through the palace's tube system and to the Rezidencia at its heart. I sit between Natalya and Volkov, my hands between my knees, heart hammering. The lift and the tube are mostly made of diamantglass, so it feels like we're soaring through open air. Looking out, I watch the palace's buildings flick past, and beyond them, the transparent veil of the perimeter shield shimmers like an oil stain.

The pod slows to a stop in the center of a wide circular chamber inside the Rezidencia, where glass walls look out to the rest of the floating palace. I recognize the room from the holomap. Voices echo off the walls; even whispers are amplified in the wide space.

"Princess Anya," Volkov says as he helps me out of the pod. "Welcome home."

I suppress a shudder. This place feels nothing like home.

Red-clad vityazes await us in orderly rows, snapping to attention as Volkov strides past. I bob in his wake, noting the differences between the Rezidencia of now and of before. In the holomap, these walls were decorated with imperial banners, but now only Unionist rings are there.

The direktor is dressed up today, suited in a floor-length red coat with white trim. I match him, but not by choice. When I opened my wardrobe this morning, all the clothing had been removed. Only this remained—a white gown with red trim, cut in a vaguely military style, with the embroidered front mimicking the pattern of the vityaze's armor. I can read the not so subtle message in the dress's colors: Unionist red paired with Loyalist white. I'm meant to show unity between the two factions, whether I want to or not.

I feel numb as I follow him out of the hangar, Natalya a few steps behind. I glance back at her, still searching for some sign of the real Natalya. There must be some way to override the brain jack, or to get her to wake up from her fugue. Stars, if I could get her out of here, if I could somehow return her to Riyan, that would be worth every bit of my surrender. Maybe I can convince Volkov to let her leave with Clio. I could tell him I'll refuse to cooperate unless he does.

But my hopes are faint. I know how fully I am in his control now, reduced to a piece on his game board.

Another smooth glass lift takes us through floor after floor of the Rezidencia. I press my hands to the walls and watch the levels as they flick past, losing count as the lift gains speed. Blue lights race across my skin, then slow as the lift comes to a silent stop.

We're at the heart of the Rezidencia. Because of the structure's spherical shape, it's the largest floor, nearly a mile wide. And its center, just like in the holomap, is a conservatory.

We step out into a misty, humid room. Simulated sunlight filters through leaves of every shape and color. Plants cluster around the lift tube, so that it's almost hidden. The door seals behind Natalya, and Volkov gives me a little smile.

"Your father and I used to hide in here and pretend we were Motherworld adventurers, exploring the ancient jungles."

He leads me down a plant-lined path. The floor is made of synthetic pebbles that crunch underfoot. When I pass the plants, holos pop up telling me their genus and species and planet of origin. There are palms from Rubyat nestled against algae ferns from Emerault.

Ponds display kelp from Sapphine, with little red fish darting through their depths.

I slow to a halt when the path splits into a circle around a small tree. My throat tightens as I reach out to run my fingers through the smooth slinke leaves dripping from the branches. A holo label pops up, offering to tell me more about this "unusual specimen native to the fringe planet of Amethyne."

A thousand memories stir in those swaying leaves. They flutter and hide in the slinke's depths like shy fireflies. Memories of Clio, of Pol, my parents. My home.

"Princess . . ." Volkov has noticed I stopped, and now returns for me. "You will have plenty of time to explore the gardens. Come along now."

Sighing, I withdraw my hand. The leaves fall still, but the memories don't.

◇

We board yet another transport pod, and this one carries us to the square building on the edge of the palace, where the Committee's political prisoners are housed. Volkov assures me that all the Loyalists arrested in Afka are inside.

After disembarking, I stand before the doors to the cells and draw a deep breath. My heart's banging around with nervousness and excitement.

She's here. I can feel it.

Somewhere behind that door, Clio is waiting.

I swallow hard, then take a step forward. "I'm ready."

The cells aren't much different from the one I was put in by Zhar, all blank walls and bright lights, doors made of diamantglass. The place is clean verging on sterile. I walk slowly, feeling like I'm in a trance.

I see so many familiar faces: Ravi from the diner, my mechanics instructor, a couple of guys from the vineyard. They all gasp when they see me, some calling out, but Volkov doesn't give me time to talk to them. What would I say, anyway, besides make apologies that will never begin to make up for their suffering? They all look haggard and dispirited. They run to the doors, watching me go past, and it isn't long before tears are trailing down my cheeks.

My parents aren't here, at least. Thank the stars for that. I have to believe they're still fighting back on Amethyne.

But neither is Clio.

I walk faster and faster, my chest tight, my breath short. My head swivels as I look in cell after cell, leaving behind the Amethynian prisoners and seeing unfamiliar faces—Sapphino and Rubyati and Emeraultine and Alexandrian. Humans and eeda, paryans and zherans and aeyla.

None of them my Clio.

Finally, we're back at the prison's front door, having walked every row in the building. Natalya stands silently by, while Volkov presses a button to summon a return pod.

"Well?" He raises his eyebrows. "Are you satisfied they've been treated well? Once you and I have finished our business, we'll see about returning them to Amethyne."

I shake my head, my mouth dry. "Is this all of them?"

Volkov nods. "Who did you expect to find? Your so-called parents, the kidnappers?"

"Clio." Her name is sand on my tongue. "My friend Clio Markova."

Might they have taken her away someplace, to use her as leverage against me? Or to torture her? My heart squeezes at the thought. I hadn't given Volkov her name before now, worried they might do just that if they learned how important she was to me. Could they have figured it out, anyway?

He grunts and opens a tabletka, finger flicking across data streams. He shakes his head. "No Markovas here. Your friend must still be on Amethyne."

"No, I saw her. On the broadcast, with the other prisoners. I *saw* her."

Panic rises in my chest. I fight for breath, my hands knotting into fists. As I grip the wall for support, I dimly hear Volkov speaking. Natalya pulls me away, half dragging me into the pod because I'm too shaky to walk.

She's not on Alexandrine, Stacia.

Stars, was Pol right after all? He tried to tell me, and I wouldn't listen. But what could he possibly know about Clio that I don't?

"I want her found," I say. "I want to know what happened to her."

"My people will look into it, Princess."

◇

The rest of the day passes like an endless nightmare. I'm fed, I'm bathed, I'm dressed in another red-and-white gown. They try to take away my multicuff, but I fight them until they give up. It's my last piece of home.

After dinner, Volkov finally takes me before the rest of the Committee. Twenty-three men and women sit in a round room, chairs against the walls, holodisplays flickering over their armrests. Natalya stands guard at the door.

The Committee stare at me with probing, curious eyes. Like Volkov, they're dressed in deceptive simplicity, structured military robes in Union colors. They all appear to be Alexandrians; there are certainly no eeda or aeyla or any other adapted races among them. To my eye, they blur together: silent, hungry faces. A few I vaguely recognize—the Head of Education, whose visage often appears before my math or civics lessons, and the Head of Press and Public Affairs, who gives official announcements over the newscasts. But it's clear where the power in this room lies; I wonder if they are even aware of how they adjust themselves around Alexei Volkov's presence, shifting slightly in their seats so they are facing him more directly, their eyes glancing at him even though I am apparently the focus of this meeting, as if they are gauging his reactions before deciding on their own.

There is another face there, though, a familiar one: Dr. Faran Luka, alive and whole. He is standing against the wall, clutching a tabletka, looking thinner and grayer than he was when I last saw him. He catches my eye and gives me the slightest of nods.

My moment's relief turns to anger, thinking he must have betrayed Zhar by joining the enemy. But then I see the metal collar around his neck, indicating he's a prisoner.

"So this is her, Volkov?" asks the Head of Press and Public Affairs, leaning forward in her seat. I can't recall her name, though I must have heard it a thousand times. Her hair is dyed white, contrasting with her black eyes. She has very long nails, and they click on her armrest.

The direktor Eminent nods. He has me stand in the middle of the room, his hand against the center of my back. "Esteemed members of the Grand Committee, this is indeed Anya Petrovna Leonova, the youngest child of the late Emperor Pyotr and Empress Katarina."

"Not much to look at, is she?" laughs a large man seated behind me. I believe he's the Head of Defense. "To think, this little mouse had the Union's finest chasing their tails for weeks."

"Well?" Press and Public Affairs peers at me; she looks much older than she does on the newscasts. They must edit out her wrinkles. "This genetic code that contains the coordinates of the Prismata—does she have it or not? Was all this expense we've gone to worth it?"

Volkov raises a hand to Dr. Luka. "That is what we will now find out."

"Princess," the doctor murmurs as he approaches to prick my finger, drawing a blood sample. He keeps his eyes lowered.

I take the chance to whisper, "What happened to you?"

"The base fell," he replies. "I was arrested by the vityazes when they took the asteroid. How is Mara?"

"Fine, she—"

"Doctor," Volkov says, in a warning tone. Dr. Luka's eyes flicker down, and he backs away with the sample. The Committee watch like hungry dogs.

Dr. Luka runs the blood sample though a small device, then holds up his tabletka to project a hologram in the center of the room: a helix of DNA. It rotates from floor to ceiling, shimmering bands of blue slowly twisting around each other. The doctor presses a button, and a portion of the strands lights up red and flashes.

"The Firebird code," Dr. Luka says. "It's inactive, but it's there. She is assuredly a Leonov."

I stare at the DNA molecules rotating above me. The whole time I was at the Loyalist base, he knew that the code was hidden in my genes. He didn't trust Zhar with it, but I suppose when he realized Volkov already knew the truth, there wasn't a point in denying it. How deep in the direktor's pocket is he? He helped me once before. Do I dare hope in him again?

"Here," he says, dismissing all the DNA except for the bright red section, which he magnifies until it fills the room, scrolling over the faces of the Committee. "This is where the cybernetic code begins, but it's waiting for the right stimulus to awaken it from its dormancy."

"So how do we activate it?" asks a pretty, dark-haired woman, who I think may be the Head of Commerce.

"That," Volkov says, "is the question upon which the fate of our galaxy rests. Thankfully, we have the mind of Faran Luka on our side." He smiles and places a hand on the doctor's shoulder. "He is the preeminent authority on the Leonovs and their genetic research. I trust him fully."

Dr. Luka's gaze flickers to me, racked with guilt. If I could get close, I'd whisper to him that I don't blame him for anything. That I'll get him out of here too, if I can, with the Afkan prisoners and Natalya. Now that I know he's alive, I have to try to return him to Mara.

My list of people to save is getting so long I'm going to have to start writing it on the back of my hand.

The meeting concludes, and Volkov walks me to my room. It's a luxurious suite that seems familiar, with a window open to the rest of the palace compound. Buildings and ships drift by like boats on a river, lights softly strobing. Beyond them, the stars shine, dimmed by the veil of the security shield. A bench sits under the window, and several small, clear crystals dangle in front of the glass, refracting beads of light across the room. Not Prisms, but similar in shape and color. I run my hands through them, watching the flecks of light dance in response.

"Do these accommodations suit you?" asks Volkov. "I thought you might be most comfortable in your old room."

I freeze, my hand resting on the window.

That's why the room felt familiar. This is Anya Leonova's nursery.

This is where, in the holo version of the palace, I saw the emperor and empress holding a baby. The crib stood where the bed is now.

I back away from the window, my hand dropping to my side. This is just like the trick with my father's wine. The direktor is trying to keep me off balance. He's *toying* with me.

"Oh, I nearly forgot." He turns back from the door. "My people looked into the records of Afka-on-Amethyne. They looked at everything—school logs, medical histories, residential listings. There's not a person on that planet we don't have a file on."

I turn to face him. "And? Did you find Clio?"

"No."

The air rushes out of me. "But she has to be there. If she's not on Alexandrine—"

"Princess, you misunderstand. I'm not saying she isn't there now. I'm saying she was *never* there."

I blink. "What?"

"No record of your Clio Markova seems to exist." He shrugs as he pulls my door shut. "Perhaps your friend was not who she claimed to be."

CHAPTER TWENTY-FOUR

Volkov doesn't waste any time. The tests begin the next morning.

A lab has been set up on the top floor of the Rezidencia. Volkov brings me there at dawn, when the edge of Alexandrine burns gold as the sun creeps around its girth. Inside, Dr. Luka and a team of scientists are still unpacking machines. A half-reclined chair waits for me, and as I settle into it, I try to quell the flutters of panic in my stomach. The scientists swarm around me, taking blood samples, saliva samples, scanning my fingerprints and retinas, poking and prodding until I want to scream.

I think of Clio.

I didn't sleep a minute last night. Instead, I paced my opulent room, trying to reason why Volkov would lie to me about her. Perhaps she's filed under a different name. She's a war orphan, after all. They may have changed her name when she was sent to Amethyne. Her original "file" could have been lost.

Even if she isn't here, she has to be *somewhere*. And knowing she's important to me, surely Volkov would produce her—even if it were to threaten her to make me cooperate. It's a worst-case scenario, but a believable one. So what does he gain by lying?

It doesn't make sense.

Unless he's right, and it's Clio who's been keeping secrets.

But that sounds even *more* absurd. Clio is the most honest person I know, the person I trust most in the entire universe. She could never keep anything from me. And besides, I *saw* her on that newscast, boarding a prison transport with the same people now sitting in the palace prison. All the others were there—so why not her?

"Well, Luka?" asks Volkov, after an hour has passed. "Where are we?"

"We've isolated the code," says Dr. Luka, bent over a tabletka. "It's right there, but in its dormant state, it might as well be an alien language to us. We'd hoped we might use the code extracted from Natalya Ayedi to crack it open, but there are too many differences between them."

"Any progress on how to activate it?" asks Volkov.

Dr. Luka shakes his head. "Whatever the switch is, the emperor took it to his grave. Genes can remain dormant for a person's entire lifetime. It takes certain conditions to activate them, but we have no idea what the conditions are. If they were normal, organic genes, we'd still be able to sequence them. But this cybernetic stuff operates by different rules, and the original Leonovs left none of their research intact for us to follow."

Volkov curses. "You were the imperials' primary physician for *decades*, Luka! How could you be so ignorant of this crucial element of their physiology?"

Anger deepens the wrinkles in the doctor's face. "You know as well as I do, Alexei, how closely they guarded the Firebird. They *died* to protect its secrets. All I was ever allowed to know was that it existed, and that it was the source of their . . . abilities. I don't know how it was created, or how it gave them control of the Prisms' energy. Nor do I know how it can be woken."

Volkov turns away from him, his jaw tight.

"When she's ready to rule, the Firebird will guide her," he murmurs. His eyes slide to me, probing. "Does it speak to you, Anya?"

I swallow, pulling away. "Find Clio. If you can't guarantee her safety, I'm not giving you *anything*."

The shadow falls over his eyes again, the one I got a glimpse of in the astronika. His voice drops to a low murmur. "We've been generous with you up till now. But I see that we're going to have to be more assertive."

The genteel host I met on the astronika is beginning to fade, and someone far more menacing is taking his place.

"Do it," he says to Dr. Luka.

The incision is made before I even know what's happening: a swift cut at the base of my skull. They must have anesthetized the spot without my realizing it, during all their prodding. The brainjack unit is popped inside, but I can't see it or feel it. Even so, my chest tightens with panic.

"All right," Dr. Luka says softly, his face pale. "Turning it on."

I feel a sort of zap in my head, and then I go into convulsions.

Scientists swoop in to grab my hands and head and hold them still, while foam bubbles from my lips and the room tilts wildly around me. Pain rolls through me, hot as flames.

"What's wrong?" Volkov shouts.

I lose all sense of the room, my eyes rolling back. It seems to last forever, the pain and the shaking and the metallic bile in my throat.

"I'm cutting the power!" yells Dr. Luka. "It's killing her!"

All at once, the pain stops. Relief washes over me. With a gasp, I roll over and land hard on the floor, jarring my bones. There I collapse, spreading on the cool tiles with a sob. Someone wipes the spit and tears from my face.

My body is still trembling. I can't even stand.

Volkov and Dr. Luka are looking at a three-dimensional holo of my brain, shaking their heads.

"Defense mechanism," says Luka. "She *can't* be brainjacked. The Firebird won't allow it."

"So it's active after all?"

"Seems to be a sort of automatic function. She's probably got other latent attributes, parts of the code that can't be totally deactivated."

The doctor studies me curiously. "I hear you have a knack for mechanical engineering, Princess, and for shooting."

I look up, my gaze unfocused.

"I'd guess that's evidence of the Firebird, giving you an affinity for Prism-powered tech. But we need more than that. Let me look at the reaction the brainjacking sparked. Maybe there's something in the reflexive code we can work with."

Dr. Luka helps me up, back into the chair. I can't fight him off. I'm too weak, too shaky. He does something to the back of my head I can't see or feel, but I glimpse him holding the little chip between a pair of tweezers. It's bloody and tangled with fine wires. He tosses it into a tray with a look of disgust. Another scientist closes the incision, her fingers gentle as she seals the cut with a skin patch.

"Why are you doing this?" I whisper to Luka, while Volkov is busy studying the scans.

He winces, not meeting my eyes. His reply is soft enough that only I can hear it. "When the Firebird activates, you must use it, Anya. Destroy this traitor. Destroy all of them."

I stare, speechless, as he returns to his work, sifting through streams of data and exploring the map of my brain.

Every few seconds my whole body quivers, the effects of the failed brainjacking still rolling through me in waves. I focus on breathing, not letting panic take control of me, because I know if it does they'll just drug me. I have to keep a clear head. I'll never escape this otherwise.

Clio, Clio. Where are you?

They run more tests, but nothing as invasive as the brainjacking, thankfully. I drowse through most of them, my brain still foggy. Holos of my DNA string across the room like festive lights. I watch them swirl and twist, my body's instruction manual displayed for all. What does it mean, to not be entirely human—not even entirely organic? What does that make me? Some sort of monster? That's what everyone said of the Leonovs. Volkov called them gods. I don't feel like either. I just feel like a girl who's been wrung out, a girl with all the questions and no answers. A girl adrift in the cosmos, stripped of everything that mattered to her.

"When she is ready to rule, the Firebird will guide her . . ." Volkov's murmur is soft, musing. He stands over me, studying my face. "You're not ready. Why are you not ready? The Leonovs were made of diamantglass, but you're fragile. You have so many weaknesses." His hand finds my hair, pulling a strand between his fingers. "You're not *worthy* of the Firebird yet."

I turn my face away, feeling a tear trickle down my temple.

"How do we make you strong, Anya? How do we make you worthy?"

Stars, how I hate him.

"Your father was strong. He blew up Emerault's moon and everyone on it, trying to take out our revolution. Could you do that, Stacia? Could you *want* that? If I put your finger on the trigger, would you pull it?"

"I don't know," I whisper.

"Hm." He studies me thoughtfully, and the look in his eyes makes my spine shiver.

"Here," says Dr. Luka suddenly, pointing to his tabletka. He sounds excited and draws Volkov's attention away. "This is the part of the code that activated when we tried the brainjacking. This is what fought back. I've managed to isolate it and get a look at it. It's only a partial of the full sequence, but it's more than we had to begin with."

"And what does it tell you?"

"Well, for starters, our genetic code has a limited 'alphabet,' if you will, with each letter representing a type of nucleotide. The human genome has two base pairs—G and C, A and T. But Anya's genome has *eight* nucleotides, in four pairs, interweaving with the existing DNA, making it possible for her genetic code to contain exponentially more information than the average human being. And these two pairs repeat over and over, forming a sort of wall around the rest. I think this is the part that acts as the rest of the code's on and off switch."

Volkov taps the tabletka, activating the holo function. The four letters spin above us, split into two sets. Other information streams around them—diagrams of protein structures, complex formulas, twists of DNA.

But I stare through all the noise at those four letters, shining in bright blue above me.

I stare as my mind unravels.

As my blood turns to ice.

As everything I thought was real turns to ashes on my tongue.

C-L

I-O

The code has a name.

That name is *Clio.*

CHAPTER TWENTY-FIVE

I start to hyperventilate.

Dr. Luka runs to my side, helping me sit up, telling me to breathe.

"No," I gasp. "I don't understand. It has to be a coincidence."

"What is?"

I let out a sob. "She's real she's real she's *real*."

"*Who* is real?"

"Clio!"

Panic rakes through me.

I roll off the chair and push past him, looking for the door. I have to get out of here. I have to escape this nightmare.

I push aside a cart that's in my way; instruments spill off and clatter on the floor. Dr. Luka tries to catch me, but I grab a metal tray and swing it, bashing his head. He curses and stumbles, reaching for me again, but I scramble over a table and finally spot the door. I run for it—only to have my feet pulled out from under me.

I yelp as I flip upside down, hanging in midair, my hair swinging under me. The room tilts and sways, and I struggle in vain to free myself.

Natalya is by the door, her hands splayed and her eyes intent on me as she tessellates. The air cracks with that awful grating sound, and a black mask spreads around her eyes. My feet are trapped in her stress field.

Volkov appears in front of me, studying my face with disappointment. "Enough, Princess. Calm down, or we'll sedate you."

Natalya lowers me. I land on the floor in a heap, and two of Dr. Luka's assistants drag me back to the chair.

This time, they secure my wrists and ankles with straps. I lie limp, heart racing, staring blankly at the ceiling.

"I want Clio," I whisper. "Tell me where she is. Please. *Please*."

Dr. Luka glances at the holo letters, then back at me. "Anya, who is Clio?"

"My best friend." I break into sobs, pulling weakly against my restraints. "She's *real*! I saw her, I saw her on the prisoner transport. She was there the day the Red Knights came to Afka. She's *always* been there, and you can't have her."

The truth is there welling up in me, but I can't face it.

It's too terrible.

Too *impossible*.

"I think I'm beginning to understand," Dr. Luka murmurs. "She's a Leonov, after all. I've dealt with this sort of thing before."

"So have I," says Volkov, with a look of disgust. "It's the madness. It's taken her already. I should have seen it sooner."

Dr. Luka kneels in front of me, peering at me with concern. "I saw many of your family deal with this, Anya—seeing people who weren't there, hearing false voices. But they knew not to trust their eyes. They knew how to edit their realities, culling the false from the true. This Clio is not real. She's a *side effect*. You must let her go."

The ache from the brainjacking was nothing compared to the pain I feel now. Someone's climbed into my skull and is drilling into it. I could rip through the walls with my bare hands to escape it, but it's like all my strength has been drained from me. I moan and shake my head, willing them to just disappear. Maybe the brainjacking worked after all. Maybe it made me crazy.

"What's wrong with her?" asks Volkov.

Dr. Luka shakes his head. "She's been living with this delusion for a long time. With the others, we usually caught the signs early. But Anya was alone, with no one to truly understand her condition. I'm sure her foster parents tried their best, but they must have given up attempting to cure her. It won't be so easy to do it now, given how long she's been affected. She needs time to process what is and isn't real."

"She's *real*," I whisper. "Stop saying she isn't. Please. *Please* stop."

Volkov snaps. "We don't have time for this! No wonder it isn't working! She's consumed by denial." Pushing aside the doctor, he grips my wrists, forcing me to look at him. "Who are you?"

"Wh-what?"

"Who are you?"

"Stacia Andr—" I cut short with a gasp as he tightens his grip.

"That's the problem. You still don't believe the truth of who and what you are. How can you inherit the Leonov legacy if you won't even accept their name? Your old self is still in the way. That is where we must start. If Anya Leonova is to live, then Stacia Androva must die."

◇

It's midnight, and I'm sitting in the corner of my too-large room, tucked into the wall. I stare at the floor, chills running over my skin like I'm feverish. When I close my eyes, I can feel their needles pricking me, their fingers prodding. My body aches from the seizure the brainjacking caused. Even still, I feel tremors in my fingers.

But none of that compares to the moment I saw Clio's name written in my DNA.

Rocking back and forth, I relive my entire life, trying to make sense of the chaos raging inside my skull.

I work backward, sifting through my mind and grabbing at every memory I have of Clio. I turn them over desperately, looking for confirmation of what I know to be true—that Clio is a girl with blond hair and blue eyes, that she's funny and kind and wise, that she's my best friend, that she's *real*.

The memories seem real enough. I can picture her so clearly. I can hear her voice.

"Your name is Clio," I whisper, hugging myself and staring hard at the white carpet. "You are seventeen years old. You're a hopeless romantic. You're madly in love with Pol."

Pol.

Pol would tell me she's real, if he were here. He would laugh at the very *idea* of Clio being some sort of hallucination. He'd tell me a hundred reasons why that was ridiculous, and then he'd tease me for ever considering it might be true.

Except . . .

Except he *told* me Clio wasn't on Alexandrine.

He didn't want me to come here. He tried to stop me.

All along, I've wondered how he wasn't as concerned about Clio as I was. He always hesitated when I mentioned going after her. I thought it was just because of his continued belief in his "mission." But what if that wasn't it at all?

What if he *knows*?

With a cry, I burst to my feet and begin pacing the room, my hands knotting in my hair, my breath coming fast and ragged.

"Your name is Clio. You are seventeen years old. You love sleeping late and romance shows and you're terrible at math. You live in . . ."

I stop dead.

My hands lower to my sides, curl into fists.

"You live . . . in a house . . ." I shake my head, fighting through the fog that envelops my mind. "You live in a house in Afka. Right? Or . . . an apartment."

Slowly, I raise my eyes to the diamantglass window, to the reflection of the girl standing there. She is disheveled, pale, frightened. She is a ghost of myself, thin as the air and fragile as a spider's web. Beyond her, the lights of Alexandrine flicker like strange, indifferent stars, reminding her how very far away from home she is.

"Clio," I whisper. "Where do you live? Where do you sleep? Stars, I *know* this! I have to know this!"

But the more questions I ask myself, the more gaps I uncover.

Who else was Clio friends with?

Who did she dance with at Solstice Fest last year?

What did my parents give her for her birthday?

Stars, when *is* her birthday?

And who raised her? Her parents died in the war, but who took care of her after that?

I have no answers. All the questions, but no answers.

These are basic facts I would know about any other person. Why don't I know them about my best friend?

I sink to the floor, sitting cross-legged, the way Riyan did when he meditated. I rest my hands on my knees and shut my eyes, and for the next few minutes, I simply breathe. Deep, steady, slow. I push out all thought and focus on the rhythm of air rushing into my lungs, sighing out again.

Then, when I am as still inside as I can possibly be, I dive into my memory.

I reach back, back, to the beginning. I swim through a river of images, until I find my very first memory of Clio Markova.

My parents were inside Ravi's Diner, ordering flavored ice to carry back home, but I stayed on the sidewalk because the mayor's new dory was parked there, and I wanted to look at it. I was lying on my back on the road, under the ship, studying its brand-new hover pads and how they were connected to the engine.

Then there she was: a pair of red shoes standing on the other side of the dory. I scooted out and stood, and we blinked at each other. She was skinny and bright-eyed, her yellow hair in a curly topknot. I'd never seen her before, but then, I didn't know many of the town kids

"Are you getting ice too?" I asked her.

"Yes," the girl said. "I like grape, but strawberry is the best."

I smiled, and knew at once we would be friends, because strawberry was my favorite too.

I release a gasp, curling over. How could something feel so real, and not exist? How could someone I've known so intently be nothing but empty air and my imagination? How could I love a lie with all my heart, and not know what it truly was?

I pick up memory after memory like shards of a broken mirror, staring at each one until it becomes too sharp to hold. She is in all of them, but it seems the more I try to remember her, the fainter she becomes, until I'm not sure anymore which memories to trust. I think of a day when we found a nest of baby mouskas in the stable, and we knelt and named them one by one. Pol was there, I know. And Clio . . . Clio is a shadow in the corner of my eye, kneeling in the hay and cooing over the little furry creatures. She was there, wasn't she? I'm not sure anymore.

I'm not sure of anything.

At the bottom of my pile of broken memories is one I can barely look at, one I've never fully recalled until this moment: my mom, sitting me in the chair in her office, telling me Clio was not real. How easily now I slip back into my six-year-old body, pressing my hands to my ears, screaming wordlessly until she gives up and walks away.

"If I keep pressing her," Mom says to Dad, who's pacing the room, "she could break entirely. It's happened before, with some of her ancestors."

"Then we don't press her," he says.

The memory plays over and over, and each time it seems a little more detailed, until I can recall the plastic of the seat sticking to my thighs, the soft lavender sunlight lancing across the floor, and the smell of the antibacterial soap by the sink.

Finally, I end up lying on the floor, spread-eagle, staring blankly. A loose thread curls up from the edge of the carpet. I pull it, and it keeps coming, unraveling along the length of the wall with a sound like tearing paper.

Nothing in my life has been real.

My parents were not my parents.

My best friend never existed.

My name is not my own.

The only person in the galaxy who might care about me—about *me*, not Anya—I shot and left behind. He probably hates me now. Why shouldn't he?

I'm the girl who left him for a lie of her own making.

I was born to inherit a legacy of madness, and that curse has been with me all my life without my realizing it. It's been eating me from the inside out, like the red fungus that grows in the slinke trees. It starts at the core and weakens the tree from within. Yet years will pass and the tree will seem perfectly healthy on the outside. But then, all at once, the trunk will buckle and the tree will fall.

My mother and my father, Pol and Spiros, everyone in the vineyard and in town.

They knew.

They *had* to have known. And either they didn't tell me or they gave up trying. My mind feels full of gaps that I never knew were there, because I was always looking from the wrong perspective. But now I can't help but see that my memory is a tangle of incongruent parts, the real and the unreal all entwined until I don't even know where to begin sorting them.

Finally, the string breaks from the carpet. I wind it slowly around my finger, around and around and around, watching it cut into my skin until the tip of my finger turns purple.

Alexei Volkov said that for Anya to live, Stacia Androva had to die.

But Stacia Androva is already dead.

CHAPTER TWENTY-SIX

I still have my string the next morning, when they come to take me to Volkov. The night passed in a haze. I'm not sure if I slept or if I simply stared at the wall for hours on end. In either case, I'm lost in a fugue as I rise and dress. Breakfast is laid out—eggs, tea, fruit—but it looks as appetizing as sand. I leave it on the tray.

As I follow Natalya through the Rezidencia's white hallways, I twist and untwist the string, feeling like it's the only thing tethering me to sanity. If it breaks, I am lost.

These are my first steps into a universe without Clio. It's like walking into an alternate reality, a world that doesn't feel real. I'm just a hologram floating along, empty light flickering over the walls. My body is here, but my heart is a thousand light-years distant.

Instead of the lab, I'm brought to a large, round room encased by arching diamantglass windows. I know what this place is, not just because I've been here before in Zhar's holo but because I've seen it in history documentaries so many times. It's perhaps the most famous room in the galaxy—the imperial throne room.

Or as it was known in the Empire's days, the Solariat.

The throne is still in place, which surprises me. I would have thought it would be the first to go when the new regime moved in. Maybe they keep it as a trophy. Maybe Volkov likes to sit in it and play emperor. Shaped like a crescent moon, the throne is fifteen feet tall and made of mirrored black stone, polished to a shine. The upper arc curves over the seat below, and from its tip hangs a round glass sphere. Inside it flashes a melon-sized Prism, one of the largest I've ever seen. It must power the whole of the Rezidencia.

The rest of the room is open floor, smooth glass tiles patterned with spheres and lines. It seems every material in this room was selected to mirror the throne and its occupant. Though these days, the great seat is empty.

Volkov waits for me along with the whole of the Committee. Their backs are turned to the door, but when I enter with my guards, heads swivel. They're not wearing their formal robes today but fancy gowns and suits, as if they're all having a party later. The rings on the Head of Commerce's fingers alone could probably rebuild Afka. They flash as she raises a glass of white wine to her lips, her blue eyes scanning me head to toe. Beside her, the Head of Defense leans in to whisper in her ear, eliciting a smirk from her lips. The others watch me with a blend of curiosity and skepticism, as if I am a pet brought in to perform. Only the Head of Press and Public Affairs gives me a smile—but that's probably just reflexive, given how much time she spends putting on a friendly face for her newscasts. I still can't remember her name.

I'm dressed up today—a filmy black gown with a train, long sleeves, bare shoulders and collarbone. Crystals have been embroidered onto it, trickling like diamond rain from the bodice to the hem. The only thing about me that feels even remotely right is my multicuff, which I now twist back and forth until my wrist begins to chafe.

The moment I saw the dress laid across my bed this morning, I knew something was up.

I just couldn't find it in myself to care.

As I walk across that shining floor in that shining gown, I feel hollow as the night, a mechanical, emotionless void. It's like my heart is beating but no blood pumps through it.

"Anya," Volkov murmurs, his eyes sweeping over me. "You look like an empress."

He takes my hand and escorts me to the front of the room, the others parting for us.

A week ago, I would have felt sickened to be at the center of the entire Committee's attention. Now I just want to lie down and sleep. I've never felt so weary. The people in front of me seem no more than ghosts. Maybe, like Clio, they too aren't real. Maybe all of this is one endless dream manufactured by my broken mind. I can trust nothing anymore, least of all myself.

"Today," says Volkov, his voice is raised for the benefit of everyone in the Solariat, "we will see the Firebird step into her birthright."

He's unusually confident for someone with no more answers about the Firebird than I have. But his eyes are bright, his face flushed.

I feel a tingle of unease down my arms.

"This had better not be a waste of our time," calls out the Head of Commerce, and a few other Committee members nod in agreement. "Really, Volkov, is all this ceremony necessary?"

"Why do we need to be here, anyway?" asks Defense. "I've got a full-blown rebellion to handle on Amethyne. Couldn't this have been relayed by holo?"

"Kostya, my friend." Volkov's eyes flick to the man, betraying a flash of irritation. "After today, the rebellion won't matter. All our jobs will be a great deal easier."

"*If* this Firebird is what you claim it is," says Commerce stiffly.

The direktor's lips press thin. "Observe, if you please."

He waves a hand, and the doors of the Solariat swing open. A row of vityazes march in, three by three. They walk through the center of the Committee and spread before Volkov and me. I watch disinterestedly; I've passed so many Red Knights since arriving at the palace, it's hardly news to see a few more.

Then I realize the middle three are not vityazes at all. What I took for red fatigues are really red prison uniforms, jumpsuits with identification numbers stamped across the fronts.

My stomach drops into free fall.

"We found these three attempting to broach the outer shield," says Volkov. "But for your sake, Princess, we took great care to bring them in alive, when it would have been much easier to simply shoot them out of the sky."

I stare at Mara, then Riyan, then Pol.

They gaze back, silent and defiant. They're a wreck; Mara's braids are undone, her hair knotted and snarled. Pol has a fresh bruise on his jaw. Their hands aren't even bound, so why aren't they fighting back? Are they brainjacked too? I lock gazes with Pol, heart fluttering, trying to see if he's still the Pol I know. He stares back rigidly.

Then Riyan's eyes find Natalya on my left, and he stiffens. His lips part, and he takes a half step toward her.

"Natal—"

He cuts short as he suddenly topples over, howling with pain, and it's then that I notice the thin black bands around each of their necks, the same as Dr. Luka wears.

The collars are wired with electricity.

Riyan curls up on the floor, gasping, his body jerking. Pol and Mara flinch but must realize they'll only end up like the tensor if they move, because they freeze in place.

"Stop it!" I scream, lunging forward, but Volkov holds me back, his fingers digging into my shoulder through my gown's thin fabric.

"Enough," he says, and the vityaze controlling the collar releases the charge. I recognize the man from the attack on Afka—he's the same one who stopped my family's dory and escorted us to town. Judging by the bars on his uniform, he's been promoted since then. At his feet, Riyan sags with a long exhale.

Through all of this, Natalya stands impassive, seemingly unaware that her brother is only steps away.

"What've you done to her?" gasps Riyan. "You monsters—"

Another jolt of electricity sizzles through him, and I struggle, trying to get past Volkov. Even the Committee is looking uncomfortable with the scene. Several of them look down at the floor; Commerce is pale and wide-eyed, and opens her mouth like she's going to protest, but then Defense lightly touches her arm and she clamps her jaw shut. There'll be no help from them.

Riyan is released again, and this time the vityazes pull him back to his feet. There he hunches over, watching Natalya with haunted eyes. Beside him, Pol and Mara exchange looks, and Mara's hand moves to her collar, shaking a little. All three of them look traumatized, and I realize this mustn't be the first time their collars have been activated since they were captured.

Tears trace burning lines down my cheeks. I feel utterly useless and sick with shame.

What were they thinking, coming here? That they could break into the most secure bit of space in the galaxy and just snatch me from under Volkov's nose? I shake my head at Pol, my heart crumbling. He had to know this was impossible.

But he came, anyway.

Pol catches my eye, and the corner of his mouth quirks in the smallest of defiant grins, as if even now he is urging me to fight back. Saying this isn't over.

But it *is* over.

Stars, it's been over for longer than either of us knew. Maybe since before it even began. If this was where we would end up, why did we ever run in the first place? I ran and I ran and I ran, and still, I couldn't escape this moment.

"What is this?" I whisper to the direktor. "Why are they here?"

"It's time you accepted the truth of who you are," he replies.

Volkov sets up a tabletka and projects a hologram of an aerial view of a battlefield. Hills and buildings spread over the great Solariat floor like a miniature world, seen through a slowly strafing camera. From this angle, it takes me a moment to realize what I'm looking at.

Afka.

I pull my eyes from Pol to stare at my home, which is now smoldering ruins, the slinke forests burning. My family's vineyard is gone completely, nothing but a scorch mark on the face of Amethyne. Distantly, I wonder what happened to Elki and the other mantibu. All I can think is that I hope they were let out of the stables. Maybe they disappeared into the hills with their wild kin. I focus on that; it's easier than processing the whole of the truth before me: that my home is gone. *Obliterated.* The hills where Pol and Clio and I— I wince, amending that thought. The hills where *Pol and I* played are burning by the acre, most of the land blackened and prickled with charred slinke trunks. Of Afka itself, few buildings are still intact.

Volkov walks slowly through the hologram, his steps falling on the homes and fields of my neighbors. The hologram fractures into pixelated blocks of light around his polished shoes. His eyes never leave my face. "We've withdrawn our troops. Only a few Loyalist factions remain in Afka, but not for long. Before you can heal a wound, Anya, you must first cut out the dead tissue. As long as these dissenters remain at large, their poison will spread, infecting the whole of Amethyne and the galaxy beyond. Their violence and bloodshed must be confronted with definitive strength. And so we have ten interstellar Prismic missiles inside the palace armory, awaiting your order. They can make the jump in ten minutes, faster than any ship."

He hands me a small transmitter; the screen on it displays the coordinates of Afka and the status of the missiles—armed and locked onto their target. Below that, a red button reads *launch.* All it's waiting for is someone to press it. There is no option to disarm the missiles or change the coordinates. Despite its small size, the device weighs like a brick in my hand.

"It's not an easy choice," says the direktor. "But it's the right one."

Across the room, the Head of Defense is nodding, his eyes glinting with appreciation.

"You . . . want me to wipe out my home?" My voice cracks.

"*Stacia Androva's* home, not yours." He crosses to stand between Pol and Riyan, putting a hand on either boy's shoulder. They flinch at his touch, Pol's lips pulling back to show his teeth.

"Prove who you are, or I will be forced to strip away, bit by bit, every remaining piece of Stacia Androva. Claim your place or be dragged into it."

I stare at him in horror.

Pol jerks away from the direktor. "Stace, *don't* press that—"

He drops to his knees with a howl of pain as the collar on his throat activates. He shudders, one hand gripped around the metal band, until the charge fades. But still he grimaces with pain, the blood draining from his face. All the while, Volkov stands behind him, his expression impassive.

I clench the transmitter, my chest compressing. My mind flashes back to that terrible day on Afka, my father pulling me away as the vityazes beat Pol, telling me that interfering would only get him killed. It feels like we've come full circle, like everything between then and now has been for nothing.

"Please stop this," I whisper to Volkov. "I'm begging you. I'll do whatever you want."

"Then *do* it. Prove you are a Leonova. Prove you're strong enough." His eyes are cold; my friends' pain doesn't affect him in the least. "Once

I have what I need, all this will end. You will be free. Your friends will be free. Just give me the Firebird."

A vityaze hauls Pol back to his feet. Sweat runs down his temples, and his skin is pale and drawn. He raises his eyes to mine, and this time, I can barely see his defiance for the pain that creases his face. It's as if the shock aged him five years.

I look down at the button.

One simple press, and it would be over.

No one in Afka would ever know. My parents probably aren't even there anymore.

I could save Pol and Mara and Riyan; I could give Volkov what he wants, and then he could deliver on his end of the deal: letting my friends and me disappear.

We could walk away from all this. I could have Pol; I could find my parents.

We could be *free*.

"End this war, Princess," Volkov murmurs. "We have a real chance to create lasting peace, you and me. I am not your enemy here."

Not my enemy?

I look up at him, my eyes focusing on his.

He craves to be a hero, Lilyan Zhar had said. Here he is, torturing my friends, forcing me to make this terrible choice, casually igniting genocide. And even *still*, he wants to be the hero. He wants me to believe his way is the right way. Stars, he probably believes it himself. He's totally bought into his own propaganda.

But I see through him.

This isn't about ending the war.

"You don't care about peace," I say. "All you want is the Firebird code. You want to use it to control the Prismata, so nobody can ever threaten your power. You're just another tyrant."

He looks at me with those second eyes, those eyes like black holes. "I have no such intention. I don't want your power or the Prismata. Humanity will not be ruled by gods, Anya Leonova."

I blink, my conviction faltering. "Then . . . then what is this about? What is all this for? If you don't want control of the Prismata, then what do you *want*?"

He spreads his hands, as if the answer should be simple. "I want to destroy it."

CHAPTER TWENTY-SEVEN

A pit opens in my stomach. *"What?"*

Gasps echo from the Committee members, some of whom stare at Volkov with jaws hanging open. They seem as stunned as I am. The vityazes are unreadable behind their helmets, but several of them shift in place, their hands moving to their guns.

As if unaware of the reaction he's caused, Volkov just looks at me. We might as well be the only two in the room.

"The Prisms cannot be allowed to exist," he says. "They are the greatest threat in the galaxy, bombs just waiting to go off, just like they did on Emerault's moon. As long as they power our worlds, and as long as the Prismata exists to turn that power against us, we will never be safe. We will never be *free*."

His eyes alight with fervor, even as behind him, the Committee members begin to murmur among themselves.

"Give me the Firebird, Anya Leonova, so that I can do what should have been done centuries ago—rid our race of the Prisms for good."

Shouts of protest and anger rise from the Committee.

"Here, now, Volkov," says the Head of Defense, stepping forward. "What in the stars are you talking about, man? You said we would *control* the Prisms, not destroy them!"

"Yes!" cries Commerce. "You can't destroy the Prismata. It powers everything in the galaxy! Warp travel, every city and station in the Belt, all of it would be lost."

"The man's gone mad!" says Education. "Every ship in the sky would fall, cities would shut down, hospitals and schools—millions would die!"

Defense steps forward, his face red.

"Stand down, Volkov. We never authorized this!"

Their voices rise and blend, their faces contorting with anger. My heart rises, hope flickering.

The Committee will never let Volkov carry out this madness. They might be ruthless in their rule of the Belt, likely each of them more deserving of a prison cell than an office in the Rezidencia, but even they see that he has gone over the edge. I don't fully understand the Prismata, but if it's the source of all Prismic energy, then even I can see how devastating its loss would be. I can't imagine what Volkov's motive is—unless he really has gone insane.

The Committee shouts at the vityazes, calling for the direktor to be seized. In response, the soldiers draw their guns, falling into attack formations, calling commands to one another. They move like machines, precise and deadly. Pol, Riyan, and Mara huddle together, watching in shock, but the men guarding them are too attentive. No chance of them breaking free, even with the activity bubbling behind them.

Then Volkov just shakes his head and raises his hand.

And the vityazes all turn, weapons aimed—at the Grand Committee.

The men and women fall silent, eyes wide. The wineglass falls from the Head of Commerce's hand; it shatters on the floor, a pale pool of liquid spreading around her expensive shoes.

"What's the meaning of this, Alexei?" calls the Head of Defense, moving to shield her.

"Friends, friends," Volkov says, his hand still raised. "I know you are confused. But trust me. All of it, from the beginning, has been for the greater good. A cause that I would gladly sacrifice my life for. But until I've seen it to the end, I cannot let anything stand in the way. Humanity will not be ruled by gods, and so the gods must be slain."

The members of the Committee start to panic, some of them

bolting for the doors only to find them blocked by soldiers, and I realize it a moment after they do: Volkov was ready for this. He *wanted* it. He had to know the Committee would never go along with his true plan, and he never intended for any of them to leave this room alive. That's why he wanted them assembled in person. He's been three steps ahead of us all this entire time, the way he always was when he forced me to play Triangulum. I keep underestimating him, but so does everyone else, it seems.

"Volkov!" shouts the Head of Commerce, her dark curls slightly undone after the scuffle. "You wouldn't dare—"

He drops his hand, and deadly Prismic rays erupt from the vityazes' guns.

I quickly turn away, covering my eyes, but cannot block out the sound of two dozen bodies hitting the floor. It seems to last an eternity, the sickening thuds, the whine of the guns, the screams.

And then it's over.

A terrible silence falls.

I wait another moment before turning, horror bitter on my tongue.

Unable to look directly at the carnage, I stare instead at Pol, and he stares back, his face pale, his eyes wide. He shakes his head slightly, as if he doesn't know what to make of it. As if he's asking *me* what to do.

But I am utterly at a loss.

This is so much worse than we could have ever imagined.

The Grand Committee, the feared iron hand controlling the galaxy, is *gone.* Wiped out in moments by a madman with dark aspirations far greater than anything my cursed ancestors ever dreamed up. The only people who might have stopped him are dead, littering the floor of the Solariat, where the Leonov family also met their end. This room is soaked with the blood of the past and present, and all of it, all of it comes down to one man.

In the midst of the bloodbath, Alexei Volkov stands with his head cocked, as if he were watching live theater. The vityazes wait in silence, guns lowered, their faces shadowed by their helmets.

Volkov slowly lowers himself to a crouch and reaches out to touch the face of the Head of Press and Public Affairs; her curated smile will never again greet the citizens of the Belt on the morning news. Smoke rises from the holes riddling her body.

I suddenly remember her name: Esfir, the Rubyati word for *star*.

"Such is the burden of the visionary," Volkov murmurs. "The masses never understand. They never see the long game, and inevitably turn on the hand that would save them."

"Save them?" I echo in a rasp. "Save them from *what*?"

He's the one killing people. He's the one who would let millions die. He says he fears another tyrant will use the Prisms to target their own people, but can't he see he *is* that tyrant? Nothing could justify all the blood he spills. It doesn't make sense. How does killing the Committee and destroying the Prismata make him a hero?

"You don't understand yet," he replies. "But you will soon, when the Firebird awakens and you learn what the Prismata really is."

"Why are you like this?" I whisper. "What is *wrong* with you?"

He turns to me slowly. I flinch when his eyes settle on me, for in them I see the depths of his depravity.

"All I want," he says softly as he begins walking toward me, "all I have ever wanted, was to protect humanity. And to do that, Anya, dearest Anya, I need *you*."

"Stop!" I plead. "You're mad! Don't you see it? Don't you see this is insane?"

He stops by Pol, putting a hand on the aeyla's shoulder. My stomach clenches.

"Every moment that you hesitate, someone dies. These are the choices a ruler faces. These are the decisions your father had to make. And until you are strong enough to make that choice, you will never be granted the Firebird."

"The emperor knew what you intended to do, didn't he?" I whisper. "The Leonovs all knew. And they chose to die, rather than let you destroy the Prismata. They really did poison themselves."

That must why he created the fake footage of him shooting the imperial family. The real recording would have exposed his true plan to the galaxy. Likely Emperor Pyotr died with the truth on his lips, cursing Volkov for his mad ideas. And the direktor knew he had to cover it up, or he'd be destroyed by his own followers. Nobody, Unionist or Loyalist, would stand for this plan.

Volkov's eye tics; I've angered him, bringing up that day. "You are weak, Anya. You are *broken*. And so I must fix you. Now, for the last time, will you accept your legacy?"

All I wanted was to run away from this war, to save Clio and disappear. I was terrified of what I would become if I accepted the truth: an orphan. A girl cursed by madness. A girl who can't walk away from this fight. Now, no matter what I do, I become as monstrous as he is. No matter which way I go, the cost is too high.

I drop to my knees, my strength seeping away. I press my palms against the floor, the floor where sixteen years ago, the Leonov family sacrificed themselves to keep this man from destroying the galaxy.

No, not the Leonov family.

My family.

Pyotr and Katarina, my parents. I force myself to think their names, to picture their faces. My sisters, Lena and Kira, and my brother, Yuri. They made this choice all those years ago, and they chose to die here, rather than to betray their people to this monstrous man.

It strikes me that the moment history names as Alexei Volkov's greatest triumph, he must see as his greatest failure. After all his cleverness in overthrowing the Empire, the Leonovs still defeated him in the end, depriving him of the prize he truly sought. Volkov, who was always three steps ahead of everyone else, was outplayed at his own game.

He was the only person who ever beat me, Volkov said, the first time he challenged me at Triangulum.

A memory comes to me of my dad—my real dad, Teo Androva—so vivid it's like he's standing right beside me, his hands animated as he coaches me through the game.

What's the first rule of Triangulum, Stacia?

"Time's up," Volkov says. He grips Pol by one of his horns and forces him to his knees, then draws his gun. Pol never once looks away from me, his gaze steady, but I can see his chest rising and falling as his breath quickens.

"Wait!" I cry, still on my knees, one hand raised. "Please, I just need one moment . . ."

If you can't beat them, make them play by your *rules.*

I frantically consider the pieces in play. What can I sacrifice? What can I use? What is my strength?

I look at my multicuff.

The transmitter in my hand.

There are twenty Prismic missiles aimed at Afka right now.

And I am holding the key to them.

The idea is half-baked and clumsy, but it's all I've got. I've never attempted anything like it. I don't know if it will work, and if I waste what precious seconds I have on a plan I can't execute, then I might as well shoot Pol myself. If I touch the wrong wire, I could set off the charge that launches the missiles, and Afka and everyone in it will be obliterated.

This isn't something I can rush.

I need *time.*

I look at Pol, sickened by what I'm about to ask of him. But this is the only way—the blasted amethyst gambit.

I tap my bare wrist in the universal sign for *time*, and mouth, *Please.*

His eyes widen with understanding. He whispers hurriedly to Riyan and Mara, then throws himself sideways, crashing into Volkov. The direktor falls with a startled shout. He starts to look my way, but Pol yells, "Death to the Union!" and draws his attention away with a kick to the direktor's thigh. It's a wonderful sight, but I have to look away and focus on my own work.

I rip off my multicuff and pull out a few tools, hiding it in the folds of my skirt. At least this dress is good for *something.* Everything—*everything*—depends on this. I have to trust that I can do it.

Me. Not the Firebird, or my ancestry, or anything else.

The vityaze activates Pol's collar. As Pol is forced to his knees, his teeth gritted against the pain, Riyan and Mara lunge at the soldier.

The man activates all their collars as the other knights rush to help. Meanwhile, my fingers are a blur, sorting through my tools and jamming them into the transmitter, exposing its circuitry. I'm mostly just guessing at what I'm doing, trusting my instinct and my hands.

Riyan fights through the pain and tessellates the air around the man, trying to crumple the tabletka he's using to control their collars. For a moment, my heart leaps, as I realize Riyan still has his power; they must have fled Diamin before his sentence was carried out. Maybe we have a chance after all.

Then Natalya steps in.

Her hands spread, and the air fills with cracks. The sound is deafening, splintering, shuddering, and even the vityazes step back, looking uneasy as the Red Tensor unleashes her power. She twists the air and focuses her stress field on Pol, Riyan, and Mara. They fight back with everything in them, Riyan managing to tessellate just enough to keep them from being crushed.

Wrenching my eyes away, I focus on the transmitter. Volkov and the vityazes are so intent on the three prisoners that they don't notice my busy hands and the parts hidden in my skirt.

I just have to stop my fingers from shaking. They're so weak that my tools keep slipping, and I have to pause to wipe my clammy palms. The longer it takes, the more panicked I grow. Volkov was right. I am weak. I am broken. I can't even fit a wrench around a bolt.

C'mon, Stace, a voice echoes in my head. *Pull it together.*

I freeze as a pair of hands covers mine.

Slowly, slowly, I look up, and catch my breath.

Clio's blue eyes stare into mine, her face solemn, her hands around my wrists. She looks *so real* that I glance beyond her to see if anyone else has noticed. But Pol and Riyan are still fighting against Natalya's control, while Mara struggles to pry off her collar. Volkov is watching them, his back turned. And no one sees the golden-haired girl kneeling in front of me.

"You can't be here," I whisper, looking back at Clio.

Stars, how I ache to throw my arms around her. But I have to keep working. I have to save the ones who *are* real.

Eyes on the prize, Androva.

The words she always yelled from the sidelines during my geeball matches. They echo through me like an aftershock. She's the ghost of a girl who never was, but she's *my* ghost. Her presence soothes my spirit, focuses my thoughts.

Good, she murmurs. *Now, which circuit controls the transmitter signal? Which one will blow up Afka if you touch it?*

I work faster, drawing strength from her presence. I can hear her, feel her, see her, like she's right in front of me, holding me steady. She might not *be* real, but she certainly feels like it.

That's it, Stace. Us against the universe.

Done!

My hands tremble so much it takes three tries before I get the transmitter back together.

Nice work, says Clio. *Now come and find me.*

"What?" I look up—but Clio is gone.

Of course she is, I tell myself, even as my heart sinks.

She wasn't there to begin with. She was just a shadow cast by my overtired, overstressed brain. But the strength she gave me is real. I can still feel it, coiled like a lion between my ribs.

Looking back at the transmitter, I turn on the screen and hold my breath.

This is the moment of truth. Either my tinkering worked, or we're all dead.

The screen flickers on and displays a loading gauge and the word *Calibrating* . . .

I stifle a curse.

I won't know if my hack worked until the calibration is finished. Which means I have to stall before they can kill my friends.

Rising to my feet and snapping my multicuff back on my wrist, I shout, "Alexei Volkov!"

He turns, eyes narrowing. Riyan and Mara are lying flat on the ground, held in place by Natalya's stress field. Pol is on his knees, grimacing as Volkov grips him by one of his horns and presses a gun to his temple.

An unstoppable wave rises in me, higher and higher, water

beginning to break. That wave is my fury, a snarling, blazing tangle of teeth and fangs. Barely holding it back, I square my shoulders and lift my chin. The transmitter is hot against my palm.

"Enough of this," I say, surprised at the firmness of my voice. My knees are still wobbly, but he can't see that. "Stop hurting them. This is between you and me."

Volkov's eyes flick with annoyance. "If you think you're in a position to make demands, Princess, then you're deluded."

"Maybe I am," I snarl, "but I am *not* broken."

"Then prove it. Press that button. Show me you can rule the stars."

I glance at the transmitter. It's at 30 percent calibration.

Looking back at Volkov, I shake my head. "If ruling means making these choices, destroying lives as if they were pieces on your game board, then I don't want to rule. Not if it means turning into *you*."

He narrows his eyes. "I told you, I only—"

"You only want to be a hero, yeah, I know. I know all about you. But you're no hero, *Alexei*. You just murdered twenty people. Does that sound heroic? You'd murder my friends and torture me. You'd wipe out half of humanity just to make yourself feel important. But you know who was *really* important? My father, Pyotr Leonov. He knew what you were, and he knew it was better to die than surrender to you."

Dark fury rises in the direktor's eyes. I've touched a nerve.

The transmitter calibration is at 50 percent.

I press harder.

"He trusted you, and you betrayed that trust. You betrayed *everyone.* You caused the deaths of my family in this very room. You obliterated anyone who threatened you. And despite all that, you *still* lost, because a few brave people managed to smuggle me away from you. They hid me for sixteen years. But I'm done hiding."

Seventy percent.

He drives the barrel of his gun harder into Pol's temple. Pol winces but doesn't make a sound, his eyes locking on mine. Trusting me.

"Are you?" asks Volkov, his eyes sharpening with interest. "Are you really?"

"Isn't that what you want to hear?" I ask. "Stacia Androva is dead. There. I've said it."

Ninety percent.

I need fifteen more seconds.

I draw a breath, and look him in the eyes.

"My name is Anya Petrovna Leonova." For the first time, the truth of those words sinks into my heart and takes root. "I am the heir to the Crescent Throne and the Guardian of the Jewels."

Ninety-five percent.

"I am the Firebird Princess and the last of my name."

Ninety-nine.

"And I will *destroy* you."

Calibration complete.

I'm in.

I look up, face flushed with triumph, and raise the transmitter, hitting a button to transfer the data on the screen to a hologram. The words shine between us:

Self-destruct activated. Awaiting command to proceed.

Volkov's face goes white. "You wouldn't dare."

"Alexei, if there's one thing you need to know about me, it's that I *always* push the red button."

He says nothing, just waits, while behind him, Pol and Riyan and Mara stare at me as if I'm a stranger. I have to ignore them for now and focus totally on the direktor. I can't trust him for a minute.

"Let me tell you how this will go," I say. "You let me and my friends walk out of here, or I'll blow up every missile in your armory and take this whole palace—"

I cut off with a cry as pain bursts in my head.

I stagger, grabbing the throne for support, pressing the heel of my hand to my temple. I drop the transmitter with a clatter. My thoughts speed and blur, like my brain is shifting into warp. With a gasp, I double over. I hear Pol cry my name, and I raise a hand to stop him from running to my side. I can't see for the blinding white light that seems to surround me.

I can just barely make out the vityazes with their guns pointed at me as they begin to close in. Then I have to shut my eyes and grind my teeth together, my knees weakening beneath the onslaught of pain and noise in my skull.

Did they shoot me?

Am I dying?

Will they kill Pol and Riyan and Mara next?

Squeezing my eyes open, I search for them—only to catch my reflection in the glass wall of the Solariat.

I freeze.

There in the glass I see a girl wearing the cosmos for a gown, and around her head burns a crown of crimson light, two fiery wings encircling her brow. The Firebird Crown, dropping sparking feathers of light that burst like embers on the floor, the floor stained with the blood of both my enemies and my ancestors.

I raise shaking fingers to my head but feel nothing. The crown is a hologram, fueled by raw energy that streams in glittering ribbons from the Prism above. I'm caught up in the glow, trapped in a terrible spotlight. The energy doesn't just pour from the crystal above; it streams from every light in the room, from Volkov's tabletka, from the guns clipped to the vityaze's belts, from every scanner and wire and screen in the room, even from the devices in the pockets of the dead Committee members. Waves of Prismic energy rush to sweep around me and gather around my brow, burning so brightly that the vityazes and my friends alike are forced to turn away, raising their hands against the shine.

I curl over, lifting my hands to my face, overwhelmed by the pain in my skull. My thoughts are like a flash flood, too many and too quick to be understood. I stagger under the onslaught. The only rational words in my mind aren't mine at all but a strange, cold, female voice deep in my subconscious, stating robotically:

Firebird code activated.

Identity confirmed: Anya Petrovna Leonova.

Time inactive: Sixteen years, eight months, six days.

Welcome back, Princess.

The direktor slips an arm around me, and I'm too distracted by the rushing chaos in my skull to fight him off. He pulls me up, away from the throne, one of his hands closing around mine, and his voice is a triumphant hiss in my ear.

"Finally." His fingers snake around my jaw, locking my eyes against his. "The Firebird awakens."

Then he presses his gun to my temple and pulls the trigger.

CHAPTER TWENTY-EIGHT

I dream that I'm standing in the Solariat, surrounded by glass walls. The lights are off, the chamber dark but for the ambient light that flows through the windows. The others are all gone: Volkov, Pol, Riyan and Mara and Natalya, the dead Committee and the vityazes.

Am I dead?

If so, this is one crappy afterlife. I remember Volkov putting his gun to my head, and the burst of light before I blacked out. I decide he must have stunned me; he still needs my DNA, after all. I force myself to believe that he needs my DNA *alive*.

Outside, the indifferent stars burn. Alexandrine is a dark curve in the left window, visible only for its glittering cities, their lights outlining the continents where the people are living their distant lives. Falling into bed, watching holovision, stressing over school, scheming and laughing and whispering, completely unaware of one shattered girl in a broken sky.

Feeling the weight of eyes on my shoulder blades, I turn but see only swirling darkness. The sense of being watched doesn't leave me, though; I know I am not alone. In the shadows, forms coalesce and then dissipate, playing tricks on my eyes.

So I close my eyes. I wait several moments, my hands folded against my chest, feeling my heart pound. I know this place isn't real, and that I'm trapped in some sort of dream. But is it a good dream, or a nightmare? I can hear whispers at the edges of my perception.

When I look up again, I start.

A circle of figures surrounds me; this time, they don't vanish when I look at them, though their forms waver like cloth in the wind. Solemn and indistinct, they watch with hollow eyes, and on each one's brow, a golden bead of light burns. Row upon row of them wait in silence, and though my skin prickles and my heart races, I don't sense malevolence in them. I'm not even sure whether they're conscious or just phantasms of cybernetic code, less real than memories—the echoes of memories. They wear fine clothing, some of it centuries old in design, accented with jewels and gold; some wear crowns.

"Who are you?" I whisper.

But I already know, though I couldn't say how I know it. I feel their names when I look at them: Vera and Ruslan, Galina and Zoya, Maksim and Fredek. There are scores of them. They stretch to infinity; I see a bit of myself in each of their ghostly faces. Emperors and the sons of emperors, empresses and the daughters of empresses. All of them Leonovs, with the Firebird pulsing in their genetic code, shining bright on their foreheads, their power and their curse.

This is my family.

I walk to the throne and stand before it, sensing my ancestors around me. The constant, pressing *presence* of so many—always at hand, always watching, always whispering. No wonder my ancestors all went mad.

I hold my hands to my ears, whimpering as I kneel before the Crescent Throne. I bend forward until my forehead touches the floor.

"I don't want this," I whisper.

I don't expect an answer from them; they're just blips in a stream of code. But then one separates from the others. She is tall and dark-haired, with a confident set to her shoulders. She steps forward and smiles at me. Unlike the others, who wear exquisite and elaborate garments, she's dressed in a white lab coat.

"Anya." She takes my hands. Her touch feels real, her skin warm. "Welcome. We've been waiting for you."

I stare with open apprehension. Hers was the voice I heard when the code activated, but now her tone is warmer, more lifelike. "What are you?"

"I'm a message, the most important message you'll ever receive. And I've been waiting for you for sixteen years."

Is this what Clio was? Some string of code unfurling in my DNA? The woman's skin is detailed enough that I can see the pores on her nose, the individual strands of her eyebrows, the green-blue depths of her irises.

"Am I dead?"

She shakes her head. "Asleep, but very much alive."

"I can't do this," I whisper.

"Of course you can." Something almost sympathetic shines in her eyes, but I'm reluctant to trust it. "The Firebird would not have activated if you were not ready. You have accepted who you are, and what's more, you've shown that you control your own mind." She steps back, pulling me to my feet. "And now it's time you learned what every Leonova must, upon coming of age: Your origin. Your purpose. Your legacy."

I pull away, shaking my head. "You're not real. I'm just going crazy."

She smiles. "Oh, Anya, you are many things. But you're not crazy."

I fall back into the throne, pressing myself into it like a cornered animal. "I dreamed up my own best friend. I'm delusional. I chased a lie across the stars, and look where it's got me. No family, no hope, no Clio."

"Come with me, and I'll tell you about Clio."

I look up at her. My heart stands still. "What?"

"I can tell you the truth," she says. "But are you ready to listen?"

She holds out her hand. I stare at it, wondering what more she could possibly tell me, what truth I've still not yet uncovered. And it frightens me, to think there might be more—another twist, another secret. I'm so weary of secrets. But this ghostly woman knows precisely which pressure point will shatter my resistance. After everything, Clio's name still works on me like a hook, tugging me forward, always calling me deeper and further.

I crossed a galaxy for her. What's one more step?

I stand up and take the woman's hand again. "I'm ready."

The Solariat blurs away like smoke, to be replaced by the curving walls of a spaceship.

I flinch, caught off guard by how *real* it feels. The cabin we're in is long and boxy, with high, narrow windows looking out to the stars. Tables line either wall, cluttered with scientific-looking but long outdated equipment. I recognize a few things as old versions of Dr. Luka's machines—gene sequencers, microscopes, brain scanners. There are food wrappers and empty coffee cups scattered around. The windows are covered in markered equations; in some places the numbers have been scribbled out by a frustrated hand, the lines sharp and angry.

After taking it all in, I realize who the woman is.

"Danica Leonova," I whisper. "You're the first empress."

"Not yet," she replies. "This was my only dominion in those early days."

She pulls me down the deck, her eyes shining. "My sister and I bought this ship, made it our lab for our less . . . legal experiments. Human augmentation and genetic enhancement were our business, but our society frowned on such things back then. We had to take our work offworld, into no-man's-sky. It was here, aboard the *Firebird*, that we developed our most powerful cybernetic codes."

"Like the code the tensors have?"

She nods. "It was our first big success. After that, we began working on a new neural enhancement, a code we hoped would spark telepathy. The joining of human minds, the most powerful form of communication that could exist."

I pull my eyes away from the lab and stare hard at her. "You said you could tell me about Clio. Not ancient history."

"If you want to know who you are," she replies, "you must understand who you *were*."

The air around us blurs, and we seem to rush forward without ever taking a step. We're still on the same deck of the ship, only at a different time. A dark-haired woman is lying on the floor—another, older version of Danica herself. She looks exhausted, defeated, surrounded by lab equipment and flickering holograms of neural networks. Now the windows are so covered in messy equations and formulas that I can't see the stars at all. The mess of cups and wrappers has deepened; there's hardly a bare spot on the floor or counters. It looks like the lair of a madwoman, and the other Danica perfectly fits the role. Her hair is a mess and her lab coat is covered in stains. She doesn't look like she's slept or showered in days. Her bloodshot eyes stare without blinking. As I watch, she picks up a small object and cradles it in her hands.

I catch my breath. "I've seen one of those before. The tensors call them Legacy Stones."

The metal flower unfurls over the other Danica's palms, and then long, searching tentacles, thin as hairs, sprout from its center. They reach for her, wrapping around her head and inserting their tips into the skin at her temples and the base of her skull. That is something the tensor's Stones definitely did *not* do. Perhaps over time, theirs had broken down, unable to perform their original purpose, instead becoming nothing more than relics. But the object Danica holds is still new. I hold my breath as its filaments begin to gleam, beads of light trailing along their lengths and sinking into her brain.

My guide looks down at herself, eyes soft. "All my efforts to activate human telepathy failed. But we had sunk everything into this project, and we couldn't afford to lose. In my final moments of desperation, I grafted the experimental code to my own DNA." She shakes her head. "But it didn't work. My sister, only a deck above, couldn't hear anything of my thoughts, no matter how hard I broadcast them."

The Danica on the floor vanishes like smoke.

My Danica turns to me, a slow smile spreading across her face. "But my failure would become our first connection with something even greater. A discovery that would change the course of civilization."

She wipes off some of the equations on the window, and through the glass, I make out a tiny object spinning just outside the ship, like a bright, curious butterfly.

"Is that a Prism?"

"It's the very first one we found, drifting in the void of space. And not by accident." Danica looks at me. "We'd tried to project our thoughts to each other, and failed—in *hearing* them, but not in sending them. The messages were getting lost in transmission, adrift in the dark channels of space-time. And as we soon found out, someone *else* was listening."

"The Prisms . . . *heard* you?"

She nods. "They heard, and they came looking."

I stare at the crystal outside the window, then notice another appear beside it.

Danica presses her hand to the window, smiling fondly at the Prisms, which begin to multiply, more and more materializing out of darkness and clustering at the glass. "Soon, we were finding a new Prism every few days. All we had to do was close our eyes and *reach*, and we could feel them spinning in the dark. So we gathered them up and studied them, and learned we could even manipulate the energy they produced, using the telepathy code. Before long, we realized they were leading us somewhere, bread crumbs scattered across the stars. And the deeper we went into that sky, the farther we chased the trail they made, the more they called to us. We were terrified of what we would find, of where they would lead us, but all our lives we'd sought the answers to impossible questions. So what could we do but follow?"

The scene changes again, to a larger ship, this one equipped for warp. A Prism in a rudimentary diamantglass box spins on the dash. Danica stands at the controls, with another woman close enough in appearance that I know they are sisters. The new one must be Zorica Leonova. They both look older now, perhaps forty or fifty.

The ship wades through space teeming with spinning Prisms. They are thick as sand in a Rubyati wind, thousands, *millions* of them glinting in the darkness.

"We finally found the main cloud, in a bit of space we'd come to call the *Vault,*" Danica says. "We had made a fortune such as no human has ever known. We were already rulers of Alexandrine in practice, thanks to the Prism trade. But the crystals still called to us, drawing us deeper and deeper into the cosmos, light-years away. And this is where the trail ended."

She points at an orb shining ahead, which I at first mistake for a star. But as the ship drifts toward it and the cabin floods with golden light, I realize it's only a little larger than a moon.

I stare at the thing hanging in space, my breath still, my heart suspended.

"The Prismata," says Zorica, turning to smile at me. "This is where Prisms are born." As we get closer, the Prismata takes shape, less a glowing ball of light and more a defined structure. Unlike the simple diamond-shaped Prisms, the Prismata is a complex, tessellated form with hundreds of points. A beautiful, sparkling crystal that burns like sunlight at its core. It spins slowly, generating just enough gravity to form an orbit of Prisms in a brilliant ring. Its many facets flash and shimmer as it turns, light playing across the ship and glancing off my skin.

I cannot speak for the beauty of it. Overwhelmed, I stare until my eyes begin to burn.

"Who knows how long the Prismata spun in the void of space, all alone? How startled it must have been to have heard my voice calling out, light-years away." Danica smiles at the great Prism. "In all humanity's trekking across the galaxy, we'd never found another sign of life. Until now."

"It's . . . alive?" Tears prick my eyes.

She looks at me, the Prismata's light shining on her face. "Haven't you heard its voice? Haven't you heard it calling you?"

"The code was deactivated . . ."

"The door was closed, but you heard the whispers behind it."

I blink, and a tear drops, runs down my cheek. The beauty of the crystal takes on new meaning as I stare into its heart.

"It's *Clio*," I whisper.

Danica nods.

I shake my head, unable to comprehend it, but feeling the truth of it in my bones. "All along, she *was* real. She was the Prismata, connected to my mind. But—but how did I imagine that *thing* as human?"

"How else would a child's mind make sense of the vast consciousness linked to hers? With the help of the Firebird code, you gave that consciousness a face, a voice, a personality. The Prismata was the soul that inhabited a mask you yourself created."

She looks back at the crystal, her gaze fond but also a bit sad. "You aren't the only one who knew Clio, Anya, though she's worn many faces over the centuries. I was haunted by a boy with a violin. Zorica often saw a woman with one blue eye and one brown. The Prismata took on a different form for each of us, shaped by our individual personalities. But the consciousness behind them was always the same. We called them *Clio* after the cybernetic code which made them possible."

Danica turns to me again. "She has always been with the Leonovs; her voice has whispered in the ear of every emperor and empress to rule the Belt. And every iteration of Clio was as unique as the person to whom it was bound. Knowing what they were, we saw through them and understood it was the crystal's consciousness we felt, while the faces were fabrications of our own minds. But you, Anya, you had no one to tell you the truth, to explain that what you saw was the Prismata, transformed by your imagination into the figure of a girl."

So Clio *was* partly my own creation, my mind's way of understanding this alien life-form to which I've always been linked. But how much of Clio was me, and how much of her was the Prismata? Will I ever know where I ended and it began?

I look back at Danica. "Why did she—*it*—never tell me what Clio was? Why let me think she was a person?"

"The Prismata doesn't speak, not the way we do. It communicates through feeling, emotion. The words it used were *your* words, Anya, so how could it tell you what you did not already know?"

"And my parents—my *foster* parents—they never said anything. They thought Clio was part of the Leonov madness."

"It's likely they feared breaking your delusion, lest they break your mind. They could have tried everything to cure you, but it wouldn't have worked. Until you knew the truth about who and what she really was, Clio would always be there."

"And they needed the princess more than they needed Stacia," I mutter. "That was always their first objective: to use me in their war."

I shake my head, looking from the Prismata to Danica. "And what about Clio? Where is she? Will I see her again?"

"You don't need Clio anymore, now that you know the truth. This is how we cured ourselves of the hallucinations—by remembering what and who was truly real. You may glimpse her in the years to come, but she will never again be as clear as she was."

Of course I need her. I'll *always* need her. She might be a part of me, but my connection to her is still real. She is scattered throughout my memories, intertwined with me in every way. Maybe her body doesn't exist, but her soul does.

I'm staring straight at it.

"But why *hide* all this? Why not tell everyone there's an alien life-form powering their whole society? That we're not alone in the universe?"

"We tried, in the beginning. We told the ruling council of Alexandrine about the Prismata, as soon as we returned from our voyage to discover it. And the moment they heard that the thing powering our world was sentient, they launched every battleship we had, determined to destroy it. They feared it would come to resent us for harnessing its power, and that it would one day turn against us. By then, Prismic energy was already integrated into our everyday lives. We were rediscovering the other human colonies, piercing the stars with our faster-than-light ships. But the council feared the Prismata more than they dreamed of unifying humanity. They didn't understand that the power we drew from it was given freely. We'd never asked for its light—it had offered it to us in friendship. For all our flaws and ephemerality, it loved us. And in return, we tried to kill it."

She shakes her head, her eyes darkening. "We stopped them, but at a high cost. Zorica died defending the Prismata. The rest of us swore our bloodline would protect it from then on, and tell no one of its true nature. We took control of Alexandrine, temporarily, we thought. But then someone whispered the word *empress*, and . . . well, here we are."

"Yes," I murmur, an acidic taste on my tongue. "Here we are, the great House Leonov, who took that energy—so freely given, you say—and turned it into a personal fortune and an empire and a superweapon to knock down anyone who threatened us. Aren't we the *greatest*?"

Danica blinks at me, her expression impassive. Of course. She's not the real Danica, just a message, and my anger doesn't seem to register with her. I'm not even sure who *wrote* this message. Most likely, I suppose, it was Emperor Pyotr. Maybe he composed all this in the days before the palace fell, in case he didn't survive, and plugged it into my infant DNA like an update to a computer system—or a virus—at the same time he deactivated the Firebird code.

She continues as if I hadn't spoken at all. "Now, as the last of our name, it is *your* job to protect it, for the sake of all humanity and the sake of the Prismata itself. There are many who would fear it. Some, like that ancient Alexandrian council, would stop at nothing to destroy it."

"Volkov," I whisper, my eyes going round with realization. "Volkov knows."

Humanity will not be ruled by gods, he said.

He wasn't talking about the Committee or the Leonovs.

He was talking about the *Prismata*.

And now the only thing standing between him and it . . . is me.

"If the Prismata is threatenened, Anya, then you are the only one who can defend it," says Danica. "The Prismata needs you just as *humanity* needs you. For you see, our fates are bound together."

I blink at her.

I'm seventeen years old and barely old enough to pilot a dory. But now they want me to defend an ancient alien consciousness on the edge of space, in the midst of a galactic power struggle, all because I'm the only person who happens to have a cybernetic telepathic code fused to my DNA?

Oh, sure. No problem, ancestors.

Panic spikes through me, followed by black despair.

But then I think: *This is Clio.*

All my life, I've protected her. Even when I didn't know why, the instinct was driving me. Guarding her isn't just integrated into my DNA—it's in my *soul.*

No matter what form she takes, no matter how deep in the sky she burns, she will always be a part of me.

And for her, I would do anything.

CHAPTER TWENTY-NINE

After Danica and the ship vanish, I struggle to wake, to even find my body. I am a million particles of light, shooting through wires and circuits, bouncing between rooms, tracing the small hidden spaces of the Rezidencia. I am a drop in the tide of Prismic energy that flows through the imperial infrastructure. I am nowhere and everywhere.

Danica explained the link between me and the Prisms is a telepathic one, so I'm not just connecting to the flow of energy—I'm communicating with it, absorbing information through its senses. As I fight to disconnect, I am barraged with images and sounds that filter through cameras, recording devices, even the vibrations of footsteps that cause ripples in the Prismic energy flowing under the floors. It's a whole new way of seeing, and it overwhelms my brain.

The images come in hazy glimpses: vityazes playing Triangulum in the barracks, mechanics arguing over how to repair an engine in the docks, guards recording the daily prisoner log in the gulag.

And it's there that I "see" Pol and Riyan and Mara, locked in separate cells. I feel a surge of relief that they're safe. I try to think of a way to communicate with them—but then a twinge of pain jolts through my head. I realize how little I know about what I'm doing. How far can I stretch my consciousness until it snaps? I retreat, pulling myself back as quickly as I can, like a turtle withdrawing into its shell.

I wake with a start, to find myself lying on the examination table in the laboratory.

Holos of my DNA spin all around the lab, with scientists poring over them. I lie still, tasting blood that must have run from my nose. My head aches terribly; the pain pounds in my temples, blurring my vision.

"Well?" Holos play over Alexei Volkov's skin as he crosses the room.

Glowing strands of DNA curl over his face. I pretend to still be unconscious as dread opens a pit in my stomach. "What's the status? Did you copy everything?"

Dr. Luka looks up from his work. "It's finished. Now that we have it, it's only a matter of time before we translate it."

Streams of data fall like holographic rain around the two men, symbols flitting too fast for my eyes to follow. Through slitted eyes, I can recognize one of the words as it flashes and then vanishes, tucked in the reams of letters: *Firebird*, just like in the tensor code.

"And the coordinates for the Prismata?" asks Volkov.

"We should have them soon. There's a huge amount of data to sequence, so it could take a day or two. All the best people are on it, direktor. It won't be long now."

"Good," says Volkov. His face softens, and he reaches out to clutch Dr. Luka's shoulder. "You've been an invaluable asset, Doctor. I always admired you, you know, even as a boy."

The doctor looks up at him, his face tight, as if he's holding back words. Then he looks down again, hunched over a screen. His hand absently scratches the metal collar clamped around his neck.

I see Volkov's hand reach inside his coat and realization bursts in my mind. "NO!"

I lunge upright, but it's too late; the shot is quick and neatly placed, and the sound it makes is an earsplitting crack. Volkov doesn't even flinch as he does it; he is as passionless and cool as he was the day he shot Ilya Kepht's mother back in Afka. He kills as if he is picking a crumb from between his teeth.

Dr. Luka slides to the floor, dead before he can say a word. He sprawls below me, eyes wide, mouth slack, a trail of blood oozing from the hole between his eyes. The tabletka he was holding lies beside him, the screen cracked.

I stare at him in horror, feeling my stomach roll. That was no ordinary Prismic bolt, which sounds like a hiss when fired; Volkov's gun is the ancient kind, loaded not with energy but with a metal bullet.

All I can think of is Mara, losing her dad twice. While I just sat here uselessly.

"So, you're awake," Volkov says, his tone cruelly casual. He doesn't even look at the dead doctor lying at his feet. "Tell me, how does it feel to finally be who you were meant to be?"

I blink hard, tearing my eyes from Dr. Luka and meeting the direktor's gaze. My head is still reeling from all the things Danica told me, and it takes a moment for my perspective of Alexei Volkov to shift. It's like he's finally come into focus. I see him as I haven't before. I understand why he killed the Committee and why he's killed so many other people. I know how close he is to achieving his great purpose, and I understand why he thinks he must do it.

I understand him fully, but I don't hate him any less.

"You know." I stare at him flatly. "You know what the Prismata is."

His eyebrows lift. "You mean that it's a living entity, an alien mind whose living energy pumps through every inch of our society? Yes, I know, Anya. I know it controlled the Leonovs, poisoning their minds and turning them into tyrants. And I know it's the most dangerous threat our race has ever faced."

"No. You know *nothing*. The Prismata isn't a monster. It's—"

"I know that if it wished, it could turn on us at any moment. It could wipe out humanity. How do we know what it wants? How do we know what it *thinks*? If the truth was revealed, there would be chaos. People would do just as I have done: everything in their power to stop it. Or worse, they might worship it and make it into some sort of god. And we know what sort of evil people can do in the names of their gods. Look at your own family: The Leonovs, in their greed for power, harnessed all humanity to this thing. It was not their right. And now I must set us free."

"If you destroy it, what happens to all the Prismic energy? If it dies, *we* die." The machine next to me is monitoring my pulse; now it beeps in alarm as my heart begins to pound faster. "Millions of people, in ships and orbital stations like this one."

Volkov nods. He's thought of this. He's thought of everything. The galaxy has always been his Triangulum board. "And if I don't destroy it, it could wipe us *all* out. We have survived against all odds, Anya. We survived when our first world died. We survived voyages into the stars in little more than metal cans with rockets strapped to them. We survived harsh new planets, tamed them and made them ours. Are we to end at last so that we could have more power to fuel our tabletkas?"

"Warp travel won't be possible. The system will fall apart, back into isolation."

"We learned how to warp once. We will do it again, a better way. These are the hard choices, Anya. You understand that now. That's why the Firebird awoke in you."

"*You're* the one who doesn't understand! The Firebird didn't activate because I played your stupid game—it activated because I chose *not* to!"

He shrugs, waving a hand in dismissal. "It doesn't matter. What does matter is that after sixteen years I'm *finally* ready to finish this. The Prismata cannot be allowed to rule us."

My hands curl into fists.

"I can't let you do that," I say quietly.

"You don't have much choice, dear." Volkov smiles pityingly. "The galaxy will thank you, Anya Leonova, the last of your name. Your contribution to the security of the Belt will not go unremembered."

He raises the gun.

Before he can shoot, I lurch off the table, ripping free of the wires suctioned to my skin. They release with small pops, tentacles unsticking, the pain sharp but fleeting. Little red circles march down my arms and across my chest like a rash.

Volkov fires, and the bullet zings past my ear. I dive behind a table before he can get another shot off.

"Stop her!" he shouts, throwing open a door to the corridor.

Three vityazes who must have been on guard outside move toward me. I stumble across the lab, knocking over equipment and blinking hard as the holos blind my eyes. There's nowhere to go but the one door, and they're blocking it. I back away, breathing hard, then kick the table in front of me. It crashes over, spilling glass vials and tabletkas and wires. The vityazes jump back and I jump forward, but I'm too slow. One of them steps in my way, thrusting his shock staff. I gasp as it prods my stomach, electricity surging down its length.

But nothing happens.

The energy sizzles across my body, sinks into my skin.

Hits my brain like a bolt of lightning.

I gasp, my eyes opening wide, as a sensation more powerful than anything I've ever felt takes hold of me. Instead of passing out or feeling pain, I seem to *absorb* the charge. Of course—the staff is fueled with Prismic energy. My heart races, my ears crackle with static, and all across my body, golden triangles begin to glow beneath my skin, like subcutaneous armor made of light. For a moment, my entire body shines.

All this happens in a heartbeat. Then my eyes meet the vityaze's. He looks stunned, hands locked on the rubber grip, still sending the crackling current into me. Behind him, I glimpse Volkov watching, his expression hard but unsurprised.

"Your weapons are useless!" he says. "Get out of the way!

He's raising his ancient gun again, and now I realize why he has it—it's meant for *me.* Prismic bolts can't stop me, but a metal bullet sure could.

The vityaze is slow to move, blocking Volkov's shot. I grip the bare staff with my hands and focus on the energy humming inside me. With a thought, I push it back.

The current reverses. It races up the staff, and as I shove it toward the vityaze, driving it into his chest, the charge leaps on him like a spider with lightning legs. He seizes and drops, blue charges still rippling over his body.

Volkov fires, but I've already rolled aside. Still, I feel the bullet whiz just inches above my head. The sound of the shot makes my ears ring. Volkov pushes forward, trying to get clear aim again.

Spotting a power dock in the wall, I raise the staff, twirl it, and slam it in, sending a current of electricity into the system. The lights around us swell brighter and brighter, until I'm blinded by the glow.

Then, with a pop and a shower of sparks, the power shuts off.

Volkov curses. "Catch her! Now!"

The vityazes flick on the lights fixed to their guns, but by the time they train them on the sparking staff jutting from the power dock, I'm already gone.

I slip around them and toward the door, figuring the power outage is only localized. It'll take just minutes for the system to reconfigure, rerouting power to this sector of the palace. When the lights come back, I need to be gone.

Through the door and down the corridor I go, shining my multicuff's flashlight ahead. Glancing back, I see the vityazes spilling out, heading my way. Volkov takes another shot; it bites into the wall over my shoulder, and bits of plaster explode into my face. I yelp and scramble onward, wondering how many bullets he has in that little gun.

Panting, I slide through a security door and slap my hand against the lock mechanism, but there's no power. Swearing under my breath, I fumble with my multicuff, popping open a panel in the wall and jamming my hand inside. Normally, I'd expect to be shocked into senselessness, even with the power down, but with a little thrill, I realize I don't have to worry about things like that anymore.

Volkov and the soldiers have almost caught up. He fires again, trying to hit me through the window in the door, but though the glass splinters, it doesn't break. I have a few more seconds.

I pull wires out of the wall until I see it—the manual door override, a little lever that probably hasn't been touched since it was installed. I yank it now and feel a rush of relief when I hear the heavy metal bolts in the doorway slide in place. The door is locked tight. It won't open until the power's back on, buying me a few precious minutes.

Even so, when Volkov slams into the other side, I freeze for a moment, terrified it will open for him. But when he scans his palm over the unresponsive lockpad, the door holds fast.

Our eyes connect through the fractured glass window. He looks distorted through the cracks, more like the madman he is.

"You're too late," he says, his voice muffled by the door. "I've got what I need. Nothing will stop me now, Anya."

Swallowing hard, I back away from his crazed stare, only to bump into someone.

I whirl, automatically going into the fighter's crouch my dad taught me, but then I see my fists are pointless.

The person standing in front of me is Natalya Ayedi.

She catches my wrist, and when I try to pull away, she tessellates. The grating sound drowns out my cry of pain as she increases the gravity around me, pulling me to the floor. I land on my hands and knees, struggling to stay upright. Natalya watches in silence, her eyes empty.

"Please . . ." I cough as breathing becomes harder. She is impassive, cut off. It's like she can't even hear me for the brainjacking in her head.

Behind me, Volkov shouts through the door, "Kill her!"

My hand finds Natalya's ankle. I grasp it hard, reaching out with the only instinct I have left—the Firebird. At first, nothing seems to happen.

Then I sense it: the chip in her skull, the only part of her where Prism energy pulses. It's faint and small, like seeing a distant candle's flame in the midst of a storm. With a cry, I focus on that little pulsing spot, willing it to power down, hoping I'm not killing her in the process. When Dr. Luka tried the jack on me, he was able to power it down remotely. Can I do the same?

It seems not, because she tessellates even harder, and the air is pressed from my lungs in a raspy exhalation. My cheek grinds into the floor, and I can feel my ribs compressing. The pain is like nothing I've ever felt; it's as if a ship has landed atop me. An image of Riyan crumpling Pol's gun flashes through my mind, and I can see myself going the same way—being crushed into a little cube of matter, small enough to fit in Natalya's pocket.

I try to cry out, but I have no breath left in my body. My mind starts to dim, the pain swallowing me whole.

Then, suddenly, Natalya gasps and stumbles backward, releasing me. The cracks in the air vanish and I throw myself forward, awkwardly tackling her ankles, my limbs stiff and clumsy with pain. Her head strikes the floor, and my hands find her wrists, pinning them to the ground.

I suck down air, releasing a sob of relief. I'm trembling, my muscles are on fire, and my bones ache, but at least I have control of my own body again.

Behind me, Volkov pounds on the door in a rage. I can still ignore him, though not for long—the power will come back on any minute.

Natalya's eyes are wide, glancing around in confusion. She doesn't fight my grip. Her chest rises and falls, as if she's filling with panic. "Who are you?" she moans. "Where am I?"

Stars above. It actually *worked*. The chip must have shorted out.

"There's no time!" I stumble upright and pull her to her feet. "We have to get out of here."

She groans, hands going to her head. I have no idea what she's aware of or what she remembers, but I can't leave her here like this. I can only hope the brainjacking is permanently shut down, and that it won't reactivate and turn her against me.

I pull her along. She resists at first, but when she sees vityazes trying to break through the door behind us, she lurches into motion. Her bewilderment is clear, but at least she recognizes trouble when she sees it.

"Who are those men?" she asks. "Why are they chasing us? Oh stars, my head aches . . ."

"Are you okay?" I ask as we sprint for the lift tubes. My gait is uneven, my bones still aching from her attack.

"I— It's all foggy. I think . . ." Her eyes widen and she skids to a halt, jerking her hand away. "I saw Riyan. Oh stars, oh skies, I attacked my *brother*—"

"Natalya!" I pull her onward. "We can deal with that later!"

We reach the lifts, but without power in this sector, they're not operating, stuck several floors above. No one has caught up to us yet—it seems the only vityazes on this floor were guarding the lab—but I know we don't have much time.

"Honestly!" I shout, kicking the door. "Why are the lifts *never* working when I need them?"

Yanking off my multicuff again, I use a wrench to wedge open the door, then shove it the rest of the way, cursing all the while. A dark chute opens at my feet, stretching the height of the Rezidencia.

"Can you lower us down?" I ask Natalya.

She blinks, eyes dazed, and sways on her feet.

Hearing voices, I glance back to see incoming vityazes. They must have finally broken through the door, probably by knocking out the window. Volkov will be right behind them with his metal bullets. "Natalya, hurry! I need you to focus!"

She nods, then says, "Go. I'll be above you."

There is no time for second thoughts.

I jump.

I can't help the scream that bursts from my throat as I drop down the tube. It must be several hundred feet to the bottom, and if Natalya doesn't come through, I've just leaped to my death.

Deeper and deeper I fall, until I'm sure the bottom must be inches away, that any second now I'll be smashed. At least it'll be a quick death. I scream the entire way down. My voice echoes off the close walls, amplified until it stings my ears.

Then, without warning, I jerk to a halt and nearly choke on my own scream. The stop is so sudden it gives me whiplash, and for a moment, I dangle in midair, a few inches from the floor.

Then I drop, landing hard on my stomach and feeling the wind rush from my lungs.

Natalya descends lightly beside me. "Sorry," she says. "My timing's a little off. This headache—"

"We made it," I growl, shoving open the door. We stumble out into one of the tubes that branch away from the Rezidencia, leading us to the docks. There are metal tracks running the length of the floor, where the lift would usually run. We race over them. On either side, glass walls open to the palace's enclosed atmosphere. The white length of the Rezidencia stretches above. I can only imagine the frantic activity going on inside there, as Volkov and the vityazes scramble to find out where Natalya and I went. It won't take them long. We probably have less than a minute to get out of here.

Instead of an open hangar, the ships are anchored to a long, narrow chamber like leaves attached to a stem. Dozens of dock portals line the walls. I can hear voices—mechanics trying to get the power back on. The outage stretched farther than I'd thought, but I can't hope it will last much longer. On the other hand, without power, we can't even access a getaway ship. It'll take more than my multicuff to open one of those hermetically sealed dock doors. I need just enough power to activate their controls.

"Keep an eye on those mechanics," I tell Natalya, as I pick up a drill from a tool bench by the wall. I have no idea if this will work, but if it doesn't, we're screwed. The mechanics haven't noticed us; they're totally absorbed in their own tasks.

I pop open a panel on the drill and remove the battery inside. A light gauge on the top indicates it's half charged, thank the stars. Drawing a deep breath, I cradle the battery in my hand and then *pull* on it, activating that new sixth sense that lets me tap into Prismic energy.

At once, power flows out of the battery and into me; I feel its sizzles in my veins. The hairs on my arms rise as it passes through me and flows out my other hand, which I have pressed onto a control panel in the wall.

At once the screen and buttons on the panel light up, startling me;

I can't get used to how the energy simply reacts to my thoughts. I put down the drained battery and crack my knuckles. A shiver of static electricity ripples over my hands. I can feel my roots prickling all over my scalp, and when I run my hand through it, golden sparks dance in my hair.

"Whoa," says Natalya, staring at me. "Who the hell are you, anyway? And . . . *what* are you?"

"A friend of your brother's." Frantically, I search the log of docked ships, pausing at the last one with a grin. I press a button, opening a dock door farther down the chamber. "This way."

We race down the chamber to the last portal. The mechanics finally notice us and begin shouting, but they aren't soldiers, and they don't try to get in our way. The door I unlocked waits for us, opening to the familiar air lock of the *Valentina.*

"My father's ship," Natalya breathes. "How did you—"

"Later. Let's go!" I unceremoniously push her inside, then sprint through the bridge to the upper control deck. There I pause, blinking at the array of controls, unsure where to start. I've never flown anything this complicated before. At least I don't have to worry about power; the Prism is spinning beautifully in its case on the board. I give it an uneasy smile, knowing now that it's as conscious of me as I am of it.

"Hey, you," I murmur to the Prism. "Want to give me some pointers on how to fly this thing?"

"We've got company!" calls Natalya from below. She's locked and sealed the door, and is peering through its circular window.

I pull up a rear camera to see vityazes storming the portal. They've got some sort of explosive device that they're attempting to fix onto the door of the *Valentina*.

With a deep breath, I press my hand to the control board and stare at the Prism spinning atop it. I reach the way I did with the drill battery, trying to connect with the crystal.

"Let's go," I whisper. "C'mon, Val, old girl. We're in a bit of a hurry."

The *Valentina* responds as easily as if I were speaking directly to her. I suppose I am, in a way. The dock clamps release and we sail away from the Rezidencia, leaving the vityazes to scramble to shut the dock door before they tumble out into the palace's artificial atmo.

"That was close," says Natalya, climbing the stairs to the bridge.

Then she stops, staring at the hand I have planted on the control board. From my fingertips and up my arm, triangles of light burn beneath my skin, tingling faintly.

"Um." She points at my hand. "You're glowing."

"Yeah, thanks. Got that." I grit my teeth and concentrate on directing the ship, guiding it through the palace's framework, narrowly dodging the struts that connect the various buildings. All I do is think of the direction I want to go, and the *Valentina*'s computer adjusts course accordingly. But the effort is making me dizzy, and I lean against the board and struggle to blink away the spots in my eyes.

"Do you mind giving me an explanation now?" asks Natalya, in a barbed tone that implies if I *don't* talk, she's going to make me.

"I'm Stacia," I say. "I mean, Anya. Stars, I don't even know anymore."

"The princess," she murmurs. Then she presses her hands to her head. "Ugh! Why I can't I remember anything clearly?"

"You were brainjacked, but that's over now. You can trust me, Natalya. I'm a friend of Riyan's. He's been looking for you."

"Is Riyan all right? Where is he?"

"There." The prison is directly ahead. I'm angling for it hard, sacrificing finesse for the sake of speed. But controlling the entire ship is pushing me to my limit. Now I know how Riyan felt when he was trying to navigate us through the Diamin Wall. I feel blood starting to run from my nose, but I can't let up yet.

"Let me fly!" Natalya says. "Whatever you're doing, it looks like it's killing you."

"I'm fine," I gasp. "I need you to get the prison doors open."

"The doors?" She shakes her head. "Think bigger, princess."

I hold on just long enough to see her begin to tessellate, her hands spread before her. Then, with a mangled groan, I release the control board and collapse into my seat, wiping blood from my nose. The glowing lights under my skin fade. Engines whining, the *Valentina* hovers in place as Natalya focuses on the prison.

"Here we go," she mutters.

I drag myself from my seat to watch, leaning heavily on the board. The entire wall of the prison begins to crumble, not falling away but folding in on itself. Natalya crumples it like a sheet of paper. Plaster and metal crunch into fragmented triangles, collapsing into smaller and smaller bits. The sound must be terrible, but I can't hear anything inside the ship. In moments, Natalya has peeled away the entire wall and reduced it to a single cube of condensed matter no bigger than my head, exposing the cells behind it like a split honeycomb. Startled prisoners stare at us.

I spot Pol at once.

He can't possibly see me through the tinted glass of the cockpit, but he has to recognize the *Valentina* and put two and two together. He vanishes for a moment, then returns with Riyan and Mara. They're still dressed in red prison jumpsuits. I can only imagine the chaos inside the prison as the inmates take to the halls. No guards appear to stop us from pulling alongside the exposed cells and opening the lower hatch. Cool, breathable air filters in from the outside and rushes through the air lock.

Natalya sits down, looking exhausted from tessellating the wall. Her face is masked in black. When I ask if she's all right, she only shakes her head and waves me away.

"Go get my brother," she gasps.

I make my way to the back of the ship, where the hatch has opened and the entry ramp lowered, nearly scraping the edge of the prison. Wiping the blood from my nose onto my shoulder, I hang on to the struts and hold out a hand. Pol jumps aboard, grabbing on to me, and the other two follow.

"Stacia! What in the blazing stars—"

"No time! We've got to get out of here."

"You're bleeding."

"I'm fine. Mara!" She's the last aboard, and Riyan helps her into the air lock. "Can you fly us out of here?"

"On it."

"Pol, pull up some schematics of this system and find a place we can lose any pursuers."

He nods and climbs up into the main cabin.

As the hatch rises and locks into place, I finally turn to Riyan. He looks angry, and his hands lift, finger flexing.

"Nat's here, isn't she?" he says. "Did she hurt you?"

"No, Pol. She's fine, I—"

"Get down!" he shouts, and before I can react, he pushes me aside while his other hand rises defensively at his sister. She stands at the bridge balcony, looking down at us.

"Riyan, it's me!" Natalya puts her hands behind her, the tensor version of indicating she's unarmed. "I swear, I'm myself again."

He flinches, still wary. I rise with a grunt and put a hand on his arm, pulling it down.

"She's better now," I say. "Riyan. She's your sister again. I deactivated the brain jack."

He stares at her, and his eyes begin to water. His chest heaves as he tries to hold back his emotion; it's like he can't make himself believe it's her, and is waiting for her to disappear into the air.

"Little brother, it's me," Natalya murmurs again.

As Mara turns the ship away from the prison, Natalya walks slowly down the steps from the command deck, her eyes uncertain. She's nervous, watching her brother as if he might still attack her. I wonder if she's starting to remember more. Is she recalling the things Alexei Volkov made her do while she was under his control? Maybe she fears Riyan won't forgive her for running away in the first place.

Instead, Riyan pulls her into his arms. He presses her to his chest, his eyes squeezing shut. "I found you," he says, his voice breaking. "Oh, Nat."

"More like I found *you*," Natalya laughs. There are tears on her cheeks as she traces the new red tattoo on his forehead.

Feeling my own eyes water, I leave them to their reunion and climb up to the control deck, where Pol is hunched over the computer and Mara is navigating us out of the palace. I watch them for a moment, my fingernails digging into my palms. They're haggard and hollow-cheeked, with the metal collars still clamped around their necks. Beneath the bands, their skin is raw. Anger roils in my stomach and buzzes in my ears. I could tear Volkov apart for what he's done to my friends.

"Are you all right?" Pol asks, glancing up at me.

"I will be once we're far away from here."

"Enemy incoming," Mara warns. Multiple vityaze destroyers pop up on the scanner, blinking like deadly fireflies. "They're closing in fast. And the palace shield is still up. That's a problem."

"Not for me." Leaning between them, I shut my eyes and press my hands to one of the screens, diving into the flow of Prismic energy.

It pulses all around me, a vast golden network of streams and rivers, unseen by physical eyes but bright as sunlight to my new sixth sense. I can make out the vague outlines of buildings and ships just by the concentration of energy they hold, like looking at a planet at night and seeing continents' outlines marked out by their cities' glow.

It's all connected.

Every wire and circuit and control board, every tabletka tucked into someone's pocket, every computer, every light, every screen broadcasting sports and news: Prismic energy flows through it all as one vast, living system. Just like Riyan said, the Prisms are connected to one another. Touch one, and you can touch them all. And now I know that this pulsing energy flows back to one source: the Prismata, somewhere in the depths of space. What I sense around me is an *organism*, a being of pure energy, stretched over the whole of a galaxy. It flows around billions and billions of people going about their lives, never knowing that each and every day they're interacting with an alien consciousness, using it to power their ships and refrigerators and cameras.

They have *no idea* what their world is built on.

Only the Leonovs ever knew. Only they could see the golden threads that I'm seeing. And only they could reach out and pluck them, sending vibrations across the whole of the galaxy.

But I'm getting distracted, overwhelmed by the immensity of it all. I need to focus on getting us out of the palace, and I need to do it fast.

Surrounded by the shining Prismic map, it takes me a moment

to orient myself and find what I'm looking for: the great energy shield that spreads over the palace. That much energy cast over such a wide area isn't hard to find. To my mind's eye, it looks like a spherical, geometric net, composed of billions of brightly burning dots joined by golden lines. It's beautiful, but there's no time to stop and admire.

"Go," I murmur. "Now!"

Opening my eyes, I see my entire body is alight with residual Prismic glow. I look like I've tattooed myself with phosphorescent ink, and now it burns beneath my skin. Mara and Pol are both staring.

"That's incredible," Pol murmurs.

"Go!" I repeat, gesturing at the controls.

Mara raises her eyebrows but accelerates. Moments from impact, I send a mental command shooting through the Prismic network. The shield flickers and parts just enough for us to shoot through it and into space beyond, then it reseals behind us. The rear cameras show the vityaze ships either veering away or crashing into the barrier, where they pop like firecrackers. I try not to think about the pilots inside. I tell myself they're probably equipped to their elbows with emergency foam.

That, or I just toasted half a dozen human beings.

"More trouble," Mara announces, and then she curses. "They've got a missile lock on us! It's a Prismic warhead—we can't dodge that!"

It might be one of the very same missiles Volkov wanted me to fire at Afka. I've seen videos of those things detonating—they could take out an entire astronika. We're helpless against something that size. Riyan and Natalya rush onto the deck.

"Can we warp?" Riyan asks, watching the blip on the defense screen, which shows an angry red bullet streaking toward us. We're pushing through space at full thrust, all the boosters hot, but we'll never outrun that missile—it's charged by probably a dozen or more Prisms.

Mara shakes her head. "The engine's not cool enough. It needs forty minutes."

"We'll be dead in forty *seconds*!" says Pol.

I clutch the control board, cold horror rushing through me. There's nothing we can do. The *Valentina* isn't built for battle. We have no defenses, no way of dodging or diverting the missile. Alarms scream all across the board, lights strobing in warning. *IMPACT IMMINENT* flashes on every screen. In desperation, I try to find the missile through the Prism network, but either I'm too blocked by panic or I've already pushed myself beyond my limits, because when I close my eyes, all I can make out are sharp bursts of gold light, like fireworks behind my eyelids. They send splinters of pain through my skull. With a hiss, I blink and turn to the tensors.

"Riyan! What do we do?"

We stare at each other, and for a terrible heartbeat, I know we will die. That these are the last breaths I will take. That the last thing I will see will be Riyan's dark eyes filled with panic.

Then Natalya puts her hand on her brother's arm. "I'm still too weak, Ri, especially after breaking open that prison. But you can do this."

He looks at her. "Nat. No."

She puts her hands on his shoulders; they're of a height, but still, at that moment it's clear she's the older sibling, her eyes steady on his. The red emergency lights strobe across their faces. "Riyan. I know how much respect you have for tensor law, but right now, I need you to break free. I need you to *lose control*."

Pol, Mara, and I stare at them helplessly as the missile closes in.

Thirty seconds to impact.

For a heartbeat, Riyan's eyes are torn. Then he turns and spreads his arms.

"Step back," he says through gritted teeth, and even before we've complied, he begins to tessellate. Natalya watches him with glinting eyes, her hands in fists at her sides, as if she's willing him strength.

"Turn the ships around," she says to Mara. "Fast. We need to face it."

Mara looks skeptical but does as Natalya says. My stomach tumbles as she engages all the starboard thrusters, slowing and turning as the same time. It's an impressive bit of flying.

"He can turn the missile away?" I ask Natalya.

"No. It's moving too fast. But he can do *this*."

Bewildered, I turn and peer through the diamantglass screen that curves around the control deck. Alexandrine fills nearly the whole width of the view, with the palace like a bright silver toy suspended in orbit. I can't see the missile yet, and know I likely won't get the chance—by the time it's close enough to be seen, it will be too late.

The ship sensors warn of impact in twelve seconds.

A pained cry slips from Riyan. Alarmed, I glance up and see his face is masked in black lines, and his irises glint like silver plates. His teeth are ground together, lips peeled back, his arms roped with veins and tendons straining.

The space in front of the *Valentina* ripples.

I grab hold of a chair as a shock wave rocks the ship, my heart in my throat. I can't take my eyes off the spreading dark knot in front of us, a writhing, snapping black storm cloud shot through with bursts of light.

This looks *nothing* like his usual stress fields.

Most terrifying of all are Riyan's eyes, which shine silver from end to end, even the whites obscured. He looks alien, devoid of emotion and thought, less human than cosmic force bound by gleaming dark skin and ragged robes.

This is Riyan out of control.

He has the same look as when he attacked Pol and nearly killed him, as if some other force has possessed him. It is terrifying and entrancing all at once. And I remember all too well what he said could happen when a tensor loses control.

The missile is five seconds away.

My grip on the chair tightens until the blood leeches from my fingers. Mara lets out a frightened sob.

Three seconds.

Riyan's head ticks slightly, the smallest mechanical tilt to the left, and in front of the ship, the gravity storm *changes.*

It happens so fast I almost miss it: the teeming darkness parts and forms a perfect circle, a round, terrible, and almighty black hole the size of the *Valentina*. Riyan has gone beyond a stress field and instead ripped open space-time itself, opening a portal so strange and powerful that the *Valentina* begins to shudder. Mara yelps as the ship lunges out of her control and starts to slide toward the hole. I feel the strength of it in my teeth—a merciless hungry strength that pulls at my every atom. It sucks us in, and Riyan lets out a deep, guttural cry as he fights to keep it open.

Then a bright flash of light bursts on the edge of the black hole; it must be the missile intended to blow us to pieces. Instead, it vanishes into the darkness, and with a final cry, Riyan releases his hands. The hole snaps shut and vanishes, so quickly I almost believed I imagine the whole thing.

Riyan collapses. Natalya catches him before he hits the floor, her cheeks damp with tears. She murmurs and strokes his face, kisses his forehead. "Good work, little brother."

A moment passes in which none of us can speak or breathe. We're all still staring at the spot where Riyan opened the black hole and sent the missile hurtling into stars know where—another dimension? A limitless void? My mind can't even begin to make sense of what I just saw, but I do know this: I've never been so grateful to have Riyan on *our* side.

"Mara," I say quietly, "get us out of here. Someplace we can hide until we're ready to warp."

"I've got coordinates," says Pol, and he keys them in.

I sink into the chair between Pol and Mara, locking my harness in place and trying to ignore the queasiness in my gut. Natalya helps Riyan to the lower deck. He's conscious, barely, but doesn't look like he'll be doing any more tessellating for a while.

Mara angles us away from the planet and throws the *Valentina* into full speed. We fall into our seats and strap in, the ship rattling hard from the stress of acceleration.

Finally, Mara lets autopilot take over. She pushes back her hair, letting out a long breath of relief.

"Well, that was fun." She turns and looks at me. "Now what?"

The *Valentina* hums as it idles in the shadow of an uninhabited gas giant adjacent to Alexandrine. It took us five hours to reach the spot, dodging vityaze patrols all the while. The ships thinned the farther we got, and now the massive planet's emissions hide us from their scanners.

Riyan, Pol, Mara, and I stand in a huddle on the control deck. Natalya is below, having fallen asleep after complaining of a headache. No wonder. She's had the roughest day of all of us, after I basically fried a circuit implanted in her brain. Riyan keeps glancing at her worriedly, but she seems stable. In fact, he looks worse than she does. Opening the black hole left him gaunt and wreathed in shadow. I don't know how much of it is the effect of his mighty exertion and how much is guilt from his shattering the tensors' most rigid law, the one he's upheld every moment of his life till now. But he says nothing of it, only focuses on what's ahead.

They tell me the short and bitter story of their half-cocked, and ultimately failed, mission to rescue me from the Committee. They had to flee Diamin quickly, Mara and Pol smuggling Riyan out before he could be stripped of his ability to tessellate, while the tensors were distracted by the Committee ships. I guess their first thought was to come after me, even though they knew it would probably end terribly.

When they're done, they listen as I relay the events in the palace, both before and after they were nearly executed by Volkov. The only thing I don't mention is Clio. I skip over the part where I searched for her in the prison, the awful night when I realized the truth about her, and the part of Danica's message that connected Clio with the Prismata.

I'm having trouble looking at Pol. I know he must be aware that I've learned the truth about her; he's been side-eyeing me ever since we escaped the Palace, like he's itching to ask me about it but isn't sure how. And I haven't been ready for that particular conversation, but I know I can't put it off much longer.

"They copied the Firebird code," I finish. "All of it. And once they translate it, they'll find and destroy the Prismata."

"Because it's . . . *alive*," Pol says, looking as if he still doesn't quite believe it. "And because its life energy fuels our entire civilization."

I glance away. "Right. And if Volkov destroys the Prismata, the entire galaxy will go dark. Ships will crash, cities will collapse, billions of people will die."

"Why would he want that?" asks Mara.

"Because he knows the Prismata's alive, and he's afraid of it. It's why he revolted against the Leonovs in the first place—he thought they were being controlled by this alien mind, that the Prismata could wipe us all out if it decided to. He doesn't trust it."

"So his plan is to wipe *most* of us out?"

"To save the rest, yeah. At least that's how he justifies it."

"This is bad," says Riyan.

"I know it's bad! You think I *wanted* them to tie me to a table and steal my DNA?"

"Easy!" The tensor puts his hands behind his back. "I'm agreeing with you here."

"Sorry. It's been a long day." I sigh and rub my eyes. "So Volkov's going for the Prismata, but we could get there first. Now that the Firebird is activated, I know the coordinates."

Come and find me. Clio's voice echoes in my thoughts. She's out there in the darkness, waiting for me. Needing me.

"You're forgetting we have only one Prism," says Pol, "while Volkov probably has thousands he could burn through. He could leave a week after us and still beat us there."

"Not if we give the *Valentina* everything we've got," I counter. "We could be there in less than a day, probably, if we drained the Prism dry."

They fall quiet, staring at me.

Then Mara nods. "We don't have a choice."

"Of course we have a choice," Pol interjects. "If we burn through our one Prism, we'll be stranded."

"At the *source* of all Prisms," I point out.

"Even if we could scavenge a new crystal, we'd have no way to evade the vityaze ships if they arrived on our tail. We'd be floating like a dead rock, the perfect target."

"Like Mara said, we don't have a choice." I look at Riyan. "It's your ship, your Prism. What do you think?"

He glances at Natalya. "Whatever it takes to stop that man, we have to do it."

"I'm in too," Mara adds. "If the Prismata falls, we all go down, anyway. It must be defended."

Not just for that reason, I think. To some extent, the Prismata is Clio. My life's instinct to protect her may have been a warped manifestation of the Firebird code, but it's still at the center of who I am. Her form has changed, but she's still mine to protect.

"How would we do it?" Riyan asks.

I shrug. "When we get there, I can . . . I don't know, *talk* to it. Try to get it to move or something. Or to fight back and defend itself. I'm not exactly an expert on it, okay? I only *just* got dumped into all this."

"If it doesn't work," Pol growls, "we'll be target practice for the Union ships that are probably already prepping for flight. I can't let you walk into the middle of a firefight, Stace."

"Or maybe you're just a coward," snaps Mara.

"He's not!" I say. "Stop it. Both of you."

"I'm not going to let you die." With that, Pol stands and storms into the back cabins.

Sighing, I turn to the others. "Let me talk to him."

"I can chart the course," Mara says. "Just tell me where to go."

I nod and touch my fingertip to the control board, letting the coordinates flow into the ship's navigational system.

As I climb down from the control deck, I watch the triangles of light glow and fade on my hands. The lights must be like the dark mask the tensors get when they use their abilities. They seem harmless enough, even pretty, but they make me feel like an alien in my own skin.

I find Pol bent over a tabletka in his bunk, looking at planet schematics. He sees me walk in and flings a holo my way—a small ringed planet springs up between us.

"Obsidiath," he says. "It's not on the fringe, not in the center, but tucked nicely in between. It's riddled with caves and tunnels, and I've heard entire colonies live under its surface, completely off the grid."

"Pol."

"Don't like it? How about this one?" He throws up another planet. "Rubyat, my father's homeworld. You like sand, don't you? We could become desert smugglers. Change our names and our faces."

"Right. Because we really nailed the whole disguise thing back on Sapphine. We lasted, what, three hours before we were spotted?"

His mouth quirks into a dry smile, but it doesn't reach his eyes.

I sit beside him, running my palm over my face. He finally lowers the tabletka, letting the holos dissipate.

"When I woke up on Diamin and realized I'd lost you," he whispers, "it was like something woke in me. Something terrible and savage. I could have ripped the sky in two to get you back. I can't lose you again, Stace."

"I know what you mean." I felt it too, at the Loyalist base, when I attacked Zhar after I thought she'd killed him.

"Would you really have hit that button?" he asks. "Blown the palace and all of us to pieces?"

"No. I don't think so, anyway."

"I wasn't sure. I thought, Stacia would never do it. But you're not just Stacia anymore, are you?" His gaze probes mine, the worry line between his eyes deepening. "I don't know Anya. I don't know what she's capable of."

"Oh, Pol." I shake my head. "Anya's just . . . a little stronger, I think. I'm not entirely sure what she's capable of, either. She scares me too."

For a moment we sit in silence, listening to the air recycler churn. Pol's pinned a photo—an actual paper print—above the vent, and it flutters softly in the draft flowing out. It shows my family and his, before his mom died of violet fever when he was six. We're all standing in the vineyard, surrounded by barrels of grapes. I remember that year; it was our best harvest, and that vintage would win my dad the most coveted award on Afka.

In my memory, Clio was there too, standing beside me. I know I've seen that photo a hundred times, because Pol used to keep it in his room above the stables, and I know Clio was in it then.

But now when I look for her, there's only empty space.

I feel a clutch of grief, but it's not as strong as it was. I know she's still out there, waiting for me, calling to me. And I may be the only one who can save her. How can I make him understand that?

Pol's hunched over, rigid with tension. I can sense the weariness in him; it's the same weariness that drags at me. We've been running and fighting at every turn for the last three months. He's ready for it to be over, and so am I.

"Are we going to talk about her?" he asks softly.

I suck in a breath. He must have noticed how intently I was staring at the picture, searching for someone who isn't there.

He waits a moment, and when I say nothing, he begins gently, "Your mother said it was the psychosis that infected all the Leonovs. She was one of their physicians, so she saw it regularly with the imperials. When you were little, she tried to treat you, to make you understand Clio wasn't real. But it pushed you over the edge, and you went into shock. She was worried you would sustain some worse form of mental trauma."

"So she went along with it," I whisper.

He nods. "She said the problem would take care of itself eventually, and that Clio wasn't doing any harm. So we fell in line. We saw Clio too. We talked to her, included her, made her a part of our lives. All of us in Afka, even the people who weren't part of the Loyalist cell. But it was all fake. It was for the princess, to keep her sane, because we needed Anya, and Anya needed Clio. So Clio stayed."

I think of everyone I know back home, and how they must have seen me as the town crackpot. But instead of shaming me, they made me feel safe.

And what did I give them in return? The Union's missiles and soldiers, razing their homes to the ground.

"How could I not have seen it?" I ask. "She was there my whole life. She was . . . *real*, Pol. There had to have been hundreds of times where Clio wouldn't have made sense. What if she asked you a question and you didn't answer it? What if I asked you to give something to her, pass her a pencil?"

"We were never really sure," he says. "But your mom suspected that a part of you always knew Clio wasn't real. For example, Clio never *asked* me questions. You never had me hand her an item, because maybe a subconscious part of your mind knew Clio wasn't there. It seemed that when anything happened that contradicted the reality of Clio, your mind rejected it. Erased it, even. I remember once, an aeyla moved into town and got a job at the diner. He didn't know about Clio. You ordered lunch for you, me, and her. He brought two drinks instead of three, and you told him to bring one for Clio. The guy insisted there were only two of us sitting there, and you got angry, and we left. The next day we went back to the diner and it was like you'd forgotten all about it."

I look down at my hands. "I don't remember that."

"It was a week before the astronika appeared, Stace. A little more than three months ago. That's what I'm talking about—you just ignored events that didn't fit with your reality. Your mom said it was normal for your family, the Leonovs, to do that, especially when they were young."

"Why were our parents loyal to them, then? Why would anyone have followed them if they thought they were insane?"

He shrugs. "The way my dad always talked about them—and it was rare he did, they were all so secretive—it was like they were gods. He said they knew things, *did* things that were beyond normal human capacity. That their madness was nothing compared to what they could do. They understood the universe on a different level. I guess that was the Firebird, only nobody knew it."

"And you put up with me all these years?"

"Stacia." He hesitates, then turns and takes my hands, his eyes staring intently into mine. "Clio was a part of you, and so she was important to me. Acknowledging her, including her, it became second nature. There were even times when I could almost see her, when I could have sworn there were three of us climbing the trees above the house, or sitting in your room watching geeball matches."

I watch him with a feeling of desperation, trying to see my past through his eyes.

"Still," he adds softly, "there were times I wished she *were* real, times when you'd burst out laughing at something she'd said. Because I knew she was a part of you, a part of you I couldn't see or hear or touch. It was like I only ever knew half of you."

I lower my face. "I feel like half of me has been ripped away."

He pauses, then asks cautiously, "Is she . . . gone?"

"Not exactly. Pol, the Prismata . . ." I draw a deep breath, meeting his gaze again. "It's *her*."

He frowns, clearly confused. "What?"

I rise and pace, raking my fingers through my hair. "Danica explained it. Remember how I told you that Prismata is alive, and that I can sense its energy stretching all around us? Well, the infamous madness of the Leonovs wasn't really madness at all, just the effect of being mentally tethered to this enormous consciousness. My family could see and feel this creature no one else saw, so everyone thought they were crazy. Meanwhile, their brains interpreted the Prismata as people—sort of like imaginary friends—because otherwise, their minds *would* break. They, *we*, had no other way to comprehend it. It's so huge, so strange . . . it's *alien*, and it's always there, whispering and hovering just out of sight." I stop and face him, spreading my hands. "Clio's real, Pol, not a figment of my imagination. She was the Prismata all along. This living, ancient being out there in the stars, linked to my mind."

He studies me, his brow creasing. I half worry that I've completely spooked him, and he'll think I really have lost it. But he just waits, patient as the stars, trying to understand.

"All my life," I add softly, "I've felt this instinct to protect her, and this is why. I was *born* to protect her, or it, whatever it is. So you see, this isn't just about stopping Volkov or saving the galaxy. I have to do this for *her*."

He draws a deep breath. "I only have one question, and I want your most honest answer."

I nod.

"Is this what you *want*, Stace? This isn't the code talking through you or influencing you? Because if it is, then we'll find a way to cut it out of you, set you free. I have to know this is your choice."

I wonder if he realizes he's touched on the exact question that's been burning in my mind ever since the Firebird awoke in me. The truth is, I don't know. I don't know how long my life has been controlled by the code in my DNA, or what choices were ever truly mine. I'm not even sure who Stacia would be without Clio or the Firebird. Maybe she never truly existed at all, like Clio herself, and was just a mask created to hide the dangerous truth.

"It's what I *have* to do, before I can have what I want."

"And what do you want?"

I sit by him and stare into his eyes.

"You idiot," I whisper. "Don't you know?"

Every part of my life till now was a lie—every part but him.

My parents were not my parents. My name was not my name. Nothing I thought was real has lasted. My family and my home and my identity: I've lost it all.

All except for Pol.

He has been my constant. In a galaxy where even the stars rearrange themselves and the laws of gravity can be broken, he does not change.

I lean into him, breathing him in. Pol, familiar, steady Pol, who I think will always smell faintly of the vineyard: fresh soil, ripe grapes, leaves damp with rain. He smells of home, and I can't get enough of it. I raise my hand to his face, my fingers slowly trailing down his cheek. He stares at me with wide and startled eyes.

It stuns me that I can touch him in this way, that doing so is like opening a side of myself that I never knew existed.

I love him.

The thought bursts in me like a supernova, sending scorching particles racing through my body.

For years, I thought he was Clio's, that *she* was the one who loved him. But it was me all along. Her thoughts were my thoughts. Her dreams were my dreams. I was afraid of my feelings for him, so I projected them into her.

But her Pol was *my* Pol all along.

Something releases in my chest, and a flood of need surges through me. Years of suppressed desire flood me with heat, a rushing fire that ignites my every atom.

I turn and press my lips into his, hot and fierce and hungry. He seems surprised by my tenacity but leans into it, returning every touch. My fingers drag at his hair and his shirt, my mind filled with sparks.

My fingers explore him inch by inch, following the veins up his wrist, his forearm. They slide over his bicep, jump to the hollow of his throat. While my fingers are busy, so are his, injecting bolts of lighting into my skin wherever they touch: my neck, my jaw, my temple. His fingers weave into my hair. He pushes it over my shoulder, leans to press his lips to the side of my neck, near where the skin patch still covers the incision Volkov's scientists made.

My stomach caves with longing, and before I know it, I'm on my knees on the bunk, tilting his face to mine, pushing his hair back. His dark curls tumble, and he shifts, moving closer, his hands gripping my waist as I lean over him. One of my hands finds a ridged horn and grips it, tilting his face to mine. Stars, he's hard and soft in all the right places, his body yielding to mine, offering himself for my taking.

I'm awakening to a part of myself I never knew I had, and I have years of catching up to do.

His hands squeeze my hips, urgent, hungry, and my body responds with a shudder. He is not the Pol I once knew, once picked on and teased and fought with. It feels as if I'm rediscovering him, finding someone else behind that familiar, handsome face. The fierceness with which I want him terrifies me. I give in to it utterly.

When we finally break apart, we're both breathing hard. His lips are still slightly parted, full and flushed, his pupils dilated. His gaze is steady, certain, hungry for more of me. In his hands I can feel his reluctance to let go.

"You have no idea," he murmurs, "how long I've wanted to do that."

I trace the ridges in his horns. I think of all the time we've lost, and all the time we may never have if we take up this fight. Because he's right. Standing between Volkov and the Prismata is a suicide mission. Even with the Firebird, even with two tensors on our side, we're facing the greatest power in the galaxy. Volkov won't hold anything back, and he'll gladly wipe us out alongside the Prismata.

But I made my choice even before I knew what Volkov intended to do, even before I knew that the Prismata holds Clio's soul inside it.

I knew the moment Volkov put a gun to Pol that I wasn't going to back down from this fight. Because that was the moment I realized that when I have this much to live for, I have something worth dying for.

"Pol," I whisper, letting my forehead rest against his, "I have to do this. You understand that, don't you?"

He says nothing, only lets me sit back. We knit our fingers together, palms down, his fingertips playing over my knuckles.

After a long silence, he murmurs, "I'm not sure I understand anything anymore. But I trust you."

"I trust you too." My fingers tighten in his. "You'll come with me, then?"

His smile is slow and crooked and a little shy, but this time, it shines in his eyes as they rise to meet my gaze. "If it means another kiss like that, Stacia Androva, I'd follow you over the edge of the universe."

CHAPTER THIRTY-ONE

"Holy skies," breathes Mara. "Where are we?"

I stare through the *Valentina*'s front screen at the space ahead, my stomach still rocking from the drop out of warp. The ship's Prism lies at the bottom of its case, useless and dark, its energy spent. When I try to connect with the ship's systems, there's nothing to connect *to* except a bit of auxiliary power. There's not enough to do much besides run the ship's minimum systems.

"This is the Vault," I say. I don't need to check the coordinates to be sure. I can feel this is right, that this was the end of Danica and Zorica's long journey across the stars, following the trail of Prisms.

We crowd onto the bridge, and even Natalya has roused herself to join us. She stands close to her brother, arms folded. It took us sixteen hours to make the jump, pushing the Prism and the *Valentina* to their limits. We've gambled everything. Unless we find a new source of power, there's no going back.

"This place isn't listed on any atlas." Riyan scans the *Valentina*'s database, shaking his head. "Its star isn't even registered."

The system is empty. It has no planets, no significant features.

Nothing, that is, except the massive, glowing crystal ahead of us.

I smile, raising my fingers to the beam of golden light that shines through the front window. "The Prismata. We're here."

It's more impressive in person than it was in the code's message. The nearer we get, the sharper it appears. The individual points take shape, spiking in every direction. The light that burns in its heart is white, but it reflects gold and pink and red in the many arms. From far away, it looks like I could reach out and grab it, but the computer measurements betray that it's the size of a small moon.

"So this is you," I whisper, drawing a look from Pol. I stare so hard my eyes begin to water, but I can't blink. I can't move, for the awe and terror that ripples through me.

For the first time in my life, I'm truly seeing Clio.

Or part of her, anyway. The part I didn't create—her soul.

All this time, Clio was a mind suspended in crystal, a thousand light-years away. How can this thing, so inhuman, so strange, so beautiful, be my best friend? If I reach out to it, will I recognize anything of her?

We all flinch when something pings off the ship's window and spins away. Then another object strikes, and I catch a glimpse of it as it deflects aside, a skitter of light.

We're sailing into a cloud of Prisms. The little crystals spin all around us, thick as flies. There must be millions of them. The more I stare, the more I see. Farther away, they seem thick as dust. They're most concentrated around the Prismata, in a vast ring encircling the much larger mother crystal.

"Aha." Riyan taps the scanner. "There's something that doesn't belong."

I peer at the scan, noting the blip that appears in the Prismata's outer orbit, at the edge of the ring of crystals. "Take us there."

Two hours later, we reach it: a station orbiting the Prismata. It's completely dark, and when Riyan tries to hail it, we get no reply.

"It's the Leonova research station. That's where it all began." I turn to Mara. "Can we dock?"

"Only one way to find out," Mara mutters, concentrating as she activates the thrusters, directing the ship into the docking port. The silence of the engines, the creak and groan of the ship, it all reminds me of when Pol and I were trapped in the dead caravel. The *Valentina*'s backup systems are more sophisticated, so we're not as helpless as we were then, but even so, if Volkov's ships were to drop out of warp this moment, they'd have all the time in the world to shoot us down. We have no guns, no shields, nothing.

Mara makes connection with the station, the *Valentina* latching onto the docking port like a lamprey fastening to a shark.

"Nice flying," Natalya comments, her eyes lingering on Mara appraisingly.

"Thanks." Mara blushes, something I've never seen her do before.

◇

We put on space suits, topping off our O_2 supply before depressurizing and opening the dock hatch at the back of the clipper. Then we file out, floating into zero g inside the old station.

I lead the way with Pol at my back, a gun in his hand. Riyan has his staff. Mara brings up the rear. Natalya stays on board the clipper at Riyan's quiet request; he still doesn't trust her, even though I know the brain-jack chip is dead. And judging by her demeanor, Natalya doesn't trust herself.

I find a control panel and switch on the artificial gravity and lights, doubting they'll even work, but then we all drop an inch to the floor as the gravity generator cranks on. The life-support systems are down, though. We can walk, but we can't breathe. Our helmets stay on.

I recognize the bay we're in—it's the same one Danica took me to, where she and Zorica first discovered the Prismata. They must have transformed the ship into a permanent station, and from here, their descendants would monitor the Prismata through the centuries. It's less cluttered now—no coffee cups or trash, and most of the scientific equipment is gone. While the windows are clean, in one corner I spot a few smudged numbers, proof that the sisters were here centuries ago. I touch my gloved fingers to the equation, and a shiver runs through me.

The station controls require a password, but figuring it's equipped with a biometric scanner, I remove my glove just long enough to press my bare hand to the screen. My touch bypasses the lock and takes me into the station's mainframe. A chill runs down my spine at the message that pops up.

DNA match confirmed. Welcome, Empress.

I delete the words before the others can read them.

Thanks to my DNA, I have full security access. More screens light up, grainy images showing close-ups of the Prismata. It looks like the Leonovs used to run drones to monitor the crystal, but they've all broken down by now. Their last transmissions are frozen on the screens, displaying data that indicates the Prismata has been steadily growing for centuries, at a rate of about a millimeter per year or so.

"Look at this," Pol says, tapping a screen.

It's running looped footage of one of the Prismata's spikes. As we watch, the tip breaks off and floats away, a perfect diamond, to join the masses like it that cluster in space.

"So that's how baby Prisms are made," I murmur.

While the others study the Prismata data, I pull up the station log.

"Last time anyone was here was seventeen years ago. The emperor and the oldest prince, looks like." I pause, swallowing. "The day Emerault's moon blew up."

"They did it from here?" asks Riyan.

I nod, pulling up a record of their visit. "They could reach any Prism in the galaxy from here, through the Prismata. All the crystals are still connected to this core, drawing energy from it. Send a high enough surge of that energy into a Prism, and it and every piece of tech connected to it will explode."

"It's all one vast, living organism," Riyan murmurs, staring at the Prismata through a narrow window. "Pure energy."

"And we've pulled and stretched that energy, woven it through billions of circuits and wires and batteries, across nine star systems."

"And if Volkov destroys it . . ."

"All that energy will vanish."

We stand in silence for a long moment; I know the others are thinking the same terrible thing: How many would die? Would our civilization ever recover from such devastation? Volkov seems to think it an acceptable risk, but I can't.

Pol breaks the silence with a cough. "Guess we'd better do what we came here to do."

"Which is *what*, exactly?" Riyan turns away from the window to raise an eyebrow at me. "We came here to stop Volkov from destroying the Prismata, but how are we going to do that? It's not like we can move a thing that size. We can't defend it, either—the five of us against the whole of the Union fleet."

"Mara's got the most military training of all of us," I say. "Mara, what do you think?"

She jumps when I say her name. She'd been staring, not at the Prismata, but down the corridor, fidgeting with her gun.

"You all right?" I ask her.

She swallows. "Yeah, of course. This place is creepy, that's all."

Suddenly Pol's head jerks. "Did you guys hear that?"

"Hear what?" I ask.

"I didn't hear anything," Mara says.

"Something hit the station. I heard a thump."

"There are probably a hundred Prisms bouncing off this thing every hour," I point out. "They're like gnats out there."

"No, this was different. Heavier." He frowns. "It came from the docking bay."

Riyan stiffens. "Natalya."

"Wait," I say, before they can charge off. I shut my eyes and press my hand to the control, then attune to the flow of Prism energy running through the wires and circuits beneath it. This was something I practiced on the *Valentina* during the brief journey to the Vault—following Prism currents and learning out to read them, drawing data directly from the ship's computers. My sense is still hazy, and I have to focus hard in order to read the messages the current is bringing me now.

What I find makes me suck in a breath, eyes shooting open.

"There's another ship. The dock next to ours has been activated." I meet Pol's eyes. "Someone *followed* us here."

"Could it be Volkov already?"

"Why would he bother docking? He could just—"

I'm interrupted by the pulse of a gun behind us, and Pol and I whirl to see Riyan slump to the ground, unconscious.

I freeze as my eyes rise slowly to Mara.

"I'm sorry," she whispers, raising the gun to me. Her eyes glisten with tears, but her hand doesn't waver. "I really am. But I can't let the Committee get control of this place."

"Mara," I say very carefully, "what did you do?"

"What I had to, for all our sakes."

Footsteps sound down the corridor, the unmistakable heavy plod of space suits, moving quickly in our direction. Pol curses, his hand flinching as if he might try to grab his gun. It's still holstered; he had no reason to draw it when we landed. We were supposed to be the only people around for a hundred light-years. But I shake my head at him, not doubting that Mara would drop either one of us as easily as she did Riyan.

"You never deserted," I whisper. "You were spying on us all along."

She shrugs. "'Go along with the princess' were my orders. No matter what you did or where you went. Waiting for you to find the Firebird, only to find out you *are* the Firebird. I was just doing my job."

"*You* helped us escape Zhar in the first place!"

With a sigh, she shakes her head. "That was my father's plan. He didn't tell me about it until we were already aboard the *Valentina*. I never intended to let you off the base, but then my father hit me with that sleep patch. *You* were the ones who signaled the Committee and got my people captured. You're the reason my dad died back there."

She has no idea her dad survived the Union's attack, only to die in the Autumn Palace. I decide now might not be the best moment to inform her of the truth.

My mind races. If I could reach the control panel, I could tap into the Prism energy fueling the station and knock out the lights like I did in the palace. It's just out of reach, but Mara could drop me or Pol before I made it one step.

Before I can conceive even half a plan, it's already over.

Loyalists swarm around us, twenty or more of them; it's hard to keep count. Their faces are blurred behind their helmets, their voices muffled as they shout. But it's clear what they want—an easy surrender. I can't even make it to the wall before they've hemmed me in, so there's no hope of shutting off the power. I can't connect with the Prism network unless I'm physically touching a machine fueled by it.

Pol puts up his hands, his face rigid and eyes blazing.

Riyan is quickly bound, his hands placed in a special cuff to keep him from tessellating when he wakes. They strip Pol of his gun, then bind him. I wonder what happened to Natalya. Stars, if they killed her . . .

"ZHAR!" I spot her bringing up the rear. Seething, I try to push through the Loyalist soldiers, but they hold me back. "You don't know what you're doing! You have no idea—"

"Stacia?" says a soft voice.

I go absolutely still.

My body is numb to the soles of my feet. Everything around me seems to freeze.

With a sob rising in my throat, I whimper, "Mom?"

And there she is, her and Dad both, flanking Zhar. They're encased in space suits, but that doesn't stop me from lurching free of the soldiers and running to embrace them. My helmet clacks against Mom's; behind her visor, she's crying. Dad hugs me fiercely, and even he's got moist eyes. My grizzly, stodgy old dad—I've never seen him cry before.

They look terrible. Even though all I can see are their faces, I can tell their bones are standing out, their figures gaunt. Mom's limping, leaning on Dad, both of them carrying guns. They look like strangers, poor imitations of my parents. But they're undeniably mine.

I've had to hold strong for months, keeping myself together like a beat-up dory patched with tape. But now I can finally release, can finally sit back and let them fix everything.

I don't have to be strong anymore.

"Baby girl," Dad murmurs. "We've missed you *so* much."

Mom grips the shoulders of my space suit and studies my face. "Are you okay, sweetie?"

"What are you doing here?" I ask. "*How* are you here?"

"We slipped through the Union blockade around Amethyne a month ago. By the time we met up with Zhar, you'd already gone. Oh, my dear, why did you do that? You should have known we would never send you to anyone we didn't trust."

"Trust! You can't trust *Zhar*! She's—" I realize I'm shouting, and lower my voice, gripping both their hands with my gloves. "She's totally insane. She's on some kind of revenge mission. She *shot* Pol."

They exchange looks.

"Come with us," I whisper. "We'll get out of here together, you and me and Pol and Riyan. Please, Mom, Dad, if we hurry we can—"

Mom shushes me, still smiling and crying as she shakes her head. "My darling, my darling. We are so close. I promise, this will all be over soon."

"Yes," says Zhar, interrupting our reunion. "It will all be over soon."

Even behind her visor, Zhar's eyes practically glow with anger as she approaches me. I step to meet her.

"You're a monster," I hiss. "You're as bad Volkov."

"Am I?" Her voice is chilled. "What are you, then, Princess? Half my people died fighting when you called the Union down on us. You chose the wrong side."

"The only side I chose was Cli—" I pause, gritting my teeth together. "Was the Prismata, and everyone you and Volkov would destroy."

"Stacia, *please*," Mom urges. "Trust us. We're doing this for you."

"We're doing this for the Belt," Zhar says. She presses a gloved hand to the window. The Prismata reflects on the front of her visor. "Pyotr would have wanted this. We, his most loyal of companions, securing his legacy. Wielding the power of the Prisms against his enemies." She turns to us, eyes fervid. "This is how we take back the galaxy. This is how we put Anya Leonova on the throne. We will eliminate the usurper and all his kind."

My father nods. "For Pyotr and Katarina, and the children."

"Your family," Mom adds to me. She squeezes me close. "Oh, Anya, I wish you could have known them. How strong they were, how inspiring. You carry that strength in you, and now you can finally claim your birthright. We are so proud of you."

My joy at seeing my parents is starting to fade, as I realize how squarely in Zhar's corner they stand. They still see the Leonov Empire as something good, something worth dying and killing for. My stomach sinks even as my mom holds me close. I was naive to think they would fix everything. I was naive to hope they could ever be just my parents again, as if the Teo and Elena who raised me are totally different people from the Teo and Elena who smuggled me out of the palace when I was a baby. Anya has always been their first priority.

"Mara told us you'd found the Firebird," Zhar says impatiently. "Do you have it with you?"

I clamp my jaw shut. It's childish; I might as well stamp my foot too, for all the good it'll do, but I don't want to make this easy for her.

Mara speaks up. "Commander, Anya *is* the Firebird. It's a code in her DNA, passed down from the other Leonovs. I've seen it—she can control the Prisms with her mind or something. Apparently it's what made them insane."

My parents stare at me while I shoot Mara a dark look.

"Oh," Mom breathes. "*Oh*. Sweetheart, is this true?"

I feel suddenly claustrophobic in my tight space suit. My fingers itch to yank off the helmet. "I'm not insane. None of the Leonovs were. If you'll just listen, I can explain everything!"

"So we had the Firebird all along," Dad whispers. "The key to the whole war was running around our vineyard, playing in the mud, and we had no idea."

I look away, unable to stomach even the sight of him right now. My own parents never saw me as anything more than a means to an end.

I'm forced to stand in silence while Mara tells them everything. She hands over the secrets I'd entrusted to her without a second thought, a soldier reporting to her superior in a flat, mechanical tone. She doesn't even feel guilty for it. All our conversations she repeats back to Zhar in a clipped voice, wrung dry of emotion. Watching her betray me is like feeling a knife slide into my gut; the final twist comes when she tells Zhar how she pretended to forgive me for her father's death. Her eyes flicker to me then, her disciplined facade fracturing just enough for me to see the bitter anger in his eyes. She *always* blamed me. All this time, she's been hiding her true feelings, playing at being my friend.

Pol has gone absolutely still, watching Mara with violence in his eyes. I find myself grateful they handcuffed him. I'm not sure he wouldn't attack her and get himself shot—again—in the process.

"Stars," Zhar murmurs. "No wonder they were so secretive about the Firebird. All along, *they* were the greatest weapons in the galaxy."

"It's not what you think," I whisper. "I'm not a weapon. That's not the *point* of the Firebird. That thing"—I point at the crystal—"it's *alive.* Don't you see? The Leonovs protected the Prismata, and in return, it gave us Prisms to power our ships and cities. It's a living creature, and it's my job to keep it safe."

"Alive?" My mom glances at the Prismata through window, her brow furrowing.

I clench my fists in frustration; how can I make them believe something they cannot see or hear or experience? How can I make them understand the Prismata isn't something to be used for death, but for life? They're making the same mistake the Leonovs made, and that led to the war that killed millions. This time, it's going to be worse. Even my parents don't understand.

I thought I'd come here to protect the Prismata from Volkov, not my own *family.* How can the people I love most be so blind? How do I make them see that they're fighting for all the wrong things, and that there can be a better way?

"Commander!" interrupts a Loyalist soldier, a hand pressed to his comm patch. "Word from our people in the palace. Volkov departed hours ago, destination unknown, but he's taken the majority of the Union fleet with him."

My head jerks up. "He wants to destroy the Prismata. That's why he overthrew the Empire in the first place—to get to it! He has the coordinates, and he's coming *here*."

Zhar stares at me, then slowly nods. "He once told me, back when he was only thinking of revolting, that the Leonovs were never the real threat. That the galaxy was controlled by something terrible and unknowable."

"Volkov thinks it will wipe out humanity. But I *know* it, and it wouldn't do that."

"So," she says, "if your job is to protect it, then protect it. The Leonovs used the Prismata to destroy all threats. So can you. We stick to our original plan."

She wants me to blow up Volkov's fleet the way Pyotr Leonov blew up everyone on Emerault's moon. All I'd have to do is connect to the network of Prismic energy all around me and, well, *ask*. The same way I flew the *Valentina* and turned on the systems in this old station. The Union fleet will be bristling with Prisms. One word, one *thought* from me could obliterate them in a moment. The Prismata would be safe then, and the war would be over. We'd have control of the galaxy. I'd become an empress. My family would be reunited. I could save anyone I wanted, and all it would take is the sacrifice of a couple thousand Unionist soldiers. Soldiers who would shoot me on sight.

But can I do that? Can I just wipe out Volkov and all the people on his ships? They might be enemy soldiers, but most of them are still innocent people with families and homes and dreams. Killing them would make me just like Emperor Pyotr or Alexei Volkov, using people like game pieces, discarding the ones I don't like with ruthless efficiency.

Yet again, I'm being asked to make a choice I cannot make.

But this time, I don't think I can open my multicuff and tinker my way out of it.

There *must* be another way. There must be an answer to all this, a path to peace. If I wipe out Volkov's fleet, then I'm just another tyrant, exploiting power I don't deserve. More will rise up in the direktor's place, and the killing and fighting will go on and on. We won't have to worry about the Prismata destroying us. We'll destroy ourselves.

But what can I *do*?

I'm tired of being told which path I should follow. Even my parents can't help me, and I'm not sure I need them to anymore.

I'm not the helpless girl who was dragged from her home three months ago.

I am the Firebird, and I was born to guard an ancient being at the edge of the universe.

I'm a girl who loves her best friend, enough to risk everything.

I think of her now: the most peaceful person I know, the one who could always be counted on to see the best path. The person I trust more than anyone else in the galaxy, who always saw the best in everyone.

I have to talk to Clio.

Everyone around me is still arguing about what to do. Yelling at one another, at me. Pol and my parents and Zhar and Mara—it's chaos. Riyan starts to rouse, and when he sees Zhar, his eyes open wide and he begins struggling. The air around him pops and crackles as he tries and fails to tessellate.

Sandwiched between Zhar and my parents, I can't get to any control consoles. I have no way of reaching the Prism current.

I shut my eyes and try to think, try to focus. I twist my multicuff—

Of course.

The cuff is powered by Prism energy, just a thread of it coiled in a tiny battery that powers the flashlight, but that might be enough to access the wider network around me.

It *has* to be enough.

I wrap my hand around the metal, stilling myself. I let the chaos surrounding me fade away. I feel the quiet, slender current of Prism energy pulsing through the tiny wires inside.

For some reason, it's Natalya Ayedi I think of at that moment, telling her brother that now is the time to lose control. No more hesitation, no more fear, no more doubt.

Instead of just observing the network of light spread around me, I fling myself wholly into it and don't look back.

CHAPTER THIRTY-TWO

The Prism network sweeps me away.

It's like diving into a river and finding the current is much stronger than you'd anticipated. There is nothing I can do but let it take me. I lose all sense of my physical body, instead inhabiting a new state of being, a disembodied mind. My consciousness is ripped from my flesh and bones, leaving my parents and Pol and everyone else far behind. Do they notice that I'm gone? Am I standing still, or has my body collapsed onto the ground? Will I even be able to find myself again?

I am reduced to a cloud of particles borne on a golden tide. I am a scattering of leaves torn from my tree by a storm-driven wind. I am stretched wider and farther, like ink through water, following the lines and channels and streams of Prismic energy that branch across space. All around me is light: pure, cleansing light that tumbles like water, a cascade of luminescent energy.

I fight to stay in control of myself, because the current threatens to rip me apart entirely. Here at the heart of the Vault, the Prismic flow is infinitely stronger than it was in the palace. Stronger, and deeper, and stranger. This close to the Prismata, I can *feel* its pulse, like there really is a heart somewhere in that massive structure. But oddly, I don't feel panic. Even as my consciousness unravels and my senses explode with alien sensations, I am not afraid. There's no room for fear in me, because I am filled to the brim with wonder.

This is where all Prismic energy in the galaxy begins. This is the living light that sustains all humanity. I can feel it all—the billions of tributaries branching away from the source, threading the stars, flowing through every inch of the Belt. But the energy doesn't just flow out—it also returns, carrying with it a jumble of information, like birds returning to their nest with scavenged treasures.

The Prismata is *collecting* things—intangible bits and pieces of humanity. It gathers moments and feelings and memories, draws them into itself, the way it's drawing *me* in. I catch fleeting glimpses as these treasures hurtle past, reflected in the bright, gleaming facets of the Prisms themselves: the pattern of lichen dappling the back of a great Emeraultine sky whale, seen through the Prism-powered binoculars held by an excited little girl; the curse of a pilot trying to start the engine of an old and cantankerous racing ship; the flash of a neon sign in the orbital cities drifting over Alexandrine, advertising a night with a beautiful escort to a lone man standing below; the delighted laugh of a young programmer when the companion bot she has built powers on for the first time; the sob of an eeda looking at an image of a lost love on his tabletka, his webbed fingers pressed to the screen.

The moments the Prismata collects all have a similar theme. Each one is taut with emotion: excitement, frustration, desire, joy, grief. It isn't the sights or sounds of the humans the crystal wants—it's their feelings. That's why it sent the Prisms to meet Danica and Zorica Leonova all those centuries ago; this is why it still sends them to us. The Prisms are its errand-birds, collecting human emotions and sending them back to their nest, nourishing it with human love and desire and rage.

The Prismata speaks in emotions, Danica said.

Now I understand what she meant.

The closer I get to the Prismata itself, the more fragmented the images become, until I can't tell where they come from or who they're about; everything tangible is stripped away until only the emotion remains. The light around me shimmers with a hundred different colors, and every color has a name: fury and lust and sorrow and happiness, many I have no name for but have felt before, like the feeling of music taking hold of you until you can't help but dance, the oddly sorrowful aftertaste that sometimes follows a moment of delight, the expansion of the soul when looking at a beautiful sunset, the pleasure of being the first to share good news. All these wash over and through me, pulling me farther apart, spreading me thin, dizzying me. I nearly lose myself in them entirely. I have to struggle to remember who I am and why I'm here.

The Prismata. I have to reach it. I have to find Clio.

There's no need to search for it. All I have to do is wait and let it reel me in. From Prism to Prism I bounce, reflected through space, borne on the unseen golden threads that bind all the crystals together. Threads that, inevitably, lead back to the center of the network, veins returning to the heart. I'm just a single cell in its bloodstream.

I know the moment I arrive, because everything goes still.

The halt is abrupt, leaving me jarred and dizzy. Though I don't have any physical sense, the part of my mind where the Firebird connects me to the Prismata—where a tiny fraction of its energy passes through my neural synapses, weaving me into its vast network—is wide open. I'm exploding with sensations that are almost *like* seeing and hearing and smelling.

It reminds of the nights when Clio and I would sneak out for a swim in the lake near the vineyard. Out in the hills, there were no artificial lights, only the dusty, glinting stars above. They reflected on the lake's smooth surface, so when I floated on my back, I couldn't tell water from sky. Weightless, I'd imagine I was floating in space, my every atom lighter than air. That's what it's like now; separated from my body, from all physical sense, from gravity—I am free.

Gradually, I become aware of the Prismata's pulsing song. It's not music I hear, but a feeling that's *like* music. It's not something I could ever re-create, even if I had all the musical talent and all the best instruments in the galaxy. Here, the stolen moments I glimpsed on my strange journey have all been distilled down to their emotional cores. They gather and mingle and coalesce, colors blending until they're all the same bright, dazzling gold. That one feeling, composed of so many others, is stronger than all the rest, and soon it wraps around me, pushing everything else aside.

That feeling is love.

The Prismata knows me. It welcomes me. It invites me deeper, to commune with it fully. And even though I can't feel my physical eyes, I know I am weeping. I don't doubt that back in my flesh-and-blood body, there are tears running down my cheeks.

I reach out and feel the mind around me reach back, curious about me, enjoying my adoration. It knows I'm here and it wants to experience me as much as I am experiencing it. I hold nothing back, but let it see everything: my fear of failing to save it, my anger at Mara and my parents and Zhar, my love for Pol. All the emotions that bind me together and make me who I am, like a different sort of genetic code. The Prismata sifts through all of them, its gentle love suffusing my being.

Stars, it is purer than I could have imagined. No wonder the Leonovs felt compelled to protect it. This is what I always sensed in Clio—a clarity of spirit far beyond my own. A soul untouched by greed and hate, existing in perfect harmony.

Volkov's fears of it turning against us are completely absurd. If he could just *know* the Prismata, if he could connect with it the way I am connecting with it now, he would see how perfectly affectionate it is, an entity incapable of violence. The attacks the Leonovs made using its power were their own dark nature; it had nothing to do with the Prismata. They exploited it in the name of protecting it.

But enchanting as this strange entity is, I have to remember why I am here.

Clio? Are you here?

My words feel small and inconsequential compared to the Prismata's much greater existence. It's like tossing pebbles from the shore to get the ocean's attention. But still I try to find a point of connection, a way of making myself heard by it.

You have to leave, please. You're in danger!

I can feel it react, a thread of green curiosity flickering in and out, brushing over me like a slinke leaf. So it must hear me—but does it understand?

Stars, this would be so much easier if she could talk to me! Is Clio even in there? Or was every knowable part of her a result of my own subconscious?

Where did I end and she begin?

Did I get it all wrong?

They're coming to destroy you. They don't know what you are. Please, you must let me help you!

I have to find her if she's here. Whatever part of the Prismata clung to me all my life, shadowed me in the form of my best friend, I have to find it now. It's the only way I can stop Volkov and save the people I love.

It's the only way this war can end.

As hard as it is, I have to let my mind clear. I must put aside the words and the pleas, and unearth something deeper. Something more instinctive, that the Prismata will understand.

I start with an image.

We are thirteen years old. We sit under the grapevines, spying on a shirtless Pol as he washes the mantibu. But then a slinke spider drops from the vines and lands between us. We scream and Pol sees us, then chases us with a bucket of soapy water. He trips and spills it on himself, and you and I laugh and laugh . . .

Warmth spreads through me. I can recall the day so clearly, and the purity of our happiness.

We are ten years old, sitting on the floor of my bedroom. The window is open, and we can smell the rich wine in the presses below. I draw a spaceship and you color it. We name it Starchaser. *We list the planets we'll visit and what we'll do. It takes us hours to plan it all out, and finally we fall asleep, back to back on the carpet.*

No one knows me like Clio does. No matter what she is, she's my best friend, for as long as I live.

We are eight years old. It's night, and we've snuck away from Pol's birthday party to sit on the top of the house, looking up at the stars. I point out Alexandrine, and you say we'll go there first. "You and me against the universe," you add, and we link pinkies and swear to be friends forever.

I lay everything before the Prismata—every moment, every smile, every whisper. Every fight we had, every make-up, every prank we pulled. I lay out our love for Pol. I pour our friendship into this ancient being's mind. And I give it my fear and horror that I might lose her.

I feel heat rising, softness closing around me. The Prismata is changing, shifting. I struggle to understand, and then—

"Stacia."

Her voice.

As clear in my thoughts as it ever was.

Relief floods through me. "Clio? Is that you?"

Her excitement rises around me; I can *feel* it, like soap bubbles popping on my skin.

"I asked you to come to me," she says, "and you did."

"Yes, yes! I'm here, Clio. Stars, I am here. I'm sorry it took so long."

A pause, as the current of the Prismata swirls around me. My mind floods with color, curls of yellow and red. And then, out of the misty hues, a solid form materializes, appearing before my mind's eye like fog taking shape, colors assembling into the form I know and love so well.

Clio walks toward me and takes my hands, and I realize I have my body again, or at least the sensation of one. I can see and feel and hear her as if we were standing in the vineyard back home. She's wearing the blue sundress she had on the last day I saw her, and her hair flows around her shoulders, as golden as the light around us. I'm in my favorite outfit—the tank top and cargo pants that I had to abandon on Sapphine, and even my multicuff is on my wrist. My hair is braided over my shoulder.

I pull her close, hug her tight, until tears run from my eyes. She squeezes back, and somehow, she feels more herself than she's ever been before.

"I miss you," I whisper.

"I was never far." She pulls back to look at me. Her eyes aren't blue anymore, but all the colors of the Prisms, swirling endlessly. "So. Are you going to tell me *all* about it, or what?"

"Tell you . . ."

"About Pol, stupid!" She grins. "You kissed him. *Finally.*"

Unreal as this body is, it can still flush furiously. I press my hands to my heated cheeks. "I'm sorry! It just—it *happened* and I didn't know how to stop and—"

Clio laughs, bright and sparkling as rain on a sunny day. She grabs my hands and pulls me close. "He's lucky, you know. Don't you ever let him forget it."

I stare at her, the *realness* of her, like seeing a dream come to life. My Clio. My dazzling, laughing friend, my twin moon. I want to grab her hand and steal her away, keep her all to myself. I want everything to be the way it was. I want to live our beautiful lie, all else be damned. But I may as well want the stars for a necklace. Clio isn't mine to steal; she's only mine to protect for as long as I can.

"This is you, isn't it?" I say. "I mean, you're the Prismata, not just my imagination. But Danica said you couldn't speak the way we do."

"For all her cleverness, Danica never totally understood me. Not many of your ancestors did. They never believed in me the way you do, with the whole of their beings." There is a touch of sadness in her smile.

"I think I understand." The other Leonovs resisted accepting Clio, knowing she wasn't real. She was just a ghost to them, never a person. But I grew up believing she *was* real, and so I could love her in a way they never could. Our connection must be deeper than any Leonov has ever had with the Prismata. I wonder: If they had known her the way I do, if they could have *heard* her the way I'm hearing her now, would they have used her as a weapon? Would the course of history be totally different if my ancestors had just loved her the way I have?

"Clio, there's one thing I can't make sense of. Why did you leave me on Amethyne? Why did you let me believe you'd been captured by Volkov? If I've been connected to the Prismata all this time, why couldn't I just blink, and there you'd be?"

She tilts her head, giving me a skeptical half smile that's so familiar, so *Clio*, it aches to look at her. It's the expression she always gave me when I asked a stupid question. Then she'd just wait, amused and patient, while I worked out the answer on my own.

Like I do now.

"You didn't leave, did you?" I whisper. "I pushed you. I told you to get far away from me and you . . . you listened."

"I've always been as you believed me to be," she says. "Your greatest fear was that I'd be captured by your enemies, and you feared it so much you began to believe it was true. And so it was."

"It was all in my head," I murmur, feeling sick. "All the panic and dread I felt, thinking you were being tortured—that was me torturing *myself.*"

She plants her hands on my shoulders, her eyes looking directly into mine. "I was always with you, stupid. Even though your own brain wouldn't let you see me, I never left. You and me against the universe. *Always.*"

"And . . ." I swallow, then ask impulsively, "Is that what you *want*? For us to be linked so inextricably? To feel yourself stretched across the light-years, woven through our silly human lives?" These aren't at all the words I had planned to say, but they well up anyway, from the bottom of my soul. "Say the word, and I'll fight to set you free from us. I don't know how, but I'll find a way. If that's what you want."

"You're done fighting, Stacia." She smiles and raises a single finger. "Let me show you what I want."

Her finger presses to the center of my forehead, and I gasp as a flood of emotions pours into me.

I feel what it's like to be a billion years old, to burn in the darkness for eons. To feel the centuries turn while I never change. To be a being of light and love and sharp, brilliant lines, lost and alone in the cosmos, the last of a once innumerable species, mourning my lost kin through the millennia.

Because, I realize, the Prismata was not always alone. There were others. Hundreds, maybe thousands of Prismatas once filled the galaxy, communing, connecting, sustaining one another. But then they began to die, their lights dimming and their songs fading, until at last, only one remained.

She's the last of her kind, just as I am the last of mine.

But then—

I feel the burst of excitement and curiosity when out of that infinite darkness, a lone voice calls out, the voice of a desperate, mortal human mind trying to *connect*. And I feel the joy of making that connection, of experiencing companionship after millions of years of solitude. I feel the pleasure the Prismata took in us frail humans, its immense affection for these ephemeral creatures that burned, lived, and faded like sparks from a fire. How pure her happiness was, to be joined again with others.

How could I return her to that lonely dark?

With a gasp, I open my eyes, and Clio lowers her finger. It takes me a moment to recover from the force of those emotions, so much deeper and stronger and older than anything I could ever experience in my own brief human lifetime. Already they begin to fade, but not before I capture their meaning.

I stare at her, eyes watering. "I understand, but I'm frightened, Clio. Bad people are coming for you, and I don't know how to stop them. I don't know how to end this fighting. What do I do?"

She smiles, like this is inconsequential. "Hope is born in darkness. Peace is born in trust."

"But what does that *mean*?"

She pulls me close and whispers in my ear, "Who will you trust, heart of my heart?"

Trust?

"You don't understand," I say. "Volkov wants to destroy you. And if I use you to destroy *him*, this will never end. More will just come for you, and it'll go on and on. Tell me what to do!"

"I'll tell you who *I* trust," Clio says, with a sly sort of smile. She reaches up and frames my face with her hands, then tilts my head and kisses my brow. "I trust *you*. And I trust you will find the path. Now go. You must go."

All at once, she dissolves like a drop of wine into water.

Clio? I call out, reach for her, but I've lost my hands. I'm formless, voiceless again, just a spark in the sun. *Clio!*

Then the Prismata hurls me away.

It throws me aside like a hurricane flinging a grain of sand, and I panic. But my fear is meaningless against the tide of the Prismata's surging energy. It sweeps over me and carries me off, and then I feel it:

A cluster of Prisms speeding through space, getting closer and closer.

Missiles.

Volkov is here. He has already opened fire.

And the Prismata, Clio, does *nothing*. She could stop them. She could absorb them. I know how powerful she is now. If she wanted to, she could snap the Prisms powering those missiles or turn them around and blast Volkov out of the sky.

But she doesn't.

She just *waits*.

I rush backward, borne helplessly away from her, a scream trapped in my thoughts.

One moment, Clio burns in the sky, ancient and golden and brilliant.

Then the missiles strike her heart, and she shatters.

CHAPTER THIRTY-THREE

I wake with a gasp, my heart knocking in my chest. The shock of being slammed back into my body leaves me blind for a moment, and I cast out for something to grab hold of. I'm completely weightless, I realize, drifting in zero gravity. Panic grips me; I imagine that I'm floating in space, untethered and alone. I grapple at the visor of my helmet, trying to rip it off, before my senses kick in. Whatever's going on, my helmet may be the only thing keeping me alive.

My vision begins to clear, but everything is tinted green. The lights must be out, and my space suit visor has activated its night vision. But it's blurry and disorienting; I manage to get a grip on the wall, anchoring myself so I can make sense of my surroundings. Everything looks different in the grainy green haze of night vision. But I manage to make out the counters and cabinets of the old Leonova lab; I'm in the same place we were when Zhar found us. The room is a jumble of bodies and screams, figures in bulky space suits struggling in zero gravity. Someone collides with me, knocking my hand loose, and I careen through the air, crashing hard into the far wall. Rebounding back, spinning out of control, I find myself crushed by bodies. Everyone is shouting; someone's elbow hits my helmet, and a crack splinters across my visor.

"Stacia!" A hand reaches out; the night vision makes it impossible to distinguish between the limbs and torsos and bulging helmets around me, but I'd know that voice anywhere.

"Dad?"

I try to reach him, but someone pushes me aside and I crash into the wall. In the collision, the crack in my helmet's visor branches out like a spiderweb. My night vision flickers and then returns.

The soldiers are trying to make for the docks, but in the zero gravity and close confines, it's sheer chaos. A space suit drifts past me, the visor shattered; inside, a pale face stares blankly, mouth stretched in a rictus of agony. I don't know the soldier, but he died terribly.

I grab an air vent and press myself against the wall to keep from being crushed like that poor soldier.

"DAD!"

My voice is lost in the current of shouting and screams. But someone pushes free of the soldiers and grabs my arm.

"Stacia! This way!"

"Pol!"

He pulls me down the corridor toward the docks, shoving aside any soldiers who get in the way. Keeping our arms linked, we drift along, nudging the walls and floor to keep ourselves propelled in the right direction. The station is completely powerless; the walls groan and rattle around us, the way the *Valentina* did when Riyan took us through the Diamin Wall.

"You okay?" he asks. I can't make out his face; his visor is just a blank green screen on his helmet. If it weren't for his voice, I'd have no way of recognizing him.

"What happened?"

"You passed out. Then Volkov fired on the Prismata. The power went out. Gravity, lights, everything is gone. Even my gun is dead. Stace, it's bad."

My stomach sinks. I dare not look out the window, but I have to. I have to. Feeling nauseated, I push away from him and grab hold of the nearest porthole—and my heart drops.

The Prismata is gone.

Where it was, there's only a cloud of sparkling dust expanding outward in the darkness. The sky is fuzzy and green. The night vision only makes the scene even more surreal.

I would scream, if I could find the breath. But everything in me locks up, my body turning to ice. Horror opens in my stomach like a black hole.

"We have to get out of there!" Pol says. "The debris will rip this place apart. Hey! Riyan!"

A space suit drifts toward us, effortlessly graceful even in zero gravity. "There you are!" Riyan says. "We need to get away—"

"I know," Pol says. "Stace, come on. It's gone. There's nothing we can do."

He has to peel me away from the porthole.

They destroyed Clio.

The one thing I was meant to protect. A being far older and purer and more complex than we'll ever know, and she's *gone*.

I shut my eyes. I'm shaking in my suit, my teeth chattering. Pain splits my head like an ax. Pol and Riyan pull me along, but I'm barely aware of them. Riyan is tessellating, moving aside soldiers who block our path; their bodies pinwheel past, arms and legs flailing, their screams burrowing in my skull. I feel frayed inside, like some essential wire has been cut, disconnecting me from my own body. I'm dead weight, towed behind my friends like a defunct ship.

"My mom and dad," I whisper. "Where are they?"

"I don't know," says Pol. "But we have to keep moving."

"I can't leave them behind again!"

There's a scuffle ahead. Some soldiers are fighting to get to the dock, but there's too many of them to fit through the narrow doorway leading there. One turns and shoves another, and we hear a pained cry as the soldier crashes into the wall.

"Mara," I whisper. "That's Mara."

"So?" Pol says harshly.

I pull away from him and push myself to Mara's side. She's rolling in midair, clutching her leg.

"Help," she groans. "I think it's broken."

Seeing her in pain, something stills within me. I can't do anything about the Prismata, but here is someone I *can* help. I link arms with her and turn back to Pol and Riyan.

"Someone's got to fly us out of the field of debris," I say. "And Mara trained in an asteroid belt. She's the best chance we've got."

Pol hesitates, then nods. "We need to move faster. Brother?"

Riyan flexes his hands. "On it."

My stomach sinks first, then the rest of me, as Riyan tessellates. It must take a monumental effort, but he manages to restore enough gravity to the corridor so that we can run. Mara leans on Pol and Me, and Riyan follows behind, our boots heavy on the floor. Startled shouts sound from the soldiers who find themselves suddenly gravity-bound again. When they try to intercept us, Riyan crushes them to the floor.

"Have I ever told you," Pol pants, "how freaking *cool* you are?"

Riyan gives a short, dry laugh.

Together we guide Mara down the corridor and into the docks. Similar to the palace's configuration, the docks are a long, narrow chamber with round ports opening to the ships. Ahead, a group of soldiers is spilling *into* the dock—soldiers in Union red. They're facing off against the white-suited Loyalists, but everyone seems to be hesitating. With all the Prismic energy dead, they can't use their guns. They have no weapons to fight with, and hand-to-hand combat in space suits is just awkward and pointless.

The vityazes must have attached to the station before firing on the Prismata, maybe in hopes of taking some of us alive.

Pol curses, pulling us aside into an empty alcove. With the soldiers in the way, we can't reach the *Valentina*.

"Can you handle them?" he asks Riyan.

"Wait!" Mara shakes her head. "It's him! The direktor!"

We peer around the corner and see two soldiers have stepped forward: one Unionist, one Loyalist. Their helmets nearly touch as they circle each other.

"You fool," Zhar says. "You've killed us all!"

Volkov curses. "I do what is right, Lilyan. Why can't you ever see that? You always took Pyotr's side, in everything!"

"There's too many of them," Riyan says, his voice strained. "If I were fresh, maybe, but I've been holding this stress field too long already. I can't do it much more."

"Stacia!" calls a muffled voice.

I turn automatically, looking back the way we came.

My parents are gliding toward us, and with a sob of relief, I release Mara and meet them; we form a little circle, helmets pressed together.

"We've been looking everywhere," Mom sobs.

"Are you all right?" asks Dad.

"No, I'm *not.* The Prismata—"

"We know. We saw it all." Dad looks past me. "We have to get on a ship. *Fast.* That debris cloud will be here in less than a minute."

Riyan gasps. "I'm . . . losing it . . ."

I can feel myself getting lighter, lifting until only my toes are on the floor. Even through his suit, I can see Riyan straining to maintain the stress field. The soldiers are starting to turn, feeling the change in pressure, and both Zhar's and Volkov's visors fix on me.

"Kill her!" Volkov shouts, and the vityazes burst forward, taking Zhar's Loyalists by surprise. Zhar slams her fist into Volkov's helmet, shattering the visor, and then I lose sight of them as the soldiers charge at us.

Mom, Dad, and Pol step in front of me. Mara screams. My gaze shifts, horrified, to the crack on my visor, which begins to splinter and branch, probably due to the shifting pressure of Riyan's stress field. The thin wail of escaping oxygen fills my ears. I'm losing precious air by the moment. I can't even call out for fear my voice will shatter the visor completely.

Then, out of nowhere, Natalya Ayedi comes whirling like a red tornado. She's wearing no space suit, only a black oxygen mask clamped over the lower half of her face. Her hands spread, her braids swirling around her head like black vipers.

The vityazes stop in their tracks, just before they can clash with my parents and Pol. They hit the floor hard, screaming in pain as Natalya's stress field pushes them into the ground. My feet sink down again, gravity restored for now. Farther down the docks, the Loyalists hang back, staring at the tensor girl with obvious fear.

"Yes, Nat!" Riyan calls, his hands dropping to his sides. "Where have you *been*?"

"Unconscious!" his sister shouts. "They got me with a stunner."

"Everyone always shoots the tensors first," Riyan says.

"Not always," Pol mutters. "Let's go!"

We jump over the vityazes and run for the port to the *Valentina*, which Natalya's left open. She's suspended in the air, her toes several inches off the ground, her eyes burning as she stares at one vityaze in particular—Volkov. She's got him and Zhar on their backs, their bodies twisted in agony, and I know the pressure on the direktor is probably ten times what she's putting on the other soldiers.

"Stace!" Pol's holding out his hand to help me. The ship's air lock is open, and the dark interior of the *Valentina* waits.

Tearing my gaze away from Zhar and Volkov, I hand Mara to him.

He pauses. "Her people are right there. We don't have to take her. Let her go with them."

"I made a promise to her father," I say. "She comes with us."

Pol shrugs, and he and Riyan pull Mara into the clipper's air lock. Once she's through, I follow, navigating clumsily in my space suit.

I wonder what the point of all this is. If the Prism is down, there's no power to the Takhdrive. No warping, no boosters, nothing. The *Valentina* has a solar backup supply, so we'll have a bit of power, but even if there's rudimentary life support, it won't last us long.

Halfway through the door, I pause, hearing an odd sound. It's like hail on the metal roof of the winery back home, which seems like a totally *wrong* sound to hear in space.

Until I realize it's the Prismata's debris starting to pummel the station.

"Go, go, go!" Pol shouts.

Natalya is in, gliding on her own little shimmering stress field. Riyan's on the bridge above, tessellating Mara up beside him and strapping her into the pilot's chair. The ship interior is lit by the *Valentina*'s pale blue auxiliary lighting.

"The Prism's dead!" Riyan reminds us.

"Thrusters," I murmur. "The solar backup should let us use the thrusters."

Pol catches my eye and nods.

"If we undock," he adds, "we can use the thrusters to generate enough force to break free of the station. If we stay attached, we die. We'll have a better chance of surviving that way, making ourselves a smaller target, but we have to do it *fast*."

"No use," Mara says, falling into the pilot's seat. "The solar backup can't power both the thrusters and the unmooring clamps. I can't undock from this side."

"From this side?"

"There are analog controls in the station, but there's no time to make it back aboard—"

Behind me, the hatch seals shut.

Pol and I whirl around to see my parents on the other side. They stare at me through the hatch's round glass window. Their eyes are sad, but they're smiling.

"No," I whisper. "No, no, no—"

"Go, Stacia," Dad says, his voice muffled. "Whatever life you choose, we know you'll make it a good one."

"We do love you," says Mom, pressing a hand to the glass. "No matter what, you were always our Stacia."

"NO!" I reach for the door lever, but my parents shut the station's paired hatch, sealing us out.

I look up, unable to speak or think or breathe, as they engage the manual undocking equipment. I can see the sweat on Dad's chin as he hauls on one large lever, while Mom frantically opens a panel and operates the gears behind it.

The clamps holding the ship in place give way with a clank, and Mara immediately fires the thrusters while yelling at us to hang on. The *Valentina* sails free of the station, and in the last glimpse I have of my parents, they're holding each other, visors pressed together, hands on each other's helmets.

"We're sorry." My mother's last words are a crackle of static in my ear, over my comm channel. "And we love you."

As the *Valentina* pulls away, I can see the Committee ships spread across the sky, and the smaller transport shuttle Volkov must have used is docked at the far end of the station. The remaining Loyalists seem to be trying to pull free on their large, bulky battleship, but they aren't fast enough.

The wave of debris from the Prismata rips through the station;

it's like watching a paper crane go through a shredder. Panels go spinning, glass shatters, walls rip and tear free. Some of the debris pelts the clipper, and the *Valentina* shudders but holds firm. Riyan and Natalya tessellate a stress field around us to block the larger pieces, but turned away from the cloud, we are a much smaller target. Even so, Mara has to work hard to dodge the bigger fragments. The clipper dives and spirals wildly, and we all hang on hard.

In moments, it's all gone—the station, the Loyalist ship, the Committee fleet. Zhar and Volkov.

My family.

I sink to the floor, shaking. Pol kneels beside me. Together we stare through the hatch window, watching the destruction fade away.

Debris becomes dust, and dust becomes nothing.

I let out a long breath and curl over, drawing breath in raspy heaves. Pol pressurizes the air lock and then removes my helmet. My hair slips free, sticking to my sweaty face. I dig my gloves into the floor and hear a sob rip from my throat.

Pol puts an arm around me. He says nothing, just holds me, his breath as ragged as mine. Tears run from his eyes, cutting dark paths down his cheeks.

◇

Hours later, Natalya rouses us. I don't remember drifting off, but my throat is still sore from crying, and Pol looks terrible. She wordlessly hands us a canteen of water, then slips out of the air lock and back onto the bridge. Soft auxiliary lighting casts a blue haze over the *Valentina*'s interior, and through the air lock window, there's nothing but inky darkness and the distant stars. Mara is asleep on one of the sofas, out of her space suit, with her injured leg propped up.

I stare at her, unable to summon the anger I felt earlier. Whether she betrayed us or not, I suppose it all would have ended the same.

And she was just trying to do the right thing, as best she could. We all were. And we all failed.

Pol hands me the water. I drink deep, then pass it to him. I feel exhausted, wrung out. All I want to do is hide in my cabin and burrow into my bunk and do nothing, ever again. Just sleep.

"You guys might want to buckle in," says Natalya, reappearing.

"Huh?" Pol stiffens. "More debris?"

She shakes her head. "We're going to warp."

Pol and I exchange looks.

"But . . . there's no power," I point out, as if informing her that water is wet.

She shrugs, and then Riyan calls down from the control deck, "Not anymore! We were out for several hours, but it's back up now. The Prism sort of . . . woke up. It's weak, so it's taken a lot longer to charge the Takhdrive, but I think we can make it now. Just tell me where to go."

I look at Pol, and he looks at me.

"How is that possible?" he asks. "We drained the crystal on the way here, and we *saw* the Prismata explode. All the Prisms went dark."

"I'm not an expert."

"Stacia, you're the *only* expert when it comes to this stuff."

I struggle to my feet, feeling wobbly. Putting out a hand to brace myself, I shake my head. "Maybe—"

I pause, staring at my multicuff.

It's *glowing*, light shining through the seams in the metal.

I pull off my glove so I can unlatch the cuff. I pry open the panel on the inside, where the Prism battery is stored. It's supposed to last a lifetime, but when I expose it, I gasp. The thin wires around the battery are frayed, filaments splayed and bare and sparking. And among them, nestled like a pearl, is a tiny glowing ball.

Breath held, I gently reach into the wires and grasp the little thing. It's hard, no bigger than a pea. Extracting it and setting it onto my other palm, I stare in astonishment. It shines golden white, perfectly smooth, perfectly round.

I raise it up between my thumb and forefinger again and, peering closely, see it start to push out a tiny little crystal, like a seed sprouting. Closing my eyes, I reach for it with my thoughts—and gasp when it reaches back. Its touch is no more than a feather's brush against my mind, but it's *there*. The seed is alive, conscious, pulsing with potential.

Hope is born in darkness.

Clio knew. She knew the missiles were coming. She knew the Prismata would not survive. Maybe she even *chose* not to.

And she gave herself to me.

This is the soul of the Prismata; that great, massive life reduced and compacted into this tiny seed. It must have fled a moment before it exploded, a spark of energy sent back to the station with me, after it cast me away. It was with me the whole time, burning against my skin. *She* was with me, as she always has been.

Pol leans over, eyes wide. "What is it?"

Letting out a shuddering breath, I reply, "Hope."

CHAPTER THIRTY-FOUR

"Are you ready?" Pol asks, the doors of the Solariat tall and imposing behind him.

"Is it too late to run?"

He grins. "You say the word, Princess. We could be in Rubyat in five days."

With a sigh, I tug at the tight fabric around my waist. The structured blue dress, the shoes, the jewelry—all of it feels wrong. Like a costume. Worst of all is the crown atop my head, heavy as a shackle.

"Why should they listen to me?"

Pol takes my hands and pulls me close. "Because you turned the lights back on."

When we limped into Emerault's system, twenty days after my parents died, we learned that the Prismata's destruction had caused a galaxy-wide blackout for five hours. Casualties were low, considering. Each system lost several thousand lives, people from stations or ships who had no backup, non-Prismic power. Still, it was a price that should never have been paid. I have to remind myself their deaths are Volkov's fault, not mine—but it's hard not to feel guilt, to wonder if I might have saved the Prismata if I'd only been faster or smarter.

"Hey." Pol's fingers brush my chin. "We keep moving forward, okay?"

I nod, not quite meeting his eyes. He's an inch taller than he was when this all began.

"I don't like it when you get that look," he says. "Like you're slipping away. You don't have to do this, you know. You don't owe anyone anything."

"I'm all right."

It's been six months since the Prismata exploded. Most of the galaxy has begun to move on, the blackout another painful footnote in our tumultuous history. But for me, for Pol, for everyone at the center of things, these six months have been one long period of chaos.

With the collapse of the Union, trade routes shut down, food and water shortages became catastrophic, and most of all, the struggle for power—literal power, the energy to power ships and buildings and tech—resulted in violent outbreaks across the galaxy. With the Prism power still far weaker than it once was, everyone has been affected. But slowly, the Prismic energy has been getting stronger.

All thanks to the seed, nestled in the little case that hangs around my neck. I raise my hand to it and squeeze. Pol leans forward until his forehead presses against mine, and we both shut our eyes. I relish a quiet, stolen moment with him; we don't get nearly enough these days.

"Ahem," says a voice directly behind us. Pol and I both jump, my heart clawing its way up my throat.

"Riyan!" we say in unison.

The tensor's robes are still fluttering from his silent touchdown beside us. He gives a little smile. "Sorry."

"You're never going to stop doing that, are you?" I ask, shaking my head.

He raises a hand. "They're ready for you."

Ahead, the door of the Solariat is open. I draw a deep breath, squeeze Pol's hand, then walk in.

I have to see this through. It's my responsibility, as the last Firebird.

The last time I was in this room, I'd just unlocked the code, and it feels like an entirely new place now. The old Crescent Throne is gone. I don't know where it went, and I don't much care. The room feels smaller without it, but the view of Alexandrine is just as stunning as it always was.

The Allied Council has assembled here: four presidents, a gold-skinned zheran prime minister, a delicate paryan queen, the Lord Tensor, an aeyla spokesman, and an eeda admiral. They're seated in a wide circle, with various staff arranged behind them.

Each of them represents one of the Jewels, most chosen according to their planet's pre-Empire traditions. Once diplomats, royalty, and generals under the Empire, many of them were prisoners here at the palace all through the Union's brief but bloody rule, and helped the galaxy find stability after the eruption of the Prism network.

It's strange to see Riyan's father again, after everything that happened on Diamin. He hasn't spoken to his son, and I don't think Riyan is ready for that, anyway. So although they're in the same building, they might as well be strangers. As long as Riyan doesn't return home, his father can't enforce his sentence. It makes me sad, to think there are still some rifts that can't be mended, but at least Riyan has Natalya now.

I'm not the only one who's nervous around the Lord Tensor, although the Council leaders have different reasons. Some of them, I think, didn't want Diamin to be part of the Alliance at all. They still don't trust the tensors. But I made it clear I wouldn't do this unless all nine planets were represented. Beyond that, I can't do anything to help the tensors. They'll have to find a way to fit in on their own, and the other planets will just have to get over it. Maybe Riyan's dream of seeing his people accepted will come true eventually, but it's going to take time.

The Council watches me in silence, most of them with expressions of suspicion. I don't blame them. What I am and what I can do with the Prisms has become widespread knowledge, but the stories have gotten out of control. I don't doubt these rulers have heard some pretty monstrous versions. I wish I could make them understand what

I truly am—a girl who still has to pick up the pieces of herself every morning and carry on, no matter how much she wants to break down.

"Anya Leonova, welcome." The queen of Sapphine greets me with a smile, at least. She sits beneath a spray of mist, to keep her eeda skin comfortably damp.

I bow to her as a pedestal rises from the floor in front of me. I walk to it and set down the small tabletka I'm carrying. With a touch, I send a hologram glittering into the air.

"Esteemed Council of the Jewel Alliance," I say. "I am happy to report that the Prismata is healthy and growing."

I raise a hand to the holo, which depicts the small crystal. It turns slowly, all twelve points shimmering. I've made it larger so they can all see, but in truth, it's still no bigger than the tip of my thumb. Its growth rate has led us to believe it will be several hundred thousand years before it's even half the size it was when Volkov attacked it. So that they can be assured it's still safe, I raise the little egg-shaped case around my neck. Made of black diamantglass, a press of a little button on the top clears away the dark tint, revealing the shining pearl inside. After they have a chance to see it, I let the glass cloud again, safely hiding the most precious object in the galaxy.

"Power across the Belt, as you know, is still extremely low. But thanks to the solar farms on Sapphine"—I nod to the queen—"and the wind farms of Rubyat, we're making do."

The galaxy still needs Prismic energy, especially to power Takhdrives, but I don't think we'll ever be as fully reliant on it as we once were. That's a lesson we learned the hard way.

"Has it . . . spoken to you?" asks the aeyla spokesman, hesitantly.

They all look at me with interest, and some skepticism. I know from our previous meetings that many still have trouble believing the Prismata is a living being.

"No," I say, hiding the ache of sadness in my chest. "It's still quite weak. I'm not sure it will ever speak to us again, perhaps not for thousands of years. But it lives, and that is what's important. As long as we protect it, understand it, and trust it as it trusted us, we have nothing to fear."

"We will be the judge of that," grunts the president of Rubyat.

I nod, glancing worriedly at him. He's the least receptive of all of them; Rubyat was the last of the Jewels to join the Alliance. In this room, all the systems are equal but independent. No emperors, no direktors, just nine sovereign worlds trying to find a way to get along. I'm just glad I'm not in one of those seats. Forging peace after everything our galaxy has been through in the last two decades is no easy thing. My job has been simple in comparison: to monitor the Prismata and keep the lights on, so to speak.

"I have what I promised," I say, "and I offer it freely, under the terms of the Prismata Accords."

I plug a data stick into the tabletka. When it clicks into place, the holo shifts into a revolving scarlet bird, the seal of the Leonovs.

"The Firebird code. It's all there, from beginning to end."

"According to the terms," says the eeda queen, "we will now present our candidates for the office of Firebird."

Each system puts forth two chosen ones, most of them young and brilliant, plucked from top universities across the Belt, of races both human and adapted. One thing's for sure—each one is way more qualified than I am for this job. They bow to their leaders and approach me, solemn-faced. Forming a circle, they hold up data pods, and I transmit the code to each of them. It's a symbolic gesture more than anything. Soon, they'll undergo the months-long procedure that will graft the code to their DNA. By the end of the Alexandrine year, they'll all be Firebirds. I won't be alone anymore.

Ours is a symbiotic relationship—the races of humanity and the strange, living crystal from the edge of the galaxy. It powers our world, and in return, we give it our joys and sorrows, our anger and our love. I know now what we mean to the Prismata, how we saved it just as it saved us. We need it to survive, and it needs us so that it isn't alone. Sometimes, in my dreams, I still feel the current of emotions rushing toward the Prismata, and glimpse the faces and moments and sensations the crystal had collected.

My part of the ceremony is almost done. The Firebird candidates return to their spots behind the circle. The heads of the Belt watch me expectantly.

Stars, it's hot in here.

I remove my tabletka and hand it to an attendant, then stare a moment at the bare pedestal in front of me. This is the part I've actually been looking forward to—probably since that awful day back on Amethyne.

But still, I hesitate.

The Leonovs had many faults, but they also did what had been thought impossible: reuniting all the lost tribes of humanity, founding an empire that would forever change the course of our race. They discovered the Prismata, created the Firebird code, and ruled—by means both foul and fair—for centuries.

All that ends with me.

I raise my hands and lift the crown from my head. Slowly, I set it on the pedestal, where it glints, rubies dark as blood, emeralds glinting, sapphires blue as the Sapphine sea. One jewel for each system, bright and brilliant.

"I, Anya Leonova," I say softly, "hereby renounce the throne of my ancestors and formally dissolve the Alexandrine Empire." Raising my eyes, I add, "May the stars grant us peace."

To my surprise, they murmur it back: "May the stars grant us peace."

That done, I turn and barely keep myself from sprinting out of the Solariat. Pol's waiting at the doors.

"Well?" he says, searching my face. "How'd it go? Was it hard?"

I shrug. "Stars, no. The thing was giving me a headache."

◇

We stand at the edge of the conservatory, looking through the glass at Alexandrine. Behind us, dignitaries and trade delegations walk and murmur in small groups, planning the future of the human race. More than happy to leave them to it, I spoon strawberry ice onto my tongue, letting it sit there a moment to melt. Ships come and go, bearing the newly minted colors and flags of the nine Free Worlds. My eyes fix on a courier, bearing the violet-and-white crest of the new spokesman of Amethyne.

"You did the right thing," Pol says. "This is how it should have been from the beginning, people making their own choices."

"I didn't do anything. They did it themselves."

"You brought back the seed, giving us the energy to run our entire civilization."

"I was just the messenger. The Prismata gave me its own heart, even though we destroyed it, all because it knew that was the only way to peace. It wanted nothing in return, just to connect. To love and be loved." I stare down into my now empty bowl. "It didn't deserve what happened."

He turns to face me squarely. "Neither do you."

I swallow hard and nod, even though I know it'll be a long time before I really believe it.

"Anyway," I say, "even that credit goes to Clio. All I did was think about what she told me, about peace being born from trust. That was the problem all along. The Leonovs didn't *trust* anyone except themselves. They should have shared the truth about the Prismata with everyone. If Volkov had known what it's like, that it's not some evil, murdering monster, maybe he wouldn't have tried to destroy it."

"Now they'll know, thanks to the new Firebirds."

"I hope so."

I hope I haven't made a terrible miscalculation. I hope I can trust them, those nine in the Solariat with their newfound power and their eighteen Firebird candidates. Each system will have its own ambassadors to liaise with the Prismata. For some, like the Sapphinos and Amethynians, this means protecting themselves from stronger systems who might try to move against them. With their Firebirds connected to the Prism network, they'll know ages in advance of any significant military actions. And for those systems more skeptical of the Prismata—like Rubyat and Alexandrine—having Firebirds will help assure them that the crystal is not a threat. I wonder if this really could have worked with Volkov, or if he was too far gone.

"You know . . ." I slip my spoon into Pol's bowl, scooping out some of his ice. "I have a few months before I have to be back here, to train the new Firebirds."

He raises a brow. "And?"

"And . . . I was thinking about your plan to become desert smugglers."

"You know I'd make an excellent smuggler."

"It's true. We could smuggle all sorts of things. Treasure, food . . ."

"What do you say we ask the crew?"

He laughs and puts an arm around me, pulling me close.

Behind us, Riyan is talking with Damai and his other sisters, here from Diamin as part of their father's entourage. His father won't speak to him, but that didn't stop his sisters from mobbing him and Natalya the minute they landed. They've hardly been apart since. Their chatter seems to fill the whole of the Rezidencia, and though Riyan seems a little dizzied from their noisy attention, he looks happy. I glance at him, our eyes connecting for a moment, and he gives me a little nod.

Nearby, on a bench beneath an Emeraultine willow, Mara and Natalya are whispering and laughing. Those two have become inseparable in the past few weeks. I guess between Mara's betrayal and Natalya's time under Volkov's power, they've found something to bond over, and I'm starting to think it's even more than that. As angry as I was at Mara, somehow none of that seems to matter anymore. She tried to apologize once, about a month ago, but the rest of us wouldn't hear it.

"I think we're all ready to get away for a while," says Pol. "And as nice as a life of crime sounds, I'd settle for a few nights on the dunes with my favorite princess."

"Ah!" I wave my spoon at him. "Not a princess anymore."

He cocks his head. "If you're not a princess, then that must mean I'm free from my vows."

"Oh." I set down my spoon and fold my arms on the counter, looking at him seriously. "Does this mean you're leaving me, Appollo Androsthenes?"

"It means . . ." He leans toward me, until his lips are an inch from mine. "I'm asking if I might have the honor, Stacia Androva, of whisking you off on a romantic voyage to Rubyat."

His lips are cold from the ice, but they warm quickly against mine. He tastes of strawberry and Amethynian wine. I slide forward on my seat so I can lock my hands behind his neck, and his fingers dig into my waist.

When we pull apart, we're both blushing, sensing more than a few eyes on us.

"For a kiss like that," I whisper, "I'd follow you over the edge of the universe."

Acknowledgments

This has been a fantastic voyage of storytelling, and I've been blessed with an amazing crew along the way. First and foremost, my editor, Zack Clark, deserves as many thanks as there are stars in the Belt. His imagination and insight made this story possible, and I'll be forever grateful for his openness to some of my nuttier "what-if's . . ." Writing this book with him has been a delight and privilege. My deepest gratitude to production editor Melissa Schirmer, her squad of copy editors and proofreaders, and the entire Scholastic team. And thanks to designer Nina Goffi and artist Luke Choice for the stunning cover.

As ever, thank you to my agent, Lucy Carson, for ushering this book along and believing in me even when I doubt myself. I couldn't ask for a truer or fiercer guide on this wild publishing journey.

Buckets of gratitude to some of my favorite crewmates, whose advice and encouragement enabled me to take risks with this story I could never have dared on my own, and whose friendships spurred me through the toughest early revisions: Marie Lu, Morgan Matson, Jennifer Wolfe, J. R. Johansson, Andrea Cremer, Suzanne Young, and Beth Revis. Jessica Brody deserves every star in the sky for her unflagging support and enthusiasm for this story, and for becoming Stacia's earliest cheerleader.

Special thanks to my dad for being available 24/7 to answer random spaceflight and astrophysics questions, and to geek out with me over Teslas in space.

I could never have written this book without some truly dedicated babysitters, so many thanks to Mama, Noma, Papa, Mimmie, Pop Pop, Katharine, LeslieAnn, and Madelaine for giving me so many hours. Your support is beyond calculable.

Always and ever, thanks to Ben for being my master chef, tech support, believer, husband, and best friend.

About the Author

Jessica Khoury is the author of the Corpus Trilogy and *The Forbidden Wish*. In addition to writing, she is an artistic mapmaker and spends far too much time scribbling tiny mountains and trees for fictional worlds. Her spare hours are spent video gaming, hiking, or cooking badly. She lives in Greenville, SC, with her husband, daughter, and sassy husky, Katara. Find her online at jessicakhoury.com.